# Ice Cream Man

Charles Puccia

# Contents

## II. Too Much

# I

# Office Politics

# Chapter 1

## The Mendacity of Truth

The moment Vinnie walked into the room, he knew something was wrong. His boss was standing behind his desk, surrounded by scattered papers, watching the numbers on his fancy atomic clock tick upward: 8:43:10 . . . 8:43:11 . . . 8:43:12. This was not an ordinary Wednesday, the last day of a bright September.

But the dead giveaway that something was wrong was the way Dan greeted Vinnie: "A complete fucking screwup."

Vinnie froze. Dan didn't curse—never cursed. In fact, he was offended by others cursing, and Vinnie's own cursing had almost cost him his job.

Learning not to curse had been Vinnie Briggs's first lesson from Dan. Two years earlier, Vinnie had approached the interview chair, looked out the window behind Mr. Dan Livorno—senior executive at DV&N—and sung out, "Fuckin'-A view. You can see fuckin' Queens."

While no other job applicant would start an interview with that kind of language, Vinnie couldn't help himself—which was probably why he was so desperate for a job. To Vinnie, cursing was like breathing: it just happened. But apart from this unfortunate proclivity, Vinnie was otherwise an astute, polite young man, barely twenty-two.

Dan sat in his prestigious corner office in the Hawthorne Building, above Second Avenue and Forty-Fifth, with a spectacular view of the East River, Queens, and on a good day, planes in flight at La Guardia. He fixed his interviewee with a stare. "Mister Briggs, there's no need to curse. Lacing an opinion with curses reveals nothing meaningful about a person's thoughts. And I would prefer that you not curse in my office."

*Fuck*, Vinnie thought at the time. *So much for getting the executive assistant position at Del Vecchio & Neale.* After that, Vinnie saw no reason to sit—his interview was doomed. He knew that Dan had only included him among the final eight—culled from two hundred—because Dan's sister-in-law, Rachel, had twisted the man's arm. It had been a lucky break, and ten seconds into the interview Vinnie had already blown it.

"I've fuckin' screwed this, haven't I?" he said. "I'm sorry to have wasted your time, sir. I'm truly fuckin' sorry."

Squinting his eyes, Vinnie waited to be dismissed, watching the seconds click by on the atomic clock that sat on the executive's desk. But Dan extended his hand. "No, Mister Briggs, you can sit. You've just expressed your thoughts very succinctly. Let's continue and see what surprise comes next... with less cursing, please."

Three days later Vinnie called Rachel: "Rach, you're talking to the new administrative assistant at DV&N! I fuckin' told Dan he wouldn't regret it, and he said, 'Let's hope I fuckin' don't.'" For two years after that, Vinnie liked to tell people he was Dan Livorno's last "fuck."

He wished now that had remained true.

Dan never regretted hiring Vinnie, despite his foul mouth—and to be fair, Vinnie did manage to curtail his cursing by perhaps seventy percent. And two years later, they were best friends. Vinnie knew Dan's ways as well as he knew his own, so to see Dan's office in a mess was a surprise, and to hear him cursing was a shock.

Bending down to pick up some papers strewn on the floor, Dan mumbled to himself. He turned to Vinnie and his mouth slightly opened, but then it closed again, holding back whatever he had been about to say.

"Talk to me, Dan."

Dan sighed and looked at his computer screen, frowning. "I was working on my economic model, and Bill's voice came booming across the room. He burst in here with his usual yappy good morning..."

Vinnie's mouth barely opened. "And? Are you okay?"

"He came in and stood there." Dan pointed to the door. "Had the nerve to say, 'Good morning, Dan.' Good morning, my ass."

Vinnie's head shook.

"Told me the proposal presentation has been moved from Monday." With his fingers pulling on his lower lip, Dan made a contorted grimace. "You know what he said? I'll tell you. 'I know it's a bummer, but you'll be fine.' And then he laughed. 'Har har, har har.'" Dan imitated Bill's notorious laugh with its harsh R sound, a good imitation. "I heard him belch from across the room. Big man Bill Barrington, fucking executive VP at Del Vecchio & Neale, Incorporated, and he belched. He'd been drinking before nine o'clock. The man I report to, drinking before noon."

"So, how long's the delay?"

"Delay! No, Vinnie, not delayed. The meeting's been moved *forward*. Moved to *tomorrow*. Bullshit. This is plain bullshit."

The presentation was the final step before the DV&N board decided whom to promote to the new Executive Director position—heading up the newly created European Operations office in Paris. Dan was one of two finalists; the other was Linda Lords, his counterpart at the DV&N California office.

Vinnie thought Dan looked capable of eating him, the furniture, the entire thirty-fifth floor.

"No way. That's fuckin' ridiculous. He can't change it in one day."

"That's what I said. I argued, but Bill had all his bases covered. I reminded him about the delays in retrieving the crucial European data—data I've been promised. I've waited weeks for that data, as you know. And it was Bill who promised to fix the delay in the first place!"

Again Vinnie's head shook. "Son of a bitch. Dan, let's talk to Gary." Gary Del Vecchio, co-founder and president of Del Vecchio & Neale, could overrule Bill Barrington.

With his head bowed toward the desk, Dan sighed. "You know what else he said to me? He said, 'Dan, you're always prepared. You're an Eagle Scout. I have every confidence in you.'" Dan looked up. "He's a bullshitting drunk, that's what he is. He told me the rescheduling couldn't be helped. All due to some crisis in LA with our Northrop Aviation account."

The rest of the story came in spasms, but Dan had already hit the high note: the Paris presentations would be tomorrow morning—ready or not—and would be followed by the board's decision. A decision that was suddenly looking not at all favorable to Dan, seeing as he didn't even have his core data yet. Apparently they needed to accelerate the schedule so that Linda could be back in California on Thursday night, followed by Bill on Friday. They wanted to show Northrop that DV&N's senior executive VP could make on-site decisions.

"He said it's the same for Linda as it is for me," Dan continued. "Level playing field; might even be worse for her. Reminded me that Northrop is our biggest West Coast client, even cited the DV&N motto, 'Clients first, that's the DV&N way,' as if I don't know."

Dan had suggested to Bill several alternatives that seemed, to him at least, far more reasonable. "But nothing I said convinced him," he finished.

"Anything… else?" At this point, Vinnie was almost afraid to ask.

Dan picked up a ruler, letting the sharp edge roll over his shirtsleeve and then slapping his palm with the flat side. "The usual Barrington gossip. Gave me Gary's itinerary. Next week Argentina, then a Miami break. Bill said, 'Screwing his boyfriend up the ass.' Classic Bill." The ruler slapped twice. "Asked if Gary forced me to hire you to increase the number of office faggots. Told me what I need is an assistant with big tits, not a little queer. I hate that man, and he's my supervisor."

Vinnie rocked quietly on the balls of his feet. Did he imagine his squeaking rubber heels reverberating through all thirty-five floors above New York's canyon at 9:15:42 a.m.? The telephone squealed, went unanswered.

"I'm sorry, Vinnie. I shouldn't have repeated that."

Each man knew evil had been in the room. Vinnie wanted a declaration of war. Dan slapped his palm, ran the edge of the ruler over his forearm. Vinnie thought, *When you're fucked, you're fucked.*

"I'll stay all night," Vinnie said. "You'll still outshine Linda. And as Bill said, it's the same for her as you. Stop worrying over the missing data. Big deal."

Leaning across his desk, Dan said, "Vinnie, you're missing the point. The data..." He inhaled, sputtered. "The goddamn data. My forecast model is a breakthrough—it predicts what happens when markets collapse. But I need the 2001 and 2008 data to prove it. Without it, all I have is extrapolation and speculation. I've invented a completely new way to respond after market crashes, against convention. But in today's investment climate, no financial services company would try my model unproven. Even Gary's belief in me won't go that far.

"I put DV&N at the head of the financial pack. Now *this* is my shot to set a whole new paradigm. And you and I both know the board won't accept my word without data. They won't risk Europe. It's over. I'm screwed." Dan's hand moved swiftly, wiping moist eyes, a Vinnie move.

"I still believe you'll win," Vinnie said quietly. "But if not, you'll have this job—and a quarter-million salary plus the bonuses, I might add. Sure, matters are complicated if Ginny takes her Bloomingdale's Paris job, but you can afford to commute. You've said you don't see her much during the week anyway. What's with the feeling so fuckin' sorry for yourself?"

The ruler flew from Dan's hand across the desk. Vinnie ducked. "It's not the goddamn money, Vinnie. I don't want to talk about it. Please leave, I need to think."

Vinnie backed away. He knew it wasn't the money, knew it really had to do with Dan's marriage. And knew better than to tell Dan that he knew.

With a pause before he closed Dan's office door, Vinnie turned to catch a glimpse of his boss swiveling in his chair to look out the window. *What's he see? Paris?*

* * *

Back at his desk, Vinnie muttered aloud. "I fuckin' love my boss. Best boss ever. Best friend, too. There's more to this than Northrop, more to Dan's upset. Look at him, hunky, handsome, with a cute bubble ass…"

Using a slightly higher voice, Vinnie answered himself: "Now, Vinnie, keep your mind off Dan's ass."

Vinnie snapped back: "Yeah, fuck you."

Vinnie made a resolution. "I'll help Dan and I'll find a way to screw that homophobic Barrington." After all, Bill had screwed Vinnie over, too, in addition to denigrating him.

Joining Dan in Paris had never felt right for Vinnie. He had told Dan, "I'll never leave the City." So Dan had somehow arranged a DV&N scholarship for Vinnie to attend NYU's Stern School for a master's in marketing. And Dan had been emphatic that the scholarship stood, independent of Dan winning Paris. But Vinnie didn't see it that way. In his mind, his fate depended on Dan moving to Paris. Dan would start his new life, and Vinnie would start his own.

His future, his friend's future, and his own dignity depended on finding out what Bill Barrington was up to. Vinnie would show him who was getting screwed up the ass.

# Chapter 2

## Daydreams and Nightmares

The mouse pointer wandered aimlessly around the screen in response to Vinnie's idle pushes. He was ruminating, struggling to understand. Why had Bill decided to keep Dan from getting the Paris job? Surely that's what this was about. And fuck Barrington with his anti-gay remark. If victory's not possible, revenge is.

Like a dog at a car door, Vinnie poked into the corridor: go or stay. Vinnie returned to his desk, deciding to call Blanca rather than chance running into Bill. Blanca Santos, Bill's executive secretary and Vinnie's close work friend, answered her phone.

"What the fuck, Blanca?"

"Uh-oh," Blanca replied. "Sounds like I better take my shoes off for this one."

Vinnie loved Blanca's fascination with shoes and her boast that she had more shoes than anyone at DV&N. Six-inch heels gave Blanca her distinctive click-clack clawing sound along DV&N's hallways. The two friends were soul mates, bound by differences and similarities. Blanca, Puerto Rican, married, had two young sons and lived in a single-family Garden City house. Vinnie, a single gay man with no partner, resided in a West Village one-bedroom. Both had grown up in tough neighborhoods and had suffered humiliation from the epithets flung at them—Blanca's were usually Rican or island monkey, while Vinnie's were wop, mick, or faggot, depending on the bigot in question. But they'd long ago realized that their biggest difference was their bosses. "Chalk and cheese, Vinnie," Blanca had said. "Mine's a *fondillo* and yours *un santo*."

Asshole versus saint.

Vinnie gave Blanca a rundown of events. "Blanca, why? A fuckin' last-minute problem in California?"

"You're right, Vinnie, sounds like Shithead's up to something. I had no idea."

Like Vinnie, Blanca knew her boss well. It was during a happy hour game for the executive staff klatch—which typically included Vinnie, Blanca, Shareen Cooper, DV&N's office manager, and Maria Benfatto, executive assistant to CEO Gary Del Vecchio—when Blanca chose Bill's hypothetical Facebook nickname and *nom de guerre*, Shithead.

"And what's up with Dan?" Blanca added. "I mean, sounds like he's nearly in tears."

A small cough almost gave Vinnie away. He had intended to tell Blanca about Dan's marital problems—it was Vinnie's one secret from Blanca—but wouldn't betray that information until after Dan was safely ensconced in Paris.

Blanca grumbled. "I have to agree, Bill's up to something, and it probably involves Linda too. I'm stumped."

* * *

Behind his closed office door, Dan's thoughts went in a thousand directions. Vinnie thinks I want more money. If only he knew. He thinks I'm as crass as Bill and Linda.

Like Vinnie, Dan believed he'd lost. Unlike Vinnie, he didn't mean only the job; he and Ginny *needed* Paris, to resolve their marital issues.

Last night, Dan had hoped to end the last year's pie-sliced marriage: good, bad, awful. At first, the long silences had seemed like nothing, easily explained. But after a while, that nothing had become something.

He still remembered the exact day when his lust for Ginny had begun. She had entered the lecture room with her treasure-packed body. He loved her silky voice, the melodic way she spoke. Their first sex sealed his love, but it also triggered his anxiety over rejection.

Now, his teenage torment resurfaced. Someone would steal Ginny from him. He had the cheerleader stolen from him, his first love, and he'd been humiliated by it. He'd never forgotten. It could happen again.

Sex, thought-provoking conversations, debates, and engagement in each other's work had filled their first years of marriage. In hindsight, the day they moved to Central Park West was the day they lost their synchronicity.

"Dan, he's so big and strong. You can see his muscles from across the room. He trains me hard, and I feel the difference." This had been Ginny's non-stop refrain for weeks.

"That's great," Dan said as if it were nothing. Teenage angst returned. Is this oversized man seducing my wife? Is he the football captain incarnate that takes the cheerleader from me, like last time?

"I'm training late, so eat without me," became another commonplace refrain.

Dan complained. "Ginny, 'eat' will become 'live,' and soon you'll never be here." Dan held back his other thoughts: home after nine... ten-minute quickies, if at all. He imagined Ginny doing it with her freakish muscle-bound trainer.

"Vinnie, how do you know if someone is unfaithful?" He regretted using the old ruse, "Doctor, I have a friend with a problem. No, not me..." He hoped Vinnie didn't know he was talking about himself.

But Vinnie did. Ginny had relayed Dan's complaints to her sister Rachel with the touch of a speed dial. There were no secrets among sisters, according to Swinburne family tradition. And Rachel had phoned Vinnie, which was Rachel's tradition.

Now Dan pressed his palm flat against the glass of the thirty-fifth-floor window and peered between his fanned fingers at the street below. Polka dots scurrying to and fro. He remembered Ginny bursting out that she'd been offered Bloomingdale's Paris chief of bureau. *And* that she had wangled responsibility for organizing this year's annual November Paris extravaganza, the Spring Collection show.

Paris was going to change everything for them.

Dan drifted to the handcrafted filing cabinet across the room, his index finger running across the wood. *We had fantastic sex for a week.* After Ginny's big news, she had reduced her training, needing more time at home to organize her Paris show.

He had helped her plan, and she had given him sex in return.

"I'll transfer to DV&N's Paris office," Dan had said. He had intended to take a lower position, doing mundane analysis; he didn't tell her that it was because he'd do anything to get Ginny away from her muscle-bound trainer. And then, out of the blue, DV&N announced a new Europe division, Paris-based, with an executive director position open. Everything was finally falling into place.

"Ginny, it's too good to be true."

Dan drummed the filing cabinet with a cadence of defeat: It *was* too good, wasn't it? By mid-June, Ginny had resumed full-time training, which Dan blamed on his working long hours on his economic model to win Paris.

Oh well. Doesn't matter now.

And just like that, they went from marital bliss to a near sexless marriage. Dan's hand slid across his forehead. What happened last night? Returning to his desk chair, Dan swiveled and faced the outside window. *What* did *happen?*

* * *

*The Night Before*

Meandering to the bedroom, Dan mumbled his exhaustion and Ginny grunted. He'd had a grueling day: rising at six a.m., twenty-five pool laps, working until seven-thirty p.m., dead tired by ten. For no reason, he hissed, "A dumb jerk going across lanes collided into me on my tenth lap."

"What are you talking about?"

"I threw him across three lanes. My bottled-up energy I guess, so I tossed him like a piece of paper."

Ginny's words rolled out. "Really! So strong. You must be working out to be able to lift and throw a man."

"Not really. We were in water."

"Yeah, but once he was out. Let me feel those muscles."

Three steps on long legs and taut calves brought Ginny next to Dan. "Make them bulge, the way you did when you tossed that nitwit."

Dan raised his arm, Ginny's fingers cruising the surface. Her other hand pulled the fabric taut, melding shirt to skin. "How hard. The guy must have been scared."

"And he complained, too. Management wasn't happy, but DV&N's corporate membership saved me from being barred. The jerk received a warning about pool etiquette, which was fair."

"Or you'd have crushed him, right?"

"Uh, no, I wouldn't. Why would you say that?"

"But you could if you wanted to, right?"

"I suppose. I certainly have bottled-up energy. I could probably crush a dozen guys at once."

A sorcerer's words to Ginny.

Minutes later, on the bed's edge, his shirt and socks removed, Dan watched Ginny sally over to him in clinging sheer lingerie unseen for months. Beneath were matching silk bra and panties.

"Are you wearing high heels?"

Breasts advanced on Dan. She saw his desire and anticipated her own by embellishing the pool toss narrative: Dan's brute strength had destroyed the puny speck of a man.

Whether that narrative was real or imaginary, the advance of Ginny's crème Chantilly-filled breasts plunged Dan's face into Purgatory Chasm. He accepted Ginny's invitation to explore, both above and below. His tongue felt her firm nipples. Eternity passed as Ginny's freshly painted Andy Warhol mouth pressed against his lips. She endorsed the rise in his pants.

"Take them off. Make your cock rise as high as you can." Ginny's sex talk had never excited Dan, but he accepted her banter. Her hips raised and her squeeze tightened. "These big muscles are so strong. Make them harder. Show me the strength you used to toss that wimp."

Dan's body arched, his chest tensed, and he flexed. Ginny's breasts pressed into him, her grip tensing as Dan's pelvis jerked.

With each jolt his testicles ached, Ginny's fingers pushing them up. He watched her wide smile as he ejaculated. Harmony had been restored.

Completely spent, Dan barely heard Ginny's whisper. "I love you."

She meant it, and Dan said the same with glee, a truth he had never abandoned.

"We'll be happy in Paris, won't we? Do you promise, Dan?"

* * *

Less than twelve hours later, Dan sensed his broken hallelujah. His office chair creaked, loaded down by his thoughts. What did Ginny really want? Didn't she realize he wanted to take her away from her trainer?

With the promise he'd made the night before now broken, Dan rose and half-sat on the desk, anticipating heavier thoughts. Twelve hours ago Paris had been a certainty; now it was certainly gone. Worse: the original idea he'd had—to take a lower-level position—had now become untenable, too. *I'll never work under Linda. I won't be humiliated.*

Dan imagined Ginny in Paris without him—and their eventual breakup.

He had needed that data in order for his proposal to win. His only hope now lay in his desperation to defeat Linda, his missing data notwithstanding.

Dan's thoughts turned to Bill. Bill never comes to my office; he always asks me to his. Something's wrong. Something with Linda, and it's not good.

It's not about Northrop, but what?

# Chapter 3

## Meeting of Crows

Sandwiched between Dan's office at one corner of the hallway and Linda's temporary office at the other was the executive suite, a dual-purpose room that doubled as a mini conference room for small gatherings and a private dining facility for executive staff. The top four administrative assistants also gathered here for lunch sometimes, when the room was free and time permitted.

Vinnie had made sure that the others would come. Blanca arrived early with Vinnie, and Shareen and Maria arrived ten minutes later. When everyone was seated, Vinnie began. "It doesn't make sense to me. How do you change something that's been set in stone for three months?"

"Things happen, Vinnie," Maria answered, the others deferring to her higher rank.

"Sure, but I don't see what could be so important in California that they'd allow all hell to break loose."

Blanca put down her sandwich. "I knew nothing about this California crisis before Vinnie told me, and that in itself is weird. I should've been in the loop. Am I chopped liver?"

"See, it stinks," Vinnie said. "I told Dan that Blanca hadn't been informed, and he was surprised about that, too."

"Just because something's out of the ordinary doesn't make it nefarious." Maria paused to drink her coffee before continuing, and she gave Vinnie a disapproving glance. She didn't condone office gossip. "There have been many… well, not many, but a few times when Gary has failed to inform me of his agenda. These men don't always take us into consideration. They need us, they depend on us, and unfortunately, they also ignore us."

Shareen lifted her head and chimed in, "Amen to that, sister. Most men, Vinnie excepted, don't give a shit about us women. I've seen it too many times. But still, something's not right about this. I'm Linda's temporary assistant here in New York, and I should've been told, but I wasn't. One assistant out of the loop is understandable, but two seems fishy."

"Fucked up is more like it," said Vinnie.

Maria scowled.

"Sorry, Maria. This change is tough for Dan. He still hasn't received the European data that he requested months ago. What the *fu*—er, hell. Can I say hell, Maria?"

Shareen leaned in to Maria. "And that's the other thing: Linda didn't seem upset about it at all. Is she just that much better prepared? What frozen food market did she crawl out of?"

Mimicking Shareen, Blanca leaned forward. "Same for Bill. He was matter-of-fact, even cavalier about updating his calendar. Tells me *he'll* contact the travel agent—but I always do all the travel. He gave me a story about a planned family vacation in San Diego next week, which his wife had organized. Then he has the nerve to say he prefers to keep family activities separate from business. Yeah, right! Like how many birthday gifts have I bought for his wife and kids? *Gilipolleces!* I'm with Vinnie on this."

The three junior members of the group stared into their lunches, waiting for Maria.

She apparently wasn't convinced.

"None of this is enough to accuse anyone—and what would be the accusation? What's the motive? I don't see where we take this."

Maria's pronouncement was the administrative equivalent of a firewall. Vinnie slumped.

"Start with what seems odd." Shareen's baritone bounced across the room. "Let's go with the calendar dates."

Blanca agreed, adding, "I'll go through Bill's calendar on my computer and compare it to the one on his computer. He doesn't like me to look at his computer, but if he questions me I'll say Maria requested all executive calendars be coordinated because of the changes needed for the Northrop crisis." Blanca gave Vinnie her conspiratorial smile; she had just co-opted Maria into her scheme.

For solidarity, Shareen said, "I'll do the same with Linda's calendar, here and California."

Maria pressed her lips together and nodded agreement. "Okay. It makes sense and follows protocol. I'll send a memo to make it official."

Maria had thrown Vinnie a bone.

Vinnie turned to her. "Thanks, hon, you're the best."

"Don't 'honey' me. And Vinnie, *you* do nothing. Understand? Nothing! Let Shareen and Blanca take the first steps. We'll talk when we learn more.

And this goes offline. No more discussion at the office. Can everyone meet tomorrow after work at Café Momo?"

"That's too late," said Vinnie. "The presentations are tomorrow morning. We need to act before then."

"Vinnie, I'm sorry, but nothing can be done about the presentations. Go help Dan prepare and leave the rest to Shareen and Blanca."

"Then why bother?" Vinnie said. "Fuck, fuck, fuck. I don't care if you don't like me saying it, Maria, but fuck!"

Maria ignored the outburst. "Tomorrow after work, Café Momo." She rubbed Vinnie's shoulder as she left the room.

Vinnie motioned agreement, not with Maria, but with himself. He knew what needed to be done, and he would do it.

# Chapter 4

## Office Lamb

Inside DV&N's Spec Room—shorthand for the pretentious Spectacular Room, named because of its panoramic view of New York—the two candidates faced each other across the long table, waiting for the others. Linda came dressed in her power suit, and she'd chosen it well: professionalism without the appearance of a man hidden inside a woman. Dan's suit had been chosen by Ginny and approved by Vinnie. Dan had complained—"I'm selling my ideas, not a suit"—but Ginny had made sure he looked his best.

The two candidates smiled and uttered perfunctory greetings before taking their assigned seats at the midpoint of the ellipsoid table, which was rumored to have replicated Gary Del Vecchio's surfboard. Linda faced the outer window, while Dan faced the corridor through a glass wall that ran from floor to ceiling so that anyone passing could enjoy the view. Gary Del Vecchio had designed this room to counter high-rise claustrophobia among DV&N employees nestled in interior offices. And he had succeeded. He also intended the open-environment plan to minimize office politics. At that, he failed.

Yet Gary's main focus was the bottom line—and that meant the expanding European Union markets that rivaled those of the US. By the end of 2013, the EU had grown to twenty-eight countries and over five hundred million people—nearly twice the United States population—and a GDP ten percent larger. So DV&N needed a better position in Europe, which the board felt was achievable with better coordination among DV&N offices across London, Paris, Milan, Vienna, and Frankfurt, among others. Today they would be picking their first-ever European chief executive director.

And now, Dan and Linda, the final candidates for the position, presented a battle of two VPs with completely different management structures in mind for addressing the European challenge. Bucking current management trends, Dan favored an arrangement that would encourage direct and reciprocal communication at the individual country level, whereas Linda favored a traditional chain hierarchy. She ran the San Francisco office like a kingdom, and she felt that approach would be even more appropriate in Europe.

As the board members filed into the Spec Room, most of them made a bee-line to the back wall buffet where fresh fruit, yogurt, and juices were served. There was not a single donut or bagel in sight, in keeping with DV&N's health-conscious corporate culture. The DV&N board had more diversity than most: one male African-American, one male Latino, two Caucasian women, and one disabled, male veteran, along with four other members of the standard-issue white male variety. The board generally met twice a year, yet the members knew each other well. They met frequently on the "circuit board," which was not an electronic reference but a modern-day variant on old-school nepotism: I'll invite you to join my board, and you invite me to join your board. Guffaws echoed from the rear buffet—commiserating over golf handicaps, no doubt. But when they took their seats around the table, the men and women of the board donned serious faces, matching those of the two stone-faced candidates.

The four partners completed the board. Bill Barrington was at the buffet first, followed by Brian Neale, Chief Financial Officer, co-founder, and senior partner. Neither said a word as they took their seats near the head of the table. At the head of the table sat CEO Gary Del Vecchio, the other co-founder and senior partner, his power drink in hand, nodding like a dashboard hula figurine to no one in particular. Last to enter was Maria Benfatto, Gary's executive assistant and a junior partner. Maria grabbed a glass of sparkling water before sitting next to Gary. The two presenters had brought their personal assistants: Vinnie Briggs for Dan and Shareen Cooper for Linda; Shareen had been temporarily assigned to Linda in lieu of her usual assistant, who had remained in California. The only other person in the room was a recording secretary who sat at a small table behind Gary.

A coin toss placed Dan first in the lineup. He was nervous, which was unusual for him. He stooped behind the front room dais, farthest from the four clustered partners, and his backbone curved. He vacillated between speaking and clicking his laptop mouse for the next slide, and his presentation was filled with caveats and hypotheticals: "… and if I had the data I could show the rebound in the second quarter… you'll have to accept my hypothetical result based on similar, published data… I wish the data was here to show how my model accuracy improves with each quarter after a downturn…"

For forty-five minutes Dan rambled, making errors that would embarrass a first-year business student. He even spilled juice on his paper handouts, which were the best substitute he could manage for the data not in his Power-Point slideshow. Vinnie quickly soaked up the liquid, but he couldn't salvage Dan's dignity.

Dan's apologetic closing hardly sounded like that of a potential director.

He fumbled his analogy to Feynman's *Challenger* disaster analysis. He stuttered. He heard himself substituting tautology for analysis. Like a US presidential candidate who blows a debate with rookie blunders that leave pundits incredulous and voters stunned, Dan had his Obama second-term debate moment, complete with his lame "trust me" conclusion.

Finally, it was over.

Linda ambled to the dais as Dan collected his notes. She tilted her head to him and spoke quietly, but her words were audible throughout the room: "Very good, Dan. You're a hard act to follow." Later in the day, Vinnie would relay to Blanca his translation of Linda's words. "She gave him a slap on the back and the old nyah-nyah-nyah-nyah. 'You were bad, really bad. Ha ha. You're a fucking schoolboy.'"

Dan passed the screen pointer to Linda. Her demeanor contrasted with Dan's in every way. She stood tall, her arm outstretched, pointer held like a baton as she bellowed: "Europe needs strong direction. Markets are not subject to votes. Europe is in chaos and my plan does not need twenty-eight diverse opinions. Let me show you what *real* data means to a model."

*How is it possible?* Each of Linda's flashing tables of data stabbed at Dan. Linda highlighted first-quarter growth followed by a decline in the second. Her model would have anticipated the second-quarter decline and created buy/sell opportunities. In Paris, she'd avoid the delay of a flood of independent counsel from each European capital. Her data analysis cried for decisive action, a profit-making guarantee. Dan watched the presentation stoically, but on the inside he cringed: Linda was a European Director.

Yet her churning graphs and sonic voice weren't what caused Dan's queasiness. It was her data that caused his discomfort. She had replicated the widely accepted second-quarter volatility after bear markets—but she had failed to include the exceptions, like the Frankfurt Stock Exchange and Berne Exchange, in four out of seven years. What's more, she had chosen only *specific* DV&N investments during the volatile years—not the entire portfolio. She might be correct for the targeted sectors, but she'd need to know ahead of time which sectors, and when. Could Linda have made these *a priori* judicious choices in larger cap stocks at the time? Dan doubted it. No one among DV&N's European analysts were that savvy. Her conclusions were applicable only if she were able to choose specific stocks ahead of a dip—and clairvoyance cannot be programmed into an economic model.

Dan whispered to Vinnie, "That's wrong. How would she know ahead of time? Don't you see?"

"Shh, Dan. We'll talk later. Have more juice." Vinnie reminded Dan of the rule that candidates would not criticize each other.

Dan drank his juice.

The board deliberated in private before speaking to the candidates. They complimented Dan on his thought-provoking theoretical presentation, and congratulated Linda.

Like a trained seal, Dan also barked congratulations to Linda, who responded with conciliatory words and passable modesty. Despite voting secrecy, Dan soon learned that he hadn't impressed anyone. Bill revealed this to Linda as they walked into his office, and his remarks were overheard by Blanca. Blanca called Vinnie, who told Dan.

"Only Maria? What a joke. I wish she'd voted for Linda. It looks like a sympathy vote."

"If I know Maria, she was sending the board a message. She knows something's wrong," said Vinnie.

"And just how would Maria know? Does she have the data? Does Maria know Linda's data was perfect? *Too* perfect? Maria did me a disfavor with her vote."

"Come on, Dan, I know you're upset, but don't blame Maria."

A long silence followed. Dan sat in his office chair, studying the wall.

Vinnie broke the silence with a scream. "Fuck, fuck, fuck! Linda and fuckin' pimp Bill rigged the whole fucking thing. Fuck 'em."

"Drop it, Vinnie. What's done is done. You think every bad event must be criminal, but not everyone has a brother like yours."

Dan stopped himself, then held up a hand in apology.

"I'm sorry, I shouldn't have said that. I'm upset."

"Forget it. You're right. My brother is a criminal, and the fact that he's been behind bars for two years proves it."

Dan acted as if he heard nothing. "I'm taking the rest of the day off."

"Good idea. Talk to Ginny, drink good wine, and tomorrow you can..."

Before Vinnie could even finish his sentence Dan was at the elevator. He glanced to his left down the hallway and saw Bill patting Linda's shoulder.

As the elevator pinged, Dan heard another sound. "Har har, har har."

Dan boarded the elevator and let the doors close behind him. *Vinnie's right,* he thought.

Fuck 'em.

# Chapter 5

## Celebration

A long office corridor separated Linda and Bill from Dan at the elevator, and neither even looked in his direction. Their eyes remained fixed on each other.

Linda whispered, "Meet me in the lobby in ten minutes. We'll go to my hotel. I'll go over a few details in my proposal I didn't address. You can give me the thrust of the board's deliberation."

"And you'll get lots of *thrusting*, too. Har har, har har." Grinning widely, Bill patted Linda on her shoulder before returning to his office.

Linda went into her temporary office and looked at Shareen. "I'm leaving now to finish packing for my flight."

"Of course. And congratulations."

"Thanks. I did a great job, didn't I?"

Shareen turned away, touching her keyboard without typing.

A similar discussion took place at the other end of the hallway, as Bill gave his own departure instructions to Blanca.

"Gotta go. Need to pack and prepare for California. Only send me urgent emails, and don't call me the rest of the day unless the building's on fire. You can wait until you're outside before calling. Har har, har har."

"I'm here if you need anything," Blanca said. Of course, what she thought was, You're a fucking asshole, Shithead. I would rather burn in a fire than call you. You think you're so superior, but you're nothing but slime. Tener mala leche. She'd have to mention these thoughts in her Saturday confession.

"That-a-girl. I'll be back in two weeks. And don't do anything I wouldn't do. Har har, har har."

Bill walked out the door.

Blanca held her breath until she was sure Bill couldn't hear her. Then she muttered, "You fucking pig. I would never do anything *you* would do. Your balls should become infected with gangrene that spreads to your legs and feet so you can crawl around like the snake that you are. Goodbye, Shithead, take as much time as you need. I won't be answering your phone."

Kicking off her high heels, Blanca relaxed. Saturday's confession had just become longer.

* * *

The New York Hilton Midtown on Sixth Avenue—officially "Avenue of the Americas," though no native New Yorker would call it that—had a standing reservation for Linda, although really the six-person suite was a generic reservation for Del Vecchio & Neale, Inc. kept available for visiting clients or board members. Bill entered to find Linda closing a suitcase. "I'm glad the asshole board guy from Texas brought his family and requested the Park Plaza instead," he said. "Goddamn cowboy. This hotel is much better for our purpose."

"And what purpose is that, Bill? The view?" Linda twirled the suitcase combination lock.

"You're such a slut. I love it when your mind goes to the gutter. Shall we get started? I mean on the plans for the proposal. Har har, har har."

"We do have a meal waiting for us," Linda said. Food had been served to the room at Linda's suggestion; she wanted to at least give the appearance of a more proper meeting. It was true that Bill had every right to be at the hotel, but she still felt they needed to show discretion from this point forward.

"Fine by me. We'll eat first, then we'll fuck."

Her lips curled. Linda turned away and shot a furtive glance toward the bedroom. *This will be my last act and final hurdle before Paris. Then I won't have to be with Shithead again, ever.* She smiled, remembering her surprise when she first overheard two staff members in the ladies' room use Bill's nickname. *It suits him.*

"Tell me about the board discussion," she said.

Bill poured wine into their glasses. "Not much to tell. Dan's poor performance took everyone by surprise. To be honest, I think they felt sorry for him. If he'd done better in style they might've overlooked his lack of data. Going in, he was the favorite by far."

Linda swirled the wine in her glass. *Fuck them. Fuck Bill too, for telling me.* "How did they decide?"

"Gary summarized the arguments. Took him twenty goddamn minutes, too. Questions came up on the models. Maria raised a nontechnical question, which might have been a problem. She suggested the board consider the reaction of the European directors to you and Dan. In her opinion, Dan would inspire confidence and trust. You're lucky I was there. I told them how you're admired by your California group… lied through my teeth, but it did the job."

"Fuck you. Lied through your teeth? Fuck you."

"Hey, hold on. What's the problem? You won. I did my part, didn't I?"

Bill reminded Linda that it was he who had blocked Dan's access to the data. *And* he had helped her *manipulate* the data, a fact no one had caught, not even the meticulous nerd Brian Neale. "Come on. Don't be so sensitive. You were great. *We* were great. It's over. Let's celebrate and plan for Paris."

A half hour later, with the bottle of wine finished, plus an additional four ounces of scotch for Bill, the two engaged in sex that could have taken center stage at Madison Square Garden.

Afterward, Bill was putting on his pants as Linda emerged from the bathroom.

"Did you review the estimated profit for Europe?" he asked. She knew he wasn't referring to the figure she'd given the board; he was talking about the real figure, the figure that was just between them.

"Of course. It's just as I said." If all went as planned, she and Bill would each be pulling in double-digit millions. And that was her lowball estimate.

"I could cum just thinking about it." Bill smiled. "I'll be rid of my disgusting wife. Of course, my spoiled brat kids will want to visit their superrich Daddy, but not a goddamn chance unless I can bribe them to hate their mother so she commits suicide. Now *that* would be worth a visit." Bill removed spittle from his lips with the back of his hand.

They left the room together. No reason not to, since supposedly they'd shared only a meal. Linda carried her laptop slung over her shoulder, and a bellhop toted her luggage to a waiting limo arranged by DV&N. She had three hours until her flight, but she was eager to escape the cooling New York temperatures—and Bill's chilling comment. She understood crime for money; that made sense. But Bill's unrestrained malice toward his wife was something else entirely.

As she climbed into the limo, Bill leaned over and snickered, "We're on our way, babe. Nobody can stop us now."

The limo pulled away from the curb, leaving Bill behind. As Linda opened her window to rid his breath from the car, she wondered just what Bill was capable of doing.

# Chapter 6

## Unnatural Defeat

Even with twenty by twenty feet of space and a larger prep room out front, Ginny's Bloomingdale's office confined her pacing. Dan had promised to phone by eleven a.m. with news of his success, and eleven-thirty had passed with no call. Ginny didn't take this entirely as a bad omen, but it sure wasn't good, either. By noon she had covered half a marathon. Enough; time to act. She telephoned Dan's office. Her call went straight to Dan's voice mail.

She called Vinnie next. "Vinnie, I can't reach Dan on his cell. What's happened? Tell me. I can guess, but I want to hear you say it."

She could hear Vinnie sigh. No doubt he hadn't expected to be the one to break the bad news. "I'm sorry, Ginny. The board selected Linda. It was a fucking farce… pardon the language. I'm angry. It was a goddamn circus."

"Where's Dan?"

"He went home. I don't blame him. He took it hard. We all did."

* * *

The front door flung open and Ginny burst in to find Dan in the living room, a glass of red wine in one hand and a near-empty bottle on the end table.

"Ginny, you didn't need to come home. I'm indulging in self-pity."

"Can I join you?"

Ginny went to the kitchen for another wine glass. "Tell me what happened." She poured what was left of the bottle.

"A disaster. Without the data, I fumbled around. Worst presentation I've ever given. Worst presentation *anyone* has ever given. A total mess."

"I'm so sorry, Dan. I love you." Ginny was under no illusion that her words would ease his pain or repair his pride. Her Dan *never* came in second, at least not academically. She'd heard him talk of third place, even fifth at some college swimming competition, and he had laughed about it. He wasn't cut out to be an Olympic swimming medalist, and he didn't want to be. His Stanford swimming scholarship was perfunctory; they needed to fill out the squad and he couldn't turn it down. But it was math that excited Dan—math where he sought his fame—and he had never before had to experience real failure in that area.

Dan's knees touched his chest. "You know, she fudged the data."

"Linda?"

"Who else? I could tell. Her premise was flawed, but I can't prove it. She made up the data so that it looked perfect. She outwitted me. She tricked the board."

"I'm so sorry. What can you—what can *we* do?"

"Nothing. Nothing at all." Dan walked to the window, finishing his wine. He stared at Central Park "Damn it. How can life continue as if nothing has changed?" He pointed. "Look, see, the people hurrying around, the horse-drawn carriages with tourists, the darting yellow cabs. They have a purpose. Everyone down there has a *purpose*. What's mine? More of the same? What should I have done better?"

Ginny had seen Dan withdraw from normal routine life before. He'd done so when working on his grad school thesis, when wooing new clients, and of course recently, when preparing for the executive director proposal. But what she saw now was different.

Looking at Dan's colorless, gray face, his mouth half open, the tip of his tongue visible, Ginny saw a different man. Dan's pigeon walk, with his arms glued to his side, epitomized despair. She had never seen Dan like this.

Of course, he'd been sulking this entire year, but that was her fault—because of her obsession. He complained and brooded, but he still responded to her; he'd argue with passion and anger.

He never once came home early to drink. Never.

Ginny knew a thing or two about battles with inner demons. They never ceased, not completely, and victory was only temporary. She knew that their recent sex proved that those demons could be beaten—but only in the short run. Today should have been a day of joy, for Dan and for her. It should have been another reprieve from *her* demon, not the creation of a new one for Dan. She had anticipated Dan telling her that he had crushed Linda and Bill, tossing them like the man in the pool, metaphorically anyway. Instead she found Dan wrapped in misery, weak and indifferent.

Ginny's anticipated passion morphed into sympathy. She curved her body into Dan's rear and clasped her hands around his chest, her head on his shoulder. "Let's go to bed."

"Ginny, I couldn't possibly have sex now."

"I know. I don't mean sex. We'll snuggle, hold each other, like we used to do. That's all."

Her fingers tightened on Dan's expanding chest. This was good—for her. She felt his spreading laterals pushing her forearms out, his firm ass pushing against her pelvis.

Dan bowed his head and jerked away. She pulled back. What is this? Depression? Has self-pity overpowered him? Why does he care about tiny people on the sidewalk?

"I'm not a loser. I need air. I need to think. I'm going out."

"I'll change my shoes. We can walk in the park."

"Thanks, but I'd rather be alone."

"Wait, I'll just be a sec..."

The front door shut behind him.

# Chapter 7

## Sign On the Dotted Line

Alone in the room, Ginny saw the walls, the floor, the ceiling as if for the first time—like on the day when she and Dan had moved in. And a strange day that had been.

Unlike many couples, their first anniversary did not include dinner, champagne, or an exhausting night in the bedroom. Well, it did include exhaustion, and sex, but the exhaustion was not from sex alone.

Ginny and Dan's anniversary came on the same day they relocated to their newly purchased condo on West 70th overlooking Central Park.

Adjustments to their new location had to be made, and a new gym was Ginny's highest priority. On her last trip from the moving van with yet another box, Ginny asked Fred, the doorman, for a recommendation. He suggested a place called UltraFit Gym on West 68th, around the block. With the elevator door closing, Fred yelled out: "The owner's a professional bodybuilder."

Upstairs, she found Dan kneeling among half-unpacked boxes, and she breathlessly told him the news.

"Dan, there's an Olympic-size pool and state-of-the-art equipment." She'd found it on UltraFit's web page, which she'd pulled up on her phone on the elevator ride up. "Should we apply for a spousal membership?"

"I'm fine. My gym is convenient for my morning schedule."

"Okay." Ginny had immediately gone to her laptop to learn more. She followed UltraFit's link to owner Ben Hausen's personal Facebook page. Her computer screen filled with a picture of Ben in a poser suit, accepting the Mister America trophy. Ginny became Ben's Facebook friend, gaining access to even more photos.

The next day, she arrived at the gym bright and early. UltraFit's ground-floor glass windows revealed a modern gym: highly polished chrome machines, wall-mounted flat-screen TVs, stationary bicycles and treadmills in formation. Marionettes swayed in cadence to heavy thump-beating music that cascaded into the workout hall from the lobby. Thump. Sweat. Thump.

Sweat. She knew from the website that the floor below housed showers lined with imported tiles, spa-like changing rooms, male and female saunas, and private massage rooms. And at the far end of the floor was the restricted-access windowless X-room.

She walked up to the reception desk, where a wall of photos and trophies, all Ben Hausen's, was prominently displayed. The day manager, Steve, greeted her. He was muscle-buffed and varnished. Her eyes wandered over his stretched T-shirt, his accentuated pectorals, the nipple just below his pinned-on nametag. Ginny watched as Steve's eyes lingered on her chest. *Good.*

Ginny's wardrobe had been chosen specifically to impress the owner. Torpedo tits filled her push-up bra, while her plunging neckline seemed made for a Lunar Rover testing ground. Below her abdomen were silk trousers, molded to her hubcap derrière.

"Hi, I'm Steve. Can I help you? Are you interested in membership? We have state-of-the-art equipment. May I show you around? The locker rooms have private showers. We supply fresh towels, all extra large. The sauna's ready early in the morning. We have our own scented soap. We supply alternative shampoos and individual blow dryers. Can I show you around? We have a great facility."

Ginny liked Steve's rapid-fire nervous cheerfulness. She moved behind the desk to help him catch his breath. Steve froze.

"Hi Steve, I'm Ginny Livorno. I'd like a membership. Any chance I can meet with the owner?"

"That's not a problem, except Ben's away for two weeks. He's always available to members. You'll like him, everyone does. He's impressive, too." Steve pointed to the photos. "He has the best arms and the biggest chest on the circuit."

With her back arched, Ginny gave Steve doubts about his last statement. "Great. I look forward to meeting him, arms and chest included. You're pretty good yourself." Ginny reached up and squeezed Steve's arm, then swished her hand to brush his chest.

"Nice pecs. I see you've done good separation." Ginny picked up the membership application, not waiting for Steve to unfreeze before she was out the door.

Ginny spent the first week at her new gym nosing around. In particular, she persuaded Steve to give her an X-room tour, even though that was strictly for bodybuilders only.

The X-room was an iron room: bridge iron weights, railroad-sized iron bars, and iron men. Thighs wider than waists, necks that were wider than heads, and forearms made for walking. The women were men with halter tops. The X-room made jumbo jet men. The women carried ordinary men in their gym bags as accessories. One-hundred-percent pure processed beef, a stockyard of cattle in contrast to the ground floor's hopping sparrows.

Ben approved all X-memberships. Steve told Ginny that each interview ended with Ben's edict: "Work out, work hard, and don't fuck around."

Voyeurism, drug-selling, and soliciting or offering sex to other members was forbidden. In five years, only two people had been booted out—due to overt solicitation. Steve hinted that Ben turned a blind eye to the other rules in the months before a contest: pills were known to be exchanged; needles were magic scepters; and the steroid-enhanced, high-octane, testosterone-fueled bodies made it likely that someone would fuck the vending machine. And if they did, it wasn't a rule violation.

Within two weeks, Ginny had established her UltraFit routine. She was doing cardio on a stationary bicycle when a double-decker bus parked next to her.

"Hi, I'm Ben Hausen," the bus said, hand extended.

Ginny dismounted, pulling her T-shirt down to stretch over her sports bra as she did. Ben's jaw moved. Ginny waited.

"Wel… welcome to UltraFit. I hope you have everything you need. Don't hesitate to ask any staff member or me for help."

"Hi Ben, I'm Ginny Livorno. Thanks. Steve's been great. You've got a great setup here." They shook hands, but Ginny didn't let go.

"Thanks."

"Everything's perfect. Keeps me motivated to get stronger."

Ginny pulled her arm in to bring Ben closer—except she moved, not Ben. Her left hand rested on Ben's arm.

"Like you. Nice bi. I disagreed with your second place at your last contest. Your symmetry was better than the winner's." She squeezed.

Ben instinctively flexed; it was a habit formed over time, as people would often touch him and request he "make a muscle." Ginny might have said Ben's arm felt like a bag of crushed stones, but she didn't. Instead she said, "This curls more than the one-fifty posted on Facebook."

According to Ben, Ginny had been the first and only member who had grabbed his arm on the first meet *and* could recite his training weights.

Four weeks passed before Ginny followed Ben down the staircase to the X-room. As Ben keyed the access code and swung open the door, he was startled by something touching his back.

"What the hell? Oh. Hi, Ginny."

Ginny's form-fitting workout clothes could make cotton cry. She watched

Ben's eyes move from her forehead to her chin, and then linger on her bosom. *Oh yes, Ben, they're real.*

Her inhale distracted Ben further, which provided enough cover for her stealth move into the X-room. Ben followed.

"Got a minute? I'd like to talk to you about my training."

"Ah, okay. Shall we go to my office?"

"Can I take a look around?"

Ginny rubbernecked. She imagined there wasn't a piece of equipment that didn't shudder when the door opened at six a.m. Rustproofing saved the iron from disintegrating in this room that steamed with fire brigade sweat. But mostly she surveyed the members: men bigger than tanks, fueled by steroids.

"Nice equipment."

In another corner Ginny spotted two rafter-size men, dripping with testosterone. "Are those two preparing for an event?"

"Just Billy, in the blue mesh T, for the Manhattan Classic under-twenty-ones. He came in second last year."

*Unreal,* thought Ginny as she watched Billy curl a loaded barbell direct from a shipyard foundry. His veins were stoking his body and he looked like a bag of nails.

"Under twenty-one? I'd be worried about skin stretch. We'll be hearing more about Billy, won't we?"

Ben opened the door. "Shall we go to my office?"

Although she had several UltraFit staff as alternatives, Ginny wanted Ben for her personal trainer. If not, Steve was next, she supposed, but she really craved Ben's high-def muscle and his dual-core sixty-four-bit processor brain. Ginny knew he was smart due to his blog commentaries on movies, novels, music, education, and social politics. He quoted *The New Yorker.*

However, Ben's self-imposed rule was to only train competitive body-builders. And with two bulls in his schedule already, a third wouldn't fit. Yet a *non*-bodybuilder could... *if* he changed his rule.

"You'd be my first non X-member," he said. "You know that, don't you?"

"Yes. And I'm just as serious as your other trainees, even if I'm not in competition."

"If you weren't serious I wouldn't consider your request. I'm going to be up front, Ginny: I'm doing this for myself. I spend so much time here that I miss intelligent conversation on topics other than weights and diet. Don't get me wrong, the guys need to be dedicated, and they have no time for books, especially since... well, let's say some of them would strain to read a picture book. If I take you on, it'd be for me as much as you. You'd be my relaxation."

"That's fine, Ben. A mutual benefit is good, as long as we know it'll be intellectual and nothing more."

Ben recoiled, and Ginny quickly moved forward. "Sorry, Ben. I didn't mean to be rude. Some gay men have tried it with me. I guess they were bis—if bisexuals really exist. Are you offended?"

"No. Actually, I'm glad you said it. I can guarantee this is a *professional* training relationship. Now let's pump. Er, iron I mean."

After that, Ginny quickly fell into a routine with Ben.

He really was a great trainer, and Ginny loved the workouts. But training wasn't *all* that interested Ginny. She also loved to watch Ben's bulging arms, his striated legs, and the bulbous glutes of his buttocks as he moved to spot her lifts. On heavy presses, she would watch him inhale, his pectorals inflated. She even went with Ben to the Manhattan Classic and cheered Billy on to first place.

But she only observed. It was harmless.

Until the day sthenolagnia took over, six months ago.

That was the day she walked out and closed the door on Dan, metaphorically speaking. She knew something had happened; Dan did not.

Today, they both knew.

# Chapter 8

## End Run

Weaving between the crowd, Dan walked the New York City streets, his head bent as he examined the sidewalk pattern. He headed west to the Hudson River, the breeze from the water chilling his neck and matching his cold inside. He ambled by the river until the edge of Hell's Kitchen, then changed direction to go across town along 59th until Broadway, where he stood at the foot of the Christopher Columbus statue.

Dan imagined what the explorer would have done in his place. Columbus must have questioned his voyage. What would he find? Would he survive? Would his men? Would they return?

Dan's voyage back to his condo brought recriminations, not questions. *I should've insisted the presentation be postponed until I had the data. I should've been better prepared even without the data. I should've challenged Linda's data and model regardless of the stupid rules.*

Throughout the night Dan tossed in bed, sleep eluding him. Sometime in the dark predawn he rose and moved to the couch in the living room. He examined the failures in his life, starting with Ginny. He'd been inadequate for several months, which he blamed entirely on her trainer. No, Dan revised, it was more complicated than that. Maybe Ben had been the problem at the start, but it was Dan who had devoted too much time to working on his model and his presentation over the last three months. He had ignored Ginny, and as a result he had missed the signs of her emerging obsession—her so-called *stethy*—and her infatuation for bodybuilders. Ben wasn't the problem. *He* was.

Failure was the byword, and Paris was just the next installment. He gave a shoddy presentation, and he knew it. *I should have been better prepared and not fixated on the missing data.* The result was a big loss not only for him, but for Ginny and their relationship. The failure would also impact DV&N: Linda's proposal would fail, Dan was sure of it. Dan hated himself for his performance.

The room seemed even darker, even though a bit of daylight now lit the sky outside. Why did I wait so long for the data? Why did I not investigate with IT? Why did I not complain and make a big issue of my request? Why did I rely on Bill Barrington? Why didn't I insist on a postponement? Why didn't I question the nature of the emergency situation with Northrop that a technical team could have handled?

Dan didn't return to his bed until seven a.m., just as Ginny was rising for work. "I'm going to stay home," he said. "I'm exhausted and I didn't sleep last night."

"Good idea. Would you like me to stay with you?"

"No. I'm going to sleep. You shouldn't lose time over me."

Ginny had stopped dressing. "Just sleep? You're not going to do anything rash, are you?"

"Of course not, it's just—I've got to talk to Gary about Linda's data."

"Dan, you can't just call up Gary with an accusation. I'm sorry, but you have to accept the board's decision. Don't torment yourself over what's already past. You'll get 'em next time. And Gary couldn't change the board's decision anyway, even if he does agree with you."

Dan nodded his agreement, and after Ginny left for work he slept a couple of hours. But at nine o'clock he dialed Gary's number on his cell.

"Gary, can you meet me? It's important."

"Look Dan, I know you're disappointed. Frankly, I wish it had gone better for you. But there's nothing to be done."

"Gary, please. This is important. It goes beyond the Paris job. Can't you at least extend me the courtesy?"

* * *

Dan found Gary sitting at the rear table of the Fresh Fruit Cafe, a Tropical Special frappé in front of him. Dan sat down opposite the CEO and asked the waiter for another of the same. Gary had already explained that he had a tight itinerary—he had an afternoon flight to Argentina—so Dan knew he would need to be brief. But Gary spoke first.

"Dan, before you say anything, I appreciate how much you wanted the position." Dan tried to interrupt, but Gary raised his hand. "I know this was important. It was important for me, too, and for DV&N. But we made our decision and we'll live with the consequences, good or bad. That's business; you know that as well as anyone. Some decisions are good, and some aren't, but you've got to keep looking forward, not second-guess the past. I'm sorry, but I'll be blunt. You didn't present a good case."

"And I would have if the data had arrived," Dan said. "Gary, I'm seeing a disaster about to happen and I'd like to prevent it. Please let me examine Linda's data for you."

The two men paused as the waiter returned with Dan's drink. Then Gary continued.

"I'm sorry, but no. You are not to snoop around. It will only create friction within the organization. I appreciate your concern, but it's over. Period."

"Sure, sure. But listen a second. I've talked to our branches in Europe this morning, and Linda's data doesn't fit what I've heard. Her premise is invalid. You'll have a stampede of clients to our competitors."

"I know this is emotional for you, Dan, but we asked these questions, too. Bill confirmed her data and several of her points. We're not stupid. You need to stop this, now."

"But don't you see? *Bill* was the one who didn't get me my data. He's helping Linda and—"

"Enough." Gary's tone was firm. It was clear that, for him, this conversation was over. "Dan, you can't accuse a senior executive of... well, I don't know what. This has to stop. This *will* stop. Do you understand? Look, I appreciate your concern and I know you're disappointed. You worked hard. But you lost."

Dan looked down at his Tropical Special and swirled his straw around without taking a sip. "I admit this was important to me. I really wanted this, and I accept that I screwed up royally. But I'm talking here about DV&N, not just about me. This will blow up in *your* face. This is not my pride speaking—this is me giving you my professional advice as an analyst."

"And I've heard you. You're a valued employee and I consider you a friend. Now take *my* advice and move on."

Dan began to protest. "Her data are flawed. Her analysis relied on parameters that she extrapolated out of thin air." Dan choked, coughed, and raised his hand with a finger extended. "She—"

Gary held his hand up. "I said, enough. You're ranting."

"No, I'm trying to tell you—"

"Stop now. I've changed my mind. I'm not giving you advice now. I'm *telling* you to take a week's leave of absence. If you go to the office in the next week, starting now, or if you in any way attempt to access Linda's data, I'll have you fired, as sorry as I would be to lose you. I can tell you're upset, and I don't blame you, but I won't have you creating havoc at the office. Do not call Europe again. A disgruntled employee makes for a bad workplace."

The two men barely shook hands as they left the cafe, one going to Argentina, the other to sulk.

# Chapter 9

## A Lunch Klatch

Vinnie, Blanca, Shareen, and Maria walked to O'Neil's Pig 'N Poke, an upscale Irish pub. It was Maria's choice, both for the alcohol and for the privacy afforded by the booths. The women settled in while Vinnie placed their orders: Guinness for Shareen, Dos Equis for Blanca, white wine for Maria and him. As he sat down, Blanca asked Maria, "Is it true about Dan?"

"Yes. Gary met Dan and he's on forced leave for a week. I'm to call security if Dan shows up. Vinnie, you better keep Dan away." Vinnie nodded, and Maria continued. "Dan accused Linda of cheating, of fudging her data. He called the European offices about it, which upset Gary."

Vinnie wagged his finger. "But you know Dan's right, don't you? That fuckin' bitch did something. Dan knows it and I know it."

Maria was visibly shocked. "Vinnie, I will not tolerate that language."

"Shit, Maria, you're right. I'm sorry. I'm angry and upset."

"That's no excuse. Do you think you can control yourself?"

"Yes, I promise. I'm a fucking idiot."

The three women laughed, acknowledging Vinnie's sincerity.

Vinnie explained, "It's just, this puts me in charge of the office while he's away. And don't forget, I'll be in charge again in November, when Dan's off with Ginny, in Paris of all places. It's not fair. I should be at NYU, not running a department." Blanca's look reminded Vinnie that he had chosen to withdraw from the MBA program over her protest. And over Dan's, too.

Maria patted Vinnie's hand. "I'm in the same boat. With Gary and Bill away, it's me and Brian Neale in charge, and he never leaves his office."

Shareen's husky voice percolated up her six feet. "I'm sorry, Vinnie. I know this is bad for both you and Dan. How is Dan? How can I help either of you?" Despite fifty-five years in Brooklyn's tough Bedford–Stuyvesant, and with two brothers incarcerated and a few other family members dead due to either drugs or gang conflict or both, Shareen was as compassionate as anyone Vinnie had ever met. And she was smart, too: she was among the few

African-American women of her age to have attended Columbia University. Smart, tough, and kind—all packaged into one.

Maria preempted Vinnie. "To be honest, I don't know what I'd do if Dan shows up. 'Immediate dismissal'—those were Gary's words." It was unusual for Maria to allow herself to gossip like this; she must have felt overwhelmed by this particular responsibility.

Silence hung over the booth. After the drinks arrived, Blanca removed her shoes and explained the oddities of Bill's schedule. Before the Northrop crisis broke, he'd had a family vacation planned, a Tuesday night flight on the original presentation date. After the crisis, his calendar showed his new flight on Friday. "But guess what," she said. "The calendar update was made *before* the Northrop crisis even happened. I missed that detail the first time I checked. So out of curiosity, I emailed Bill's travel agent for his itinerary. And according to his itinerary, his departure was *always* for Friday, never Tuesday."

Vinnie stopped drinking his wine. "I don't understand."

"It means the calendar dates were artificial. Bill never had a Tuesday departure. Unless the travel agency didn't email me everything; I mean, I suppose it's possible there was an even earlier itinerary than what they sent me. But if not, it's like he *knew* the Northrop crisis would happen and had planned for it in advance."

The conversation paused, as if everyone was letting this sink in, and then Shareen piped up. "I was in the lobby a few minutes after Bill left the office. He got into a cab with Linda. What's *that* about?"

Blanca grimaced. "Pig. I feel really bad for Mrs. Barrington. I liked her when we met at Bear Mountain for the picnic last summer. She took an interest in my boys."

Shareen smiled. "Me too. She wanted to know all about my church choir."

Blanca cursed in Spanish. "Typical men: betrayal and deceit. I'm sorry, Vinnie, but it's true."

Shareen twisted. "You know, I'm sorry for Dan, like everyone here. And I've spent enough time with Linda now to confirm that she's both mean-spirited and condescending. But still, Blanca's information isn't actually incriminating."

"It's certainly fishy," Vinnie said in a flat voice.

Shareen turned to Vinnie. "Blanca said the agency might have omitted the original itinerary. Unless we have access to his entire travel file, we're jumping to unfair conclusions."

"I can get it. Log in to his computer," Blanca said quickly.

Maria put down her wine glass. "I don't think so. That'd look suspicious.

What would be your reason?"

"I don't know… maybe Bill's an asshole?"

"Really, Blanca. That doesn't help."

Vinnie's voice remained flat as he spoke. "There's got to be more. Has anyone noticed anything at all funny, especially around scheduling?"

Maria closed her eyes. "Now that you mention it…"

Vinnie looked up. "What?"

"Well, it's just that, when the presentation was moved to Thursday, I remember thinking that it worked out nicely, because I already had the Spec Room reserved for Bill for that time. Two weeks ago, Bill had asked me to set up a reservation for that very day."

The Spec Room really was spectacular, which of course meant that everyone wanted it for their meetings. As a result, the room required special reservation, and all reservations had to go through Maria.

Maria continued: "Bill said he needed the room for a client meeting. He used that tone of his, you know the one, Blanca?" Blanca nodded. "He 'wasn't to be questioned.'"

Vinnie raised his hand. "That's some coincidence…"

Maria interrupted him. "Now that I think about it, he asked about Gary's schedule, too—Gary's availability. He said Gary had to meet this client. He wouldn't give me details, just said he'd talk to Gary about it. I never heard more about the mystery client, and after the presentations came up, he never said a word about rescheduling the original meeting."

"And you don't think that's fucking suspicious?" Vinnie's voice rose.

Maria gave him her *wash-your-mouth-out* look.

Shareen's deep voice rumbled. "I think we should look over the calendars again. Look for anything, no matter how trivial. Start with the week before the presentation, maybe two."

* * *

As they left the Pig 'N Poke, Vinnie said to Blanca, "I'm going to do more than check Dan's calendar."

Shareen overheard and took Vinnie's arm, pulling him ahead. "Vinnie, tread carefully. Office espionage is illegal. You could lose your job or even go to prison. And if it comes down to it, I *will* report you. Be smart, Vinnie. You're too sweet to lose."

They soon split up and went their separate ways, and only Vinnie and Blanca remained, both headed toward the 42nd Street shuttle.

"Vinnie, what's the matter?" asked Blanca.

"It's nothing. Don't worry about it."

"That won't wash with me. You're down, I can tell."

"Fuck yeah." Vinnie's voice had a tinny sound. He swayed, holding on to Blanca as they quickened their subway descent to avoid an oncoming shower.

"Please, don't stonewall me."

No response.

"Come on, Vinnie, talk."

Vinnie sighed. "I guess I'm just depressed, is all. I didn't realize how much I wanted to go to NYU."

"You still can, Vinnie. Dan made that clear. You've been guaranteed the DV&N scholarship."

"I can't leave Dan."

"Why not? Dan's a big boy. He'll easily get another assistant."

Vinnie winced at that, and she noticed his eyes crinkle. Vinnie was barely audible when he said he didn't want to talk anymore. Blanca said she'd call him again after her boys were in bed.

* * *

The TV was tuned to Hitchcock's *North by Northwest* when Blanca called Vinnie.

"What is it really?" she asked. "You could attend NYU. Dan will survive without you."

"But what about me?"

"What do you mean?"

"… It's complicated."

"Of course it's complicated. It involves *you*." Blanca's little laugh wasn't reciprocated. So she waited—her usual successful tactic with Vinnie.

"Fuck, Blanca, I love Dan. And I don't mean like him a lot. I fuckin' love him. You know what that means, don't you?"

This time Blanca's silence was unintended.

"It's stupid. I'm a gay man and Dan's so fuckin' straight you could use him to draw lines. He loves his drop-dead gorgeous wife. Paris would have solved everything."

"I… I don't know what to say. You're right, this *is* complicated."

"Fucking right it's complicated. I thought I might meet someone like Dan at NYU, someone who was gay and available."

"You still can. There's still time to enroll."

"I can't. I want to *be* with Dan, even if I can't have him. And not for sex— which we don't have, just so we're clear. It's the way he talks. He's smart and has fantastic ideas. His math is beyond me, but I get the concepts. And he actually asks for *my opinion*, Blanca. Believe it or not, Dan says my ideas are good. With Dan, I use my brain in ways I've never done before."

"I'm still at a loss here."

"You and me both. Fuck… that's why I wanted Dan to move to Paris. With him gone, I would've had a chance to start anew—a real chance to meet smart people like Dan. Maybe find someone for me."

"Vinnie, you will. You're a great guy. I'd fall for you, gay or not gay. You're handsome, funny, intelligent, and considerate. I can't imagine anyone *not* falling in love with you."

They talked for nearly an hour. Blanca tried hard to boost Vinnie's self-esteem. Vinnie moaned over Dan and his lonely life. Neither heard the other's point of view. Vinnie felt he was "addicted" to Dan, which Blanca thought overly dramatic.

Then their conversation took a turn that alarmed Blanca. Vinnie suggested that he could do more with regard to the investigation of Bill and Linda.

"Vinnie, you heard Shareen. It's espionage. Leave it to us."

Vinnie agreed—but far too readily. "Sure. Goodnight, Blanca."

Blanca did not sleep well that night.

# Chapter 10

## Bill Has Mail

Del Vecchio & Neale, Incorporated had twenty-first-century executive offices outfitted with top-of-the-line amenities: electronics, cables, Mac computers, Bluetooth, WiFi, wall-mounted flat-screen TVs, adjustable ergonomic chairs, private bathrooms with showers. Ninety-five percent of the work flowed through computers, tablets, and cell phones; the electronic cloud knew all, from shared calendars, data, reports, and spreadsheets. The business had always been both hard-core and hardball; the modern office had merely added the hard drive into the mix.

And it only made sense that assistants' calendars were linked up with those of their bosses. The assistants were, after all, the ones in charge of making all the updates. When entries changed, each executive was kept up to date in real time with an instant refresh of their calendars and agendas.

"I've pulled up the first recorded calendar entry for the Paris presentation," Vinnie said to Blanca from his office telephone. "It was set up three months in advance. Maria put it on the general office calendar."

Vinnie tapped more keys then added, "The first meeting change came a week after the original schedule. Maria moved it from morning to afternoon. No reason given. That's the thing with calendars, they don't provide reasons."

"Yeah, I know," said Blanca. "I'll look around on mine and Bill's DV&N calendars and see if I can find anything else." She clicked off.

A few minutes later, Blanca pinged Vinnie through Gmail; Vinnie had suggested that for the sake of discretion they communicate through their private Google accounts, although they both knew that even these were traceable. Her message confirmed that Bill's DV&N calendar and her own calendar both showed the same history—Maria's original meeting date, then the subsequent move to the afternoon—as Dan's personal calendar and the general DV&N calendar.

However, there was one caveat: Bill kept a personal calendar that wasn't linked to the DV&N office calendar. "Bill doesn't trust me, or anyone," Blanca wrote.

Vinnie's next message was predictable: "Can you access Bill's personal calendar?"

"Yes. He maintains his personal calendar himself, but it still has to be coordinated with the office or he'd double-book. He usually does this with me once a month, but when he's away, like now, he sends me a link and I do it for him. I'm typically only editing future events, but that doesn't mean I couldn't go back and look at earlier information."

After sending this message, Blanca called Vinnie on the phone; whatever she had to say must be too sensitive even for Gmail. "I can access his files, too," she said. "He mistakenly left his password scribbled on his notepad one time and I wrote it down, although I'm not sure why." Blanca giggled. "One more thing: Shithead's pretty computer-savvy, so he might have protected his individual files with passwords, or he might have a way to track if they've been opened."

Vinnie digested all this. "This is great. But let me access Bill's calendar, not you. I can do it from his office, which will leave less of a trail to me."

"It's too risky, Vinnie. Someone might see you. You have no reason to be there—but I do. Remember Shareen warned you about corporate espionage? Please, just leave it to me."

As Vinnie hung up, he imagined being chased by a crop duster, like Cary Grant in *North by Northwest*.

* * *

Throughout October, DV&N was a beehive. With the launch of the new European Division, everyone had been expected to be on hand at all times. Except Bill, who had wangled an invitation to be a speaker at a weekend conference in San Diego; something about "New Strategies for Volatile Markets."

"Sorry, Gary," he explained, "but this is too important for DV&N not to be represented. I'll use an extra day to schmooze with our southern California clients and make them feel special."

Bill didn't mention that the five-star Park Hyatt Aviara Resort conference venue included the world-class Arnold Palmer golf course—which in his mind greatly enhanced the conference's "importance."

He piggybacked two extra days by using the Monday Columbus Day holiday and an extra day to schmooze with clients—on the course, of course—and would be flying back to DV&N headquarters on Wednesday, arriving late afternoon.

This created just the opportunity Blanca needed. She planned to examine Bill's calendar on Tuesday—about the time he'd be on the back nine, she estimated.

* * *

The mid-afternoon sun baked Bill as he reclined on the balcony overlooking the lagoon. His golf was finished for the day, and he was bored, with no activity planned for the night. *Might as well have another scotch and check my emails; make it look like I've done some work.*

Bill opened his laptop, and in seconds he was virtually sitting in front of his New York City computer. First he pulled up his DV&N calendar to check his availability for the coming week. He had received a text while on the fairway: *New Special next week by reservation. RSVP RR by Tues.* Cryptic, but easily deciphered: Bill was a regular customer at Ristorante Roma and the special was a high-stakes card game. His work calendar showed that he had no client meetings on the evening in question, but he still had to check to see if he had any personal plans. *Better not be some fucking kid recital or basketball game that night.* Why couldn't his wife go without him?

Bill pushed his scotch aside, minimized his DV&N calendar, and pulled up his private one.

A flag? What the fuck? That's not possible.

The little red triangle in the corner of the calendar blinked at Bill. *This isn't right.* He reached for his cell phone, catching Blanca minutes before the end of the New York workday.

"Were you on my computer?" Bill barked as Blanca answered the phone. She didn't answer right away, so he added, "Did you hear me?"

"Uh, yes Bill," said Blanca. "Vinnie said Dan wanted to meet with you when you return. I didn't want to bother you. It didn't seem that important, so I checked your personal calendar rather than disturb your well-deserved relaxation time." Her voice sounded strained.

"Don't *ever* go to my computer again. I don't give a *fuck* what either Vinnie or Dan want! And how did you get my password?"

"You gave it to me before your last trip, don't you remember? You thought I might need to access files."

Bill's scotch-infused brain accepted this explanation, and he moved to the next part of Blanca's statement. "And what the fuck does Dan want to meet about?"

"I'm sorry, Vinnie didn't say. Shall I call him and ask? Vinnie's gone for the day, but I can try to reach him at home, or I can give you his number."

"Don't bother, I don't want to talk to that queer. I'll find out when I get back. Mark it on the office calendar and add a note about the subject. And stay off my fucking computer. Tell Rodney in IT to change my password."

Bill's head cleared for one moment. *Fucking lying cunt. She's up to something. I know it.*

Bill ended the phone call, poured more scotch, and settled back onto his chaise longue. He looked across the lagoon to calculate probabilities. What were the odds that Dan would want to meet with him? What were the chances Blanca wouldn't know the reason? Was he likely to have given her his password? Had Blanca given his password to anyone else? To that queer Vinnie? Scotch and shock had induced fear into the normally fearless Bill Barrington.

*Fuck Blanca, I'll call Rodney myself.*

Blanca's remark about Vinnie leaving reminded Bill that Rodney in IT would probably have left work too, so he telephoned Rodney's cell.

"Hi, Rodney, it's Bill."

"Hi, Mister Barrington. I thought you were in California."

Bill skipped the pleasantries. "My password was used on my private account by Blanca. I don't think she's secure. I want you to change it now. Send me a text with a new password."

"Of course, but I can't change it without you in the office with me. Remember, we set up a double secure system for partners and senior staff. We'll have to wait for your return."

"Shit. There's nothing you can do?"

"Sorry, sir. I can make it top priority the minute you get back."

"Fine. And another thing: I want to know if anyone's been reading my emails. Can you check on that? Don't read them yourself, just find out if they've been read. Let me know if anyone has been going through my files, too. This is your priority."

"Okay, Mister Barrington. I'll do it first thing tomorrow."

"And remember, Rodney: this stays between us. No one hears or your ass is on the line. Got it?"

Bill hung up without waiting for Rodney's response, because the question Bill wanted answered was not for Rodney:

*What does that pissant Dan Livorno want?*

# Chapter 11

## Uptown Lunch

Weekday lunch meant business, so Ginny's midweek invitation to her friends to join her at Pane e Olio had surprised them. The personable owner, Giulio, greeted his long-standing customers like honored guests. With each order he said, "Va bene. Grazie."

The ladies waited until Giulio left them to enter the kitchen, and then Sarah spoke. "So Ginny, what's up? Not that I'm complaining. Anything to get away from those whining, privileged undergrads and their bloated checking accounts. Oh wait, that was you two."

"Not funny for the umpteenth time. Enough with the privilege envy," grumbled Betsy.

"Very mature, rich girl. Okay, Ginny: spill. You sounded anxious."

"This is going to sound weird…" Ginny hesitated.

Sarah looked to Betsy, then back to Ginny. "I love weird. Kinky and sexy, too?"

"Maybe."

Sarah rubbed her breast.

"Stop that. This is serious." Ginny paused. "You know what, it's not important. Let's talk about whatever you want."

"No way. You brought us here for a reason. C'mon, I'll behave." Sarah smiled and Betsy nodded.

Removing her napkin from the table, Ginny started, "Dan's taken his loss hard. He's been distant. This is the first time his effort hasn't paid off."

"Come on, disappointment happens to all of us," said Sarah. "It's been what, five or six weeks? Dan needs to grow a pair. I'm sorry he didn't get the Paris job, but it's not the end of the world."

Betsy chimed in. "You can take the Bloomingdale's job, and Dan can join you later. He'll find employment in Paris. Maybe a few months' commuting might even be a little fun."

"It's not the commute, or a job. Dan's an overachiever. Success is all he knows. And this loss was unfair… fixed. He thought that DV&N people were good, honest people. He's… changed."

Neither friend responded, so Ginny continued. "I've told you our sex has been lousy for a long time, and I accept the blame for that. But now it's Dan. He's… off sex. I've tried everything. And I mean *everything*. I'm worried. Even scared."

"I'm sorry," said Sarah.

With a shift in her seat, Betsy tilted. "Me too. Have you suggested counseling to Dan?"

"He won't discuss it. And as much as I loathe the idea, I suggested antidepressants. He balked."

"I don't know what to say other than I'm sorry." Sarah was using her professional voice.

"Thanks, but I'm not here for pity. I want *advice*. You see, Dan's not the only one with needs. A few months ago… uh, remember my idea about Dan and me with my UltraFit Gym trainer Ben?"

Sarah and Betsy grunted. Back in the summer, Ginny had shared with them her fantasy about having Ben and Dan together. They had told her to drop the idea. In no uncertain terms.

Ginny lowered her eyes for a second before looking up to speak. "I didn't take your advice. I asked Ben if he'd be willing to pose for Dan and me. Not sex, but sexy. Remember that idea?"

Heads nodded.

"Ben declined. He even told me that my offer wasn't the first. He offered to find some other bodybuilders looking for extra cash, but I said no, I wasn't interested in a stranger, I wanted him."

Betsy waved her hand. "Good for Ben. A muscleman with common sense."

"Amen, amen," sang Sarah. "Really, how could you think Dan would enjoy that scene? Sometimes you amaze me."

Ginny stuck out her tongue. "Fine. You'll be happy to know that I dropped the idea."

After pausing to swallow her lie, Ginny began again. "But recently I've been thinking that Ben might reconsider if I say this helps Dan's depression. Ben's seen bodybuilders in deep depression losing a contest they should have won. Rigged. Judges influenced by money—or in other ways, if you get my drift."

"Every sport has skeletons. Payoffs, doping. So?" Sarah's voice deepened.

Giulio arrived then with their meals, and the women thanked him. Ginny drank her chamomile tea before she replied.

"True, but it's worse for bodybuilders, or at least it's different. These guys take years to pack on fifty, sixty pounds of muscle. And the prize money on the way up is really small—unlike, say, for tennis pros. I mean, for a professional tennis player, you don't even need Wimbledon in order to earn a good living. Besides, quantitative sports are judged on observables, like speed in track, for golf it's par, and tennis the ball's over the net. Subjective sports are much easier to fix. Ben's won USA and Universe, but not Olympia because the right people didn't back him. Bodybuilding politics are brutal. Ben's even had to stay with men after losing, one guy for as long as a week, afraid he was suicidal. I feel the same about Dan."

"You don't think Dan might do himself in?" said Betsy.

"No! God, no, I don't think so."

Sarah jumped in. "Ginny, take Dan to a doctor. Stop fooling around."

"I can't. He'd hate me. Our marriage would be over if I forced him."

"And if he hurts himself, or worse? Where's your marriage then? How could you live with yourself?"

"Sarah, this isn't helping. I wanted advice on how to convince Ben. Stop berating me and *help* me."

Betsy and Sarah looked at each other.

"Think carefully," Sarah said at last. "And please forget your sexual fantasy."

"I have; I told you that." A lie, like the one she'd told when her mother found the bodybuilding magazines under her bed and asked her if she had sexual fantasies about musclemen.

Ginny could tell neither friend believed her, though. She cursed her own denial, and her voice was loud enough to shock Giulio, who was approaching the table. He nervously piled dirty plates on his arm and avoided eye contact.

In a soft voice, Betsy said, "Grazie, Giulio. Tutti sono buoni."

"Di niente. Volete altre?"

Betsy moved her index finger from side to side with a slight movement of her wrist. "Va bene cosi." Betsy's college semester abroad in Italy had paid off.

Outside Pane e Olio, Betsy directed Ginny to the side of the front door. "Here's a thought: ask Ben to be Dan's trainer. They'll talk while Dan lifts. Man-to-man bonding. As you pointed out, Ben has experience with depressed overachieving men. He's not a therapist, but that might be nearly as good."

"Maybe even better," said Sarah. "I've had two therapists, and frankly, I wouldn't be shocked to learn they both received their degrees online."

Ginny gave a faint smile of agreement. But like a chess master, Ginny was looking several moves ahead, seeing potential benefits for herself if Dan trained with Ben.

Betsy angled her head. "You realize though that Ben can't help Dan's underlying psychology. Endorphins may lift Dan's depression, but they won't resolve his issue. He'll still need therapy. You get that, don't you?"

"Yes, but it's a good start. Betsy, you're a genius."

"Flattery will get you everywhere. Now tell me I've lost weight, I haven't aged since college, and I look just as great as I did before having two kids."

Sarah's eyes narrowed at Ginny. "Be honest. Is this still about your fantasy? Because if it is, that would be a really bad idea. Promise us you'll focus on Dan."

Ginny promised.

As her friends departed and Ginny walked away, she reflected on Ben. *Do I limit my explanation to Dan's depression, as I promised? Or do I reveal our intimacy problem? If the latter, I'm the other side of that equation, and Dan knows this. Does Ben need to know?*

She had no doubt that Ben could solve Dan's problem—and hers. Forgot her promise. Ben would pose for her—and Dan, eventually. *If I'm satisfied, then it helps Dan.* But she would tell Ben about Dan's needs first; for now, her needs would go to the back burner.

In her somnambulant walk home, Ginny passed a bus pulled up at the curb. On its side panel was a Calvin Klein ad showing a man in underwear; he had rippling abs and a chest bifurcated into twin mountain peaks. Ginny turned to the storefront window, where her reflected image was superimposed onto the Calvin Klein Adonis.

Her hand reached out.

* * *

It was her mother, Anna Swinburne, who had forced Ginny to talk to Dan after a month of marriage. Actually, Anna had forced the issue by blabbing about sthenolagnia and alarming Dan. Even as his mother-in-law softened her message, telling Dan that sthenolagnia obsession was probably controllable, and maybe not even a problem, Dan had grown concerned, and one night he expressed that concern to Ginny.

Shuffling closer to Dan on the couch in their New York rental, Ginny said, "You can't believe my mother on everything. Yes, I like watching muscular men pose, but that's all. Bodybuilding is a sport, just like your favorites, baseball and swimming. Look here." Ginny opened her laptop and pulled up the website for an Atlantic City bodybuilding contest. "C'mon, maybe you'll learn to like it too. We can go together."

"That's not necessary," Dan said. "You go. I'm not interested, and I'd ruin your fun. And the truth is, I've done some online research. Technically, sthenolagnia is sexual arousal from displaying strength or muscles, which doesn't exactly describe you. I know you like muscular men, to watch feats of strength, but you also like academics, films, music, opera, and me. And I'm strong, too. Feel this."

Dan knew the routine Ginny liked. He'd been doing it ever since their first date—on her instruction. He flexed his arm, and a round mound surfaced underneath his shirt. Ginny gently pushed him, a signal for him to move to the floor. With his sleeve unbuttoned, Ginny inserted two fingers inside.

"I love this arm." She straddled Dan's chest, helped him out of his shirt, and flung it aside. "This is good."

Next off were Dan's pants, then his jockeys. Ginny took hold of Dan's engorged penis and rubbed it against her vaginal area, over her trousers. With his non-flexed arm, he pulled Ginny's stretch trousers from her narrow waist until they hinged on top of her pelvis.

"Slip them down."

Her trousers clung to her ass, pulling her panties with them. Now naked, she slid down until her firm buttocks rested on Dan's knees, her vagina fully exposed. For a half hour their spooled bodies, corded by flexing muscle and taut skin, channeled sweat created in a fairyland.

Ginny loved feeling Dan's strength. And she loved that her stethy distracted him from his fear that he'd lose her, his freak complex. She commanded and he obeyed. "Make them harder." "Get bigger." "Flex your pecs."

From Dan's broad smile and his tiger's teeth on her bosom, she knew Dan was satisfied. And now he'd be even more satisfied. She spread her legs to eternity, but kept Dan at bay until he cramped. She waited for him to beg.

"Put me inside, please."

She did; and once he was in, only Ginny would decide if he'd ever emerge again.

His final spasm shook Ginny, and his hard muscles tightened. Protected and secure, Ginny had taken refuge in Dan's striated sinew.

* * *

The bus pulled away and the reflected Calvin Klein man vanished. Ginny continued on home, satisfied with her conclusion: her obsession *helped* Dan. It gave him security and sublimated his jealousy. He never quizzed her about bodybuilders she knew, or her attendance at competitions; never about Ultra-Fit or brawny office colleagues. Yes, her obsession helped their marriage. If ever she needed to harness her stethy it was now. And Ben was her harness.

After Paris, she'd make another request of Ben. And this time he would agree.

# Chapter 12

## French Connection

American Airlines Flight 103 from Kennedy reached its assigned bay at Charles de Gaulle airport on time. Ginny was out of her seat at the initial chime. She and Dan sailed through immigration to retrieve their luggage from the baggage carousel.

From the bathroom, Ginny's voice fluted across Le Meurice Hotel's large living room suite. "What will you do about JJ?" She used the American shorthand for Jean-Jacques, their friend and Dan's Paris counterpart at DV&N.

"I don't know. I feel like a fool." Dan looked out across the Jardin des Tuileries to the temporary structure erected for Ginny's "Bloomies" fashion show on Espace Ephémère Tuileries. The hotel was too far from DV&N's Paris office, which was in the prestigious sixteenth arrondissement, to allow for a quick drop-in.

"You're acting foolish, Dan, but you're not a fool. JJ was the best man at our wedding. He and Marion are our best friends."

With their suitcases nearly unpacked, Dan sat on the edge of the bed. "Did you have to invite them?"

"How could I not? The papers, TV, and fashion magazines will cover the show. I'll be interviewed. How would I explain to our closest friends we hadn't invited them? Tell them you weren't in the mood? It won't be me who ends a friendship."

Ginny was right. Her friendship with JJ was a long one—a byproduct of Harvard's MBA program. JJ and Ginny had been classmates, and after Dan started dating Ginny, he became good friends with JJ too.

Placing his suitcase in the walk-in closet, Dan parked himself on the edge of the hotel bed, allowing his closed eyes to help him maintain his semi-hypnotic state. Dan's prevailing thought ever since they had left home had been the same: *Ginny's in charge of my life.*

Before the trip, Dan had even hinted that he might stay home. And now, here he was in Paris. Two days until the big gala. Ginny would be busy preparing for the show, while Dan would be left to roam the museums and wallow in his depression.

Dan lay back on the bed. He was exhausted already.

* * *

The ten solid minutes of applause affirmed the show's success. Models had spiraled a figure-eight runway that was designed to avoid gridlock, while flames had shot from a panoply of kettledrums. The cheers had rivaled those at a Springsteen concert.

Dan had never doubted that Ginny's show would be a huge success. And he was happy for her. But her success contrasted too sharply with his failure. She had overcome her challenges: Bloomingdale's management had taken a chance on her inexperience because of her unbridled confidence. Dan had taken the opposite path: despite his qualifications, he had blown his chance due to fumbling and nerves.

In prime runway position, Marion sat between Jean-Jacques and Dan. JJ stretched across Marion: "According to the catalog, a blouse can cost six thousand dollars; whole outfits run eighty-five-thousand or more. I hope Marion doesn't ask for one."

The light banter, along with Marion's voice, the sexiest Dan had ever heard, had distracted Dan for much of the show, but the crowd's roar of applause had awoken Dan from his apathetic torpor. On the runway, Ginny was bowing to cheers, and her 3-D Amalfi-coast curves made her stand out among the plastic, wafer-thin supermodels. At the moment, Dan hated Ginny's cheesecake smile.

"Great. Ginny, that was fantastic. Very good," he whispered.

After the fireworks died down, JJ pulled Dan aside outside the tent. "What's the matter, my friend? Why so glum?" But before Dan could answer, they heard shouting behind them.

A short, compact man had stormed up to Ginny and was letting loose with a series of curses, first in French and then in English. "You slut Americans think you can come and take control of the French fashion industry! Americans are all whores and cultural imperialists. Look at the crap you showed today!"

Dan and JJ hurried back to Ginny's side.

"I'm sorry you didn't like the show," Ginny said. Her hand was on her necklace and her voice was unsteady.

The man screamed, "You offend me, you *whore!*"

Ginny moved backward. Dan stepped forward to catch the man's eye.

Even without having exercised for the last two months, Dan could have picked up the smaller Frenchman and thrown him aside, just as he'd done with the ill-mannered swimmer.

The Frenchman turned to Dan. "What do *you* want, you fucking American? You going to defend this *bitch*?"

The man extended his arm toward Ginny, clearly intending to shove her, yet Dan didn't move; it was JJ who acted. He stepped forward, but was farther away than Dan, and before he could reach Ginny she had stumbled backward in her high heels and fallen to the ground.

Only then did Dan grab the Frenchman and pull him away.

Dan had only frozen for one second at the most; he could have blamed it on reflexes. But that's not what it was. For an instant, Dan had looked directly at his wife. The woman with whom he was no longer intimate. The controlling woman. The woman who made him believe that he was all she wanted. The woman who *really* wanted brawny oversized masculinity.

And for that one second—for *only* that one second—Dan was hoping Ginny might be punished. It was a shameful thought, he knew, and he regretted it immediately.

But worse, Ginny knew, too. In his delay Dan had seen Ginny's face contort, her eyes lock on his with understanding and clarity. She knew that, if just for a moment, her husband had cheered on her attacker.

She began to cry.

JJ shouted French expletives at the man while Marion called security. Dan held Ginny until Marion returned, then Dan gave the guard his eyewitness account. Over his shoulder, Dan caught Ginny's scorn reflected in her tears.

With the man removed, Marion rubbed Ginny's shoulder. Ginny's wish to abort their dinner was countered by Marion: wine and food would give Ginny respite. Yet Marion's winning point was unintended: "Don't worry, we'll leave you plenty of time in bed with your magnificent husband."

Dan watched Ginny, knowing his wife subtracted the restaurant time from that in bed with him.

JJ and Marion struggled to keep up the conversation. The four strolled across the Jardin des Tuileries. Dan and JJ, a few steps ahead, had heard Marion implore Ginny to forget about that little French *merde* of a man. Ginny promised she would.

I'm sure she will, Dan thought. Because she'll be concentrating on her *merde* American husband.

The early morning street clamor awoke Dan. He saw Ginny stretch, her silk negligee revealing full breasts, her nipples clinging to the fabric. Dan's bent knees hid his arousal.

"I'm meeting Marion today for lunch," Ginny said. "I'm sure you can find something to do with yourself." Cool words.

A year ago, the day would have started with a gentle coo of, "Hi sunshine, I love you," followed by, "You look gorgeous, come back to bed." Then sex. Then a shared shower and wetter sex.

Now they spoke with answering machine "leave a message" intonations. As Ginny walked out the door, there was no kiss, no "I love you." Just: "I'm going. Meet in the hotel restaurant for dinner. Bye."

The door had closed before Dan's words tumbled out: "Ginny, I'm sorry."



The small bistro where Dan met JJ for lunch was in the eighth Paris arrondissement, an easy ride on the Metro from the Musée d'Orsay where Dan had spent the morning failing to distract himself from his problems. JJ greeted Dan with the traditional three kisses, then suggested the wine.

"Fine with me. As long as it's high in alcohol," replied Dan from a face that hardly moved.

"Oh, mon ami. Ça va?"

Uncertain how to begin, Dan stuttered in imperfect French, "Ah... ça va... ça va..." He stopped abruptly.

"You've forgotten your French. Not to worry. We will speak English."

Speaking English was fine by Dan, but talking about himself was not. So JJ asked instead about Ginny's well-being and her state of mind. And in an effort to cheer up his friend, he reviewed the better insults he and Marion had rained upon the stupid Frenchman.

But regret limited Dan to giving perfunctory responses, and his shame prevented him from giving JJ full disclosure. Dan had intended to reveal how his meanness had knocked Ginny over, but he couldn't. So as JJ reviewed his better curses, Dan accepted them as if they were meant for him.

"Enough delay, Dan," JJ said finally. "Tell me what those fools are doing at headquarters. No one here can understand what happened. As you New Yorkers like to say, spill the beans."

Dan gave JJ the long version: the missing data, the last-minute date change, his sloppy presentation. For the first bottle of wine Dan focused on himself. With the second bottle, Dan speculated. He drew inferences from observations, things he hadn't forgotten. He told JJ about Linda's hand on Bill's shoulder; about his belief that Linda had fudged her data.

Dan attempted to order a third bottle of wine, but JJ's wagging finger forestalled the waiter. "I must return to the office. And actually, the office is why I wanted to see you today. I should have telephoned you sooner. If only I had talked to you… What happened didn't seem important…"

JJ told Dan about Linda Lords's recent arrival at the Paris office, her taking command as European Director, and the customary meet-and-greet with staff. She had been pleasant enough, and the staff had reciprocated, concealing their disappointment that Dan hadn't been selected.

"As a senior staff member, I introduced Lords to the staff," JJ said. "Of course I knew that she had met management during the selection process, but she hadn't met any of the support staff. When she met Antoine, our head of IT, she called him 'Tony.' That *is* his nickname, but she wouldn't have known that—or shouldn't have. Tony—Antoine—blushed and stumbled."

"So they'd met before. What does that mean?"

"Everything. I quizzed Antoine about it later. Apparently Barrington was here in July to announce the creation of the European Division in Paris and a new executive director. He asked Antoine to his hotel."

Dan raised his eyebrows. "Why would he need to see the head of IT off-site?"

JJ nodded. "Exactly. Antoine said that Linda was waiting for them both back at Bill's hotel; that's when she met him. Bill and Linda told Antoine that there were some concerns about possible corporate espionage, and that as a result, all data was embargoed—and any data requests required Bill's explicit approval. Moreover, Antoine was told that in order to catch the spy, secrecy was paramount. He'd lose his job if he were to reveal this embargo, or the hotel meeting, to anyone. He only told me because I questioned him about it directly—and, I suppose, Linda had insulted him with her informality upon arrival, unlike my long-standing friendship with Tony. Frankly, he seemed relieved to get it off his chest."

Dan's face flushed. "I was told the French screwed up the request—something to do with a strike. And that a technical problem blocked the New Jersey backup archives. You're saying all of that was Bill Barrington's bullshit?"

"Yes, bullshit is a good word for it."

# Chapter 13

## Return Voyage

Papers on the desk sat in disarray, a ballpoint pen clicked in Vinnie's fingers, and he rose for the third time to look into Dan's office. He had been anticipating Dan's return, and Dan was late. Sure, the days of Dan beating everyone to the office after his thirty pool laps were long gone; no more pool, no early rise. But this was late even for the new Dan. Here it was, nine forty-five, and there was no sign of Vinnie's boss with his coffee and a bag of donuts.

*Why the fuck isn't he here? It's nearly ten.*

Vinnie had cleaned Dan's desk and checked all the plans, but he did it all again as he watched the doorway.

Finally, without fanfare, Dan arrived. Yet even then, he hesitated for just a beat at the threshold to his own office—a cat's entrance. At last Dan meandered to his desk, throwing his overcoat onto a chair and making only a small acknowledgment of Vinnie's presence.

Vinnie's blank stare hid his thought: *What the fuck happened in Paris?*

"Hi, Dan, welcome back. How was Paris? I read about Ginny's success."

With a slight lift of Dan's chin, the slow reply came: "Thanks. It was a great show. I wish you'd been there. You'd have loved it, and I could have used your help in identifying who was who." Dan stared blankly at his clean desk's empty surface.

"I'm pleased for Ginny. I read about the fireworks inside the kettledrums. That must've been fantastic."

That was apparently enough small talk for Dan, because his only response was, "Vinnie, there's something we need to talk about. But let me catch up first. I'll start with a review of your notes during my absence, and then we can look at this week's schedule. Give me an hour."

"Sure thing, boss," said Vinnie, feeling… well, Vinnie didn't know how he felt. Dan was acting weird. His responses were weird. Everything felt weird.

Vinnie grabbed Dan's overcoat and hung it in the office closet, closing the door with care as he left.

* * *

The computer hummed to attention in the time it took Dan to replace his winter boots—an early snow had dusted New York—with office loafers. He calculated the six hours' difference between Paris and New York and concluded it was mid-afternoon for JJ. As if due to his wish alone, right then his direct line rang. One ring was all it took.

"Bonjour, Dan. Did you have a good flight back? How are you feeling? How is Ginny? Did you have your special last night in Paris? Don't tell me, I will be too jealous. What is the status at headquarters?" As JJ ticked through his rapid-fire questions, Dan drummed his fingers on his desk.

"We're fine. Ginny and I want to thank you and Marion for your wonderful hospitality."

"Our pleasure. Now tell me what you've learned."

"JJ, this is my first day back and it's not yet eleven in the morning—actually ten forty-six and two seconds. I was hoping it would be *you* with more information."

"Oh, *mon ami*, nothing yet. I wanted to meet with Antoine today but he's not here. His wife's not well, so he stayed home to care for his infant. This is his right under French work laws. Let's hope his wife has a speedy recovery. I'll try again on Monday."

A few additional exchanges on weather and matters unrelated to DV&N ended the conversation. Dan had hoped for more.

His next call was to Rodney in IT.

"Sorry Mister Livorno, Rodney's with the group in a staff meeting," said the IT receptionist. "I'll let him know you called. They should be done at eleven-thirty." A glance again at his clock, and Dan considered his options. Okay, that left him enough time to update Vinnie.

* * *

The inner corridor window was shaded before Vinnie even walked into the room. Vinnie knew that meant this was either a sensitive corporate matter or he was being fired—and he felt confident it was the former.

Placing the window remote in his desk drawer, Dan quickly informed Vinnie of Jean-Jacques's revelation regarding Antoine, aka Tony, who had been instructed to hold all data.

Vinnie's response was, predictably, a sequence of swearwords; but this time Vinnie went unchastised.

"I have news, too," said Vinnie after he finished his swearing. "Bill's and Linda's calendars were adjusted for the so-called California crisis long *before* it

53

even happened. They knew it was coming. And now, with your information, we have proof that this was a setup. We should tell Gary."

"Not yet. Gary's already warned me. This has to be a rock-solid case, more Perry Mason and less Rebus."

"Don't know who you're talking about. I know about Perry Mason—saw all the old reruns with Raymond Burr, but the other one... don't have a clue."

"Rebus is... never mind. The point I'm making is that there can't be any doubt. Everything we have is circumstantial; it makes it pretty clear they were up to *something*, but at this point that alone will not be enough. We have to have actual proof that Barrington and Lords manipulated the presentation. And we have to know why. Facts alone will not be enough. Gary will want a motive."

"They're screwing their brains out. What's wrong with that for motive?" asked Vinnie.

"Two things. First, sex is less frequent with five thousand miles' separation. Second, if I had gotten the European job, Linda would have taken over my position, increasing their sexual opportunities to pretty much limitless."

"You mean I'd have worked for *Linda*? Fuck that. Never. I'd have come to work every day in farmer's overalls and a mask to cover the rude smell surrounding Miss Piggy."

"Vinnie, focus. Linda's not coming. And we had arranged for you to go to NYU, which by the way, you should still do... I want you to enroll for the spring term. What *might* have happened doesn't matter. But let's get back to the next step.

"I'm certain there's more to the data holdup than just screwing me. Barrington requested all data pass through him, so I'll check on that as soon as Rodney returns my call. In the meantime, could you review calendar dates and go back even further? Try six to eight months, especially for Paris trips for Bill and Linda."

Walking out of the office with a swagger that may or may not have been Raymond Burr as Perry Mason, Vinnie said, "Okay, boss."

# Chapter 14

## Family Membership Upgrade

The Swinburne family, like the rest of America, anticipated Thanksgiving, the busiest holiday of the year. Aside from travel plans for out-of-towners, the main focus was on the food: turkey size, cranberry recipes, traditional stuffing—with one new version—and, of course, several kinds of pies.

Thanksgiving dinner had been Ginny's most cherished event at her Connecticut homestead. Of course, the holiday did have its drawbacks, not the least of which was being sequestered with family members—boors or opinionated—for hours or even days. Even the best of friends could become overbearing after eight hours; families could be even worse. And the Swinburne household was not immune to spats—probably more than the average family if such statistics existed—often provoked by Dr. Anna Swinburne, matriarch extraordinaire, whose lack of self-censorship encouraged others to speak their minds just as plainly. Of course, Anna Swinburne claimed that her candid manner had an academic bent and was for the benefit of others: "kindness through knowledge," she said. The prevailing family opinion was that Anna's claim was nothing but a self-serving rationalization. And in the spirit of "kindness," they often told her so.

Still, for all the pitfalls, Ginny's close relationship with her family made these minor irritations irrelevant to her enjoyment of the holiday. So every year, in the week leading up to the fourth Thursday in November, Ginny looked forward to the get-together with great anticipation.

But not this year.

As she looked around the condo, Ginny suddenly felt like the furniture seemed small, and the Thanksgiving decorations—piled in the far corner waiting to be loaded in the car—were inadequate to fill the emptiness. Ginny felt an absence of the love, the sex, the laughs, the intellectual exchanges, the friendship she'd once had with Dan. Her thoughts wandered. *Dan promised me unconditional love. Did I reciprocate? For the last year I've withdrawn from him, and he from me. We're both at fault. But I can't help my actions—they're part of my psychological makeup.*

Maybe Dan's are too.

Paris weighed heavily on Ginny in the week leading up to Thanksgiving. She had to make a decision or she felt she would implode. And there was only one real decision to make: she would refuse the Bloomingdale's job. It no longer mattered. Her life was out of control; moving to Paris would only make things worse. And just as importantly, she could not allow herself to succumb to her stethy. If she couldn't surmount her personal demons, then her marriage was doomed. And not just this marriage—*any* marriage. She would never be able to maintain a serious relationship so long as she was enslaved to her irrational desire. And without love, affection, devotion, trust—she had nothing. She had loved Dan, and she would not allow that love to be smothered by an obsession.

But she still thought that Ben could really help Dan get through his depression and confidence issues. It wasn't about her fantasy; it was about Dan. Not that anyone would believe that. She knew that Ben wouldn't like her to repeat a request he'd already refused twice, and there was no question Dan wouldn't want her pushing Ben on him as a personal trainer.

So if she was to make this work, she would need two stories, one hand-tailored to each man—with overlap, of course, should they quiz each other.

* * *

Ben stood from his desk to greet Ginny, then escorted her to the guest chair in his office. "Ginny, why are you here? What is it that couldn't wait until our next session?"

Before Paris, Ginny had believed she could never convince Ben to be Dan's personal trainer, much less pose for her and Dan to fulfill her sexual fantasy. She still wanted both—there was no denying that—but she would keep her focus on Dan's need. Ginny had analyzed Ben's prior refusals, especially her fantasy about him posing in her condo. Sarah and Betsy had been incredulous when she'd told them about the idea; they'd lampooned her logic and praised Ben's refusal. But now Ginny believed she understood where she'd gone wrong in her approach to Ben.

Her appeal needed to do three things: gain his empathy, gain his sympathy, and place his need for her intellectual companionship at risk.

With a whispering hush, Ginny filled Ben in on the Paris assault, watching Ben's chest expand until his T-shirt stretched to its tensile limit. *Empathy, check.*

She sighed as she recounted Dan's hesitation. She told Ben her marriage was about to end. "Geez Ginny, I'm sorry." *Sympathy, check.*

A long pause, and then Ben lightly coughed into his closed fist. Ginny finally spit the words out.

"Ben, I'll have to leave New York. I don't know if I'll go to Paris, but I can't stay here. I just can't be around Dan much longer in his state. It's affecting me."

"I'm sorry, Ginny. And I'll be very sorry to see you go."

Ginny leaned forward. "Ben, I was wondering if… well, I would like you to train Dan."

Silence followed.

"Ben… ah, Ben… if I leave Dan, leave the city, I'll no longer be your client."

"Sure, Ginny. Just like if you had moved to Paris."

"Yes, but in that case we'd have remained close friends." Even as she said the words, Ginny felt guilty. *I'm blackmailing him.* "I'm sorry, that didn't come out right. I'm not saying it would be a conscious decision. That's just what happens when people move away. Especially if they—rightly or wrongly— feel a friend refused to help them. Ben, if you must refuse because of your principles, then of course you should."

Whack. A blind shot and a bull's-eye.

Again, silence. Ginny decided she'd have to go all the way. She had crossed the threshold anyway; now she would reveal her secret, the part she had promised herself she wouldn't tell.

"Do you know about sthenolagnia, Ben?"

"Of course. It's common knowledge among bodybuilders. Some say it's an urban myth, and some believe it explains bodybuilding, or at least why many people attend contests. I'm undecided, but… well, I've suspected you had a form of it. You know, sometimes you're kind of obvious when you go around asking men to flex."

Ginny wasn't pleased about that remark. She normally would have told Ben to go fuck himself, but not today.

"So you know the syndrome manifests differently among people?" Ginny went on to summarize her experiences with stethy, her mother's diagnosis, and various fantasies. And once she got started, the words just spilled out. Before she knew it, she had confessed more than she had ever confessed to anyone—although she had stopped short of revealing her ultimate fantasy about Ben and Dan.

"I'm going to say something I thought I'd never say," Ginny concluded. "I've become fixated on wanting Dan to have incredible power and brawn. But Paris… it's completely emasculated him. He's flabby, weak in both body and mind. I need Dan to be manly again for me, and not just his muscles, but his mental attitude. Ben, I know you can help Dan develop his physique and return his confidence."

Ben opened his mouth to speak, but Ginny held up the palm of her hand. "Let me finish. You've told me what you've done for bodybuilders, men demoralized after defeat in a competition they should have won. You rescued them—and you can rescue Dan… and me. Please help. *Please.*"

Clarence-Ginny-Darrow waited for the one-man jury to rule.

Ben examined the backs of his hands. "Listen carefully. I'm not going to try to persuade Dan. Do you understand? Dan has to be the one to ask me to train him."

Ginny's leap was the kind seen at basketball games. *Victory.*

As Ginny left Ben's office, he held the door for her, as he had on her arrival. Ginny grabbed his rock-hard shoulders and pulled—which moved her closer to him—then gave him an open-mouth kiss: her paperless contract.

Two passing female patrons commented. "I thought he was gay." "He is gay." "Maybe he's bi." "I wish he'd be bi with me." Laughter followed them into the women's locker room.

Back at the front desk, Ginny asked Steve to book an appointment for Dan to meet Ben on the Friday after Thanksgiving; she wanted to preempt the possibility of Ben "inadvertently" overbooking.

"Yes, Ben knows," she said in response to Steve's question. "And Steve, remind Ben to wipe the lipstick off his face." She smiled, her finger touching her bottom lip. Steve would pass on the message and Ben would understand: "Fuck you, Ben, for your smug sthenolagnia remark."

The front door to the condo seemed heavier than usual as Ginny pushed it open. Her second round was about to begin. She had imagined this would be an even harder sell, so she was surprised when Dan acquiesced to the idea after only two simple questions: "When? And what time?"

Ginny should have felt joy, but she didn't. She had interpreted Dan's easy capitulation as further proof of his weakness, his emasculation, and his depression.

# Chapter 15

## Hard Liquor for the Girls

At about the same time that Ginny was leaving Ben's office, Shareen and Blanca were sitting in a corner booth at one of their favorite post-work taverns, discussing their holiday plans. Like everyone else at DV&N, they were exhausted from six weeks of long, frenetic workdays. All staff had been mobilized for the European division announcement, and in addition, the two women had the self-inflicted burden of reviewing their bosses' prior six months' worth of appointments.

Shareen ordered a Jack Daniel's and soda and Blanca ordered her favorite Mexican beer—Dos Equis—with two slices of lime. Maria joined them a few minutes later with a cafe latte.

At least five minutes of chatting later, Maria checked her watch. "I guess Vinnie isn't going to make it. He's probably staying late to help Dan catch up on his first day back from Paris. He's been carrying Dan's load for too long. Poor Vinnie. I wish Dan would snap out of his depression. Vinnie's been left more or less in charge. Honestly, I think this is too much. It's unfair to Vinnie."

"Yeah, ain't that the truth. Poor Vinnie looks downright harassed," said Blanca.

They were surprised when Vinnie slid into the booth beside Blanca. He had no drink in hand, a departure from his usual routine of bar, drink, sit.

"Fuck, fuck, and fuck. I am so pissed off. This is absolute bullshit. Dan's sure that fuckin' bitch Linda doctored her data."

Maria sat up straight. Her eyes widened and her voice deepened. "Okay, stop right there, Vinnie. You're upset, but I am *not* going to listen to your foul language or have you malign a woman no matter how much you dislike her. We *all* dislike Linda, but you will not use sexist language. If you say anything like this in the office I'll have you fired! Understood?"

Shareen, Blanca, and Vinnie gaped, then lowered their heads in unison. Vinnie swayed and his soft voice cracked. "I'm sorry, Maria. I apologize…

to all of you. I hate that Linda makes me act this way. I just feel so badly for Dan. He's crushed, you know? I love my boss—and not in a gay way, but as a person. Dan's the first man who's ever treated me like I counted. He's a good person, and what's happened to him is so unfair."

Maria took Vinnie's hand. "We know. I accept your apology. We all do, right?" She looked to the other two women, who mumbled agreement.

A few minutes of small talk passed while Vinnie went to the bar for a glass of white wine. When he returned, he retook his seat next to Blanca. Maria immediately addressed the group. "Let's do this properly. Shareen, you start. Anything to report?"

Shareen reached into her large handbag and pulled out a notepad. "I found a few things that seem unusual. Nothing is incriminatory, just out of the ordinary. First, Linda's calendar is marked with a cryptic note two weeks before the original September presentation date."

Looking down at her notepad, Shareen read, "MKRSVLV FR 8. All caps. At first I thought this meant that her flight back to San Francisco was on the Friday after the presentations at eight a.m. It didn't take long to see RSV means Reservation and MK stands for Make, and of course LV means Leave. It's a no-brainer to see FR is Friday and eight is the morning departure time. Yet the calendar was marked two weeks before any crisis."

Vinnie half stood. "See! I told you."

Maria shook her head. "Wait a minute, Vinnie. Slow down before jumping to conclusions—and sit down. Friday might mean *after* the original Monday date. There is no 'from and to' destination. For all we know, Linda might have planned a weekend away with her Baltimore friends to relax before the big presentation. All we have is that Linda reminded herself to make a reservation for some Friday, to somewhere, at eight a.m. And that's *if* Shareen has correctly deciphered the message; I'm inclined to accept that she has, but still, it's hardly strong evidence."

"Bullshit. Linda knew she had to leave on Friday."

Shareen shuffled the pages of her notebook. "There's one more thing. Baltimore's out. An email from Linda to her travel agent shows that she requested a New York to *San Francisco* flight at eight a.m. on the Friday before the Monday."

Vinnie started to say, "That fuck—" then immediately bit his hand sideways to prevent himself from completing his sentence.

Maria pointed her finger to the table. "Good, it clarifies the destination. Still, Linda might have made a mistake in dates that she corrected later. What about you, Blanca? Find anything?"

"Yes. I went through Bill's computer calendar. I remember at the time he told me he would update his personal and office calendars on the flight change. The change never showed on the office calendar, yet his personal calendar had the correct new Friday flight. And—get this—the entry regarding the flight change appeared *two weeks earlier* than the Northrop crisis, just like Shareen found on Linda's calendar. Why would Bill have one flight schedule on his personal calendar and another on the office calendar? I should have caught this sooner, but I've been too busy and I haven't had time to check for discrepancies between the two calendars."

Vinnie wanted to say something, but his only thought was *That lying fuck-off shitface*, so he sat silently morose.

Everyone waited while Maria sipped her latte. "This is delicate. It seems Linda and Bill either had reservations, or at least *planned* to make them, for a departure before the originally scheduled Monday presentation date. That's very suggestive... but there could be an explanation."

"What explanation? That's ridiculous," said Vinnie.

"Well, like I said, maybe Linda made a mistake in setting up the date with her travel agent."

"Yeah, right!"

Maria looked around the table. "Okay, I know that's weak, but it's *possible*. But listen, I don't want any of you"—she fixed Vinnie with a pointed stare—"making any wild accusations until we have the complete story. All we know is that there was some fishy scheduling. That won't fly with anyone. We need to know what the travel dates mean, what they were up to, and why."

Vinnie shook his head. "We already know why. They were trying to screw up Dan's presentation."

"Vinnie, that's not logical. Linda wouldn't have known the crisis would move the date forward, would she? It could have been moved *back* a week or two for all she knew, giving Dan *more* time. And how did she know Dan wasn't prepared already?"

Slightly above a whisper, Shareen interrupted Maria. "Vinnie, I expected Dan to be prepared no matter what. Everyone did. It came as a shock to all of us that his presentation was sloppy."

"Yeah, well, he didn't have the data and that's because IT fucked up, not Dan," said Vinnie.

Maria knitted her eyebrows. "And just how would Linda have known that? And why was Bill involved? Surely Bill wanted the best proposal to win, because his annual bonus depends on DV&N profits. What's Bill's motive, Vinnie?"

The table seemed to grow smaller in Vinnie's view. He already knew from Dan that sex was unlikely to work as a motive. He blurted out, "Money."

Maria shook her head. "Bill loves money, yet I'm going to guess Dan would have brought DV&N more European profit than Linda will, and that translates into a bigger bonus for the partners, including Bill."

"Maybe Linda paid him." Vinnie's weak voice belied his lack of conviction.

"How much could she possibly bribe him? Bill's bonus from European returns could run to five hundred thousand or more. Linda couldn't top that, could she? We'll need a better conspiracy motive than that, or we have nothing." Maria paused. "Let's dig some more, after Thanksgiving. Be careful—and nothing illegal." She focused on Vinnie again. "Look through emails and notes that you have a *legitimate* reason to check. We're on thin ice."

Drinks were pushed to the center of the table, and the group rose together to leave. They all seemed satisfied with the plan, except for Vinnie, who thought: *More procrastination. We've got them and we need to find more. Bullshit.* He felt frustrated, pushed to the sidelines. *Fuck the illegality and fuck thin ice.*

He forgot to ask if anyone knew the name of Perry Mason's PI.

# Chapter 16

## First Date

For the last two months, anyone who observed Dan staring intently out his office window might have been excused for thinking he was an inspector for the New York Port Authority. However, the half a million vehicles that crossed the bridge each day were not Dan's concern. Ginny was. He refused to acknowledge that his own senseless jealousy was actually fulfilling his own fear: that he could lose her.

They had met at a joint seminar of the Massachusetts Institute of Technology Sloan School of Management and the Harvard Business School; Dan was enrolled in the former, Ginny the latter. He had been shocked by her first words: "Good job, Dan Livorno, but be careful. Someday someone will be better." If her words had shocked Dan, her body had shot him with a lightning bolt. Ginny had a jigsaw-drafted body with a starlet's face on top.

She told him later it was his smug look that had made her follow him. In particular, she liked the way Dan had looked pussycat pleased when he'd asked a question during the lecture and the lecturer, a Harvard professor, had showered him with praise.

"What's your name and which school are you with?" the professor had asked.

"Dan Livorno. I'm from the Sloan."

"Well, Mr. Livorno, MIT's lucky to have you. That's quite possibly the best question I've ever had. Do you have a solution, too?"

Starting with a stutter, Dan's voice revved up: "Yes... Professor Barish, I do..."

Ginny had singled out Dan for exactly the same reason that Professor Barish had: his brilliant mind. And, of course, for his great body and movie star looks. After shocking Dan with her opening comment, she went on to add, "I'm enrolled in Professor Levenson's 'Uncertainty Models in Economics' next spring. By any chance will you be enrolling?" Ginny was taking advantage of the Harvard–MIT arrangement to cross-register between the two universities.

"Of course. He's the best."

The joint classes started their intellectual engagement; the physical soon followed.  From that point forward, Dan and Ginny's love affair included a constant academic contest between them.

Dan rested his head in his hand as he watched the traffic crossing the East River. *Our best years.*

Is it entirely my fault?  What about Ginny?  Ginny had been sucked into her sthenolagnia, obsessed with the world of bodybuilders. Ben Hausen's not at fault. It's Ginny who's the culprit.

With a half-hearted kick he clanged his wastebasket against his desk. What about me? Don't I bear some responsibility? No! Cheaters beat me. If I had won, as I deserved, I could have helped Ginny with her obsession. This is not my fault.

Dan's thoughts drifted even further back, to high school. It had been, for him as for so many teens, a period of embarrassment and low self-esteem. The cruel cheerleader that had labeled him "freak," a nickname that had stuck for years.  It wasn't true, but truth cares not about labels.  The cheerleader had wanted out and she'd made up her reason.

Dan fought the unwanted memory: his reflection in the swimming pool, validating the cheerleader's malice.  He was poolside, his Speedo around his ankles, penis stiff and as long as the pool.  He recalled the torment of the laughing-hyena high-school seniors bellowing at their prank.  The boys laughed, but at least they never excluded him for it—unlike the girls he had hoped to date.

Stanford followed high school. Women didn't shun him in college, didn't run away; they didn't know that he had been branded. And to Dan's relief, Stanford had no cheerleaders. But still, Dan couldn't shake his paranoia. No one laughed as he crossed the campus, but he saw lips parting as he passed, and he imagined the worst. And he was certain that any coed he dated would cheat on him. That feeling was only strengthened when he finally did work up the nerve to date—only to find his date with another man a week later. He decided then that women were *all* cheerleaders, pompom in hand or not. Insecurity ate away at Dan, and he responded by substituting the safety of mathematical equations for dating.

Ginny had been the first woman ever to ask him on a date, the first to suggest sex before he did.  And the restaurants, the movies, the weekend skiing. Dan liked that Ginny didn't want to date anyone when she was with him: right from the start, she wanted exclusivity for both of them, which Dan was more than happy to oblige. He felt secure for the first time. He even told Ginny about the cheerleader, which produced a brief smile and shrug.

Then it dawned on him that Ginny didn't understand jealousy. She had no idea what being dumped was like. Sure, she had seen it with her friends and her sister, but she'd never been dumped.

Dan pinched the bridge of his nose. He'd had his happy years with Ginny. The years when her fingers would circle his cheek; when her tongue boxed his; when their lips compression-sealed and her firm breasts pushed against him.

Dan flexed his arm unconsciously as he stared at the iron bridge. Even early on, Ginny had demanded she feel his strength. She had talked about his hard swimmer's shoulders, had marveled over his striated canyon scapula. She rafted his upper torso and dug into his trapezoids. She found clever ways to move her tits closer to his cleavage line. She traced his body with her fingertips, redrawing him. Her index finger would glide along his horseshoe triceps to mount the vein of his bicep. "Flex, Dan."

Now he sat down in his office chair and flexed again; he could feel the flab underneath his shirt.

The soft hums of the office sounded to him like Ginny's old refrain: "This arm is fantastic, Dan. Flex your bis." He'd had no reason to refuse at the time, but now he knew that he should have. He should have listened to his mother-in-law. He should have paid attention when Ginny purred as she squeezed his biceps or punched his pectorals. Her acts were neither foreplay nor sex chatter.

A knock at the door stopped Dan's descent into resentment.

Rodney from IT entered. "Hi, Dan, I heard you wanted to see me?"

Dan signaled to the chair in front of his desk, his voice louder than he had intended. "Rodney, I want to ask about the data I had requested for the presentation. Do you remember?"

Rodney's head bobbed. "Yeah, sure. Archives in New Jersey had a problem."

"That's what you said at the time. I'm sure that's been solved."

Rodney crossed his legs. "Uh, yeah, I suppose. I'd assumed you didn't need the data anymore once... once..."

"Once I lost to Linda. It's okay, you can say it, Rodney. I'd like the data now. Do you think you could get the data disks for me?"

"Uh... uh... like I told you, we had technical problems..."

"Stop the BS, Rodney. There was no technical problem. I want that data by Monday."

Rodney's voice trembled. "There was a technical problem. I'm telling the truth."

"Enough lying.  Do as I ask or you'll find yourself unemployed after Thanksgiving. Bill won't be able to protect you this time."

"Dan... I... I didn't want to hurt you—or anyone. I had no choice."

"Data by Monday. Goodbye, Rodney."

The door shut and Dan reclaimed his place at the window.  The Queensboro Bridge traffic continued to flow.

Dan had achieved his goal. He could go home now.  He had nothing urgent on his agenda, although, to be fair, the same could be said of home. *Should I leave my perfunctory job to face my indifferent marriage?  Do I call clients to converse in small talk, or do I engage Ginny in banal discussion?  "Who's up for an Oscar?"  "Do you like the new lighting on Broadway?"  "I think the Sox have a chance for the pennant."*

Dan spread his fingers against the office window, tapping his index and middle finger, alternating thoughts between beats: Linda was in Paris.  The pathetic French *merde* stole his marriage. Ben Hausen would become Ginny's toy. What had Bill and Linda stolen?  What did they want and why? I know the data will reveal at least the latter, and maybe resolve other issues.

Fifteen minutes passed before Dan shuffled back to his desk.  His lackluster performance since Paris had piggybacked on his rocky marriage; DV&N's former rising star had turned into a pencil pusher, and his body had turned into a jelly donut. Gary Del Vecchio had been blunt: "Start showing initiative, Dan. Show me your creativity again, the reason I recruited you." Maria Benfatto gave Vinnie a different version of the same sentiment, quoting Gary: "People think DV&N is a charity.  Well, these people had better understand I give to *real* charities because of the profits earned from hard work here." Maria was tacitly encouraging Vinnie to gossip—to tell Dan what Gary was thinking. Vinnie did, but was met with only a shrug.

With nothing better to do until he had the data, Dan went home.

# Chapter 17

## Blanca Joins Team Vinnie

Vinnie's determined quest to help Dan escalated the Wednesday before Thanksgiving when Blanca called him. She asked him to drop by her office before their pre-Thanksgiving klatch lunch because she had something to show him. This would be the first klatch lunch in the last three weeks, as everyone had been too busy preparing for the first European review scheduled for the Monday following Thanksgiving. Linda had been on the Paris job for two months now, and the partners wanted an assessment before the Christmas slowdown, which always happened earlier and lasted longer in Europe than in the US.

"Vinnie, I've got something to show you," said Blanca as he entered her office. She reached into her top drawer and pulled out a long piece of wire and a small metal appendage.

"Hector brought this to me yesterday. He wanted to show Bill, but Bill had already left for the Thanksgiving break. Hector said this wire got wrapped around the bristles of his vacuum cleaner as he vacuumed Bill's office. I had no idea what it was or where it might have come from, so I brought it home to my electronic whiz husband and he immediately recognized it. This is a microphone, the kind used in surveillance. I'm thinking Shithead pulled a Nixon and bugged his own office."

The historical reference meant nothing to Vinnie, but the wiretapping did.

"Then where's the recording?"

"I don't know. Jandro"—Blanca referred to her husband, Alejandro—"said this is a Bluetooth device and requires a Bluetooth-capable recording device. So somewhere else there has to be a Bluetooth recording receiver."

"And I'm guessing Hector didn't find a recorder sucked up into his vacuum cleaner."

"Nope."

"It has to be Bill's computer, don't you think? He'd want to store any recordings on his hard drive." Vinnie thought for a moment. "Did Hector show you where the wire tangled?  If it's Bluetooth, it can't have been too far from the receiver, maybe fifteen or twenty feet, and Bill's office is at least fifty feet long and maybe wider—so if we knew where the mike was, it would help us locate the receiver. The ceiling would limit the range too, given the height and interferences with electrical wiring."

"Hector didn't say where he was when it tangled, but I can ask."

"In the meantime, why don't we go have a peek around ourselves?"

* * *

Blanca dimmed the interior windows in Bill's office, preventing anyone in the corridor from looking inside.

They found nothing in the easy locations: under the chairs, wastebasket, and potted plants. Bill's neat desk was devoid of family photos and mementos, limiting the possible hiding places. Vinnie climbed up onto the desk, struggled to move a few ceiling tiles, and found nothing.

Blanca checked underneath the modern couch in the corner, around the desk legs, and all around the executive swivel chair monstrosity. Still nothing.

Vinnie's eye caught an upright stand lamp not more than fifteen feet from Bill's desk.  He checked under the shade—and found a small, cylindrical, threaded tube next to the bulb socket.

"This is it," he said. "The mike would have threaded through here. I'm betting the bulb burned out, someone pulled it out to replace it... Hector, right?"

"Yes. Hector checks the lighting once a week and he probably did this for the long weekend."

"Hector must have accidentally pulled free the microchip wire as he removed the burnt-out bulb, and it caught in the vacuum," said Vinnie, flapping his arms.

"Get serious. Where's the recorder?"

With wooden steps, Vinnie moved to Bill Barrington's desk. "Six feet, eight feet, ten feet, twelve feet, fourteen feet. There you go, within fifteen feet, even with an additional foot for the computer. This would work."

Vinnie bent over the desk and looked behind Bill's iMac. One of the USB ports had a small insert the size of a fingernail. "See this? This is a Bluetooth micro-port receiver. I'm telling you, this has to be it. You know he would want those recordings to be on his computer. We'll just need to access it. Do you know his password?"

Blanca sighed. "I did, but Bill had it changed after he found I'd gone into his calendar—and don't give me that face. Dan trusts you, but Bill doesn't give me the same respect. But don't worry, Shareen and IT have access to everyone's password. I'll ask Shareen for Bill's password. If I can convince her Bill gave me permission—what the personnel handbook lists as exigent circumstances…"

"You mean something urgent requires Shareen to reveal all to us?"

"No, Vinnie, not *us*, only *me*. She may even refuse me, but I can guarantee she'll refuse if she thinks *you're* involved. We'd lose our jobs. I hate that I'm going to have to lie to her."

"What if she finds out that Bill didn't give you permission?"

"I'll just have to think up a plausible enough reason so that she doesn't bother to follow up. I'll say Bill called and requested notes he'd forgotten and I have to get them from his computer. It's halfway plausible, and I doubt she would check with Bill about something like that. Besides, she dislikes talking to him."

"Who doesn't?"

"And Vinnie, can you reattach this microphone? We don't want Bill to know that his recordings have stopped. There shouldn't be anything missing yet, since Hector only pulled it out yesterday, after Bill had already left."

* * *

By noon Blanca had successfully acquired Bill's new password from Shareen and passed it on to Vinnie, who copied it down on his personalized VB embossed notepad.

"Wait until Sunday," Blanca said. "Bill's away for the Thanksgiving weekend, visiting his in-laws in Florida, and he won't return until Monday. Same for Gary. I heard Brian Neale would be here on Saturday to prepare for his Sunday Washington departure, so Sunday's your best choice. A cleaning crew might come Sunday evening, on their regular schedule. Remember to darken the corridor windows. Keep all the doors closed. Make no noise. And Vinnie, be careful."

Vinnie yawned into the phone. Blanca spoke with a sharp edge: "And Vinnie, do I need to remind you to keep quiet about this at our klatch party today? Maria would fire us both on the spot."

* * *

With the mission objectives and date set, Vinnie planned his evening. A few hours on the Internet taught him all he needed to know about his new vocation. He learned about fictional characters, espionage, and surveillance, and he found page upon page regarding laws, licensing, firearm restrictions, and employment opportunities at private agencies. Digesting the volumes of information put Vinnie into overload. But one phrase had stuck with him: *The main job of a private investigator is to obtain facts—not to make arrests nor prosecute criminals.*

This wasn't the manly picture Vinnie had hoped for. Of course, not that he had sought confrontation. In fact, he liked the idea of a PI persona who only gathered facts. *I'll make a fuckin' great PI.*

But at the moment, the most pressing chore facing this would-be PI was to bake three pies for his college roommate's family Thanksgiving in Vermont. This had become a tradition for Vinnie and his roommate's family, ever since freshman year; Vinnie had a standing invitation rather than spend Thanksgiving alone. (Vinnie had told his roommate that he had no family—which was sort of true.) Vinnie was looking forward to spending time with his "Thanksgiving family," but he was also eager to return to New York Friday afternoon and renew his PI studies.

# Chapter 18

## Vinnie Briggs, PI

Nightfall arrived on the Friday after Thanksgiving, and Vinnie's refrigerator was jammed with leftovers he'd brought home from Vermont. Vinnie was sitting in his living room chair, his feet perched on the coffee table, a notepad in his lap and a glass of wine in his hand. He was getting anxious about how little time remained to prepare for his first espionage gig. And there was no delaying. By Monday the opportunity would have passed; DV&N offices would be abuzz for the next two weeks, with the European review highest on the list of activities.

Vinnie was determined to discover the recordings Bill Barrington had on his computer. He added USB memory sticks to the list of supplies he would need, then reviewed his notes. *This looks like a fuckin' grocery list. Think, Vinnie, what is it you want to find out?*

He responded aloud to his own question. "Feedback, that's what I need. Actually, I need more than feedback—I need help to focus." He needed Blanca. But he waited until eight-thirty, when Blanca's children would be in bed, before he called.

* * *

When the phone rang, Blanca checked the caller ID, although she already had a pretty good idea who it was. "Hi, Vinnie. What's up?"

"Hey, Blanca, what was the name of that PI for Perry Mason? Paul something. Paul Duck? No… I've got it: Paul Drake. Yes! That's who I'll be," said Vinnie without explanation, as if Blanca had been privy to some earlier train of thought.

"You're Paul Drake, huh?" Blanca's voice had a slightly rising lilt. "First, need I remind you that Paul Drake is a fictional character? Next, even in fiction he was a *licensed* PI. Third, or whatever number I'm on, the man was over six feet, could throw a mean punch, and could use a gun. How much of this sounds like you?"

"Okay, then I'm a fuckin' *modern-day* PI. I don't need a gun… and we're talking about fuckin' piggy Linda Lords. I could take her."

"I say this with love, Vinnie, but I don't think you could. Anyway, Linda's not the problem. Well, not the only problem. Bill Barrington is your real problem. And I don't mean his physical size, though he could easily beat the crap out of you. No Vinnie, the problem with Shithead Bill is he's a bad man in a high position. He can have you fired."

"You worry too much. I have no intention of fighting him, or Linda, and I won't get caught, so Shithead won't have a reason to fire me. *He'll* be the one getting fired. I'm going to be an intelligent PI, not your macho gumshoe type. Think of me like… Tom Cruise."

"Great, now you're on *Mission Impossible*. Vinnie, get real, you're not in a movie. There are no props or special effects people. There won't be a SWAT team to rescue you. You'll be crying by the end."

Blanca sucked the air from the room, wishing she could take back her words. She knew about Vinnie's childhood proclivity to cry and his resulting "crybaby" schoolboy label. It hadn't helped that his family came with built-in bullies: his father and his older brother Jack. Vinnie had spit venom when he'd told Blanca about their behavior. They'd told him to "stand up and fight like a man," then they'd thrown punches at him until he cried. "Crybaby" was all he'd ever heard, at home and at school.

And Vinnie had never shaken his crybaby nickname. He might have, eventually, if not for the fact that, in eleventh grade, Vinnie's father had learned that he had a homosexual son. After that, his taunting was operatic. "You'll be crying all the time, queer boy." Vinnie's father and brother had creased him with skid marks, and now Blanca had revived the crash scene with her off-the-cuff remark.

"Sure," Vinnie said quietly. "Spit my father's words at me. I'm a crybaby."

Blanca's hand covered her mouth. "Vinnie, I'm sorry, I didn't mean it like that. Let's change the subject, please."

But Vinnie apparently didn't want to drop it yet. "You know, my father loved my brother Jack because he *wasn't* a crybaby. He has two years and fifty pounds in muscle over me, and he lives in a cell in Attica—yet he's still better than me, the queer."

"You know I have a brother like yours. We're not them, Vinnie. We're better."

Vinnie broke into a hushed tone. "You're right, Blanca. Let's talk about what I need to do. Can I start with my list, and you add to it?"

Forty-five minutes later, Blanca and Vinnie had his approach to searching Bill Barrington's computer all mapped out. As she hung up, exhausted, Blanca called to the living room. "Jandro, next time *you* answer the phone and *I'll* read the boys their bedtime story."

# Chapter 19

## Gym Rescue

Dan closed the car trunk, then wedged two small suitcases between the bags of food he'd set on the front porch of Ginny's Connecticut homestead. Ginny then opened the screen door and was met with gleeful shouts of welcome. After Ginny had finished with the smooches and chitchat, and Dan with carrying everything inside, Ginny headed to the kitchen to assist in the meal preparation, and Dan pardoned himself to freshen up, thinking that all the hustle and bustle was a good shield from family probing.

The house was soon packed with relatives—more buffer against any serious questioning about Dan's and Ginny's relationship. The ensemble included Ginny's parents, her sister, Rachel, and Rachel's boyfriend, Ted, as well as two of Ginny's paternal uncles—bachelors, both—and her ninety-two-year-old grandma. There were also a variety of lifelong Swinburne family friends, some of whose names Dan remembered, some not.

Still, the evening consisted of evading a series of subtle inquiries about him and Ginny—especially with regard to whether they were planning for a family—and Dan was relieved to escape it unscathed.

Late the next morning, the bathroom fan whirred long after dissipating the steam of Ginny's shower. Sunshine cut through wide-open drapes across the bed, which had been half-unoccupied for hours. Dan lifted his head from the pillow, burping away his excessive alcohol consumption of the previous night. Looking around Ginny's former bedroom, he recalled his first thrill in this room with Ginny, their unbelievable joint shower making the bathroom fan work overtime.

Everyone slept in on the day after Thanksgiving, but still Dan entered the kitchen last, two hours after the habitually late-rising Rachel and Ted. His tardy rise surprised everyone. He drank three cups of coffee and consumed two danishes, a blueberry muffin, and four scrambled eggs, topping it all off with a large slice of leftover apple pie. And ten minutes after gulping his last drop of coffee, Dan had the car packed; he was ready to go.

He pecked Anna's cheek, expressing thanks for her hospitality; hands on her hips, Anna protested and tried to convince Dan to stay, even offering her office for his use. Moving his wife aside, James Swinburne, Ginny's father, apologized to Dan.

With goodbye waves over, Dan and Ginny sped along the highway back to Manhattan. Ginny hated having to cut short their usual long Thanksgiving weekend. She had planted excuses the week before, but hadn't liked doing so. "We've a lot of work to catch up on after Paris," she'd said. "I'm sorry, but it can't be helped." The preemptive lie fooled no one, though. Rachel had pried the real reason from Ginny during a late-night nibbling of Thanksgiving leftovers. She heard all about Ginny's problems, listened to the Paris disaster, and the predicted marriage breakup. Ginny had burst into tears when she'd related the Paris humiliation, which had freaked out her sister. Rachel understood depression, yet she thought that the sex embargo was a bad idea, and she didn't think much of Ginny's alternative.

Now, as they drove away, Ginny knew that before she and Dan had even crossed the Bronx, her sister would have spilled all to their mother. She knew this because the Swinburne household had banned the word "secret."

* * *

Dan gripped the steering wheel tightly. He was not looking forward to his interview at UltraFit. I'll meet the guy as promised and be done with it. Ben Hausen, my personal trainer? Ha. Ginny can't be serious. He caused her stethy relapse. At least if I meet him, I'll know if he's screwing my wife.

But as he parked the car in the underground garage, Dan lost his nerve and hinted that he might renege. Ginny would have none of it. "You'll meet Ben or I'll pack and leave before the car engine cools. You'll never see me again."

Dan's hands remained on the steering wheel as the passenger door slammed.

* * *

A shipyard's derrick grabbed Dan's hand. "Hi, I'm Ben Hausen. Pleased to meet you."

"Dan Livorno. Likewise."

Dan looked from Ben's eyes to their clasped hands, at his own string forearm lashed and tackled to a boom capable of lifting a thirty-ton working load. Ben's sinuous forearm flanged onto a box-beam-girder upper arm that stretched his wrinkle-free, short-sleeve Polo. Dan took a wide-angle view of

Ben's cliff chest, the 3-D UltraFit emblem practically poking him in the eye.

The pro bodybuilder had no reaction to Dan's engineering survey.

"I'll leave you guys to talk," Ginny said cheerfully. "Meet me at the juice bar." As she walked away, neither man released their hold.

* * *

An hour later, Ginny and Dan stepped out of the front door of UltraFit. To Ginny's delight, Ben had agreed to be Dan's trainer, and seemed to honestly like him.

Ginny grinned, her first real smile in weeks. "I guess it went well."

"No need to gloat. Yeah, it was okay. Ben's a good listener and has a great sense of humor. I like him—and what a body. My God, he's big. I have never seen anyone that large. He has the proverbial muscle on muscle, but in his case I think you could use an infinite series to be accurate. Unbelievable. Did I stare too much?"

"A little, but don't worry, he's used to it, and you will be too in a few weeks."

"It's still a trial, remember."

* * *

Dan had told Ginny a partial truth—the part about Ben being likable, and of course, about his size being incredible. But Dan had omitted his worries, the *whole* truth. *How can Ben change my job loss? How will he fix my lack of sex drive? And what about Paris? So I pump iron and that's supposed to make me forget how Linda and Bill beat me? Forget I allowed a stranger to push my wife?*

Everyone told Dan he would get over his job loss, but he took these as typical token remarks. No one knew his real concerns, his hidden thoughts. *I know Ginny's in love with Ben. He's a real man. He's the kind of guy she drools over. He would never have let that little Paris twit push her. With one finger he'd have cracked the pavement with the Frenchman's head. I'm a wimp compared to Ben. This is Ginny's way to make me feel small in every way. This is a mistake, but I can't renege.*

Ginny will leave me if I do.

* * *

Approaching his office, Ben shook his head. How could he ignore that Dan was drop-dead gorgeous? This is stupid: he's married and a heterosexual. And how in the hell do I help Ginny and Dan with their marriage while I'm fantasizing about Dan for myself? What the fuck, don't they know how good they have it together?

Ben knew he could have men, many men—pickup sex with men who adored his muscles, who browsed him like a bookstore shelf: look at the cover, not the content. But Ben despised that lifestyle. Only once had he ignored his own "no pickups" gym rule; it was a time when he'd been juicing hard and would have fucked a fire hydrant if he'd had to. For the most part, he wasn't attracted to the X-room mesomorph stable behemoths; Ben recognized their bodies for their appeal in competitive sport, but they weren't for him. His ideal man was lean-muscled, handsome, and intelligent—and the latter trait was not a typical pro bodybuilder attribute. But here was Dan, both drop-dead gorgeous and incredibly intelligent. And in a few months he'd be hard bodied, too, fulfilling all three of Ben's criteria.

Ben leaned back, his arms cantilevered behind his head. *And what happens then? Will I seduce Dan?*

Then there was Dan's depression. Ginny was right. Dan's soft laughs and weak smiles didn't fool Ben. Dan had avoided talking about Ginny, and he'd clearly lied when he'd said that Paris had been good.

Not the first lie Ben had heard, not by a long shot. Dan reminded Ben of Davis McGregor III, Ben's former boyfriend, lover, and partner. Davis had lied—regularly—yet, with or without the lies, Ben missed the man. *Am I subconsciously replacing Davis with Dan?*

Of course, Ben had never raised any of these misgivings with either Dan or Ginny. He hadn't mentioned that this was risky, or that he found Dan attractive.

Ben rubbed his eyes, as if stupidity could be rubbed from his sight. He justified his actions by taking a dubious moral high road: *If I go back on my word, then* I'm *the liar.*

# Chapter 20

## Hide and Seek

Trolling Bill Barrington's iMac, Vinnie screwed his eyes. This was taking longer than he had planned. Luckily, the building was wilderness quiet. The last living person he'd seen was the lobby security guard, who had barely looked up from his TV, the Giants game blaring. Vinnie had scribbled the name of the Giants' quarterback in the logbook. Blanca had said, "On the Sunday after Thanksgiving you can bet most Americans will be on a plane, highway, train, or in front of a TV."

Vinnie had found Bill's audio collection, in a media directory with five subfolders. He'd selected a folder named "Office memos," which was marked as being password-protected. But Vinnie had come back from his Vermont Thanksgiving with a secret weapon; his college roommate, a computer science major, had given him a USB stick with a hacker's decode program—a welcome addition to the leftover turkey and trimmings that still filled his freezer. As a result, decrypting Bill's folder had been as easy as apple pie.

Unfortunately, the folder had a ton of files. Vinnie decided to start with the dates when Linda had been in New York. He checked Bill's calendar. The first time Linda had been in New York this year was eight months ago, for two days. But there were no recordings on those dates. *Of course, Bill was away.*

Three months later, Linda stayed for one day, joining the executive staff, including Dan, for the Orlando national department head meeting. Vinnie played the memos from that day. Nothing but boring conversations about agendas, presentation order, subcommittee assignments, guest lists, and on and on.

Vinnie skipped ahead.

Two months before the September date, Linda had stayed for an entire week. This time, as Vinnie went through the recordings, he immediately skipped out of any conversation that didn't involve Bill and Linda alone. Even their one-on-one conversations were nothing but repetitious dull agenda litanies, but he forced himself to listen, hoping to find some helpful nugget of information.  Bill's executive chair made for easy listening; Vinnie reclined, feet on the desk, head bent back as if seeking guidance from the ceiling.

Vinnie was so comfortable and the conversation so dull, he almost missed it.  Removing his feet from the desk, Vinnie snapped to attention, checking the recording date.  "Did they say a Northrop crisis two months before it happened?  They fucking planned it."  He rewound the recording.  And there it was: Bill suggested that Linda confirm her flight for Thursday from New York to San Francisco, then on Friday morning to LA.  He would then meet her in LA to "solve the Northrop crisis."  Loud laughter cut the air.

It was the proof he'd needed.

There was nothing else of interest for the rest of that week, so Vinnie jumped ahead to the date of the actual Northrop crisis.  Skipping around through recordings, trying to find another one with Bill and Linda alone, Vinnie stumbled across one that sounded garbled.  *Was that a moan?*  At first he assumed the microphone must have malfunctioned, but when he heard Linda telling Bill that his belt was caught, the meaning was clear: "They're fucking their brains out."

The recording was filled with Bill's deep baritone grunts and Linda's higher-pitched ones.

Grunt.

Snort.

"Har har, har har."

"Stick it here."

"You missed."

"Grab it yourself, you slut."

"Fuck you, Bill."

"No, fuck you, and that's what I'm doing.  Har har, har har."

"Like this big boy inside you?  How's it feel?  Good and hard?"

"Yeah, but how's this wet cunt make your dick feel?  Warm and sloppy."

"Wait.  Don't cum yet, Bill.  I'm not there."

With his hand to his mouth, Vinnie held back his gagging.  He loathed listening to sex as pretense of lovemaking or intimacy.

Bill's last words were, "Fuckin' goo all over my finger.  I'm going to go clean up."  This was followed by shuffling sounds and a slam.

Vinnie glanced toward the executive bathroom at the side of the office; seeing it made the vision of Bill with his pants off too real for Vinnie.  He almost missed Linda's subsequent mumbling, but he did catch her final "Shithead."

Though Vinnie smiled, he was perplexed, too.  Why is Linda fucking Bill?  The man's a pig.  She even calls him Shithead.

He knew that others at the office thought the same. Blanca surely did. Once, at an after-work klatch meeting, after a little too much drink, she'd told Vinnie, "Bill preys on women after gambling." She'd found condoms in his pockets before sending his suits to the dry cleaners. Shocked, Vinnie had asked if Mrs. Barrington knew, and Blanca had burst out laughing at Vinnie's naivety. "Really, Vinnie? She's out in the Jersey boonies on a huge estate, nearest neighbor invisible... like her. Bill pays the hundred grand country club membership to keep Mrs. B from nosing around."

If Linda screwing Bill was a conundrum, Vinnie's next question to himself complicated the matter. *Why is Bill screwing Linda?* She was too old for Bill's tastes, having passed thirty a few years back, and not exactly a Vogue model. Bill was fifty-something himself, but his looks and six-foot-three trim body contrasted sharply with Linda's heavyset five-foot-ten frame and long face.

Nothing made sense to Vinnie. Linda's disparaging remark. Bill's mocking.

Vinnie rubbed his eyes, stifled a yawn. But the recording continued to play, and Bill's next sentence caused Vinnie to sit bolt upright.

"Enough bitching. Let's get down to business. What about on your end?"

"Ready to go. My virus is already installed on the Northrop mainframe. Activation begins on Tuesday at four p.m. West Coast time. I'll expect a voice mail from my team while I'm in-flight to JFK. Around nine I'll call my office manager pretending to be surprised, and I'll act upset." Two voices chuckled. "I'll call you afterward to have an official record of the 'crisis.'"

After more chuckling, the conversation moved on to another topic, so Vinnie once again skipped ahead to another recording. He chose the Wednesday when Bill had come to Dan's office to change the date of the presentation.

Bill's voice, apparently calling to Blanca: "No calls, and I'm not to be disturbed." A thud came from the slamming door.

Rustling as Bill moved around his office. Vinnie skipped ahead a bit.

"Babe, he was like a whining little kid about how it was unfair. Har har, har har. I told him you'd be in the same situation and worse. He wanted to talk to Gary. Faggot might've listened too, but I threatened to veto his proposal if he jeopardized Northrop."

"He couldn't have liked that." Linda's voice. Bill must have had her on speakerphone.

"He didn't. You know Dan, a company guy. He tried to negotiate. Postpone until next Friday. He begged. No can do, I told him. Dumbass."

"I wouldn't go that far. Dan lives for his economic models, not for the money they make. He'll never reach for the stars like us."

"That's what I meant."

"He underestimates me. My Trojan virus went off as scheduled. No one will know. You can bank on it."

"That's exactly what I'm going to do. Har har, har har. Oh babe, I could do you right now. Shall we meet tonight?"

"Bill, stop. Blanca might come in. Be cautious. Too much is at stake."

The sounds of a chair being pushed back interrupted the conversation. "I've gotta piss." The now-familiar sound of the executive bathroom door shutting sounded in Vinnie's ear.

Apparently he just left Linda hanging on the phone, because Vinnie could hear her mumbling, although he couldn't make out the words. Then the bathroom door slammed again, followed by the screeching wheels of Bill's desk chair. "I'm back, babe."

"You know, I'm going to lounge under blue skies at my private Cayman Islands resort with servants and gigolos," Linda said. "I'll be set for life. You too. This is big. But you have to be careful."

"Will do. We'll screw our brains out in LA to celebrate. In the meantime, have you sent me your updated notes on our private plan?"

"Not yet, but they're ready to be uploaded to my private Dropbox folder marked Paris-Misc."

"Fine, I'll get the details later." Bill coughed. "Just so I have some idea, run through your latest version. We had been talking forty mill each. Does that still seem feasible?"

A giggling laugh, not Bill's guffaw, penetrated Vinnie's ear.

"Oh, much better than that. I reworked the model. The details are in the file. My revision puts us over one hundred twenty million—conservatively. Of course, don't forget, we're vulnerable to depressed markets and normal variations. But still, I think we'll each walk away with fifty to sixty million. Happy?"

"Happy? Fuck yes. And I won't have to share a goddamn cent with my bitch wife. She won't get a cent in alimony because she won't find me. Har har, har har."

With tapping fingers, Vinnie said out loud, "Shithead would fuck the family dog for that amount of money."

Linda's high pitch roused Vinnie. "Have the Swiss accounts ready for tomorrow, day after at the latest. We can set up the Caymans before I'm in Paris."

They proceeded to go over bank account details, itineraries, meeting points, fake passports. Bill would become British: Derrick Chambers. Linda would remain American: Lucille Pallo. Vinnie yawned.

"And the European data you provided from IT in Paris is perfect," Linda said. "I've made a few alterations to enhance my model predictions for my presentation."

"Dan would shit a brick if he knew I've withheld that data from him. He's such a pussy."

Vinnie pressed pause. "What the fuck!" He thought about calling Dan immediately, but a crick in his stiff back held him back. So he listened to the recording for a few more minutes, but he heard nothing more of interest and decided he could hear the rest at home.

The discovery—the proof of what he'd suspected—unnerved Vinnie. One copy wasn't enough, he decided. He wanted a backup. Vinnie was flustered as he looked around the room. He would keep one USB on him and hide the second USB here at DV&N. Then he'd call Dan from home.

He made copies on two USBs, then rushed out of Bill's office. Still angry at what he'd found, and preoccupied with finding a hiding spot, Vinnie failed to notice that he'd left the interior windows darkened—or that a small USB microchip still lay next to the keyboard. He was a rookie PI, lacking training and experience.

*Now where to hide this fucking backup USB?* Vinnie thought as he hurried down the hall. He stopped at Hector's janitorial closet. As a DV&N administrative assistant, he had access. You never knew when you might have to clean up a spilled coffee.

The shelves were stocked with cleaning fluids, spare light bulbs, and paper products, with a vacuum cleaner and mop and bucket in a corner opposite a stepladder. Vinnie climbed the stepladder and pushed the USB stick behind the cleaner fluid on the top shelf. Even if Hector removed several bottles, he'd be unlikely to notice the small device.

# Chapter 21

## Hacked

It was an unseasonably warm Friday, the day after Thanksgiving, and a gust of wind blew across a sand trap on the Dunes Golf Course in Myrtle Beach. Sand blew into a golfer's eyes. "Fuck!" The golfer sliced the ball, and it barely landed on the edge of the green before tottering to roll back into the trap.

"Har har, har har" breezed across the green from the golfer holding the ninth-hole pole. Bill Barrington found misfortune amusing. The expletive reminded Bill that his wife had said the same word when she'd learned that an unexpected business meeting required he cut short his Thanksgiving weekend at her parents' Florida condo in the tony, upscale Winter Park suburb of Orlando.

"Unexpected" was, of course, not an accurate descriptor for Bill's pre-arranged plans, but he'd have preferred to drop dead than to spend five days with his wife's family. He'd made his announcement to his father-in-law as he'd walked through the front door: "Unexpected urgent business in Charleston on Friday. Can't be helped… clients first. At least I'm here all of Thanksgiving."

"Fuck," Joan Barrington had said, and would have said more had she known the unexpected business meant golfing. Bill had wormed a guest stay at the prestigious club from a member, a former Princeton football teammate. He'd planned to golf all weekend at The Dunes, departing Charleston Monday morning. The golfing was great, but best of all this itinerary allowed him to avoid his bitching wife and ungrateful kids over the long holiday break. They'd be taking an Orlando to Newark flight Sunday while he was playing the back nine.

However, Bill had decided to change his schedule a bit after receiving a text on Saturday, announcing an impromptu Sunday night poker game in New York. This meant a chance to recoup some heavy losses—as well as scratch an itch that had been growing over the past two months without gambling, Bill's longest period of abstinence yet.

* * *

The taxi stopped curbside at the Hawthorne Building shortly before five p.m. on Sunday. Outside the cab window, a figure distracted Bill. *Is that... Vinnie Briggs? Why's the little faggot here on a Sunday? Nah, can't be. These queers all look and dress the same.*

Shaking the image from his mind, Bill handed the driver two twenties. "Keep the change," he said, which amounted to a two-dollar tip. The New York cabbie shot back, in a voice heavy with sarcasm, "Can ya spare it? Big shot's afraid he'll break the piggy?"

"Fuck you."

The cab door slammed behind him and he headed for the revolving door. Bill figured he'd use the time to prepare for Monday's meetings, knowing that after a late night of gambling he'd be lucky to arrive by eleven-thirty. After a few hours' work he'd grab a pastrami on rye and make his way to the gambling table. This time he'd nab his lucky chair; he'd missed it last time and it had cost him dearly.

As Bill entered his office, he immediately noticed the darkened interior window. *What the fuck! Has Blanca been in here? I'm going to have her ass for this.* Then he placed his carry-on luggage next to the coat rack and settled into his executive chair.

While waiting for the computer to boot up, and still fuming over the darkened windows, Bill pulled the keyboard toward him. A small USB transmitter plug slid across his desk.

"What's this?"

Bill held the micro-hub, already knowing the answer to his question. He leaned over his iMac and spotted the empty USB port.

DV&N's financial insight came from advanced technology and computer models—in fact, Northrop had dropped a competitor in favor of DV&N's technological superiority—and this sophisticated expertise included safeguards against corporate espionage. Installed on all senior managers' computers was a proprietary program called ToSec. The program monitored activity on client data files and downloads, and any unauthorized activity sent a notification to upper-level managers and executives and an alarm to IT and Shareen Cooper. ToSec could be personalized as well, allowing non-client files to be flagged— personnel data, budgets, technical data, and sensitive emails. Naturally, Bill's settings monitored his recording subfolder.

Vinnie had known that he could deactivate the alarm with the master password—he had done this many times on Dan's computer. What Vinnie didn't know was that at the senior executive level—Bill's level—an additional safeguard ensured that even when the alarm was deactivated, monitoring continued.

Bill opened his ToSec log file and searched his "audio" tags. The results flashed on screen. *Son of a bitch.*

**Date opened:** Today (Sunday) 1:45pm

**Date closed**: Today (Sunday) 4:43pm

**Copied location**: Today (Sunday) 4:25pm, External USB port 2, transf 2.2GB

Bill knew port 2 was the micro-USB hub port. He knew what had been copied and who had made the copy. The person he'd seen leaving the building.

Two questions filled Bill's mind: How much had the faggot Briggs discovered? And had the internal recording file password been compromised?

Fuck me.

* * *

The phone rang, midnight long past. Linda was packing for her Paris flight to New York for a busy two-week schedule: review the San Francisco clients' needs with her replacement; report on initial European organization; propose modifications to her plan. It was too much for two weeks. Linda picked up her cell and groaned when she saw Bill's number.

She answered. "Bill, it's Sunday after Thanksgiving. I'll be there tomorrow, as planned. Can't this wait? I haven't finished packing."

"Yeah, fuck that. Sonofabitch. Bastard. Fucking bastard."

"Wait a minute. What did I say?" Linda's voice was a high soprano.

"We have a big problem. A fucking big problem." Bill was staring at his computer screen. "My computer was hacked."

"What—what was hacked? Your emails? So what? We were careful. There's nothing there." Linda stopped picking clothes from her closet.

"Not emails. The recordings. The goddamn recordings."

"Recordings? What recordings? We never talked on your office phone."

"Not the phone. The computer *office* recordings." Bill had never told Linda, or anyone, about his office recording system. He closed his eyes and put his cell on speaker. He inhaled before giving Linda a full rundown. Silence interspersed with gasps. Linda cursed him, then cursed herself for working with a fool.

"Why, Bill? Why recordings?"

"It helped me keep everything straight. That's why I hold meetings in my office. I'd later recall details that others had forgotten. It made me look like a genius."

Linda listened without interruption. A long silence. Bill poured himself a scotch. "Does it record everything, or did you turn it off when we were screwing?"

Bill answered with a hushed exhale.

"Bill, you're a fucking idiot." Linda ranted for minutes, every sentence a curse. Bill cursed himself. Another long silence. Linda's subdued voice finally reached the inevitable conclusion: "We're screwed. We'll lose our jobs and maybe go to prison. Goodbye Grand Caymans. Goodbye millions." Just when she seemed calmer, Linda screamed across the Atlantic, "You're a fucking idiot, Barrington! We're done."

Linda's rancor was beyond anything she'd ever displayed in her life. She was so angry she was afraid she might cry.

But Bill had stopped listening; he had started to *scheme*.

"Maybe not," he said. Bill explained the elaborate encoding and encryption system, including the one saving grace: the copied audio files had an automatic safeguard password, which was not the same as the master password. The NSA might break the code after two months, but short of that, no one except DV&N's IT department could open the file. "I'll alert Rodney to the possibility of a pirated recording. He'll know what to do if one crosses his desk."

Linda knew another problem remained: the intruder could have already listened to the recordings at Bill's desk. "Do you know who it might have been?" she asked.

"Oh yeah. It was the little queer, Vinnie Briggs. I'll have his ass for this. He'll be out of here so fast that even if he listened it won't matter. It's his word against mine, ours... and if he can't produce the audio, he has no evidence."

"It doesn't matter if he has *proof*, Bill. Just the allegation will screw us. We'll be watched. *I'll* be watched. The whole project in Europe is a bust. Goodbye millions. Goodbye dreams. I'll be stuck slaving in Paris on a boring project. You'll be the good hubby commuting to work from New Jersey with no new life."

Linda's despondency crept in through her panting cries. But Bill did not accept defeat—he would not be blocked from his millions. He told Linda he'd find a solution to the Vinnie Briggs problem. The call ended with Bill pouring another drink, reclining, and staring at the ceiling, just as Vinnie had done hours before.

Fucking faggot. Well, Mister Vinnie Briggs, I hope you enjoyed yourself.

When Bill left his office at last, it was to gamble, but not at cards. Fuck the lucky chair—the stakes had just gone up.

# Chapter 22

## Cappuccino to Go

Ristorante Roma was halfway along Stillwell Avenue in Gravesend, Brooklyn. The taxi dropped Bill at the front door, and he walked to the desk to inform the maître d' he'd arrived for a meeting with Carmine. Carmine Aquafreddo was at the back of the restaurant, in a small side room with the door open. Across from him at the table was a big man—a *very* big man—Sal Friscollo. Sal stood up to take Bill's overcoat, which he then handed to the maître d'.

"Hi Sal, how are you?"

"I'm fine, Mr. Barrington. How about youze?" Bill was startled by Sal Friscollo's Brooklyn accent even though he'd heard it many times. *Was this guy from central casting? What a fucking bozo.* Bill never said these thoughts out loud to Sal, to the staff at Ristorante Roma, or to anyone in Brooklyn.

Bill turned from Sal and walked over to offer his hand to Carmine. "Hi, Carmine. Thanks for seeing me on short notice."

Carmine took Bill's hand and gave it a limp shake. "Sit down. What would you like to drink? Anything to eat?"

"Cappuccino, and nothing to eat. I'm fine."

"You sure? The Pasta alla Norma special tonight is very good. How about a small plate?"

"Thanks, Carmine, but I'm fine. To tell the truth, I'd rather talk."

Carmine shook his head and gestured to Sal for a cappuccino.

"What's on your mind?" he said. "I've saved you a place at tonight's game. I know you're anxious for the chance to regain your losses. The cards didn't go your way… everyone has a night of bad hands. Don't worry, you'll find your streak soon. And I hope to organize another table in two weeks—takes me that long. It's old age. This will be the last table before Christmas though… people are too busy with families over the holidays. You'll get details next week."

*He thinks I'm here about my loss, fuckin' ginzo.* Bill had dropped twenty thousand at the last game. He'd been upset and had showed his displeasure with abuses at the table, which was a big no-no at Carmine's games. Excuses had been made, but the croupier had raised his eyebrows.

"Thanks, Carmine. I'm not here about that. I have a bigger problem, one that could cost me a lot more. And I mean more than money… my freedom."

Bill paused, and Carmine nodded.

"It's like this. A colleague and me had worked out a plan."

Carmine shook his head. *He doesn't want to know.*

"Okay, forget the details. Let's say my colleague, a female, and myself have something that will yield a big payoff if all goes well. Sometimes we celebrate, in my office."

Carmine's head looked down to the table, his finger moving in a circular motion on the tablecloth.

"Right, not important. So the tricky part is that I… well, this is unrelated, but I make recordings in my office. It's a business management thing. There's the stuff with me and my woman colleague and there's sensitive information about our plan. And anyway, someone broke into my office today and found out about the recording. They made a copy on a USB flash drive. Do you know what that is?" Bill paused and thought, *That's a stupid question. Of course even Carmine knows. I'm rambling.*

"If anyone hears what's on the recording, then my colleague and I, well, we're fucked royally."

For a second Carmine's finger stopped circling and he tapped the table.

"I need that USB flash drive, and soon. The consequences are big."

With a turn of his head, Carmine mumbled to Sal, *"Che cazzo."* Then in Sicilian, so Bill couldn't understand, he expressed his opinion to Sal: "Who the fuck tapes their conversations? It's bad enough the Feds listen in and bug everywhere, but to do it to yourself. Che cazzo…"

Carmine turned back to Bill. His demeanor, facial expression, and tone had not changed one iota. "Interesting story. Sorry to hear about your troubles."

Bill knew—from past experience with taking loans from Carmine—that help was not *offered,* it had to be *asked for.* Carmine moved three fingers across the table, scraping invisible crumbs.

"Look, Carmine, I know who took it. I can't do this. I need help to retrieve the USB flash drive for me? This faggot—"

Carmine's hand went up like a traffic warden at a pedestrian crossing. He turned to Sal, who leaned in like before, with more whispers.

"Bill, I don't know what you mean. I think you should talk to Sal. I'm an old man, and I don't understand what you're saying or how I can help. I'm too old, and I get confused. My dinner's about to be served."

A large hand pulled on Bill's arm, and the half-finished cappuccino was left on the table.

Sal escorted Bill into a back office, then motioned for Bill to raise his arms. With an agility that startled Bill, Sal removed Bill's jacket and unbuttoned Bill's shirt, sliding his hand around Bill's chest.

Sal gave Bill his jacket back. "Sorry, Mister Barrington. You know we gotta be careful. Carmine likes to do it by the book."

"Yeah, I understand. Not a problem."

"Would youse likes your cappuch brought in?"

"No, thanks." Bill thought Sal's voice had the sizzling crackle of butter in a hot frying pan.

Sal took a pad and pen from the desk and handed it to Bill. Bill understood, and he wrote down Vinnie's address. Sal read it, then took out a lighter and burnt the paper in an ashtray.

"Sal, I want to be clear. Do whatever needs to be done to persuade Vinnie to go no further. There can't be any doubt he'll reveal what he knows."

"We know our business. Don't worry, Mr. Barrington."

"Sure. I didn't mean to imply anything. You're professionals." Bill looked at Sal's face and wished he hadn't said the last part.

Then he added, "How much will this cost? Not that it matters, but I'd like to be prepared. I assume we're talking cash."

"This would normally run to fifty. But Carmine says given you're a good customer, and with your recent losses at the table this'll be discounted to twenty-five grand. Carmine's doing you a good deal. He must like you."

Bill thought he was at a Macy's sale. *All shirts are priced two for one.*

Right on cue, the maître d' entered, handed Bill his overcoat, then turned and left.

"One more thing, Mr. Barrington. It might be a good idea for you to forget the card game tonight. Walk to the Sheepshead Bay BMT to go back to the City. Forget tonight's game. No trail from here, and stay away for a while. I'll collect later tonight." Sal opened a drawer, retrieved a cell phone, waited for the phone to turn on, and read out a number. "Call me with your location."

Bill made a point to stop by the front desk at the Hawthorne Building and say a few words to the night watchman. From his office, he called Linda using his cell phone, even though it was three a.m. Paris time. When she picked up, he said simply, "Send me an email to meet you at the airport."

"What the fuck, Bill? Do you know the time? I'm due at Charles de Gaulle at six-thirty, which means I can't go back to sleep."

"Stop the bitchin' and do it *now*. I need the email. Do as you're fucking told and don't ask questions."

Bill's reply to Linda's email confirmed that he would meet her outside JFK international arrivals.

He waited a few minutes before he called Bel Jour France, a restaurant in the East Village. Reservations were needed weeks in advance, but Bill knew as a frequent customer an open table would be "found" for ten p.m.

Bill informed Sal, who told him to have a long meal, and to make no further calls. Twenty-five thousand in petty cash came out of Bill's office safe with no record made of the withdrawal. The money would be replaced in full by tomorrow afternoon.

* * *

Halfway through dessert, the Bel Jour France maitre' d informed Bill that someone outside in the parking lot had requested to talk to him, but refused to come into the restaurant. Bill nodded and stepped outside. Without a word spoken, Bill handed an envelope to the big man standing next to a late-model black Caddy.

Bill checked into the JFK Hilton around midnight. He called his wife to see if she had arrived safely with the children. The call caught Mrs. Barrington by surprise.

"Is everything okay, Bill?"

"Yeah, fine. I didn't want you to worry you as I'm staying at the airport and can't be home tomorrow morning. I'm just concerned for you and the kids. Goodnight."

The bitch will make a good alibi.

Bill opened his laptop and composed an email to Blanca for another alibi.

# Chapter 23

## Frutti di Mare

As he stepped out of the front door of the Hawthorne Building, Vinnie saw a cab pull up to the curb. He didn't give it much thought, of course—it was a normal occurrence on a weekday, if not necessarily so on a Sunday—as he was concentrating instead on his Brighton Beach train journey home. He always avoided the Coney Island line, as it reminded him of his brother in Bensonhurst, even though Jack Briggs was an upstate Attica prison resident. When he surfaced at the Brighton Beach Third Street and Sixth Avenue exit, Vinnie had a ten-minute walk to the West Village, and he pushed his key into the front door a few minutes after five-thirty.

Vinnie Briggs, PI, repeated out loud what he had been thinking all the way home: "Fuckin' rush! Better than coke. I'm on an adrenaline high. I'd better look out for low-flying aircraft."

He took a long, hot shower, omitting his normal masturbation. He was too tense. He would try to take a short nap and would then make supper—*spaghetti ai frutti di mare*—before going uptown to Dan's condo. Dan needed to hear about this, but surely it could wait a couple of hours.

* * *

Vinnie put on blue and yellow sweat pants and a matching gay pride sweat-shirt. His short nap had lasted two hours, and it was now just after seven-thirty p.m. Still on a high from his earlier escapades, Vinnie created a new playlist on his iPod to help him cook. He meticulously chose the songs and la-beled this new playlist *Spy*. By the time he'd finished it was past eight o'clock. *I'm not going to make it to Dan's tonight,* Vinnie thought as he filled the pot to boil water.

* * *

Sal stepped quietly through Vinnie's front door with a crosstown bus behind him. His companion had muscles in all directions. His street moniker was Mister Clean, and no one ever doubted what he cleaned.

Sal turned to Mister Clean. "Smells like *spaghetti alle vongole*." Mister Clean's pebble head nodded on his boulder shoulders.

At that moment Vinnie stepped out of the kitchen, carrying a plate and utensils on his way to the dining table—and stopped when he saw the two tons of muscle in his home. The plate fell from his hand and smashed to the floor, the only sound in the room. No cry. No scream. Vinnie had opened his mouth, unsure whether to breathe in or out; he did neither.

"Oops. Dropped your dinner, Vinnie. Not to worry."

Although Vinnie didn't know Sal's name, the man's voice and appearance told him two things: this man was from Brooklyn and he was mob.

Mister Clean stepped over to Vinnie, his sideway sashay giving the appearance of an ocean liner approaching a pier. Similarity in height was their only common measurement. A shovel-sized hand clamped Vinnie's shoulder; the little sputtering of Vinnie's bones signaled the first phase of cracking.

"Don't be shy, Vinnie, Mister Clean's just being friendly. Now, imagine him *unfriendly*, which will happen pretty quickly if you don't hand over that USB stick. *Capisce?*"

Vinnie nodded, and tears filled his eyes. He pointed to his laptop on a small desk. Sal walked over. "In the laptop?"

Vinnie shook his head. *No.*

Mister Clean pushed Vinnie forward the way a pitcher throws a fastball across home plate.

Vinnie opened the desk drawer and pulled out the USB stick. Without hesitation he handed it to Sal. Mister Clean's jackhammer hand tightened on Vinnie's shoulder—more cracking. Vinnie winced and gave a high-pitched wail, tears streaming down his cheeks.

"You sure this is it?" Sal said. "This is what I want?"

Vinnie spoke in toddler tones. "Yes, yes, yes, please. It's the only one. Look around if you don't believe me. Please, mister, ask him to let go. Please. That's what you want. My shoulder's hurting. Please, please. Tell him to let me go." Tears were flooding down Vinnie's face. *Crybaby. My father and brother were right. I'm a crybaby.*

With a nod from Sal, Mister Clean unclenched his lobster-claw, removing the pressure but not the pain. Vinnie rubbed his eyes, sobbing. Sal had looked around, showing no interest in anything except the plate on the floor.

"Is that spaghetti alle vongole?"

"What?" Vinnie sobbed.

"What you cookin'? Spaghetti alle vongole?"

"No… it's… it's…" A pause for more sobs. "… *frutti di mare.*"

"Ah, love that. Don't you?" Sal looked to Mister Clean. Mister Clean's pebble head nodded a few times.

"Now Vinnie, there's one more thing. You see, we know you heard the recording on this thing, and we need to know you can keep it a secret. *Capisce?* Otherwise Mister Clean will have to give your other shoulder a massage— and a neck rub, too. Imagine Mister Clean's two hands massaging your neck. Actually, I think he could manage with one hand 'cause your neck's not too big. Do you know Mister Clean bench presses four hundred and fifty pounds? Isn't that right, Mister Clean?"

The giant nodded and flexed, his shirtsleeves fashioned for stock cars.

Vinnie sobbed again.

"Come on, Vinnie. Mister Clean's playing with you. He thought someone of your *persuasion* might like to see a real man. Ain't that right, Mister Clean?"

Those last sentences upset Vinnie in ways Sal could not have appreciated. Vinnie's Gay-Lesbian Alliance Training sessions had been designed to confront homophobic taunting; in fact, he'd been preparing himself against just this kind of taunting for a long time. His training kicked in, and he ignored Mister Clean's intimidation flex; he ignored his shoulder pain. Vinnie's reaction ignored reality.

"Fuck you. I'm gay and I'm proud. I'm better than Shithead Bill Barrington and his whore Linda. Wait until you hear the recordings. I know it all, and they're not going to get away with this, even if you denigrate my sexuality. And I don't like big-assed musclemen with pea brains."

* * *

The prime location to dump Vinnie's body was in the apartment building's back alley. Sal and Mister Clean staged the scene: Vinnie's pants and jockey shorts were down to his ankles, his ass exposed, and a dildo was sticking out of his anal crack.

"Let's see how long it takes the dumb cops to figure this out." Sal neither smiled nor frowned; he never did. But Mister Clean grinned, as he'd been the one to shove the dildo up Vinnie's ass, his specialty. His dresser contained a selection of colorful dildos in various sizes. On solo jobs, Mister Clean would first stick his own dick into a fully awake victim's ass before he inserted a dildo, which proved he was a dedicated professional; and no one ever suggested otherwise.

The USB flash drive was in Sal's possession, as was Vinnie's laptop; Sal never left anything behind that was remotely relevant to the job. And Vinnie was left for dead, as far as Sal and Mister Clean were concerned. He looked dead, but Mister Clean turned to Sal. "Yeah, good enough. He looks gone to me."

"Want me to keep at it?"

Sal might have said yes, but he heard a commotion at the alley entrance, a barking dog. Having to deal with a pooch and owner would be an unnecessary complication.

Carmine's enforcers had vanished through the service doorway before the dog and its owner reached the body of Vinnie Briggs. The subsequent 911 call reached an EMT ambulance that by chance was parked right across the street at a sub shop. Within minutes, Vinnie was riding inside and had an overeager gay EMT attending to him. The homosexual rape had upset the tech, so despite finding no detectable pulse, he applied non-stop CPR after he had secured the oxygen mask and administered an epinephrine shot. While his partner drove at Indy 500 speed, the tech administered multiple electroshocks. The heartbeat came on the ninth shock—six more than allowed by the handbook—which the EMT hoped was sufficient to boost his performance evaluation and outweigh his disregard of protocol.

For six hours, not counting the life-saving ten-minute ride to the Belgravia Incare-Z Medical Center emergency ward, Vinnie received constant medical attention. Doctor James Goldoni, the attending intern, shared something in common with Vinnie—both were on the emergency ward for the first time. And Doctor Goldoni did not want to start his medical career at the Belgravia Incare-Z Medical Center with the loss of his very first patient. His med-school nickname had been "Rotty," short for Rottweiler, because once he bit into an assignment he never let go.

Doctor Goldoni called out from the emergency bay: "Move the patient to the OR and initiate a Code Blue!" Code Blue meant no ER evaluation stop, the patient wheeled directly to surgery.

The chief of brain surgery, Doctor Silverstein, had just finished a duty call to a celebrity patient, which explained why he was at the hospital that evening, instead of with his wife in their box at the Met, listening to Tosca's anguish over Scarpia's trickery. He was heading for his car, taking a shortcut through the ER, when he heard the Code Blue order.

"Who gave the Code Blue?" he asked a duty nurse.

The nurse told him it was the new attending, and she gave her opinion that the patient was unlikely to survive. "Doctor Goldoni believes otherwise though, and he's going to perform surgery."

"Would you ask Doctor Goldoni if he'd mind if I assisted?"

With his senior position, Silverstein did not require permission, yet the nurse wasn't surprised he asked, as the greatly admired Doctor Silverstein was, in addition to being a gifted brain surgeon, the most considerate among the senior doctors.

Together, the junior doctor, the senior chief, and a five-person team kept Vinnie alive, albeit in a coma. He had suffered multiple fractures: his right leg in two places, two ribs broken and three cracked, his right humerus. He had a bruised spleen and kidney and a torn anus, and his face resembled a checkerboard, although, remarkably, no facial bones had been broken, not even his nose. If he survived, Vinnie would need months of physical rehab to recover from such severe injuries. And that's if he awoke from his coma, which was anybody's guess.

Back at Vinnie's apartment building, the police quickly concluded, based on the dog owner's description of the scene, that this had been a hate crime. An interview with the EMT crew confirmed this initial opinion. The investigating detective added two facts to his notes, both of which corroborated the hate-crime hypothesis: the victim had been wearing a gay pride sweatshirt, and a dildo had been stuck up the victim's ass.

However, the victim's identity took another day to discover, as he had had no identification on him. When at last they figured out who he was—thanks to interviewing the other residents of the apartment building and asking them if they had any openly gay neighbors—they investigated Vinnie's apartment, but they found no additional information there, other than that the victim had recently prepared *linguini alle vongole*. Or was it *frutti di mare*?

# Chapter 24

## Pump and Slump

The Sunday after Thanksgiving was one of UltraFit Gym's busiest times; guilt-ridden members would clog the machines after three days of overeating. But Dan was there for another reason. As he entered UltraFit, swinging his gym bag, he thought to himself, *This is a stupid idea. Why the hell am I in a gym on a Sunday? Thanksgiving weekend, no less.* In previous years he would have swum fifty laps on the weekend after Thanksgiving in order to prevent his gut from bearing any resemblance to the recently consumed eighteen-pound turkey. But today Dan grumbled, thinking about his new personal trainer, picked by Ginny.

Added to his misery was the fact that Linda would be at the office over the next two weeks. *She'll probably make a victory lap around the thirty-fifth floor.* He found consolation by thinking about the victory lap he himself would take once Gary Del Vecchio heard about Jean-Jacques's story. But he'd have to wait until he had the backup data from Rodney first. *I can't appear bitter… but I* am *bitter, and now I've been forced to come to a gym for my mental health.*

Dan's workout began with Ben's promise of an easy routine for his first day. But it wasn't long before Dan's legs ached—the way he imagined legs ached when flesh was ripped from bone.

"Ben, we need to discuss the meaning of the word *easy*."

Ben trained newbies with lighter weights: fifteen repetitions over six sets for each body part's muscle group. He had chosen Dan's legs, a body part that was often overlooked by men, as Dan's swimming had already built up his upper body.

Another of Ben's training techniques was to illustrate the muscles for each exercise using his own body as a living anatomy chart—a method not many trainers could match. "If you extend your leg and hold it out for two seconds," he said, "you'll achieve more effect in your upper thigh. We're aiming here for the *rectus femoris*, the muscle that sits in the middle of the four quadriceps." Ben flexed his leg and a spindle popped out, tapered at each end, the midsection's wide sinews ready for high-speed rail. "We'll work the two side *vastus* muscles with a different machine." Ben's layered outer muscles became tire balloons. "Go ahead: feel the effect you want to achieve."

Dan hesitated, so Ben placed Dan's hand on his flexed kryptonite leg. Ben's was pulley cable and Dan's was tree tinsel.

But the illustration and the lighter weights did not make the session easy. On his third set, Dan's burning spread and he imagined his sweatpants aflame. Still, Ben insisted on two more sets, and Dan's inflamed legs became brittle burnt. It wasn't until Dan's allotted time with Ben ran out that Dan received respite. He requested longer rests next time. Ben agreed, but added "and a harder workout," too. Dan shook his head.

"I know you don't want *this*." Ben flexed to show surface-painted veins channel across his muscular pillars. "But you *are* here to regain your shape, and you won't get that without hard work."

Dan thought differently. I'm a twig; I'll never be his redwood size. He's what Ginny wants, not me.

* * *

Ginny greeted him at the door after he cowboy-waddled his way home. "What was Ben like?" she asked. "You look a bit shaky."

"I'm exhausted. He had me touch his legs to show me what muscle groups I was working. He's unreal."

"I know." Ginny smiled.

Dan shuffled into the kitchen for water. He didn't want to talk; couldn't. Ginny entered to fill her water bottle, and adjusted her jogging shorts as she passed. She was preparing for her run in the park with Sarah and Betsy. A year ago, Dan would have moved to block her way, no matter how exhausted he was; he would have touched her, caressed her breasts, spilled water on her, used his hand to dry her even in places the water hadn't touched. He'd have taken hold, made her body a tourniquet against his to relieve his sore muscles. And Ginny would have complied, would have put her hands behind Dan's ass to push his hard penis against her.

But today there would be none of that. Dan had noticed that Ginny had asked first about Ben. In response, his manhood shrunk, his desire was crushed, his confidence diminished. Dan saw indifference as the worst form of hate.

Ginny walked out the door, and Dan bent to rub his sore legs.

Reclining on the couch—in the only position that was even somewhat comfortable—Dan considered what he and Vinnie could do on Monday.

They'd start with the most recent event: Rodney's admission that data had been deliberately held back. Their narrative would link Rodney's admission of Bill's intervention to JJ's revelation about Antoine.

Dan's thoughts meandered. *What about my life? How much of that should I tell Vinnie?*

He decided to tell Vinnie about Paris, about the little man shouting obscenities. Dan curled his body. He would not be telling Vinnie a story, he'd be confessing. Confessing his cowardice, his self-absorption. He'd talk about Ginny's sthenolagnia and his own uncontrolled envy. Would he confess to Vinnie that he had thought of cutting off his penis as a teenager? That he'd used a razor to cut his arm?

Dan cried until he slept.

The sleep was disturbed. He awoke after an hour with a new decision, something he had sworn he would never do. He called Vinnie about work on a Sunday. Dan had always believed that Sunday was the one day of the week when no employee should ever be disturbed. But Vinnie was his friend, and this wasn't a typical work call, so perhaps this one-time exception would be acceptable. Besides, Ginny would be out late, which would leave him alone with his thoughts. And the last place he wanted to be was alone with his own thoughts.

His call went straight to Vinnie's voice mail, which was strange; Vinnie always picked up. *Why would Vinnie's cell be off?* Dan left a message: "Hey, Vinnie, I know it's Sunday of the holiday weekend, and I hate to bother you, but would you mind coming by my condo? I'd like to talk to you before work tomorrow. It's important. Of course, if you have plans, I understand. But if not, can you make it by five-thirty? I'll even make supper as an enticement. Give me a call. Thanks."

*That was lame. I sounded pathetic. I should call him back. I'd be better off preparing for tomorrow's client meeting.*

As he rubbed his legs with lotion, Dan decided he should stop shirking his responsibility with clients; after all, he'd already been warned by Gary, both directly and indirectly. And he'd lost a promotion because he'd been unprepared. *I need to do better or I'll lose my job.*

Dan would need the client folder, but his sore legs ruled out going to the office to get it. Dan saw this as a more compelling reason to ask Vinnie to work on a Sunday, so he dialed a second time. Voice mail again. Dan amended his message: "I'm sorry, Vinnie, to bother you again. If you hear this and it's not too late, could you swing by the office first and bring me my notes for tomorrow's client meeting? I hate to ask, but... I can't go myself, which I'll explain when I see you. And... I'm just not well prepared... you know how I've been. I should have taken the notes with me, I know. Listen, there's a bottle of champagne in the bottom drawer of my desk, a relic of the celebration that never happened. Bring that too—we can have it with the supper I'll make for us. If you can come. Thanks."

Dan considered this a better explanation for asking Vinnie over, although maybe he'd rambled a bit, which wasn't like him. *I'm a mess. Ginny has that right.* He'd wait until they'd both had a glass of champagne, and then he'd confess. *I know Vinnie will come. He's the best person I could have ever hired. Vinnie's my true friend… a fuckin' good friend.* Dan smiled.

Then: Where is Vinnie, anyway?

# Chapter 25

## Runners' Insights

A mob congregated at the 65th and Central Park West entrance on the warm final Sunday of the Thanksgiving break. Ginny threaded her way to find her best friends, Sarah Rubinstein and Betsy Farnsworth. Betsy and Ginny, grade-school friends, had met Sarah at college, where they had been roommates. The three of them believed there were no secrets between them.

Fifteen minutes into their jog, two men rounded a small bend at a rapid clip, causing a minor collision. Betsy was forced into the grass, and would have fallen if not for Sarah's outstretched hand.

The men stopped to mouth *sorry*. Mini-dagger glares were exchanged. Sarah feigned kicking the men in their sensitive area.

Rubbing her ankle, Betsy stopped Sarah. "Notice anything different?"

"They're wearing matching outfits," said Sarah.

"Yes, and what else?" came a slight singsong from Betsy.

Sarah played dumb, but she had noticed: their cut-off tank tops revealed muscular six-packs, and stallion legs, hugged by tiny stretch briefs, held up their large V-shaped upper bodies.

"Fuck that. Their balls are still soft." Sarah faked another high kick.

The taller man, laughing, placed one hand over his private parts, then winked at Ginny. He flexed his arm while his partner squeezed the bicep. Running away, they chanted, "Have a nice day, girls."

"Screw you," yelled Ginny. "How dare they?"

"Offended that Mister Central Park undressed you?" Sarah laughed.

"They undressed all of us."

"Not so," Betsy said.

Sarah added, "You know those hunks are gay, right?"

The three women giggled like twelve-year-olds. However, Ginny broke into a run. When Sarah and Betsy caught up with her at the S&L Health Café, they were puffing for an explanation.

Sarah started the inquiry. "What gives?"

"You'll think I'm crazy." Ginny sipped her drink and gazed out the cafe window.

"Take your time, but my two kids are with a babysitter." Betsy spun her finger.

"Something's very wrong with me and Dan." Ginny shook as Sarah looked to Betsy.

"Oh, God, Ginny, take your time. To hell with the babysitter."

Sarah leaned forward. "Say it, however you want."

"Our difficulties are unbearable, bigger than what I've told you." Ginny held back a sob.

"What?" Sarah and Betsy said together.

Sarah continued, "You're the perfect couple. Is Dan having an affair?"

"No. And how can we be a perfect couple if we're imperfect individuals?"

"Is it you?" Sarah was direct but jittery. Betsy shook her head at Sarah. "No."

"Good, no affair. But that begs the question, what's happened?"

"No more questions. I... I... I don't know how to put it."

Seconds ticked by and the women sipped their drinks. Finally, Ginny broke her silence.

"I love Dan, yet for a year we've had terrible sex. And none at all for months."

Her friends leaned forward across the table.

"We've known this. What's changed?" Betsy held her chin.

...

Betsy prodded. " 'The honeymoon's over,' you've heard that expression? Yours lasted longer than most."

"No. This is something else. And it's my fault. Mostly"

Silence.

Sarah coughed.

"Let me recap. Neither of you is having an affair but no sex at home. And it's because of you?"

Betsy shrugged, and Ginny made a rude gesture. Tears filled Ginny's eyes.

"Oh, Ginny, I'm sorry," said Betsy.

"Me too. Just tell us." Sarah stretched her hand across to Ginny's, and Betsy rubbed Ginny's shoulder.

"Uh... this is hard... uh..." Ginny swallowed, and her words rushed out. "I want to have sex with Dan while watching a bodybuilder flex—specifically my trainer, Ben. The two guys we ran into in the park are UltraFit members, and they've seen me with Ben. They know I... *admire* bodybuilders."

In classic deer-staring-into-headlights fashion, Sarah and Betsy neither blinked nor moved.

"I guess you want an explanation."

Two heads bobbed up and down.

"I've been fascinated with muscular men for a long time. You didn't know, did you?"

"I knew," said Sarah. "Rachel told me."

"Me too," said Betsy. "Your mother told me first, then Rachel. I had no idea what they meant, but I was a teenager, so nothing was really strange."

"Screw you. Screw them. I had asked them not to talk about it with anyone. They promised."

"Please, Ginny," Betsy said. "When have your mother or sister kept secrets? We've seen your fitness magazines. Big deal."

"Then you *don't* know. My mother never mentioned my addiction to strong men? Here's a flash: I adore looking at big muscles and feats of strength. My mother calls this my stethy obsession. Did you know that?"

"No, not that..." said Sarah.

"Me neither," said Betsy. "What's stethy?"

"I don't even know if it's real. The Internet is divided. The actual term is sthenolagnia syndrome: it's an unhealthy obsession with strength and muscles. Personally, I think it's bullshit, but my mother disagrees. Didn't Rachel or my mother explain this?"

"Nope," said Betsy, turning to Sarah for confirmation, then looked back at Ginny. "Why does your mother believe you have this syndrome? And why do you deny it?"

"Because as a teenager I cut up muscle magazines, compared men, circled their bodies with different colors. I compiled pro bodybuilders' statistics. Rachel called me a pervert about it once, and I knocked her over, gashing her hand. That's when my mother told me about sthenolagnia."

"You played with musclemen pictures and I didn't know? I practically camped out in your room during high school." Betsy's teenage whine came through her grievance.

"I'm sorry, Bets." Ginny shrugged. "My mother lectured me about it. For most of high school, I tuned her out. If she even mentioned sex, I stormed out. Her sthenolagnia lecture was bad. She asked if I had a sexual attraction to strong men or women. I would have run away if my father hadn't stopped me."

Betsy spoke hesitantly. "Did you know your mother asked me to... 'watch you' around big men? I just figured she was worried you'd have sex with the football players. My hope was that you'd lure the entire team and I'd get your rejects."

"Thanks, Betsy, it's good to know the basis of our friendship."

"For what it's worth, I never believed your bullshit explanation for all the bodybuilding mags in our college apartment. 'For exercise tips,' right…" said Sarah.

"Well they *were*. Only… different exercises." A sheepish grin crossed Ginny's lips.

"Oh my God, you didn't," said Betsy.

Ginny's grin grew teeth.

"You slut. I get off on women getting off on men," said Sarah.

"I've been to bodybuilding contests, too," Ginny said quietly, her smile gone. Her friends wanted more detail, so Ginny described the X-room assembly line: rocket-sized men constructed from iron bars; surface veins on rice-paper skin stretched over hardened steel-forged limbs; the volcanic, lava-hardened twenty-one-year-old, Billy.

The friends smiled throughout Ginny's bodybuilding digression. But frowns followed when she revealed her fantasy: Ben flexing while she and Dan had sex. Until Paris, she had sublimated her desire. Now her preoccupation was to fulfill it.

Ginny interpreted their silence as a rebuke. "You both think I'm crazy, don't you?"

Gulping her drink, Betsy spoke. "Not crazy, but… you won't get the satisfaction you want. Dan won't see it your way. Or Ben."

Sarah rested her face in her hands. "Betsy's right. Have you talked to your mother, or a shrink?"

"So you *do* think I'm crazy. Fuck you, Sarah."

Sarah moved back. "Hey, I'm just trying to help."

Ginny looked sideways at Sarah. "I'm sorry, I didn't mean to snap at you. I'm desperate." Ginny's gaze turned to the people outside the cafe, hurrying past. "There's more."

The waiter arrived with refills. For a half hour Ginny revised her original Paris narrative. The new version featured the little Frenchman and Dan's passivity.

"I snapped." Ginny began to cry, her tears dropping to the table. A few people looked over. Betsy passed her napkin.

"Dan was a shit, no doubt about it," said Sarah.

"He did something I didn't think possible." Ginny took a big suck of her power drink. "It made me stop loving him… No, I still love him—but I don't *like* him. Sometimes I can't stand being in the same room with him." Ginny choked, the liquid stuck in her gullet.

In a subdued voice, Ginny began: "There's not much to say, is there? How can I love and hate the same person? I can't imagine having sex with Dan. He's miserable, and I'm miserable."

Sarah spoke first. "You need counseling—both of you. I'm sorry, and you can tell me to go fuck myself again, but it's all I can offer."

Without missing a beat, Betsy chimed in: "You might as well say the same to me, because I agree with Sarah."

They don't understand what my obsession feels like. The security I gain from bodybuilders. The pleasure I used to get from Dan's strength, his arms curled around my waist to scissor-squeeze my buttocks. The joy I still get from observing Ben's massive body. My dreams about a bulkhead-sized man who crushes puny men.

Ginny tried to explain the effect on her of Dan's effete intellectualism and his limp confidence. She despised Dan's weaknesses. Yet, she was ashamed of her callous apathy.

She wanted the *original* Dan to return: virile, confident, goal-oriented, sexy. "I've never been unfaithful, to answer your original question. But I can't last much longer."

Ginny revealed that she had arranged for Ben to train Dan. While Betsy and Sarah discussed this fact, Ginny brooded and lost the thread of the conversation.

"Sorry, Betsy, could you repeat that?"

"I said, you're asking a lot of Ben. Shouldn't Dan see a therapist?"

Ginny answered without thinking. "Yes, but I don't think a shrink can help Dan with my stethy problem." Even Ginny thought her answer was lame.

Betsy replied sharply, "Then talk to Dan."

"How? We're not communicating at this level. Besides, he has another problem." Ginny proceeded to explain the other omitted Paris event: JJ's revelation that data had been withheld.

Sarah banged the table, and Betsy crossed her arms.

"Damn it, Ginny, can't Dan use that? No wonder he's depressed. *I'm* depressed." Betsy unfolded her arms to swing them around her head.

"Get Ben to beat the crap out of Bill and Linda. That's a good use of your stethy," Sarah said, making a fist.

Ginny shook her head. "The information can't be proved, and if JJ were to tell anyone about it, he would risk his own job. There's no motive. And worst of all, Dan's too weak, too timid, to do anything about it—which brings me back to my problem. I know Dan didn't set off my stethy, but his constant whining hasn't helped."

More tears from Ginny. More sipping power drinks. Ginny wiped her eyes, stretching the silence.

"Here's an idea," said Betsy. "Ask Ben about your obsession, even your fantasy."

Placing her glass on the table, Sarah added, "I agree. Maybe Ben's heard of stethy, or whatever the real name is. Isn't this what bodybuilders have?"

"Ben knows. And bodybuilders don't necessarily have it. Pro bodybuilders are obsessed with training and size—like any professional sports person. Even non-sports competitors, like chess players, are obsessed with what they do. That's normal."

But Betsy's suggestion did strike a chord with Ginny. Leaving the S&L Health Café, Ginny walked at a slow pace. Ben was already training Dan; could she persuade him to do more?

# Chapter 26

## Setup

As she went through her email on Monday morning, Blanca was even more displeased with her boss than usual. Bill had sent her a detailed email outlining his unexpected return to the office Sunday night, including his late-night dining arrangements at Bel Jour France. *Why the fuck do I care?* He had also forwarded Linda's email requesting he meet her at JFK because of the sensitive European documents. *So she could screw him at the hotel.* And finally, Bill had copied Blanca on his email to Dan requesting that he preside over the morning meetings; he had left his paperwork from Sunday night on Blanca's desk.

Extra work. Wait until I tell Vinnie. Vinnie had yet to respond to her two phone messages. And Bill's email had alarmed her. Did Bill catch Vinnie when he returned early? Did Vinnie chicken out? Where are you, Vinnie?

It wasn't until nearly one p.m. that Bill and Linda entered the office. Bill dimmed the corridor glass as he barked to Blanca, "No interruptions of any kind, understand?"

"Yes, Mr. Barrington, I'll make—"

Slam.

*Shithead. I hope you both catch an incurable disease.* Blanca's hateful thought would have to be recited at Holy Confession.

With the door closed, Linda fidgeted, waiting for Bill to explain his cryptic comment—"One problem's solved"—in the back of the limo ride from JFK. He'd placed his index finger to his lips when she'd asked for an explanation.

"Geez Bill, what did you mean?"

"Just that the homo Vinnie Briggs is no longer a problem. He's relinquished the recording."

"You bought him out? That's great. How much?" Linda was excited. Bill wasn't sure how much detail to reveal.

"It'll be fifteen grand for your share of the cost."

"What? You paid thirty thousand? Wasn't that a bit high?"

Bill took his time responding, a surfeit of ideas in his head. *I'm going to have to tell her more—although not that she's paying more than half. But why shouldn't she? I used my contacts. I took the risk. What's she going to do, ask for an invoice?*

Bill's chuckle caught Linda by surprise. "Well, Bill, I'm waiting."

"It wasn't a payoff. Vinnie had… 'an offer he couldn't refuse.' Har har, har har."

Linda put a hand up. "Don't say any more. I don't want to be involved. Not another word."

"Right. Give me your fucking morals. You're in the big league now, and this is the way the world works. You should be pleased I've taken care of the problem." Bill walked around and bent over Linda with a sneer. "No problem with white-collar crime. Just don't want to get dirty, huh?"

Bill smacked his lips. *Goddamn slut. Time to get dirty, Linda.*

He offered her a scotch on the rocks. Bill had already finished half his own drink in the time it took Linda to open a sparkling Perrier from his office refrigerator. "Oh, so French, after two months in Paris."

"It's in your fridge, isn't it, *chérie*?"

"Smartass. Now it's *your* turn to do something for the team." Bill finished his drink and wiped his mouth with the back of his hand.

"Don't give me orders. I won't be involved in violence. And what's left to do? With the Vinnie problem, how did you put it? Oh yes, 'taken care of'…"

"Vinnie Briggs isn't enough. There's still fucking Livorno. He'll be looking over our shoulders. *Your* shoulder. He's been angry ever since he lost to you, and he's been asking questions. I hear he's taken a sudden interest in retrieving the archived data that I withheld. Once he gets it, and sees that you doctored it, he'll make the leap. And that's game over. The recording Briggs stole would have exposed us immediately, and Livorno may take a few months, but they both end up with the same result. He needs to go."

"And you'll make him an 'offer he can't refuse,' too? I won't be part of it, Bill. You're crazy. You're a shithead, just like everyone says."

*First this fucking cunt refuses to take directions from me, and second—no, not second, this should be first—she called me a shithead.* Bill said nothing until he had poured himself another drink.

"We're both at risk, Linda. Dan's not a wimpy homo, and his wife has clout. You think I'm stupid—and don't even think of responding to that. But I have a plan, and you play a central role. You're going to entrap Dan on charges of rape."

"What? You really are out of your fucking mind. There's no way Dan would rape me. He hates my guts."

Bill smiled. He, too, could not imagine Dan wanting to have sex with pug-faced Linda when his wife was the best piece of ass he'd ever seen. Bill wouldn't mind having a go with Ginny Livorno—like that would happen in a million years.

"You're right, he wouldn't. That's why his rape will be based on anger."

"And how am I supposed to get Dan to try to rape me?"

"You miss the point. He doesn't have to actually rape or even attempt to rape you. It only has to look like it. Appearances are everything. You must know that by now."

"Yeah, I get it. I'm not stupid either. So what's your goddamn genius plan?"

With a quickness that surprised Linda, Bill was over her, his hands on the arms of her chair, his face inches from hers: a big dog facing down a small pup. "Cut the attitude. I've had enough."

Linda turned her head away from Bill's whiskey breath.

"Fuck it. What do I have to do?"

Bill stood up straight and took a step back. "Good girl. The rape accusation needs an independent observer, someone impartial and credible. Can you guess who? My Puerto Rican bitch assistant Blanca. It'll serve her right, because I know she helped Vinnie gain access to my office and computer. I'm going to enjoy it *so* much when she serves Dan's head to Gary on a plate." Piano key teeth spread across Bill's face.

"I like it," Linda said. "Blanca has always treated me with disdain. I'm sure she calls me a whore behind my back."

"Well, she got that right."

Bill watched Linda's eyebrows rise to touch her hairline. *How's that for instant payback, bitch?*

"The anger is good," he said. "It'll help you act. We'll set it up a few days before you return to Paris. Vinnie Briggs's incident will add to Livorno's rage."

"And why would Dan be upset about Vinnie Briggs? You still haven't told me that part."

"You'll find out soon enough. To be honest, I don't fully know, other than that the queer won't be cooperating with Dan."

"So how does this rape plan of yours work?"

"I'll invite you and Dan to my office. The pretext will be that we need to integrate your former Southwest division with Dan's East Coast. So your input is necessary, if Dan questions your presence, which he won't."

After further discussion, modifications were made to Bill's plan. They sharpened the reasons why both Bill and Blanca had to go to Maria Benfatto's office, leaving Dan alone with Linda.

"And when and how does Dan 'fake rape' me?"

"I'm not finished. While I'm out of the office, you stand up with Dan's back to the door… you'll have to improvise that part. I'll leave the door open. Keep him talking until you see Blanca in the corridor. That's when you grab Dan and push him over. You do know a few wrestling moves, don't you? I'll show you the night before—in your hotel. Har har, har har."

"Fuck you."

"That, too. Seriously though, you'll need some practice. I'm bigger than Dan, so if you can push me over you'll be able to do the same with him. Then just remember to scream and say 'rape' a few times. The more cursing and screaming the better—something you're good at. Har har, har har. Wear a blouse that you can rip the buttons off of, and where it's not too hard to tear the fabric. Then when Blanca enters the room, slap Dan's face and roll onto the floor. You'll need to improvise, but the physical show is important. Throw out your tits, too."

Bill placed his right hand, open-palmed, under his chest and motioned upward.

"Do you have to be so crude? And I'm not at all convinced I can even touch him, much less push him down. He's more likely to push me away."

"Even better! Just take hold of him any way you can. Slap him, and he might slap back, leaving a mark on your face. But none of that matters unless you're on the floor when Blanca enters. Screams, blouse ripped, you prone, and tits flying are key for this to work. Livorno on top of you is a bonus, but not essential. Blanca will have no choice but to corroborate your physical position and your screams."

Bill recognized Linda's billboard grin. "You know, this might work. I know exactly the blouse to wear: my cleavage power blouse that distracts men. The buttons are tiny and will easily rip. I can loosen some threads and slit the buttonhole to make ripping easier."

"That's the spirit. Be creative. Put your acting abilities on show. Har har, har har."

The two collaborators left for an early supper, with a pit stop at Linda's hotel room for a quick screw.

Dan's screwing would come a week later.

# II

# Too Much

# Chapter 27

## The Call

DV&N staff loitered in the hallway, with caws of "How was your Thanksgiving?" passed around like leftover apple pie. Dan avoided these pleasantries, taking long strides to his office. Only one conversation interested him: Vinnie's excuse for ignoring his messages.

The office lights were off. No Vinnie. Dan's annoyance rose. He sat at his desk, too preoccupied and fueled with anger to complete simple tasks. *Where the hell is he?*

A half hour later Dan called Shareen. "Have you seen Vinnie? Is there a staff meeting?"

Like Dan, Shareen was puzzled. Her speculations were plausible but unconvincing: Thanksgiving travel delays; Vermont snowfall; cell phone uncharged. She'd let Dan know the minute she had news.

Around eleven o'clock Dan's cell rang. The caller ID flashed Vinnie's name.

"Vinnie! Where the hell have you been? I've left you messages yesterday and this morning. Couldn't you have at least returned my calls?"

"Hello. Is this Mr. Livorno?" came a voice from the other end of the line.

"What? Who's this? Who's calling me?"

"This is Detective Schwartz from the ninth precinct. Is this Mr. Livorno?"

"Yes."

"Mr. Livorno, you were the last call from this cell phone. Are you family? I need to contact Mr. Briggs's family. What is your relationship to Mr. Briggs?"

"Vinnie... I mean, Mr. Briggs is my assistant at DV&N—Del Vecchio & Neale. What's this about?"

"Mr. Briggs's been the victim of a mugging, and he's now in a coma at Belgravia Incare-Z Hospital. His cell phone was damaged in the assault, but our technical team was able to activate the last call function, which, like I said, was you. Do you have contact info for his relatives?"

Dan was stunned. "I—yes, of course, Human Resources should have that information. I'll ask them to call you immediately."

Dan went to the conference room door and signaled for Shareen to leave the meeting. When she joined him in the hallway, his voice had a flat tone. "Vinnie's been mugged and…"

Shareen's hand flew to her mouth.

Dan explained the situation, and Shareen hurried off to get the necessary contact information to Detective Schwartz. But her shocked expression didn't help Dan's thinking. *This cannot be happening. This is the second time I've had bad news at DV&N. Fate shits all over me again.*

As he stepped back into his office, Dan covered his eyes. *I've become them. It's only about me. I equate my loss to Vinnie's mugging.*

Faced with his own selfishness, Dan resolved to help Vinnie, to prove he wasn't like Bill and Linda. He laughed at this contradictory resolution. This was how he appeared to others. He never truly thought about Vinnie's needs—nor Ginny's, for that matter.

*I should be punished. The cheerleader was right after all.*

* * *

A week dragged by, and Dan waited impatiently, like everyone else, for some sign that Vinnie would awaken. In the second week, Dan reduced his daily hospital visits to every other day. His presence there felt pointless anyway. He talked to Vinnie, but it was ineffective; Vinnie didn't answer.

Dan's temporary assistant maintained a proper decorum, which reminded him even more of Vinnie's absence. She never said, "The weather's fucking awful."

The DV&N hallway buzzed: Would Vinnie recover? How long before he woke up? Dan avoided everyone's questions, held back doctors' updates. Paris was struck from his agenda, and he forgot all about follow-ups with JJ and Rodney. He kept his distance from Linda and Bill. And he increased his UltraFit sessions, which resulted in twelve pounds' weight reduction and fifteen pounds heavier lifts. But this brought no relief from his depression—only less time with Ginny.

Linda was sent back to Paris for a while, as she wasn't needed here; under the circumstances, the transition of the Southwest territories to Dan had been postponed. It wasn't until the third week of December that Dan's new assistant was up to speed and Linda was recalled to New York.

Linda arrived on Dan's hospital visit day. Dan inevitably came back from the hospital feeling that the future was bleak—not only for Vinnie, but also for him. Ginny had become more distant, and sex had become a three-letter word for the *Times* crossword clue: "Precluded by monastic life."

The phone buzzed at Dan's desk. It was Blanca. "Hi, Dan. Bill asked if you're available to come to his office." Her short communication accentuated their remoteness. Blanca had taken Vinnie's mugging hard, and Dan sensed that she blamed herself.

"Now? What's it about?"

"I don't know. He just asked for you."

*Yeah, nothing's changed. Bill calls, no notice, I jump. Shithead.* A smile quickly pressed Dan's face. It just as quickly evaporated when he entered Bill's office.

"What's up, Bill?"

"It's about the Southwest transition to you. Linda's replacement doesn't have enough knowledge to cope with both that and California."

*Now I have to do Linda's job, too!* The old Dan would have objected—would have complained that Bill should have selected a replacement for Linda with some experience, instead of who Bill actually chose: a young bimbo with a second-rate degree.

"It shouldn't last beyond the March quarter," Bill went on. "You'll have January in Texas while we're freezing our asses off here. Har har, har har."

"Yeah, great." *Like hell, Shithead.* Dan pasted on a half smile.

The sound of tapping heels caused Dan's head to turn. The smile was wiped from his face as Linda entered Bill's office.

Dan held back the bile he wanted to spew on Linda's power suit jacket as she removed it and placed it over the back of the chair, her blouse revealing too much cleavage. His chest tightened. He was enraged. He felt a combative feeling unlike anything he had experienced. This was what he should have felt in Paris with Ginny.

His soft voice belied his emotional state. "Oh, hi, Linda. You're looking well. Enjoying your time in New York? You must find Paris exciting."

He hated himself, the scared little boy. *Ginny* should *despise me. I'm despicable.*

"Thanks, Dan. No hard feelings. Something big will come your way, I'm sure. These things take time. Sorry to hear about your assistant—er… Benny. Just terrible. Hate crime, too. We have those even in liberal San Francisco. I hope he recovers, although I understand the longer the time in a coma the less chance for recovery. Still, you'll manage. There are lots of good assistants out there."

*His name is Vinnie. And there are no assistants better than him, you cheating slut.*

"Thanks Linda, I appreciate your kind words for *Vinnie.*" Dan grabbed the chair's arm to control his flapping left arm.

The small talk came to an end. Bill said, "I've asked Linda to join us for her overview on the Texas staff—I mean *former* staff. Har har, har har. Linda's evaluation will be a rundown of skill sets, that kind of stuff, you know, not in the financial charts. Of course you can contact Linda when she's back in Paris, but only if it's absolutely necessary. She needs to focus on Europe now."

"Sure." Rub it in, Bill.

Linda chimed in: "Good people, by and large. One or two airy-fairies, nothing to worry about."

"Airy-fairy. Good one, Linda. Har har, har har."

With only a handful of sentences, Dan's venom had returned. Maybe this is good, he thought. These two have restored my emotions. Keep it up, Linda, and I'll bust your lip. Bill's too. Assholes.

Dan held tighter to the chair.

* * *

Blanca stood in the doorway, stunned. She couldn't believe what she was seeing. She had come running when she'd heard screams; now the folder Bill had sent her to retrieve was pressed tightly against her chest.

Linda lay on the floor, and Dan was on his knees beside her. Linda's blouse was ripped and her bra was half off, exposing one breast. Bill arrived only seconds after Blanca, his lips hinting at a smile, but it was partially hidden by the hand at his face.

"He attacked me! He was trying to rape me! Get him away! You fucking bastard!" Linda spoke with stage-perfect diction.

Blanca and Bill ran to Linda's side. Blanca covered Linda's breast while Bill placed a cushion under her head, whispering, "Oscar."

Standing behind them, Dan spoke: "I don't know what she's talking about. She attacked me. She grabbed my jacket, kissed me, then tripped me and we fell. That's when she started to scream. This is absurd."

"Dan," Bill said, "you should leave—*now*. Go to your office and stay there." He turned back to Linda. "Linda, are you okay? Do you need medical attention?" His baritone seemed deeper to Dan, who did not move.

Blanca bent over Linda and lightly touched the woman's arm. "Stay still. I need to check if anything's broken."

To Dan, this whole scene was a TV hospital drama.

Bill's baritone, louder now, broke the scene. "Dan, leave. Do as I've asked."

Dan exited in slow motion. He heard Blanca telling Bill that he, too, should leave: no man in the room, unless it was a physician. Blanca volunteered at a rape crisis center; Dan had learned this at some point from Vinnie, information that had at the time seemed extraneous.

From the sound of Blanca's voice, Dan knew this was bad—no matter the actual facts.

Forty-five minutes later Maria and Bill entered Dan's office with grim faces. "Dan, I don't know what happened," Maria said. "We're not going to make presumptions or jump to conclusions until we've had a full investigation. But in the meantime, we're going to ask you to leave the building. Take your personal items. This is DV&N's sexual harassment accusation policy." Marching orders, unequivocal.

"I didn't do anything," Dan said. "It's a goddamn lie."

"Don't say another word. There'll be an internal investigation. You must leave. Linda has also been asked to leave, which she did fifteen minutes ago. She can file a sexual assault charge here and with the police. Linda says there was no penetration, but that doesn't preclude the police from asking her to take a rape test. Or she can file for rape assault."

There it was. That horrible word: *rape.* Once accused, true or not, the label would stick.

Forever.

As Dan returned home, he wished he could talk to Vinnie about all this. Instead he called Ginny, who left work. She listened, consoled, and embraced. Yet Dan found no comfort from her, which had never been true before.

It was mid-afternoon and Dan lay in bed, unable to control the incoherent and illogical thoughts that colluded to form a single, horrid word. Blanca's expression scraped his skull. He felt ashamed for even being falsely accused. Yes, he hated Linda—but he would never violate her, not like she said. And Maria's admonishment made him expect that the Special Victims Unit would arrive at any moment, handcuff him, and charge him.

Dan's brain seized. Deep sleep followed, not too dissimilar from Vinnie's current state.

When Ginny rose at eight the next morning, Dan was already gone. After her third voice message, she panicked.

# Chapter 28

## The Counselors—Phase 1

Good friends sometimes say what you don't want to hear.

Betsy wrapped her hands around her coffee mug and Sarah stirred honey in her herbal tea. Ginny had called them in a frantic state, which had immediately brought her good friends to her condo. But now, Ginny was calm. Minutes before they arrived, Dan had called, three hours after her first voice message. He had been sitting with Vinnie, and now he was on his way to an extended session with Ben; he'd be late for dinner.

Now that her panic agenda was no longer relevant, Ginny decided this was the time to broach another topic: the modified form of the proposal she had presented to Sarah and Betsy months before. The new version was that Ben would pose while she and Dan had sex. Ginny reasoned that Ben's modeling would put her in the mood to provide Dan with the greatest sex he'd had in years. And now, unlike before, Dan knew and liked Ben, so the circumstances had changed.

"Fucking stupid. That's all I can say. It is the most fuck—" Sarah soprano's voice began, but she was interrupted by Betsy.

"I think what Sarah is saying—inelegantly, I might add, for an English major—is that your idea has too many ramifications."

Her mug shaking, Ginny bellowed: "*That's* your response? Too many ramifications? I expected better from you. Both of you."

"No, you expected agreement, and we gave you our honest opinions." Sarah was as vehement as Ginny. "Your wishful fantasy doesn't alter the facts. Dan will *not* find the sex wonderful, because you'll be getting off on *Ben*. As for lessening his depression… I don't even know where to begin. And don't believe for one minute that Ben will enjoy posing while you and Dan are going at it. Homosexuals do not get off watching straight couples have sex. And if he wants to participate, let's be clear, it'll be with Dan, not you."

"Sarah makes a good point." Betsy's voice seeped through her lips. "Dan and Ben will not react the way you want. And to be honest, I've not fully taken in *what* you want, or expect, to happen. My limited college psychology says you're indulging in a personal fantasy—your excessive interest in musclemen. Have you done something with Ben?"

Ginny's eyebrows chain-linked to contort her face. She gave Betsy the finger.

"I'm sorry, I didn't mean to imply you've cheated. I mean, how far does your involvement with Ben go? Paris altered your relation with Dan, yet in a bizarre way the rape allegation has readjusted the balance. You could jeopardize your new bond."

Placing her mug on the coffee table, Ginny pulled at the buttons on her sweater. She explained that the new bond they had was based on loyalty, not sex or love. Dan had been trampled again, outmaneuvered; he remained a weakling compared to Linda and Bill. His loss made her stethy flare. She had no desire for a weak man. She sought transference from Ben's masculinity to Dan, and she thought that might make it all better.

"It's illogical and wishing on stars. It's bullshit." Sarah's head seesawed as she spoke.

Betsy shook her head disapprovingly at Sarah and turned to Ginny. "I agree with her—wording aside. Can you... explain more?" Tears formed in the eyes of the hardened financial advisor.

"What else do you want me to say? It's a fantasy. It's *my* fantasy. We talked about this. My sthenolagnia syndrome, or 'stethy obsession,' as my mother calls it," Ginny said, using finger quotations. "My mother says I fit the medical definition for obsession. I don't know, but I do know that I like strong men. I like seeing muscular men flex, that's all. I enjoy it. And no one gets hurt, do they?"

"Not yet." Sarah rose to speak, thrusting her arm out. "But you want Ben to flex while Dan and you have sex. Someone *will* get hurt." She pointed to the bedroom and continued: "No, *two* people will get hurt. Dan and Ben."

Betsy pulled Sarah back down into her seat. "*Three* people, Ginny: you, too. It's one thing to admire men posing on stage, but in your bedroom with your husband... that's a whole other ball game."

* * *

Closing the door after farewell hugs, Ginny returned to her living room and cleaned up the empty mugs. What the fuck do Sarah and Betsy know anyway? I'm going to make this happen. I'll show them I'm right. And I'll show them my mother's wrong.

Acrimony between mother and daughter had started on the day Anna asked her teenager daughter to explain her interest in bodybuilders. In Ginny's view, Anna crossed the line when she suggested Ginny's attraction might be sexual. Ginny did not mistake this friendly mother–daughter conversation for anything other than an interrogation, an intrusion into her teenage privacy. She had seen too many war movies to fall for Captain Anna Swinburne's tricks.

"None of your business and you have no right to snoop in my room!" Ginny said. Then she blared the teenage anthem: "I hate you. Leave me alone. I'm old enough to make my own decisions. Stay out of my room."

Anna ignored this treatise on rights and independence and instead focused on the psychology behind the fitness magazines she'd found under her daughter's bed. "Do you want to start bodybuilding? Are you taking supplements, steroids, or doing anything to yourself? Ginny, do you fantasize about men's body parts? Is it their muscles or their penises?"

"Oh my god." Mortified. Her mother had just said "penis," so the teenager had no alternative but to run out of the room. She stomped downstairs and slammed the front door while her father rose from his living room chair, hesitated, then sat back down.

Two hours later, when Ginny finally returned, her father called to her: "Want to join me for a glass of iced tea? Freshly made." The kind tone in James Swinburne's voice appealed to Ginny. Perhaps he was an ally against her mother.

Ginny swallowed four ounces of iced tea and scrunched up her face. "Mom's crazy. She has no right to go into my room. She's cruel and she hates me."

"Ginny, you know your mother loves you. And *I* love you. We support you in whatever you want."

Ginny retrieved the sugar basin from the counter to sweeten her drink.

"Dad, I don't want to talk about it. Mom's mean and she shouldn't be in my room. Okay?"

This was an airtight defense, so Ginny assumed the discussion had been concluded, yet her father continued. He offered a rerun about her age of exploration, her body changes, and advice on not confusing physical with emotional discovery.

Ginny interrupted when he started to talk about sex. "Not sex again! We've been through it." Ginny looked away. She wasn't into sex, and they needed to stop worrying about that.

A long silence followed, until footsteps broke the quiet. Anna stood behind her husband.

James placed his hand on Ginny's arm. "Will you listen and not interrupt?

We agree, this is not about sex. Could you at least give your mother a chance? Will you do that? I'll make more iced tea."

When he got up and went to the refrigerator, Anna began in a soft voice: "Ginny, this is about a syndrome known as sthenolagnia. Let's call it stethy, for short."

"What? I don't care."

"You might, once you learn more. Maybe you don't have stethy—I'm not sure yet. But knowledge will help you be in control. Control of any obsession is important, and it comes through knowledge. This is important for you and for those you love."

The knowledge argument worked. Ginny was a learner. She had always been curious, and she loved schoolwork, extra projects, and research.

So, armed with articles provided by her mother and the Internet, Ginny researched sthenolagnia. She wasn't sure whether she had "stethy" or not, but in either case she could control her obsession.

And for decades Ginny had succeeded. She'd controlled her obsession with harmless activities. She had felt vindicated.

Until Paris. Dan's enfeeblement had repulsed her. And that had caused her to accept her full-on sthenolagnia syndrome. Her self-deception was over. So instead of denying it any longer, Ginny decided her obsession would *guide* her. Maybe at fifteen she hadn't known what she'd wanted, other than that she liked to look at men with bulging muscles. And at twenty she had used the gym, online pictures, and bodybuilding contests. Now, in her late twenties, her addiction controlled her; and to take back control she had to immerse herself once and for all. This would prove her mother wrong. Her friends, too.

Yet nagging concerns disturbed Ginny. Could a night with Ben and Dan destroy her marriage? Could she lose Ben, her trainer and friend? Could this increase her desire? Ginny weighed the risks against the potential benefits. Her doubts did not alter her resolution to proceed.

However, she did need to answer the prime question: *How to proceed?*

A few days before Christmas, Ben provided the answer.

# Chapter 29

## UltraFit—Rescue 1

White tiled walls, fresh towels stacked high, and hair blowers whirring. Ultra-Fit's women's locker room was a scrum of New York's most health-conscious females. Ginny threw two towels into the laundry bin on her way out. Her chassis glowed with a new car polish as her long legs rolled toward the front desk.

Steve stood, and Ginny's hundred-forty-horsepower XL slowed to a halt. "Ben asked if you'd mind stopping by his office before you left."

With a rear axle spin, Ginny returned down the hallway, knowing Steve was watching her tailgate and expecting that he might want a lube job later. She entered Ben's office, complete with furniture that, next to him, looked like it belonged in a dollhouse.

Without even a greeting, Ben started in. "Ginny, I've been rethinking what you asked a few months back. Now that I've gotten to know Dan, I've decided to accept your request for a private showing—that is, if you're still interested. I could use the occasion to get both your opinions on my new competition routine. I've got a contest at the end of January, out west."

Ginny blinked rapidly. "What?"

"I said I'll pose for you and Dan. Are you still interested?"

"Of course. You've caught me by surprise, is all. I'd given up. Actually, that's not true. I was going to ask you again... but I didn't have the nerve. I'm surprised, shocked, grateful, pleased... I'm at a loss for words."

"Good. Let me know your schedule over the next few weeks. He'll be okay with this, right? And this will help you and Dan? That's still true?" Ben rubbed his face with his baseball mitt hand. "Look, Dan's very upset over all that's happened at work. And he knows I never believed the accusation against him for one minute." He stood and walked to the front of the desk. "Dan talks a lot to me... not about you, so don't worry."

A smile crossed Ginny's face. "I'm sure he doesn't."

Ben crooked his head. "Okay, I don't know what that means, but never mind. Anyway, he's sure that something is happening at DV&N in Paris involving that Lords woman and Barrington. His hands are tied, and he's frustrated. I'm sure you know this."

"Yes, more or less. He needs to drop it. It's not his concern anymore. Dan has an obsession…" Ginny stopped talking and looked down at her feet. "Besides, he misses Vinnie."

The conversation continued with praise and concern for Dan. They agreed he was deeply depressed.

"So, do you think this will help both of you?" Ben asked again. "I know it will improve my routine for the show."

"Absolutely. And Dan will be delighted. He'll want to help you, and he's said he'll do anything for me." She hesitated and glanced down. "He may not admit this will be good for him, but it will." Her smile came with rising cheeks and sparkling eyes. Ben's smile followed.

Two liars grinned collusion. Ben's lie was over his real goal: more intimacy with Dan. Not full sex, but visual. Ginny's lies were many and complex. Dan had certainly not agreed and might not do so willingly, but she'd force him. And her goal was to control her stethy by yielding to her desire. Dan's improved mental state was merely a hypothesis—a secondary benefit.

* * *

His body folded like a human question mark, Dan gave tacit agreement to Ginny's declaration.

"So, I'll tell Ben you agree."

Dan nodded.

Ginny was pleased with the agreement, but not with the feeble nature of it. This was just another sign that he was a pushover. His body might have shown improving strength, but he remained weak in both character and attitude.

"This will be good for us, Dan. I think this will help our relationship."

"I suppose. I guess it can't hurt. I mean, what's the worst that can happen? I'll be embarrassed. Ben will be embarrassed. And there's no threesome. I mean, I need to be sure about that."

Ginny assured Dan of that, but she didn't reveal that they'd be engaging in sex while Ben posed. She did reveal one other detail, though: "I think to make him more comfortable though, we should strip down to our underwear."

That gave Dan another worry. Had she forgotten about his adolescent swimming pool incident? The older bullies? His exposure? His fear of an erection around men?

For a few seconds he said nothing. Ginny waited. He closed his eyes, the image of the two older boys, sixteen or seventeen, passing him poolside. One explaining his workout routine, his double-bicep pose. The other boy squeezing his arms, telling the alpha male they were big and hard. The flexing boy's teeth growing longer with his widening grin: "Sixteen inches of pure, hard muscle."

Dan's eyes grew moist with memory. The humiliation returned; the boy's flexed arm rammed Dan's face; the push away, the second boy pulling at his Speedo, his erection displayed for all to see—girls, moms, everyone.

"Have you forgotten about my incident at the pool, Ginny? Have you not given me any thought at all?"

Ginny knew about what had happened; Dan had told her. But that had been a long time ago and he had been just a teenager. It wouldn't be like that, not now.

"I don't know why it happened," Dan said. "Maybe it was the boy's hard muscle or maybe it was fear, but I became excited. Don't you get it? My penis sprang up to its full length, and probably larger than the sixteen-year-old bully's. He called me a queer. For months I worried that I was a homosexual."

Ginny moved closer to him. "When did you know you weren't gay? Or have you been suppressing it?"

"No, I'm not gay, and you know I'm not homophobic or Vinnie wouldn't be my best friend and I wouldn't be working out with Ben. My high school swimming coach is the one who helped me understand. Coach knew I wasn't gay and he told me, 'One hard-on in front of a boy doesn't make you gay.'"

Dan crossed the room, away from Ginny. She followed. Her words came out slow and soft. "You won't have a hard-on with Ben. But even if you do, it will be me in the room. Ben won't care how big your erection is, believe me."

Wine was poured, and the discussion shifted to dinner preparation. For reasons he didn't understand, Dan felt good about their conversation. It was their first real, non-trivial conversation that wasn't an argument.

After dinner, Dan went to his study, reinforced by alcohol. So what if I get hard in front of Ben? At this point my life has been reduced to nothing anyway, so I should just forget the shame. I'm going to let Ginny enjoy herself and move on.

Dan closed his study door to block out the sounds of the television. He believed his agreement would be good for Ginny's stethy, and maybe it would help their relationship, too. But he didn't see how it would help Vinnie—or the looming financial crisis at DV&N.

# Chapter 30

## Insecurity

The date chosen for Ben's "show" was the Friday after Christmas. Roles had been assigned: Dan as cook, Ginny as organizer, Ben as guest and entertainer. Ben refused the wine Dan handed him, citing his contest diet.

"I've made a protein shake for you," Ginny said. "Dan doesn't know about your diet the weeks before a contest. I made the menu too, which Dan will cook to perfection."

The dinner conversation focused on Vinnie. Ben's empathy came across, even though he'd never met Vinnie. Dan repeated his theory that Vinnie's attack had been something other than a random hate crime.

When the food was consumed, Ben revealed that he was feeling nervous, and Dan agreed. Ginny clanged her glass: "Enough talk, everyone to the bedroom."

In the bedroom, Ginny ordered: "Undress. Dan to briefs and Ben to poser suit."

Ben placed his folded clothes on a chair and applied body oil. Dan didn't move. Ginny twirled her finger, winding-clock fashion, and said with a harsh voice: "Do it." Dan obeyed.

Ginny stripped down to her bra and panties, then hugged Dan and swiveled him, his back to Ben, facing the headboard. Over Dan's shoulders, she had a full view of Ben.

The soft bedroom light glistened off Ben's oiled Doric thighs that supported a triangular upper torso; a cement-hard chest projected pectorals cantilevered between shoulders.

Music played from Ben's iPod. On beat three he started his routine: a double bicep, honey-coned peaks on peaks, then a twirl to a side pose.

Muscles percolated, flesh thinned, and veins skimmed Ben's skin. His nipples formed fireplugs, surrounded by areola quarters. His semicircle horseshoe triceps formed a coral.

With each pose Ginny touched Dan's corresponding body part. She imagined if Ben exploded, each sinew would land on Dan. Ginny's flicked her wrists, signaling for Ben to move closer.

Throughout his posing, Ben's focal point was Dan's well-defined muscles. Ben was proud of his trainee. The dresser mirror reflected Dan's Adonis face: licorice lips, high cheekbones, silky eyebrows, and crystalline eyes. Ben squatted, putting him level with Dan's curved ass, his humps accentuated by tight jockey shorts.

On an impulse, Ben massaged Dan's back, his cool hands startling Dan. Then he moved his hands down to squeeze Dan's buttocks, releasing a gasp. Ginny dug her fingernails into Ben's flared pectorals, which Ben ignored. He snaked his hand between Dan's lags to crawl beneath his genitals.

Ginny's kiss stifled Dan's outcry.

Ben whispered, "Dan, you okay with this? Is this okay, Ginny, can I touch Dan?"

Their reply stayed trapped by their kiss.

Ginny broke away. Her feathered voice in Dan's ear said, "I need this. Ben does too. You owe me." She held back, *For Paris.*

Crushed by Ginny's words and Ben's chest, Dan whimpered, "Ben, I'm sensitive."

"It's okay. I've done this before, and we have the same equipment."

Good, thought Ginny. The men are talking.

Dan craned his neck, made a half turn, and saw Superman. The striated musculature, the Alaskan pipeline veins crisscrossing underneath the skin. Ben's body had been undraped by his contest diet, revealing new details. He had evolved into a new species.

The men were transfixed by each other until Ginny removed her bra and panties. Dan's jaw dropped when Ginny pressed her naked breasts against him. With a swift squat, Ginny pulled Dan's briefs to his ankles, releasing his hardening penis. Ben's ink drop poser followed, kicked aside.

Without a cue, Ben shot a bicep pose, and Ginny moved to pinch the peak. Ginny dragged her ass across Dan's hips, taking his penis for a ride; his eyes grew to fill his forehead.

Ben spied Ginny's wide Cheshire grin as he followed her pointing finger. "Huge, isn't it?" she said. "Like a porn movie star, wouldn't you say?"

Ben said nothing.

"One of the biggest I've seen, how about you?" Ginny nodded to Ben's carrot and then to Dan's beetroot.

Dan chewed his gums. Ben's mouth curled, and his teeth bit hard against his lips. He stopped flexing, his nostrils flaring.

Ginny knew. *I've gone too far. This is Paris speaking. I need to stop.* She mouthed for Ben to resume, which he did.

"Dan, feel like you're at the gym," she said. "Ben's in contest form."

Dan looked at Ben, then to his throbbing erection. "I'm sorry, Ben. I don't know what's come over me..." Dan felt like he was poolside again; he heard the adolescent laughs. *Coach, I need you now.*

"Don't sweat it," Ben said. "It happens to lots of guys, straight and gay. It's a completely normal reaction, and I'll take it as a compliment." Ben lowered his arm and smiled.

Dan looked away when Ginny's pushing caused his stiff penis to hit Ben's abdomen. She guided Dan's hand along Ben's furrowed pectorals. She pulled Dan's hand over Ben's nipples, hard as hers. The music stopped, but Ben didn't bow for applause.

Dan cupped his hand over Ginny's breast, which was smaller than Ben's.

Ginny felt secure. *Dan's overcome his self-effacement before another man. He's forgotten his jealousy and fear of abandonment.* Her left hand moved from Ben's nipples to his eight-pack abs, then returned to his pectorals. She anchored her free hand to Dan's cock and pulled his flared tip to rub her vagina.

Dan suddenly backed away. "No."

"What?" Ginny had no lilt in her question.

"I don't want to talk about it."

"Why did you stop?" Ginny shouted.

Ben, sensing the fight, walked out to the living room.

Dan's voice sizzled. "You want to have sex with Ben."

"That's not true. I admire his physique. Besides, he's gay—or had you forgotten?" Ginny's voice was as hot as Dan's.

"Doesn't matter. Maybe he's bi. Your mother warned me that someday your fetish would take a turn."

"Leave my mother out of this." Ginny took several breaths. "And I don't have a fetish and my mother's theory of sthenolagnia is *bullshit.*"

"Bullshit's about right. Why were you touching Ben's nipples? He doesn't have muscles in his nipples."

"Because they're at the end of his pecs! Basic anatomy, Dan. People use porno films to enhance their sex, don't they? This is just like that. It's called fantasy and nothing more." Ginny was at full volume. "I love you, not Ben. Don't you love me?"

Dan scowled. "Not at this moment. I agreed to help Ben and you, but all you want is a dumb bodybuilder, not puny me."

"First, you're not puny. Second, I refused bigger men before you came along."

"More bull. You were groping Ben. Say it: you want a muscle freak to satisfy your sthenolagnia fetish." Dan was shouting now.

Ginny shouted back, "Don't you become my fucking mother! I've had enough. You're immature and your jealousy is stupid. I'm not interested in Ben as a man. I want to explore his muscles with my hands, not my pussy."

Ben came back into the room to fetch his clothes. Dan pointed.

"There he is," Dan said. "Go fuck your big muscleman."

"You're a fucking idiot."

"You're a muscle slut. I'm not enough of a man for you."

"You got that right. Chickenshit let a little French asshole push me over."

Dan's hands covered his face. Ben walked out.

A wailing cry broke the lull in bedroom enmity. Ginny and Dan rushed to the living room, where they were shocked to see Ben doubled over, rocking, weeping, his hands covering his face.

Squeezing in beside him, Ginny touched his forearm. "What's wrong?"

Dan knelt before Ben, resting his hands on Ben thighs, ignoring Ben's genitals. "I'm sorry. None of what I said was about you. This is between Ginny and me. I didn't mean my derogatory remarks. Please forgive me."

"Me too," Ginny added. "I overreacted. I like you for more than your body."

But Ben's heaving was unstoppable.

He whimpered, gasped for breath, and cried louder: a primordial anguish, and unbearable to hear. Ginny cried, and Dan joined them. This was a breakdown *they* had caused.

"Please, Ben. Please stop. Oh god, please stop," Ginny sobbed.

Ben's mouth gaped, soundless.

Dan's tears leaped to Ben's chest. Ben gasped, choking as he tried to speak. Dan fetched water and held the cup as Ben drank, sucked air, and drank again, the gulping his only sound. When the glass was drained, Ginny brought a refill. Ben finished the second before speaking.

"I'm sorry... I am so sorry... so sorry... so sorry...." A diminuendo refrain.

Ginny placed her arm in Ben's. "You have nothing to apologize for. *I* should apologize."

"Me too," Dan said. "I said vile things that have nothing to do with you." He stood behind Ben and rubbed his shoulder.

Ben sobbed, "It's not your fault."

"What's upset you so much?" Ginny asked in a soft whisper.

Ben explained that he felt he had been the fight's catalyst. It wasn't their words that bothered him—he'd become immune to insults about bodybuilders being meatheads, queers, grotesque freaks. Bigotry he could handle. But not his own lying.  He hadn't come here for their critique of his routine. He'd wanted intimacy with Dan, something he knew Dan would never have granted. So he had used Ginny.

Dan backed away.

"Not sex, Dan," Ben clarified. "Just to look and touch."

Ginny stood, her finger wagging. "You did *not* cause our fight.  So, you wanted to enjoy Dan. That's not why we argued."

"Ginny's right," Dan said. "It wasn't your touching me that was the problem. Ginny and I have other issues. Okay, you were untruthful, but we were too."

Ben's head was bowed. A tear fell on his thigh.

"There's something else, isn't there?" Ginny's hand on her mouth muffled her question.  "Our argument couldn't have caused such upset.  What is it? We're your friends; you can tell us."

# Chapter 31

## Revelation

The past was private. Ben didn't talk about his past. He asked for a glass of wine.

"Are you sure?" Ginny asked. "What about your competition?"

"Ginny, if I'm going to talk I'll need alcohol. A glass of wine won't matter now. I've already lost, given my state."

Ginny and Dan shrugged at the pumped nude god on their couch. Everyone put their clothes back on, and Dan decanted a Montepulciano. After two sips and a deep inhale, Ben started his story.

"I was married to a woman once. Marianne. We were high school sweethearts." He stifled a sob. "We had a child. Carl."

Ginny touched Ben's arm.

"I began serious weight training in college. My workout partner got me into bodybuilding. By senior year, I'd won some amateur contests. After graduation, I took State Juniors, which caught a promoter's eye. I trained part-time, around a boring pharmaceutical sales rep job."

"Is bodybuilding when you knew you were gay?" Dan asked.

Ginny put her index finger to her lips, and Ben ignored the question.

"I started steroids or I'd never have made pro. Marianne was already pregnant, so I didn't worry. I matched her pound for pound. My sales position gave me access to good stuff. Marianne lied to her parents. Don't all families pretend?"

Dan looked at Ginny and her pencil smile.

"Carl's birth was my happiest moment. Soon after, my serious pursuit of a pro card began, but I needed more training time. I wanted pro status before my twenty-fifth birthday, which few have achieved. My doping and training increased. I quit my job before I was fired. Marianne supported me. She became a second grade teacher. Carl entered daycare at three months."

Ben threw back half his wine. Ginny saw Dan's head move up and down.

"We managed, with Marianne's parents' help. I won state and regional competitions, and I earned a pro card in eighteen months. The prize money and magazine photos brought in thirty grand a year, which wasn't enough. Food, supplements, steroids, promoters' fees and travel… all that ran upwards of twenty-five-thousand."

"That much?" said Dan.

"Easily. Along the way, I came out. It sounds absurd, since I'd always known, really, but the usual self-denial and shit excuses had held me back. But as a pro, I had more opportunities with muscle groupies and gay men. Marianne's reaction was… well, you can guess. I told her I loved her, but not in the way she deserved. We divorced. For obvious reasons I didn't get custody, but I loved my little boy and he loved me. To her credit, Marianne never tried to turn him against me. She granted me weekend privileges, even over her parents' objections. I helped with babysitting for school meetings and most daycare pickups."

Ben finished his wine and Dan poured him another glass.

"I had a new training partner—and sexual partner—a gay bodybuilder. We were having sex, in the locker room, after a workout. I ignored my cell, lost track of time. Until two hours after the daycare had closed. I missed the pickup. The director gave Marianne an earful, threatening to inform Social Services. Marianne went to pick up Carl. She left me a message, cursing my irresponsible, selfish behavior."

Ben drank the entire glass of wine in one gulp.

"Do you want to stop?" Ginny rubbed Ben's shoulder.

Ben shook his head. "A drunk driver ran a red light, broadsiding Marianne. Carl died instantly. Marianne was on life support without brain activity. I was her living trust executor—she had never changed it after the divorce. Her parents pleaded for me to pull the plug. I did. I watched Marianne die in seconds."

Ben finished his story with staccato sobs, which brought tears to Ginny and Dan.

"I'm… I'm so sorry." Ginny's voice cracked on each syllable.

"Me too." Dan's voice scratched his throat.

Ben's hands covered his face. Ginny and Dan both embraced him. Ginny brought a box of tissues and they all wiped their eyes in silence for minutes.

"I… loved… them."

Ginny handed Ben more tissues. "You don't have to say any more. I can't imagine how you felt… feel," said Ginny.

"Feel? The aching is inside and out. Physical and emotional pain. I ask myself all the time what might have been instead of what is… and…" Ben bent, his head touching his knees.

"Please, no more." Tears washed Ginny's face.

Ben sat back. He folded his arms behind his head, his biceps crushing his ears. "Let me finish. I want you to know everything."

"Don't torture yourself," Ginny pleaded. Her hand slid along Ben's arm.

With only a drop of wine left, Ben reached for the water. Dan offered to pour more but Ben declined.

Hands clasped together, Ben told them that he had never moved on after the death of his child. Marianne's loss was different, although he'd never forget.

He withdrew from contests for two and a half years after that. "I trained alone, acted mean. The owner tolerated me because of my trophies—and, I suppose, because he pitied me. Things changed the day Davis McGregor—to be precise, Davis McGregor III—joined the gym. Davis was tall, not a body-builder, but a hunk, and gorgeous. Like you, Dan."

With a turn, Dan smiled at Ginny.

"He approached me, and I brushed him off. But Davis didn't give up, and you can guess the rest. He brought me back to the living." Ben paused. "We lived together off his trust fund. And the sex was unimaginable." Dan shook his head, and Ben politely skipped the details. "Anyway, we became a couple. We were perfect."

"But?" said Dan.

"Yeah, the 'but.' Davis's playboy lifestyle didn't match my monogamous one. I was his one true love—I knew that—but he had other needs. He'd be faithful for maybe three weeks at most. I accepted this, but I asked that he keep his trysts concealed. And of course I insisted on periodic HIV checks with full access to the lab results."

There was a pause as Ben stretched, cracking ligaments. Wine glasses were filled for Dan and Ginny.

"Davis left one day for San Francisco. He called to explain that this would rejuvenate our relationship, which I knew was a lie. Davis was obsessed with sex. He believed that if he satiated his obsession, over time he could control it."

Ginny slapped her thighs. Ben asked if something was wrong, to which she barked no. Ben shrugged.

"I waited for Davis to come back. I planned for us to become Massachusetts residents. It was the only state granting gay marriage at the time. But our phone calls went from daily to weekly, then stopped altogether. I trained, had casual sex."

Ben's story finished with a call from a New York lawyer and the reading of Davis's will. Davis had died of AIDS and had bequeathed his New York and San Francisco condos to Ben. He'd stipulated that the ground floor of the New York building be converted to a gym called UltraFit. The bulk of his trust fund went to Ben as well.

"Can you guess how much?" Neither Ginny or Dan tried. "Two hundred and fifty million. Undeserved. He died because I pushed him away. If I hadn't insisted on monogamy, he'd have stayed, and I would have seen his HIV reports and saved him."

Tears rolled down Ben's red raw cheeks. Ginny's and Dan's eyes moistened as well. The tissues were passed around.

"Don't you see?" Ben said. "*I* caused your fight. I'm a selfish person with my... I'm so sorry... forgive me. Please forgive me..."

Neither Ginny nor Dan answered. They both realized the plea wasn't really directed at them.

Dan reached for Ginny, and they both felt Ben's arms surrounding them, his smothering fire blanket hold.

Ginny gasped. "It's a little tight."

Ben released and sobbed. "Dan, may I?"

"Sure."

With a gravity pull, Ben crushed Dan to his chest, their two mouths sealed together. Ginny slipped on the edge of her chair.

"Uh... well, that was different," Dan said. The back of his hand rose to his mouth but he stopped halfway.

"Dan Livorno!" Ginny said. "That's all you can say? Well, I want in on this too."

Ginny mauled Dan's lips, pushing Ben's kiss down Dan's gullet. She placed her hands on Dan's cheeks. "I'm sorry for the hurt I've caused you tonight... and over the past months. I love you, and I never meant to hurt you."

Dan's new tears came with a smile.

Ben handed over the tissue box. "I'll go now. I think you two need—err... what's it called? Yes, makeup sex."

Ginny asked Ben to stay, but he declined, promising he'd call if he felt depressed or lonely.

The makeup sex was slow-motion intimacy, not acrobatic passion. It lasted a long time before climax. Dan rolled on his side, and Ginny parked against his rear, whispering, "Everything will be good again. Vinnie will recover. Tomorrow will bring good things. Don't you agree?"

With one hand under his pillow and his knees curled, Dan fell asleep, his slow soft breaths warming the sheets.

# Chapter 32

## The BIZ Hospital

A faint antiseptic smell permeated the hospital corridor. Dan could have walked blindfolded, he'd been here so often. He was uneasy on the Monday after New Year's, that day which implied a new beginning. That idea was foolish to Dan's rational mind; the day was nothing more than a dial marker for the Earth's position relative to the sun—and an inaccurate one, too. But Dan's apprehension was a result of the baggage from the disastrous evening he and Ginny had had with Ben. Each footstep made him think of another detail of Ben's awful tale: his betrayal of his ex-wife; his irresponsible behavior; his son's death; Marianne's coma; her swift death. What would be the consequences of his and Ginny's behaviors? Was Vinnie one of them?

From the elevator to Room 1432 at the Belgravia Incare-Z, Dan carried his thoughts. *I'll never get used to this trip. Never.*

Along with learning the hospital routine, Dan had learned the rumor surrounding the bizarre hospital name Belgravia Incare-Z. As happens, rumors repeated enough times become believed, no matter how absurd. In this case, the hospital name derived from a failed merger between the Belgravia Incare, or BI, and St. Ambrose. The two hospital presidents had a dispute over handicap calculations at a Kiawah Island Golf Resort fundraiser, and the disagreement spilled over into which hospital name would be first in the merger. Drinks flowed on the 19th hole, tempers flared, and, ultimately, the merger dissolved. The BI president then took precautionary measures for future mergers by adding a placeholder spot at the end of the hospital name. And so the Belgravia Incare became the Belgravia Incare-Z. From BI to BIZ—the irony missed. Dan felt irony had been written into the BIZ bylaws.

Arriving mid-morning, Dan saw two people at Vinnie's bed. He recognized them as Nurse Betty Davis and physical therapist Jimmy Janks. Dan had already had a few unpleasant confrontations with them both. Their dismissive and condescending attitudes had rankled him. He'd liked the two doctors—Goldoni and Silverstein—but had only seen them once, and they'd explained that at this point, Vinnie's life was in the hands of the physical therapy and nursing staff. They'd monitor his physical state, but they had no control over how, when, and whether Vinnie awakened.

And Dan's anxiety rose each day Vinnie remained in his coma. Perhaps this anxiety, his frustration, the waiting for Vinnie to awaken and for a full and complete recovery and recuperation prompted his action. Or, maybe that particular day, that particular moment, his tolerance for condescension had simply been breached, but whatever the reason Dan snapped at Nurse Betty.

From the doorway of Vinnie's room, he gestured for Nurse Betty to meet him in the hall. She stepped out of the room and shut the door behind her, leaving Vinnie in the care of Jimmy Janks.

"Are you sure that physical therapist guy knows what he's doing?" Dan asked.

Nurse Betty's voice was cold. "Unlike you, Mr. Livorno, we are trained staff. We know what we are doing."

*Bullshit,* thought Dan. Jimmy Janks was even worse than Nurse Betty. On a previous occasion he'd told Dan to stop asking him so many questions as it "interfered with him working."

"I'd like a word with Mr. Janks," Dan said. "I want to know about alternative means to help Vinnie recover."

"Mr. Livorno, as you've been told many times, Mr. Briggs's chance for recovery is slim, and I'm sorry to say it's even less likely with each passing day. Your best hope, and what would be best for Mr. Briggs's family, is that he doesn't last in this state too long before..." She trailed off meaningfully.

"Before...? Before what? He dies?"

Nurse Betty had a faint smile on her face, or so it seemed to Dan.

His face flushed and his throat became dry. "You've given up, haven't you? Well, *I* haven't. And I'm fed up with the defeatist attitude."

For Dan, a line had been crossed, as it has been for many who have learned that medical science admits defeat. Doctors and nurses work on statistics and evidence, not hope; family and friends, the opposite.

"Have you told Vinnie's family?" Dan was angry.

Nurse Betty turned. "Don't worry, we know what's best. Now, I suggest we leave Jimmy alone. You're in the way, and he has other patients to attend to. Mr. Briggs isn't the only patient in the hospital."

Dan had been dismissed. Told to leave. He did, with his head on the boil. He stormed out, vowing to advise DV&N and the insurance company not to approve further payment. His new purpose in life had now changed: to remove Vinnie from the BIZ, Nurse Betty, and Jimmy Janks.

* * *

"That's unbelievable. It's like a TV sitcom," Ginny said after hearing Dan's story of his hospital encounter. She tilted her head and slanted her lips. "Dan, we have to report her and BIZ to the New York City medical ethics board."

"And what good would that do for Vinnie? Our concern has to be Vinnie and his discharge to... well, I don't know where he'll go, but his discharge comes no matter what the cost. I'll insist DV&N pays. And if they don't agree, *I'll* pay... if you'll agree. I know we can't afford *all* the costs, but we could supplement, and I'm sure others will help."

Ginny paced.

"Don't you agree? We have to move Vinnie as soon as possible. Tomorrow." Dan walked across the room to the window overlooking Central Park.

Ginny stopped pacing. "I agree something has to happen soon. I'm not sure we should pressure ourselves with unreasonable urgency though. Let's aim for the end of the week."

"That's too long. They're crazy over there."

"Be realistic, Dan. A coma patient can't be moved in a day. I'm not even sure one week is enough time. Let's not focus on the time. Let's start with what we need to know. Who can advise us? Do we have contacts with private nurses? Who do we know who's used private care?"

Dan turned. He had always admired the way Ginny organized her approach to a problem. He realized he was acting emotional and reactive. He took his cue from her.

"Good idea. Let's make a list of people that might have used private care," he said. "Let's start with elderly parents. We can expand to terminally ill spouses. Also children with genetic disorders or an incurable disease."

"Yes, that's the idea. Keep going." Ginny retrieved her laptop and began typing.

Dan named a few more groups until his categories overlapped under different descriptions. "That's it for me. How about you?"

"There is one other that would be kind of appropriate to Vinnie. Well, not the same, but one common element."

"Gay men with AIDS."

"That's right. How may AIDS victims went to special facilities or were set up with at-home care? We must know someone who knows."

"What about your mother?"

"Okay, but before we talk to my mother I have another idea: Ben."

"Of course. Ben will have known gay men in hospice facilities. Call him. He'll be at UltraFit now."

"I think we should go see him in person. This isn't a telephone conversation. I'll see when he's available. He knows about Vinnie already, which will makes the explanation simpler. And after what we learned about Ben from our 'special' night together, we know that he's familiar with knowing someone in a coma, his ex-wife. I hope this doesn't upset him. We'll have to tread very carefully."

# Chapter 33

## UltraFit—Rescue 2

The X-room assembly line churned, even at nine p.m. on the Monday after New Year's. Iron-pumping addicts lived for sweat. Ben wasn't finished with his current session, so Ginny and Dan crouched in a corner, away from the monsoon men. After a few minutes, Ben finished and came over to them.

"Sorry for the delay. I added extra reps on my lats. What do you think?"

Ben's latissimus dorsi spread the way hangar doors open. Ginny and Dan made room.

"Fantastic," said Ginny.

"Yeah, great," said Dan, not knowing whether barnyard wide was the intended effect.

"Do you need more time?" asked Ginny. "We can wait in your office."

"Nope. This looks like it's important, so I'll skip my shower if you can stand my rank odor."

The three entered Ben's tidy office. Behind his desk stood a bookcase packed with trophies and an eclectic book selection: medical, bodybuilding, training, physiology, interior design, psychology, and philosophy. Wall photos portrayed a well-known bodybuilder handing Ben his first-place trophy and magazine covers promoting his routines.

Ben settled behind his desk the way a semi-trailer moves into a loading dock. "What's up?"

Ginny spoke rapidly. "It's about Vinnie. He needs private care."

Dan filled Ben in on the details of his Belgravia Incare-Z visit.

"Fuck," Ben said. "What a fucking disaster. Do you want a lawyer?"

"No. Not that a lawyer didn't cross my mind," Dan said. "But that wouldn't help Vinnie."

Ginny grabbed Dan's forearm. "Ben, we're here for suggestions. We thought you might have... er, this is difficult to express and sounds insensitive, but we thought you might've had experience with AIDS patients and private nursing care. Is that too much of a stereotype?"

"It's not a stereotype. I'd say most gays have known someone in hospice. Too many friends have died from that terrible disease… Davis among them, although I wasn't there." Ben stopped to wipe his mouth. "Too many. One guy from this gym."

Ben leaned over his desk. "I shouldn't have said that. Please don't tell anyone. The membership would flee. There's still a lot of ignorance around. Can I count on your secrecy?"

Dan and Ginny nodded.

With his hands holding the sides of the desk, Ben looked to Ginny, then Dan. "That was a stupid thing to say. Of course you'll keep quiet." He sat back, his hands in his lap, and with a smile he said, "I know the perfect person to help. I also know he's available. He owes me a favor. His name's Joe Malich. He's not cheap, but he's worth it."

Like a child in a classroom, Dan raised his hand. "We'll find the money. If DV&N won't pay, we will. We have savings, and we'll find the rest. We'll need to find a place big enough for Vinnie's needs, a hospital bed, rented medical equipment, and a room for your friend… Joe, right?"

Ben leaned forward. "First things first. Let me contact Joe."

"Thanks. This is great. We can't thank you enough." Dan shook Ben's hand and prepared to leave. Ginny stood too.

But Ben didn't let go of Dan's hand. "Wait. I'll call Joe now. Time's important, right?"

Dan and Ginny nodded. Ben released Dan's hand and dialed a number on his cell phone. After a moment he said, "Hello, gorgeous. How are you?"

Ginny and Dan could tell that this was Ben's intimate voice, rather than the instructional one they were familiar with.

"Same back at ya. Joe, I'm with two friends who want your advice. I'm going to put you on speaker." Ben placed his cell phone in the middle of the desk. "Joe, let me introduce you to Ginny and Dan Livorno."

"Hello. Nice to meet you, audio-wise," said a melodious voice from the speaker.

"Hi, Joe. This is Ginny."

"Hello, Joe. Dan here."

Ben spoke. "It's a long story, Joe, and I'll fill you in on the details later. The gist is that Ginny and Dan have a friend in the coma ward at BIZ. His coma came from a mugging, almost certainly a gay-bashing. Ginny and Dan have concerns about his treatment, and from what I've heard they have a right to be."

"Say no more. That coma ward is full of Grouchos and Chicos. Sorry, darling, I didn't mean to interrupt. Go on." Joe's voice was soft, Village-hip, with a heavy dose of gay and an underlying educated tone. Ivy League, maybe? He certainly didn't hail from one of New York's outer boroughs.

Dan summarized Vinnie's needs. Joe explained that his patients were typically not open-ended assignments like coma patients, but he'd had a few that he'd stayed with till the end.

Ben asked the key question. "Can you take on a new patient?"

"Big boy, you know I'm free so drop the candy store pretense. I know underneath all that gorgeous muscle you have a brain. It's been three weeks since I lost my last. It takes me that long to recharge, and it doesn't get easier. But I'm back in the saddle now, and I would do anything for your bulbous saddle, you hunky piece of meat."

Ben blushed. "Great. Can you handle the hospital discharge? I'll give Dan your number and you two can talk over the details." Ben looked at Dan, who nodded. "That's settled then. I can make arrangements at my place—you know, the first floor room facing the park. That'll do, won't it? What else?"

"That room's perfect," Joe said. "Don't worry your bubble butt about anything. Leave it all to me. I'll prepare a medical equipment list and have a prelim budget before we talk. Can you prepare your limits?"

"Joe, don't skimp. Include everything and we'll trim later." Dan's voice was strong yet checked for Ginny's approval. This was a major commitment for them at a time when Dan's income was uncertain. Ginny held Dan's hand.

"Ben, this is for you," Joe said. "Have Vinnie's room set up before he's discharged. I'm not fucking around with my patient. And that's the other point, for everyone. Vinnie is *my* patient and I'm in charge. I get any shit or objections, I walk away. Does everyone agree?"

Three voices responded. "Yes." "Absolutely." "Yes."

"One last point, Dan. Who's authorized to sign the discharge papers? Usually it's a spouse or next of kin, like a parent or sibling. Does Vinnie have a medical guardian? I hope he had the forethought to establish one. If not, BIZ can tie this up with delays. They've got lawyers coming out their asses."

Dan's voice wobbled. "I'm afraid I don't know. I'll contact my office to find out if they know, and I'll call his parents, although he's not on speaking terms with his father. That's a long story. I've not met either one of them."

The room went silent for several seconds until Ben spoke. "Okay, Joe, you get the ball rolling. We all know what we have to do next. Talk soon. Love ya. Bye."

No one moved. Dan put one hand on his chin, his eyes cast downward. "Ginny, this is a big decision. I hope we don't regret it." Dan looked straight on at Ginny.

"Never. Vinnie's your best friend. We'll stand together to help him. I'm with you all the way on this."

Dan turned to Ben. "And what's this about your condo? I can't ask you to take someone into your condo. It's too much."

Ben gave a snorting laugh. "Neither of you have been to my condo. I told you I own this whole building, right? My condo spans two floors. I won't be near Vinnie or Joe. They'll be on the floor below. I have fifteen thousand square feet. Do you think I fucking use all of it?"

Dan made a rough calculation based on the three thousand square feet he and Ginny had purchased at two point three million, and not on the top floor. Ben's place would be eighteen to twenty million. *Holy shit.*

"Ben, it's still too much to ask," said Ginny.

"No it's not. Are you refusing to accept my offer? What's your alternative? Accept it—no more discussion."

# Chapter 34

## Legal

The expansive office was adorned with modern decor and a health-conscious motif. Juice bar, exercise mat, state-of-the-art lifecycle, a high-def TV. Water cascaded down one wall; another held a seventy-five-gallon fish tank. Four leather coaches surrounded a square Murano glass coffee table. A sleek Italian-designer chrome desk with trussed cables to the ceiling sat at one end of the room. Gary Del Vecchio, President and CEO, had designed his office to match his philosophy.

Myron Rosenberg, DV&N's chief counsel, sat on the couch adjacent to the one occupied by Gary. Without preamble, Myron declared: "It's not good, Gary."

"Explain. What's not good? For whom?" Gary's hands were out in front, like he was pushing a car in need of a jump-start.

"I called my friend Lenny Cohen at Schwartz, Kauffman, and Klein; sexual harassment is his expertise. Lenny said that DV&N's exposure is big, given the company's net worth. Every lawyer in town would sell their family to get this case. If it weren't a conflict of interest, Lenny would take the case himself, the son of a bitch. That's what I'm talking about."

"I can't believe it. Dan's one of the most decent people I know. And his wife Ginny is stunningly beautiful. I'm gay, and *I* notice her. Dan sexually attacking Linda... it makes no sense."

"You're missing a key point. True, Dan's wife may have given every man at the holiday festival a woody—mine lasted twenty-four hours..." Myron grinned; Gary did not. "Well, the point is that sexual assault—rape, to be blunt—is not about sex. It's about power and control. Rapists are either emasculated men or men that want to demonstrate their power and position. Any schmuck lawyer will make mincemeat of Dan."

Myron cleared his throat, then spoke with a nasal intonation: "Ladies and gentlemen of the jury, this man lost out on a lucrative career opportunity in Paris—and he lost it to a woman. The plaintiff Linda Lords." Myron gestured to an empty couch. "The defendant, Dan Livorno, was emasculated by this—and so he did what every lowlife scum humiliated by a woman does: he attacked her in the most violent way possible."

Myron returned to his normal voice. "Get it, Gary?"

"Shit, shit, and shit." Gary stared across the room.

"Dan has to go. You could suspend him without pay for six months, but in my opinion, it'd be better for him and us if you give him an immediate dismissal. Sweeten it with a good severance package. Six-month suspension is a risk. Any lawyer will advise Linda to take this to civil court. If she does, you'll have to fire Dan without severance, so dismissal now would actually be doing him a favor."

Myron's glare and curling lips gave Gary the feeling he was a scolded schoolboy. "So I tell Dan six months unpaid, risking dismissal at any time with no severance, or he resigns effective immediately with six months' salary."

With a small smile, Myron added, "That'll cover us. With Dan gone, Linda either brings a civil suit immediately or she weakens her case. Of course, there are no limits on a criminal rape charge, but that's not our concern. In six months, Linda's up for a performance review, which might warrant her reassignment to, say, Bogota or Cape Town. That's a bargaining chip for later."

"What's our short-term situation?" Gary twirled a pen on the glass coffee table, a habit of his when he was making a decision.

"Right now we say nothing about a demotion to Linda, or we're complicit in Dan's alleged rape… she'd own us. If Dan resigns, our vulnerability diminishes after three months. We need to learn Linda's immediate intentions against Dan and DV&N, and Bill can help us with that."

The pen stopped twirling. "Okay, you and Bill feel out Linda's position on lawsuits, and I'll talk to Dan. This is a fucking nightmare. It's times like this I hate being the president. You were right, Myron, it's not good."

* * *

Instead of returning to Paris, Linda situated herself in the Park Plaza Presidential Suite, a sumptuous set of rooms big enough to entertain her family or friends over the Christmas holidays. This largesse on the part of DV&N was deliberate: it established their concern for Linda's health and their support for her grievance. Myron wasn't sure DV&N was getting enough value for twenty-four hundred a day. But the one piece of luck, in his ironic worldview, was that the lazy Europeans shut down until after the new year anyway, so Linda would not miss much work.

Linda had a different perspective on this situation. Her Christmas plan had been to work in Paris on the private portfolio for her and Bill, without scrutiny or distraction. Now she'd have to spend weekends at the office. Linda had asked Bill if he could alter the arrangement, but he'd explained management's thoughts. If she played her cards right, Dan would resign, and then they'd be home free. Bill even suggested she meet an attorney to consult on a civil suit. Criminal charges would be better, but Bill cautioned her not to file. "The fucking pigs or a DA can screw things up, if a zealot actually investigates and finds no rape assault."

So when Myron came by to talk, Linda spun her yarn. She didn't want to hurt Dan; she understood his anger. However, she had nightmares of meetings that included Dan. She'd have a hard time moving on emotionally. However, if Dan were no longer a DV&N employee... well, then Linda felt sure she could conquer her emotional problems. She probably wouldn't even need time off for therapy. *Ipso facto*, no Dan, no lawsuit.

* * *

All hospitals discourage self-discharge. Of course, for a coma patient, that wasn't a problem. Further, in such cases the discharge decision went by default to the hospital, rarely to a relative. So when it came time to get Vinnie out of Belgravia Incare-Z, Dan's biggest bargaining chip had been that DV&N supplemented Vinnie's healthcare costs. But even so, there was no way he would be able to discharge Vinnie without a medical-care provision—the "living will"—naming someone as his executor. Dan hoped DV&N had something on file; otherwise a legal battle would surely ensue.

Dan's call surprised Shareen Cooper, DV&N's personnel administrator. "I was about to call you, Dan. Gary would like to meet. When can you come by?"

"Now. I'm calling about Vinnie, and it's urgent. I'd like to see you, and Maria, too."

"Is Vinnie okay? Has something happened?"

"He's the same. It's complicated." Dan relayed his request that she check Vinnie's personnel file for a living will. Shareen promised to have the information upon his arrival.

Shareen met Dan at the DV&N reception desk. His visitor's badge was attached to his lapel. She told him that Vinnie's medical file gave no details about emergency care. She had queried Maria and Blanca, but neither had anything to add.

"Thanks for checking. Can you can give me Vinnie's mother's number, please?" Dan asked.

"Uh… okay, but wait here and I'll get it from Vinnie's file."

Shareen's formal tone put Dan off. "Take your time. I'll meet Gary, then I'll swing by your office. I do remember my way around." Dan flicked the visitor's badge.

"No, please wait, let me get the number first. I can use the exercise." Shareen fidgeted with her notebook.

As she walked away, Dan thought, Why should she insist I wait? Am I really that much of a threat here?

* * *

Forty minutes later, Dan had an answer to his rhetorical question. Had Shareen waited until after his meeting with Gary, she would not have been able to share Vinnie's personnel information with him at all.

Because such information can't be shared with an ex-employee.

The exchange with Gary had been short and tense. Myron sat adjacent to Gary, Dan on a couch directly opposite.

"Dan, I'm sorry, but we're going to have to let you go. This incident with Linda puts DV&N at risk. Believe me, I'm very sorry. Myron tells me there are two options."

Gary did not elaborate on the two options; there was no need. Myron suggested Dan take time to think about the options, although he would counsel that the resignation was the more favorable of the two choices.

Dan rubbed his eyes, giving himself the appearance of being overcome by emotion. But his appearance belied the fact that his brain was already working several steps ahead, like a chess player.

"I'll resign," he said. "I'll take the six-month severance. And I want it to go on record that I did nothing wrong. You'll soon find out that I had DV&N's interest at heart. Linda is going to ruin your European expansion."

"Dan we've been over this." Gary's voice crackled.

"Don't worry, I'm not revisiting anything. In fact, after you screw me, I'll be laughing when you find out *you've* been screwed. Both of you, and DV&N. I had intended to help, but not now. However, before I voluntarily resign, I want to add a condition."

"Dan, you're not in a position to bargain," barked Myron.

Gary twirled his pen. "Stop, Myron, let's hear what Dan has to say."

Myron shook his head like a wet poodle.

Dan looked straight at Gary. "DV&N covers Vinnie for private medical expenses as soon as he's discharged from the Belgravia Incare-Z hospital. What his insurance doesn't cover gets picked up by DV&N. I'd guess your bill will double or triple from its current level. If you don't accept this condition, I'll engage a lawyer for unfair dismissal, and I'll go public. That's my deal."

An agreement was reached: private care for six months, but for standard medical procedures only, nothing experimental. Dan asked for a definition of "standard medical" and Myron gave his medical definition: "Under a million."

Humiliated but not entirely dejected, Dan left his former employer's office with something. On the street he recalled a business journal interview from a year before. It had included Gary Del Vecchio's boast that DV&N's success came because he had a canny ability to recognize and pursue exceptionally talented people like Dan Livorno.

# Chapter 35

## Hello Mrs. Briggs

"Hello, is this Mrs. Briggs?" Dan didn't wait for a response. "I'm Dan Livorno. I work with… I mean, I used to work with your son Vinnie," Dan said over the phone.

"Oh, hello, Mr. Livorno. I've heard so much about you from Vinnie. How can I help?" Mrs. Briggs's voice had a lovely vibrato.

Dan was surprised. He had gotten the impression from Vinnie—and it had been confirmed by Blanca—that Vinnie had no contact with his family.

"Really? Vinnie never told me he spoke to you."

"Yes. We talked by phone once a month. Not his father. He and Vinnie have issues."

*I'll bet*, thought Dan. Vinnie had told him all about being disowned over his sexual orientation. "My brother beat the fuckin' crap out of me with my father's encouragement," Vinnie had said.

"I'm glad you know who I am. Do you know I've visited Vinnie?" Dan kept his voice relaxed, his breathing even.

"Yes. That nice Nurse Betty told me. She said you were DV&N's representative. I can't tell you how much it means to know that Vinnie's under good care because of you and DV&N. I appreciate it very much, Mr. Livorno. You are so kind and so busy, yet taking time to visit my Vinnie. You're a good man."

Those last words stung. Dan cleared his throat. "Please, call me Dan."

"Okay. I'm Ellen."

"Well, Ellen, I'm calling about Vinnie. You know about his prognosis. It's… we're all hoping for the best." Dan's voice cracked. "I'm calling about his hospitalization."

"Oh, yes. Again, thank you for covering his costs. We'd have never been able to afford it."

"Well, that's why I'm calling, Ellen."

"Oh, no. DV&N won't pay anymore, will they? Oh, my. I don't know what we'll do."

Dan heard the panic in her voice. "No, no. I'm sorry to worry you. DV&N will continue to pay. It's another matter. Can you meet me at the hospital tomorrow morning?"

Now Ellen's voice sounded even more panicked. "Is Vinnie all right? Has something happened? Oh, God, oh, don't tell me."

Dan knew that Ellen would misinterpret anything he said over the phone. "No, don't worry. Vinnie's fine. Can I come over to explain in person?"

* * *

Ellen Briggs's three-story Queens brownstone wasn't grand, but it wasn't shabby. The diminutive woman greeted Dan with two kisses, one on each cheek. She was a stunning woman in her late fifties; her figure hadn't sagged. Her beautiful face matched her melodic voice.

"Can I get you anything to drink? Coffee, tea, beer, or something stronger?" Ellen rattled off this menu as Dan entered the living room. She pointed him to a sofa that faced a large-screen TV.

"Thanks, Ellen, I'm fine. I'd like to get to the point, as time is important."

"It's not a problem. I have coffee brewed already. I can make decaf, too."

The beverage decision seemed to have become Vinnie's mother's primary interest, so Dan raised his index finger. "Coffee, no sugar and a little milk. Thanks."

When Ellen handed Dan a coffee mug, she also placed a dessert plate with a thick slice of pound cake on the table in front of him. She herself held nothing.

Dan sipped the coffee, then forked a large piece into his mouth, chewing as he spoke. "Yesterday I saw Vinnie at the hospital, and I'm concerned that he's not receiving the best possible care. I'd like to move Vinnie from the BIZ into private care—to a condo of a good friend. This friend, Ben Hausen, has a large condo on sixty-third across from Central Park. Vinnie would have a bedroom and a round-the-clock nurse, Joe Malich. DV&N has agreed to pay for this private care."

At this point Dan stopped. He was unsure how much more to share. The pound cake and coffee came in handy as he reflected. Joe and Ben were gay, but that shouldn't matter. Vinnie had always said he'd despised being known as Dan's "gay assistant." Vinnie had been adamant that ability and performance were unrelated to whom he fucked. The wording didn't thrill Dan, but he agreed with the principle. And Dan was sure Vinnie would feel the same about this: it was the nurse's ability that mattered.

"Joe is a trained hospice care nurse. Mostly AIDS patients, but coma too."

Dan paused. There was no change in Ellen's facial expression.

"This is a lot to take in, I know. Unfortunately, it requires swift action." Dan explained the discharge procedure and the medical guardianship issue. "Ellen, do you know if Vinnie has a living will? It'd be unusual for a man as young as Vinnie, but did he have one?"

Ellen blinked, but otherwise remained motionless.

Dan waited two heartbeats before asking in a strong voice, "Ellen, are you okay?"

Ellen rose. "I won't be a minute." She left the room, leaving Dan alone with his coffee and cake.

A few minutes later she returned with a large brown envelope. She handed it to Dan; it was addressed to him.

"Vinnie gave me this," Ellen said. "In addition to our monthly phone calls, we'd meet occasionally—usually during the holidays, behind his father's back. About three months ago Vinnie asked to meet me, and when we did, he gave me this envelope. He said I should give it to you if anything were to happen to him. It upset me at the time, and I asked him to tell me what it contained, but he wouldn't. He told me it was work related."

Dan stared at the thick envelope, then at Ellen for a moment before prying open the sealed flap. Out slid legal documents. Dan flipped through them; a rapid read gave him the gist.

"There are two sets of legal documents," he explained to Ellen. "One is Vinnie's last will and testament, which appoints me as the executor of his estate. The other is a medical guardianship, in which he names you as the sole guardian. But in case you are unable or unwilling, he appoints me."

"I'm confused. Does it mean *I* make decisions about him, or you?"

Dan took a few seconds to respond. "It says you make the decisions unless you would rather not. Then it falls to me. Frankly, I would prefer you do it. Vinnie's your son."

Without warning, Ellen burst into tears. Dan felt terrible. He had just informed a mother she'd be making life-altering decisions for her child—or very possibly ending it, if it came to that. He let her regain her composure a bit before speaking again.

"Ellen, this has to be done quickly. Will you approve Vinnie's discharge into the care of my friends Ben and Joe? Do you understand what this means?"

With each last sob, Ellen sat up a little straighter. Each exhale seemed to give her strength. "I've done nothing for too long," she said. "All because my husband's an ignorant homophobe. This stops now. I'll need your guidance, but I'm taking charge. What do you think is best?"

"I think Vinnie needs private care."

"Fine. I approve. Let's go." Ellen rose from her seat.

"That's great, but we have to wait until tomorrow. There are papers and lawyers to deal with first. I'll take care of all that. Can you meet me at the hospital at nine a.m.?"

* * *

Dan called Joe in the cab ride from Queens to Manhattan. Joe gave Dan a rundown of what would happen. Joe's lawyer had already started the paperwork, and Joe would arrange for him to arrive at the hospital by eight a.m. The living will would be their trump card. Joe would put in a call to the medical supplier after he hung up with Dan, and would arrange to have the medical paraphernalia delivered tomorrow. He'd also let Ben know to expedite the room preparation. A private ambulance would transport Vinnie to the condo.

Joe asked Dan to fax Vinnie's medical guardianship papers to both the lawyer and him, and to bring the original tomorrow.

Dan was pleased with Joe's enthusiasm and preparation; the man seemed to be unstoppable.

Joe finished by giggling in Dan's earpiece: "Honey, we have liftoff. Oh, I love those words, don't you?"

# Chapter 36

## In-Patient Care

The early morning influx kept the twenty-foot revolving entry door at the Belgravia Incare-Z hospital twirling. Flanking the merry-go-round door stood two additional doors that swung inward to the large exterior vestibule. Ten feet behind the entry doors were a twin gang of automatic sliding glass doors to the interior lobby. And sandwiched between these two doorways stood Dan, waiting for Ellen.

He went outside as soon as Ellen exited the cab and stepped onto the curb. She took Dan's extended arm. "Let's pull together and do the best we can for Vinnie," he said.

For the first time in years, Ellen went to meet her son not in some out-of-the-way place where they wouldn't be spotted—but here, out in the open, with one of Vinnie's friends. She'd always known her son was a good person, but somehow she'd allowed her husband to vilify him for being gay. Now, as she held Dan's sturdy arm, Ellen had a new outlook. All that homophobia, hatred, and stupidity would stop. Now. Her husband would either change or he'd find himself kicked on his ass, out the front door, by a woman who stood five-foot-two.

Ellen waited next to her son's bed, holding his hand, until Dan and Vinnie's new nurse, Joe Malich, returned with additional paperwork for her signature. Her eyes were red and her heart pulsed in sync with the rhythm of Vinnie's machines. She was no more aware of her surroundings than her son was.

Joe and Dan entered, and Joe handed over another form. "Last one, Ellen. Sign on both pages, please. My lawyer's with BIZ's legal, and they're pains in the ass over minor details. But with this one, we're done."

Ellen signed the paper, and Joe headed out to give it to Nurse Betty. But first he turned to Ellen and said, "The hospital administrator may come down to ask you to reconsider. Please—don't let him persuade you, please."

To reinforce Joe's words, Dan placed his arm over Ellen's shoulders and spoke loudly enough to be heard over the VIP room intercom: "Joe will be more help to your Vinnie than Nurse.  He'll also help *you*—unlike the way you've been ignored here."

"Don't worry," Ellen said with a sniffle. "This fuckin' place won't hold my Vinnie back if I have anything to say about it."

Ah, thought Dan. The wellspring of Vinnie's vocabulary.

* * *

Joe never left Vinnie's side, from the hospital room to the ambulance and the journey uptown. Dan and Ellen waited, calm and composed in a coffee shop; Ben would call Dan's cell when Vinnie was settled into his new room.

In contrast, Ben was sweating and anxious. He watched Vinnie wheeled to his room after he'd oriented the ambulance medical team to the condo layout. Ben swayed then stumbled. Joe was pretty sure he knew why.

"Yes, Joe, memories, *déjà vu*, whatever you want to call it. Seeing the techs lay out the plastic hoses and wires brought it back, and the flashing LED lights." Ben took a deep breath. "Worst of all is the sound. The machines seem louder in this room than they did in Marianne's hospital room. They're so inhuman, aren't they?"

Joe nodded.

"It's like... like... Marianne is..."

Ben's nightmare had been wheeled into his condo. Joe ushered Ben into the bedroom next door—his new room—and sat Ben on a chair. Then he called Dan. One patient at a time.

* * *

Ben looked around at the room's cream tones, its king-size bed and its wall-mounted flat-screen TV. Across from him was the entrance to the en suite bathroom. Ben rarely came to this floor, and he spent little time in any of the five en suite bedrooms. And, he thought now, he'd be spending even less time on this floor as long as Vinnie was attached to the machines. His penthouse floor was more than adequate. Joe could manage with this floor's smaller kitchen—smaller in comparison to the penthouse; it was still twice the size of what you'd find in most New York City apartments.

Ben could avoid Vinnie and Joe.

Standing, Ben caught sight of himself in a wall mirror. He was used to observing himself, checking on the progress of his physique. But today, a drooping face peered back, reflecting his regret at having made the offer to house Vinnie. In his zeal to help, he had acted in haste—possibly caused in part by his remorse after his exhibition disaster with Ginny and Dan. But whatever the cause, he had never imagined he'd be struck by the revival of suppressed memories.

Yet those memories from hell now screamed within him, and they spoke reality: *This is a mistake. Vinnie's going to die, and I will have given false hope to his friends and family. I'll be drawn into their darkness again. I will relive my despair.*

He felt trapped. Could he change his mind? Tell Dan and Ginny this wouldn't work? Send Vinnie back to the hospital? Or maybe pay for a temporary condo elsewhere—that's what he could do. Move Vinnie far away. *That's what I should have done in the first place: rented a condo. Maybe there's still time to make the change.*

The doorbell rang. That would be Dan with Vinnie's mother—but why? He hadn't called them yet. They had come too soon. Well, it didn't matter— now he could tell Dan that he'd changed his mind. He could suggest that alternative accommodation be found immediately. Better to do that before everyone got settled in.

But as he worked out his explanation in his head, Ben didn't consider Ellen Briggs. As Dan began to introduce her, Ellen motioned for Ben to lean down. She was incapable of hugging even one side of Ben's heirloom chest, so she balanced herself with her arms around Ben's neck, kissed him on both cheeks, and spoke softly: "You're a good man, Ben. You'll be in my prayers forever."

With her kisses and those words she had just signed a long-term lease on her son's behalf.

"Can I see my Vinnie?" she asked.

"Follow me." Ben walked slowly to Vinnie's room, head bowed. Dan held out his arm for Ellen and the two strolled behind the hulk.

Ellen's numbness prevented her from taking notice of the designer furniture lining the hallway, or the wall-mounted paintings, or the two homo-erotic pencil sketches—original and very expensive. Weary from emotional upheaval, hospital paperwork, and legal interrogation, Ellen was stoic until she saw Vinnie—then she broke. Dan steadied her, and Ben brought a chair next to Vinnie's bedside.

For five minutes, Ellen quietly cried. Then she stood, and Ben came over to her. His loose sweatshirt concealed his body the way a one-ton packing crate hides content but not the volume. Ellen stumbled, and Ben reached out, holding her forearm like a child holds a crayon.

"Are you okay? Please sit down, Mrs. Briggs." As Ben lowered Ellen into the chair, his expansive chest nearly pushed her over. "I'm sorry about your son. I don't know him, but he's a friend of Dan and Ginny, so he's my friend now. And I have to tell you, this gay-bashing attack makes me very mad,

Mrs. Briggs."

"Please, call me Ellen. I can't thank you enough for your generosity. I don't know how we can repay you. I want to help, too. I want to be part of my son's life again." Her shoulders slumped.

From the doorway, Joe spoke. He must have arrived while Ellen was crying. "Ellen, I can't tell you how much I appreciate what you said. I've seen too many parents remain steadfast in abandoning their homosexual children. I'm sure your presence will help Vinnie." Joe paused. "But I don't want to give you false hope. The longer a person remains in a coma, the less likely they'll recover consciousness. It does happen, but it's rare. There are things in Vinnie's medical chart that indicate he has a chance... but good is not a guarantee. I'm going to use all my magic and honey-making juice... and I'm fuck—uh, damn good, too. Ben, tell Ellen. Am I the best or what?"

The three men made no movement or sound; they knew Ellen had something to say.

# Chapter 37

## Mother Tells All

Ellen rose from her chair at Vinnie's side and walked to a couch at the other side of the large bedroom, near a window. The three men followed. Ben took an armchair, and the other two reclined on a settee.

"I'll never forget that day." The men knew she was talking of the day Vinnie had been banished from the Briggs household.

He had just turned sixteen, she explained, so he hibernated in his upstairs bedroom with his computer games. On that day, Vinnie's father, John Briggs, had called Vinnie for help. John's buddies called him "Big John" because of his six-foot stature, his hefty girth, and his megaphone mouth. Vinnie flew down the staircase to his father's call. Big John expected his family to respond immediately to his commands—anything less was unacceptable—so Vinnie had forgotten about his computer.

Vinnie moved two-by-fours from the garage to the basement while Big John went to his bedroom to change into his work apparel. Big John thought he heard someone in the boys' bedroom—the room Vinnie shared with his older brother, Jack—John Briggs, Jr. Indistinct grunts pushed Big John to investigate.

On the computer screen, two naked men were dueling with their stiff cocks. Then one man stuck his hard penis up the other's ass. Big John screamed, "What the fuck!"

The sting of the blow dazed Vinnie. Flat on his back, he looked up to see his father's fist pulled back. Blood gushed from Vinnie's nose. Big John's voice boomed so loud that people in neighboring Nassau County must have heard it. Ellen ran from the kitchen to the garage.

Big John yelled, "You're a goddamn *faggot*?"

He told Vinnie that there would be no queers in his house. Vinnie cried. His father called him a crybaby. Vinnie was hysterical and kept repeating that he was sorry.

By this point in her story, tears were falling from Ellen's eyes. She wiped them away with a tissue handed her by Joe.

She turned her head toward Vinnie's bed, then looked at each of the men, her hands clasped in her lap. "Vinnie admitted that he had been hiding his sexuality from us for two years. He begged for us not to hate him—to understand. But my husband could do neither, and he stormed out."

Jack, Ellen said, found out about Vinnie that night. Jack was four years older than Vinnie, tall, and muscular. He used to love it when Vinnie asked him to flex. His face would light up, Ellen explained.

It wasn't until after Vinnie's banishment that Ellen learned, from Vinnie's eldest sister, that Vinnie enjoyed watching his older brother masturbate. Jack had reportedly warned him, too: "No queers here."

So on the day when Jack learned that his younger brother was gay, he beat Vinnie to a pulp.

"I bandaged Vinnie twice that day," Ellen said, tears welling in her eyes. "I knew that Vinnie was not safe alone in that house."

As they listened to Ellen's story, Dan, Ben, and Joe shook their heads. They knew that Ellen was blaming herself. She thought that if she had only stood up for her son, Big John might have changed his mind.

"Deep down," Ellen continued, "I think John was angry because he loved Vinnie more than he loved Jack. Jack is big and manly—he boxed—and he beat up most of the men in the gym. Both inside the ring and out, which is what got him into trouble. Jack's in prison now for assault and battery with six months left on his sentence. Did you know that?"

Dan nodded yes. The other two shook their heads no.

"Crime is all Jack knows, sadly. Vinnie's better than Jack. He's smarter, better-looking, and a nicer person. My husband knows this too, but he won't admit it. He used to be so proud of Vinnie, before that terrible day. A neighbor once told me how much John bragged about Vinnie's high school grades. Jack did, too: he told everyone he had a genius little brother.

"But, in the end... Vinnie stayed with my sister until he finished high school."

Ellen started to cry again. Joe brought her a fresh glass of water.

"Stupid men," she said. "Stupid, stupid, stupid."

"That's always the case," said Joe. "Stupidity is the root of all bigotry and hatred."

Ellen mumbled, "So true."

The rest of Ellen's story took the men through Vinnie's young adult period. He lived with his sister through high school, then attended Bennington College in Vermont on a full scholarship. "And I know he's really made something of himself—thanks to you, Dan, and his job at DV&N."

Joe sat next to Ellen, took her hands, and suggested she take a break.

She whispered, "I may not know who hurt Vinnie this time, but I know who did it all those years ago." She removed her hands from Joe's. "My husband will have to accept that I'm either going to be part of Vinnie's life, or John can find a new wife. And I'm going to tell him right now. Ben, is there somewhere I can make a private call?"

The men sat with Vinnie in silence until Ellen returned.

"He's on his way."

* * *

An hour later, Ben escorted Vinnie's father into the room, without a word exchanged as Ben left the room.

John gave a quick glance to Dan and Joe on the sofa—there had been no introductions—and acknowledged his wife, who sat next to Vinnie. His eyes were fixed on the room's central feature: the large hospital bed surrounded by machines, tubes, and monitors. Vinnie's face was buried behind masks and tubes, but the bruises and blackening around his eyes were visible. John knew what had happened, but he couldn't accept that this was his Vinnie in the bed.

"John, look at our son," Ellen sniveled, tears flowing.

John moved to Vinnie's bedside. His mouth opened, but no words came out.

All voices remained silent except Vinnie's surrogate: Whump whump... whump whump. Beep beep... beep beep. Shoosh shoosh... shoosh shoosh. *I'm here. I live. I don't exist.* Whump whump. Beep beep. Shoosh shoosh.

Ellen turned from her son to look at her husband, her face streaked with tears.

Finally John found his voice. It was choked with emotion. "Who—who did this to my boy?" He turned to his wife. "Oh Ellen, what have I done?"

No one answered.

Whump whump.

Beep beep.

Shoosh shoosh.

Ellen rose, took her husband's hand, and guided it to Vinnie's forehead. That's when Big John lost control. Tears spilled from his eyes and his chest heaved. He made no attempt to wipe his face or suppress his sobs.

"I'm sorry, Vinnie. Forgive me."

Ellen burst into tears.

Joe moved to Ellen. "It's all right, dear, it's all right. This is a step. Cry your eyes out. This is what love feels like. Hold on to me, sweetie, and let's give Vinnie a kiss to let him know you love him."

With Joe's help, Ellen leaned over and kissed Vinnie on both cheeks.

As she stepped back, to her surprise Joe kissed Vinnie too, as near to his lips as possible without disturbing the tubes—in full view of Big John.

Ellen looked up, frozen—she expected her husband to grab Joe by his throat. But Big John just stared at his son. Being gay didn't matter at this moment. What mattered was possibly losing Vinnie forever. Not the kind of loss they'd suffered over the past seven years, but the forever kind of loss: eternal and evermore.

"What can I do to help?" John said. He looked to Joe, then to his wife.

At that moment, Ben entered the room. His hostility to Big John was palpable. "I'm Ben Hausen," he said to John, "and this is my condo. I'm this man's gay friend." Ben pointed to Joe.

Big John extended his hand to Ben for a handshake. With hesitation, Ben extended his own hand—then applied pressure that stopped short of cracking Big John's fingers. A grimace on John's face was followed a small grunt. Ben's vise-like grip caused Big John's eyes to tear up.

Ellen smiled, thinking that her husband was overcome with the same gratitude she felt. But the pain traveled from Big John's hand to his forearm and shoulder.

In a deep voice, Big John said, "Mr. Hausen, I think we've gotten off to a misunderstanding."

"How so, Mr. Briggs?"

From the couch, Joe jumped up. For him, this was an all too familiar scene: an angry AIDS patient's friends confronting a non-supportive family member—often at the funeral service.

"Ben, honey, let go of Mr. Briggs's hand. Go to your happy place. Time to relax those muscles. I don't have time for another patient, do I?"

Ben stared coldly into Big John's eyes, but he let go.

"Sweetie, follow my tush outside."

Dan followed Ben and Joe out of the room. He knew Vinnie's parents needed time alone, with themselves and their son. And Dan needed time, too, to collect his thoughts before Ginny's return from her out-of-town meeting. If the Briggses could talk, then he and Ginny could too. Their future together depended on it.

# Chapter 38

## Technique

Silhouetted rose walls and light lavender baseboards and insets gave the Livorno bedroom a sensual feel. Dan lay on the king-size bed; the extra mattress space was a reminder that he was alone. The light taupe ceiling became a portrait of good times past. Years before a different bedroom with a smoky-white ceiling had been a special day: Dan's fantasy day, the day his desire renewed his insecurity.

From the beginning, Ginny had scripted their activities. But that day Dan had decided he would rather die than lose Ginny. On that day, his jealousy was ignited.

He had watched Ginny on campus; had seen her demeanor around men. He sought clues that she was being seduced. He watched. And he'd quiz Ginny if they hadn't been together for several days—who did she meet, where did she go.

But on that day, Ginny had had enough. She gave him an ultimatum: he would stop these queries, or she'd leave him. Dan's quizzing stopped., but not his jealousy.

That day marked the beginning of both his dream and his never-ending nightmare.

* * *

*Four Years Before*

Her direction was strong and clear: "Dan, go to the bathroom first and prepare."

After he had relieved himself—as much from nerves as from a full bladder—he undressed. He stared into the mirror and thought he needed a shave. With the fragrant rose soap on Ginny's bathroom counter, Dan lathered his upper body. He poured mouthwash direct from the bottle into his mouth. He gave a quick flex and was pleased with his shape. He sucked in his stomach muscles, and a six-pack formed—the result of his daily swims. He knew he was in shape.

Dan removed his pants and jockey briefs, folded them, and set them on a stool. His fastidiousness prompted a quick wash of his private parts. Then he waited, a hand in front. He was unable to shake his shyness, even when it came to intimacy with his girlfriend.

The word "girlfriend" sparked a self-interrogation. *Is Ginny my girlfriend? Will she always be mine?* Years later the word "wife" would replace "girl-friend," but otherwise the questions would remain unchanged—and unanswered.

Naked and wary, he heard Ginny's call. He knocked on the bathroom door and heard a cheerful laugh. "Come out, I know you're there."

The dim bedroom lights highlighted Ginny's hair. She was like a painting, Dan thought—a lady waiting for her courtier. Dan halted and raised both hands to his chest. Ginny was lying on her side, one arm under her head, half-turned to him.

From her position, she could see Dan's reflection in the wall mirror: his back muscles, the movement of his muscular ass. She smiled as she watched Dan's large penis mount up his cascading abs. His chest mushroomed into round platters that stretched across shoulders meant for a saddle.

Blood filled Dan's facial capillaries as he spied Ginny's heart-shaped ass. He moved behind her, gazing at her spine and long neck. With one arm stretched outward, he stepped forward until he touched the silk sheets.

Dan knelt at the bed's edge. He shifted his body sideways and rested his head on the mattress, his ear listening to the bedsprings, his eyes anchored to the curve of Ginny's spine. His hand trembled as he placed his index and middle fingers on the base of Ginny's neck. He was careful not to disturb a single vertebra. His slow-moving fingers rode down Ginny's upper spine the way small boys roll toy trains along a floor, each vertebra arch a trestle. His head inched closer to Ginny's railway spine as his fingers slid and Ginny giggled. There was a momentary pause when he reached Ginny's spinal base before his fingers crossed her alpine ass. Up one side, down the other, he reached the summit and abandoned his finger train in favor of a palm full of the mounded flesh. He squeezed, kneaded, gave himself proof that this was real.

"Ouch."

Her sound had no effect on Dan. He had lifted himself up to place his face at the top of the bubble so he could peer into the valley. He kissed Ginny's hard ass, scraping her skin with his rough tongue. He wanted to consume her. He desired her in ways that should have made him blush, but the heat of his desire burned away all inhibition.

That was the moment: the woman he'd never lose. Could never lose.

Ginny's face pushed into the pillow and she raised up on her knees. Dan's fingers pressed deeper, seeking her vagina, his forearm lodged between the cheeks of her sky-high ass. His thighs spanned her lower legs as he straddled Ginny's buttocks.

Sweat perfumed the room. His pulsating penis sought entry, yet the pleasure of his hand and eyes on Ginny's body restrained him. Dan lowered his head to guide his hands; they slid down Ginny's thighs to widen her ass. With gentle exploration, his arm forded her anus as his fingers ran across her perineum to her wet labia. He wanted to have and hold forever this perfect female form.

Extending his fingers, Dan reached into Ginny's vulva. Her moan encouraged him. He wanted to comply, but his penis throbbed and the cremaster muscles tugged his aching balls upward. He rose to mount, but for Ginny's instruction:

"Turn me over. I want to see you."

Ginny turned face up. Dan's mouth opened at the sight of the firm breasts. They disarmed Dan, their perfection, sculpted, and defying gravity. They would not sag with age, these bear claw breasts and suckle-sweet nipples.

That was a night of acrobatics—and Ginny's incantation; Dan should have paid closer attention. "Make them bulge. Make them big and go high." Dan knew the drill. He lifted off his elbows, his arms parallel to his shoulders, and flexed a double-bicep pose.

"Closer. I want to feel them."

His powerful abdominals held him at a forty-five-degree angle. Ginny took hold of his arms, circumscribing his mounded biceps, releasing her sibilant sh... sh... sh. Dan knew that Ginny wanted him to have the strength of Hercules. His bulky shape had satisfied her. The same mass had cost him an Olympian swim tryout and denied him a first-place college trophy—his bulk impeded him in water but had propelled him to Ginny.

He knew that Ginny's admiration of his masculine physique was different from that of other women. When she touched his sinew, it felt like she was painting trim.

Dan had simply not understood how much this mattered.

"Let's play rough."

Following her words, Ginny's next move had surprised Dan. An index finger extended, Ginny sledded between Dan's perineum to his scrotum, and then again; on the third slide, she rested her fingers on his ass crack. Dan jumped when her middle finger ever so slightly pushed into his anus. Pain was followed by stimulation. Dan groaned as she slid in and out, each exit accompanied by a touch of his balls. Ginny kept up her rambling sex talk, but Dan heard only consonants and vowels. She massaged his testicles and his ego.

From her single digit, Ginny spread her fingers, and her open palm cupped Dan's balls in a juggler's grasp. Then, without warning, she pushed them into Dan's upper cavity—and released them to parachute down. She reversed her action, now pulling his testicles down, a vine plucking. This tugging swing nearly rendered Dan unconscious. His penis became harder than it had ever been.

When coitus began, Ginny said it felt like being beneath an oil rig, he pumped so hard. She had hissed "more... bigger", her ass rising upward.

* * *

Now alone and sleepless, Dan's eyes moved from the ceiling, and his head turned to face the wall mirror. *How naive. I should have known.* His future mother-in-law had told him about Ginny's sthenolagnia. But the warning had been forgotten the minute Ginny had him in bed.

Dan didn't need to look—he knew he was rock hard in his darkened bedroom of silence, loneliness, and memory. He flushed red. On another occasion, he might have masturbated to release himself, but not tonight. He would not defile this memory, perhaps all that might remain of him and Ginny. He had become hostage to her stupid folly, her stethy obsession, which had only grown when she'd met her muscle-bound trainer, Ben. And Dan's uncontrolled jealousy had contributed to the problem. Of course, now he knew that Ben would never have taken advantage of Ginny.

Mental exhaustion overcame Dan, and his penis flagged. He felt depressed. Tomorrow he would know his future: either he and Ginny would stay together, or he would be stuck with memory sex and a life alone. Dan's depression rendered a fitful sleep. His dream mixed bedroom scenes, muscular bodybuilders, cheaters taking his job, and scandalous accusations.

# Chapter 39

## Pleasure and Pain

Throughout lunch, Dan reviewed his checklist. Ginny's flight had been delayed, which had given him extra time to put his thoughts down on paper. But now she sat with Dan at the kitchen table, holding her coffee mug.

Dan stared at his list.

Item one. Vinnie's move to Ben's condo.

Item two. Fired from his job.

Item three. Improved marriage and sex.

The third item was his quandary. Start with Paris? Which? His failure or the fiasco? Their marriage had gone south before his screwup; even before Bill Barrington and Linda Lords had screwed him. He and Ginny needed to solve their issues or they were as finished as his job.

While Ginny sipped only coffee, Dan ate yogurt, chicken, and a protein mix—Ben's nutrition regiment for him. He decided to start with Vinnie's arrangement at Ben's condo.

Ginny stopped him, asking for details. She wished she hadn't. She was upset to learn about Vinnie's teenage beating, his banishment, his mother's guilt. She was skeptical of Vinnie's father's bedside change of heart. Could people change so quickly?

Placing his dishes in the sink, Dan moved on.

"I was fired from DV&N."

"What! Oh my god, what happened? Were you arrested? Why didn't you call me?"

"I wasn't arrested."

Ginny touched Dan's hand. "If there's no criminal charge, why were you fired? Didn't Gary promise to settle this internally? Do they believe Linda?"

After a sigh, Dan began a long, monotone description of his meeting with Gary and Myron Rosenberg, including the two options and the deal he had struck for Vinnie's private care.

"After six months we won't be able to afford the mortgage," Ginny said.

Dan paced the kitchen. Time for item three. He searched the wine cabinet, removed a bottle, and poured two glasses. Ginny sipped once while Dan's loud swallows masked the sixty-cycle hum of the kitchen appliances.

He emptied his glass and poured another.

He finished the second and poured a third.

"What's going on, Dan?"

"Us."

"Us? What does that mean?"

"It's time we face facts. We're coming apart. We have to figure this out."

Now it was Ginny who drank all her wine and refilled her glass. Then she moved to the living room couch, where she tucked her legs under. Dan followed and sat next to her, bringing a second bottle of wine.

"You're right," Ginny said. "It's me, and I admit it. Everything has changed since Paris."

"And that was my fault. I acted like a shit, a coward."

"Well, that triggered a big decline, but it doesn't explain everything. Something's been bothering me for a long time, and I think I know what it is."

"Do you not love me? Is it your Bloomingdale's Paris job? Take it. I'll come along and be the house hubby. It might be easier for me to find work in Europe. I'm sure to get something, even if not as cutting edge as DV&N."

"No, it's not my Paris job. And of *course* I love you. How could you have doubts?"

He did, but he wasn't about to explain.

Ginny unfolded her legs and placed them over Dan's lap, her hand on his arm. "This is going to sound... well, I don't know how it'll sound, but you have to trust me, it will help. I want to invite Ben over again."

"To thank him and apologize. I was thinking that too. But how is that relevant?"

"No, not to thank him—or, not *just* to thank him. To help me... us. Something happened last time. And... we need to try again, to solve my problem. Maybe it'd be good for you and Ben, I don't know. The truth is, I need help, and this is it. I've been thinking about Ben's remark—you know, how Davis told him he needed to sate his desire? Well, I feel the same."

Dan's voice was cold. "Davis died."

"Come on, that's different. The point is, Davis knew he had to immerse himself in order to control his obsession. I feel the same."

"You're talking a threesome!" Dan's voice rose. "Didn't you learn anything? Ben won't agree. And Ben's gay. And I'm not having sex with a man! How would you participate anyway? And what about Ben's feelings?"

Ginny removed her hand from Dan's arm.  He pulled back and Ginny pushed away. She gulped more wine.

"Listen, Dan, I've learned new facts. Can you stop arguing for a minute?"

Ginny explained how she believed the encounter would integrate their sexual and emotional needs.  Her mother had provided medical studies on sthenolagnia.  They were sparse, from colloquia mostly, unpublished, but enough. And Ginny had investigated online various psychological researches into human desires.

"Your parents *approve* of this idea?" Dan was shocked.

"No, I haven't told them. I don't ask *permission* from my parents—or any-one. I don't need a counselor." Ginny had decided not to mention her discus-sions with Betsy and Sarah.

"What about me? My feelings don't matter either?"

"Of course they do.  And that's why I'm asking you for your opinion on how to do this."

"We don't.  That's my opinion."  Dan's jealous anger ate at his stomach. His cheeks sucked in and his eyebrows dipped like closing curtains. With one hand on his head, he rubbed out thoughts.

Ginny raised both hands to her face, barriers to her words.  "I'm asking, how do we involve Ben? The best arrangement."

"Best arrangement for what? Us masturbating while Ben flexes?"

"No, Dan. I've heard your morning grunts. You don't need any help with that."

Dan's face reddened.  "You know why?  Because we don't have sex. But I've never cheated on you. I've been faithful!"

Ginny stiffened, folded her arms. "Me too, Dan." She softened her voice. "Me too."

Neither moved, aware that their forced statements should have been un-necessary.

Ginny unfolded her arms.  "I'm suggesting this precisely to improve our sex, repair our relationship, and save our marriage."

Dan's voice modulated.  "And how?  Has Ben said he wants to have sex with me? You're pimping me out so you can feel his muscles?"

Ginny's voice rose. "Dan, you can be truly stupid. Don't you want to save our marriage?"

There was not a twitch on Dan's face, but his eyes were like lasers piercing Ginny.

"You *know* I don't want to have sex with Ben," Ginny said, "nor for you to either. This is my fantasy, maybe my lifelong desire. I felt something the last time, before we fought. I felt a breakthrough was about to happen."

"Speak English. What do you want?"

Ginny tapped her leg. "Let's start with your biggest worry. The only penis inside of me will be yours. I love you, not Ben. Now listen again. *I love you.* And Ben will not be putting his penis into you, not if I have anything to say about it. This is to fix my problem, my... obsession. There, I've admitted it."

Tears rolled down Dan's face. "Ginny, I can't live without you. I didn't sleep last night. I felt so alone." Dan choked on his words. "I love you so much. Without you, I could never have survived all that's happened. Ben, too. We couldn't have a more supportive friend."

A tear slid down Dan's cheek and was wiped away by Ginny's finger. She brushed his lips with a quick kiss.

"This is my fantasy, but it will bring us together, trust me. Ben's physical presence gives me passion, like watching a movie with a hot sex scene."

"Maybe for you."

With a toothpaste-commercial smile, Ginny nodded. "But if I get excited, you'll have a good time too. I guarantee it."

Dan's lip twitched, and his hands opened, palms up, as if catching snowflakes.

"Somehow my stethy has returned in a bad way," Ginny said. "I need to see and feel Ben's muscles while we have sex. I can't explain it. Trust me, this will be a one-time event. What alternative solution do you have?"

Nothing was said for a few moments. Dan walked around, looking at his notes, as if an answer might appear there. Returning to the couch, he held Ginny's hands and spoke softly.

"I can't go on like this."

He tilted his head, his neck cartilage cracking, and his eyes opened wide enough for fists. Then he stood and backed away. He mumbled something more, but his words were inaudible to Ginny. He moved to the living room doorway.

"What? Dan, I didn't hear you."

He was gone.

"Dan, please, what did you say?" Ginny's voice carried to the hallway.

Dan reappeared, looking at nothing in particular. "Set it up."

Each syllable slowly marched across Ginny's eardrum. Dan commanded; he was in charge.

Tears came to Ginny's eyes. Something was different. Dan's demeanor, his face. She didn't need a psychology degree to know that something had changed in an instant. She'd gotten her wish—although she was unsure now that she wanted it.

# Chapter 40

## Mother-In-Law

Streetlights cast shadows across Dan's knees. A small lamp projected his shadow on the living room wall, his shadow hunched and rocking. He had risen in the middle of the night. What had he agreed to? Ginny didn't lie, but she didn't always tell everything. Dan's mind raced over what he knew about his wife.

Ginny Swinburne had always excelled in both academics and sports. A typical teenage girl had turned into an intelligent woman of exceptional beauty. He first learned just how complex Ginny was on the day he met her parents, at her Harvard Business School graduation.

* * *

*Graduation Day*

Ginny had obtained graduation tickets for her parents, her sister Rachel, and Dan. Rachel gawked at Dan when they met.

"It figures my sister would pick up a tall, handsome man an hour before the ceremony."

Ginny gave her sister a friendly shove. "Hey! I didn't just pick him up off a street corner. This is my fiancé, Dan Livorno."

"What the fuck! You're engaged?"

This was the first direct exchange Dan heard between his future sister-in-law and future wife. Many more would follow over the years.

A family argument ensued. Dr. James Swinburne apologized for his daughters. Dan would later learn that James's role was family apologist.

Dr. Anna Swinburne walked with Dan across the campus quadrangle. She squeezed Dan's arm as they went. "Yes, this will satisfy Ginny," she said.

Dan was embarrassed. His future father-in-law mumbled, "Please excuse my wife."

The next time he met Ginny's family was at their homestead in Stamford,

Connecticut. Anna and Rachel greeted Dan and Ginny at the door. James was out walking the family dog, Foo Foo, a yappy bichon frise. Rachel's boyfriend-slash-significant-other, Ted Akens, arrived a short while later. Ted was a talker—the kind that didn't hold anything back. He told Dan about his sex with Rachel, his drug addiction. Anna seemed pleased, and James apologized.

After a cordial family dinner, Anna took Dan to the family room. That was when she told him about Ginny's "condition."

Dan didn't understand. He just said, "I'm pretty fit, you know."

Anna squeezed Dan's arm. "Yes, and I believe that you'll be enough for Ginny. But you need to understand: she needs more than usual strong."

Anna embarrassed Dan with questions about their dates, and even asked intimate details about their sex routine. At last Dan stood, making the excuse that he'd like to go help with the washing-up.

Anna stopped him. The Swinburne family kept no secrets, she explained. "Of course, we only talk about intimate subjects in person, not over the phone or email. That's why Ginny didn't tell us about your engagement."

Dan didn't really think sharing engagement news was quite on the same level as sharing frank sex talk, but before he could say anything more, Anna launched into more details about Ginny's infatuation.

"In medical terms, sthenolagnia means a muscle proclivity, although it's usually called a fetish or obsession."

Dan stumbled over the pronunciation.

"Say it like this: steh nol neeaah."

Anna gave him the rundown of the condition. It dated back to sometime in the late 1800s, and was first identified by a German psychologist named Magnus something or other. This particular fetish could be found among both males and females. Anna explained that sthenolagnia was sexual arousal caused by being around strength or muscles.

"Ginny has a sthenolagnia obsession, a word she dislikes," Anna said. "I first noticed her fascination at ten or eleven, but it probably presented earlier. Her obsession increased in high school. James and I didn't try to stop her or be judgmental. Saying no is not the way to treat any obsession."

She took Dan's hand. "I'm telling you this because Ginny's obsession will have implications for your marriage."

* * *

*Dawn*

Dan rose at six-thirty to a winter-dark sky. He wrote Ginny a note after breakfast. "I need to go away for a short time, and I've taken the car. I'll be back by dinnertime. Love you, Dan."

Two hours later, Dan had arrived at the Swinburne home. Anna opened the door to her son-in-law and greeted him with open arms. Coffee was brewed and fresh croissants were set on the table; Dan accepted the former and declined the latter. James said hello, apologized for a yapping Foo Foo, and sequestered himself in his study.

Dan gave Anna a rundown of his and Ginny's current life together—in detail. Then he broached the million-dollar question: What could be done about Ginny's sthenolagnia?

Anna's initial response was to encourage Ginny to seek professional help. "Obsessions can change over time. Some people believe obsessions—or fetishes—shift or diminish, or become more intense. It depends on the fetish and other factors, both internal and external."

"Ginny refuses to see a shrink."

Anna raised her shoulders.

With halting speech, Dan outlined Ginny's proposed "solution"—the one he had agreed to. Had he done the right thing?

Anna took Dan's hand. "This isn't my expertise, but I *can* say that no one can predict what will happen to either of you—like with Ben's reaction on your first try."

"Why? What caused Ginny's sthenolagnia?"

Anna looked out the kitchen window. "It happened around the time Ginny was five years old. We lived in a different neighborhood, a suburban housing tract, starter homes for middle-class families. Young children were every-where. It was a good summer ice cream truck route.

"One day I was on the phone, and Ginny heard the Good Humor ice cream van jingle. It might as well have been the Pied Piper."

"I know. We had one too," Dan said with a clean smile.

"Well, Ginny went out without waiting for me, the first time by herself. By the time I reached her, Ron, the van owner was consoling her. He called himself 'Mr. Huge Humor'—and he *was* huge. He was an amateur bodybuilder and made enough money during the ice cream seasons to support his training. The kids loved him, and he loved children."

The rest of the story revealed that the kids had been bullying Ginny; she was always a small child, up until her growth spurt at age twelve. Without Anna there to protect her, the children had pushed Ginny over. She had dropped her ice cream cone, and one boy threw the ice cream in her hair.

"Like I said, by the time I reached her, Ron was wiping her down with a towel. He had chased the other children away and given her a fresh cone.

But he also said he'd protect her. He flexed his muscles, gave her a ride on his bicep, and took off his shirt. Dan, he was so big and muscle-bound, I know it impressed Ginny. It impressed me, too. After that day, Ginny received special treatment from Ron. And he flexed every time he served her."

Dan rubbed his temple. "So a muscular ice cream man protects Ginny from the other children. That caused her stethy obsession?" He shook his head in disbelief.

"I don't know if anyone can say there is one specific origin for this syndrome. All I know is that Ginny loved her Ice Cream Man. But there's probably more to it. Usually is."

Gazing across the table at the kitchen wall clock, Dan forced his next question. "Will she eventually be unfaithful to me?"

"I don't think Ginny will be unfaithful—she's too open and honest. In my opinion, if her sthenolagnia grows, she'll ask for a divorce before she'd deceive you with an affair."

On his return home, Dan found his mother-in-law's words bittersweet. Ginny wouldn't betray him—but big deal that was if he still lost her anyway. And Anna hadn't provided any advice on whether Ginny's scheme would help. Only that she was sure the results would be unpredictable for everyone: him, Ginny, and Ben.

Midway across the Bronx, Dan decided. He'd be Ginny's new Ice Cream Man. He'd prove that manly didn't only mean burly, bulging muscles. He would protect her. And to do that, he'd have to participate in her experiment all the way. No constraints, no complaints.

# Chapter 41

## A Night's Reflection

If Dan had a fitful sleep, Ginny's wasn't much better. Her return home had been fraught with anxiety, and it continued on into the middle of the night. She woke to find herself alone in bed. Peering out of the bedroom door, Ginny saw a faint light from the living room. Dan was there, his faintly illuminated form slumped on the couch. Ginny had no doubt that he was in turmoil over her proposition and his agreement.

She returned to bed and reconstructed the day Dan first learned of her sthenolagnia.

* * *

*Four Years Before*

A cool early morning breeze circled through an open window in Ginny's Connecticut bedroom. She awoke as the light silk sheet rustled; Dan was sitting on the edge of the bed. His back was to her; he hadn't seen her open her eyes.

She watched him adjust his athletic-style briefs, his hand pushing down his left leg to adjust his penis. She was fascinated by the way men's undergarments differed from women's—a more practical approach based on personal equipment. Dan must have experimented, and his particular length was probably a factor. Ginny smiled to herself. Her real fascination was Dan's well-defined body, a combination of a swimmer's low fat percent and a weight lifter's bulk. She knew too well his handsome facial bone structure, his cheeks set to highlight a short nose, which in turn underscored lips made for kissing. She loved his eyes, a lake blue that made her want to skinny dip. He was perfect; better than any airbrushed and photoshopped magazine cover model.

She'd been with men packed with more muscle, models stamped with handsomeness to sell cologne in glossy magazines. Dan was all that, but he was also something more: he was smart. His intelligence wasn't something he had been taught; it came down the birth canal.

Despite her attraction to Dan's body, Ginny didn't want a man that only saw her for her own body. She had suspected this of Dan for a while, until in a moment of honesty he had debunked her illusion. She had smirked, acknowledging her own hypocrisy. She looked at men's bodies first. She evaluated size, body shape, muscularity, athleticism. If they passed her evaluation, only then did she talk to them. Body before mind.

The last item in her equation was sex. Hers and Dan's was incredible. Her body tingled in her recollection of the previous night; she'd have to give Sarah and Betsy a fiery blow-by-blow account. Ginny giggled, and Dan turned.

Ginny sat up. "Morning, sweetie." The sheets moved down, and Ginny's breasts filled her nightgown, a soft breeze moving the sheer fabric. Sunlight shone on Dan's briefs and he moved his hands to cover himself.

"Dan, I don't think you need to do that. I *have* seen it, remember?"

"Oh, yeah. And I want to thank you for last night. That was the best ever. You are beautiful, and I'm so lucky you allow me to be with you."

Ginny's grin spread so wide it might have cracked her jaw. Who is this guy? Has he read the playbook on how to charm a woman? Is he real? A gentleman or a charlatan?

"You're welcome, Dan. Great for me, too."

"Shall we have breakfast? I'll make it."

"Okay, but you need to come here first."

Ginny tapped the bed. Dan twisted around and leaned across. Ginny took hold of his neck to kiss him, tongue deep, her breasts imprinted on his. Dan responded; no shifting of his briefs would hide the awakened giant. The rapidity of it even surprised him. "Oh, sorry, it's beyond my control."

"Sorry? Not me. Let's do something about it."

In the morning light, Ginny and Dan made love again. He devoured her, explored each breast with tongue, fingers, chin, and nose. He massaged her body, lingering on her thighs, calves, and feet. He kissed between her breasts, his desire throbbing below. She had wanted him to take her, to control her entirely with his strong arms wrapped around her. Her desire washed across her taut skin.

She pushed her breasts together, and Dan licked both nipples, his head oscillating between them.

"Sit across my abdomen, resting on your knees," Ginny demanded.

In this position, Ginny took Dan's elongated thick penis and pulled it between her breasts. Her nipples hardened to acorns as Dan's pre-cum droplets fell on her.

Like the night before and all others, she reached that point when she desired Dan's muscle.

"Flex, Dan. Flex your biceps. Make them big."

Dan made no move, so she repeated her words. Dan lifted one arm; a round bulb formed. Ginny pulled it closer, licked it with her tongue. She moaned as Dan's cock continued to rub the inner crevice of her tits.

"Show me the horseshoe."

Dan stretched his arm, producing ringed triceps. Ginny touched the striations and wetness filled her; she was on the verge of an orgasm. She pushed Dan's arm, telling him to lift up. His cock flew out as Ginny turned over to rest herself on her elbows. Her ass was high, practically into Dan's face. She gave him a view of all her parts. She wanted him to touch all of her.

With her legs spread, she tapped her backside. Dan adjusted his position, his face on her back, his cock entering her vagina from the rear. He held himself upright, one hand on her back and the other cupping her breast.

She felt his initial penetration, his delicacy. Ginny took shallow breaths with each half-inch. She thought about his chest muscles resting on her. Her ass felt the power of Dan's round glutes pushing, his inner leg adductors squeezing his balls to perform. For a half hour she let Dan fuck her from behind, with periodic cries of, "Yes. Fuck me."

Her second orgasm arrived with Dan's. His thrusting glutes had been aided by her fingers behind pushing his balls higher. After his final ejaculation he rolled onto his side. Ginny focused on his glistening sweaty chest, his rounded globe pectorals. She rubbed them, knowing Dan was too spent to flex. No matter; they felt hard and big.

He was fully dressed when Ginny came out of the shower. "I'm taking no chances with you, you Harvard sybarite. Stay away or I'll die of starvation."

They ate breakfast, knowing the afternoon would bring more sex. She would ask Dan to pose. While he contracted his muscles, she would walk around, surfing each sinewy ridge.

* * *

Sleep would not resolve Ginny's issue. She and Dan had been happy, fulfilled, everything she could have wanted. And now she wanted more. She wanted bigger bulges, sinew that sat on sinew. Muscle crevices carved and chiseled to rival Michelangelo marble. She had promised Dan this would be a one-time event, the solution to satisfy her stethy. But in the dark bedroom doubts descended: might her words be more wish than truth?

She lay motionless in bed despite her racing thoughts. She dwelled on

Dan's agreement, hoping he wouldn't change his mind in the morning. How would she approach Ben? What could she say, given the previous disastrous attempt?

She rolled onto her side. After a while, Dan returned to bed, his pelvis snuggling her rear, his arms across her breasts. Ginny's hand reached up, touching Dan's muscular arm.

# III

# Recall

# Chapter 42

## The Call

Inside Ben's large modern condo, his restless sleep pattern mirrored the Livornos'. He'd become aware that his loneliness was not from solitude. His days were filled with hundreds of gym members, two trainees, and a dozen staff members. At night he supped solo, by choice, at a marble kitchen table. And Ben had used intense workouts to create exhaustion—as a remedy for insomnia.

That solution had worked until the infamous night with Ginny and Dan.

His new solution included a change to his sleeping pattern. After his sixth and final meal of the day, Ben would take care of his bodily necessities and change into loose pajama bottoms, leaving his chest bare and unencumbered by tight cloth. Then he would retire to his nine-hundred-square-foot entertainment den, where he lay down on a small leather couch in lieu of his super-king bed. He would choose a CD from Davis's eclectic music collection until he was lulled into a semi-slumber.

But with Vinnie's arrival, even this had failed. Too many memories raced through his mind.

The next change came the weekend after Vinnie moved to Ben's condo.

Joe had suggested that Ben join him, Ellen, and Vinnie for a small party—a delayed New Year's celebration. Ben mocked the false, fake joy—it was based on hope, not reality. He knew reality, and he knew there was nothing joyous about it. Ben knew from experience.

But Joe badgered him, and Ben didn't want to upset Ellen. So they had their "party" in Vinnie's room, where Ben hadn't been since the first day Vinnie arrived. Their little party broke up before nine—in time for Ellen to book a taxi to Queens and for Joe to meet his friends for an all-night celebration of a different kind. Ben had volunteered to cover Vinnie's night surveillance, using a baby monitor placed in his den.

Yet his heavy X-room workout hours before was a breeze compared to dealing with the onslaught of memories that rushed through his mind as he listened to the sounds of Vinnie's life support machines. To suit his melancholy, Ben's CD choice for the night was *Madame Butterfly*, an opera he'd learned about from Davis. It was the Maria Callas version—his favorite.

By the time Pinkerton's betrayal was exposed, Ben's despondency matched Butterfly's.

After the finale, just before midnight, Ben decided to check on Vinnie. Ben felt so alone. No one cared about him. He was merely a body to be admired, a trophy like those on his shelf. He was liked for his largeness, not for who he was.

He looked at Vinnie. We're alone. We're numb. We're the same.

Although he hadn't planned to, Ben sat down next to Vinnie and began talking.

Solace came to him that night, unexpectedly, from just talking to Vinnie. And so Ben decided to make this a nightly routine—after Joe had gone to bed. On the following night, Ben listened to Simon and Garfunkel's "Homeward Bound" before making his midnight descent to Vinnie's room.

His monologue that night repeated the story he had revealed to Ginny and Dan weeks before. And once again, he cried when he mentioned his son's name. He described Carl's joy, smile, love of life, curiosity, playfulness. He shared his lament for all that Carl would not have.

His cries were amplified on the baby monitor in Joe's room. Joe went to the doorway to investigate, and stopped in the shadow. Ben was confessing—there was no other word for it. The faint hall light gave Ben's face a gray, ashen look; his cheeks were charcoal, his voice smoky. Joe already knew Ben's story, yet this incantation was different. Joe retreated to his room and lowered the volume on the baby monitor. This was not meant for him.

When the low winter sun awoke Ben, he was still at Vinnie's side. He looked at Vinnie, at his broken leg and arm, his bandaged torso, his bruised face, machines attached. He remembered Ellen speaking of Vinnie's father's and brother's derision—they had called Vinnie a little faggot and a crybaby. The neighborhood kids had joined in, chanting "crybaby." And Vinnie had, indeed, cried.

"You're not a little faggot," Ben said. "You hear me? You're not a crybaby."

The EEG needle made a slight jerk, just a hitch, imperceptible. Ben didn't see it.

"You're not—you hear me? You're not a crybaby. Your mother loves you. Dan loves you. You're *loved*, Vinnie. You're not a crybaby. You hear me?"

Another blip.

For three days after that, the EEG needle jiggled from time to time. Joe noticed it when he did his daily review of the tape. He reassured Vinnie's mother that this was a good thing—an active brain—although no one could say the cause, or whether it would last.

"Talk to him, Ellen," Joe said. "Sing with your beautiful voice. Let Vinnie hear you from the kitchen as you cook. Can you do that? Sing for Vinnie?"

So Ellen began singing in Vinnie's room and as she prepared meals for Ben, Joe, and herself: pasta alla matriciana, pasta alla norma, linguini al mare, chicken cacciatore, bistecca alla pizzaiola. She sang louder and made bigger portions to fill Ben's stomach until even he could eat no more. And she sang her prayers. The EEG needle danced faintly to her tune every day.

* * *

Four days after Ben's confession, Vinnie's fog lifted. He perceived only jumbled images and voices: a baseball bat, screams. His inner curtain lifted; his optic nerve reacted. Vinnie imagined a subway. He heard epithets like "faggot" and "little queer." Sounds of a creaking door and a pinging keyboard. Then words without origin: bad for your health, no son of mine, crybaby, please don't leave, you're suppose to be my friend, a setup.

Then, for the first time in weeks, he formed a thought of his own: *Dan's at risk.*

And a voice outside his head sounded: "Good morning, Vinnie. Time for your bath, sweetie." It was Joe, with his usual cheerful morning greeting.

Unlike some nurses, Joe enjoyed bathing his patients. It was his way to connect. He was gentle with those who were conscious, especially if they were shy or ashamed of their condition. He allayed their embarrassment with flowery words; his noble speeches gave them dignity. Joe would never be inappropriate, never be a Jimmy Janks, yet he didn't deny his own enjoyment at seeing Vinnie's smooth, young man's body. And Vinnie's generally healthy body was an exception in his line of work.

"Okay, let's be sure the water is neither too hot or too cold. Don't go anywhere. I'll be right back, gorgeous." Joe turned to leave the room.

"Okay."

Joe dropped his small wash-bucket.

"Vinnie! Honey, did you say something? Vinnie, did you answer me?"

"Who are you?"

Joe touched Vinnie's face and gave him a kiss on his cheek.

"Honey, it's going to be all right. Just wait, I've got to make a quick call."

Protocol required that the attending physician be notified immediately upon a coma patient's awakening. Joe reached Dr. Alvarez immediately.

Dr. Alvarez was the physician on retainer at UltraFit, and his duties extended to Vinnie, twenty-four seven, rain or shine.

Then, using the internal house phone, Joe called Ben. "Vinnie's awake! Get your big ass down here now!" Ellen received Joe's third call.

Five weeks after his assault, Vinnie awoke. "What's happened?"

Joe answered Vinnie's questions with short replies. When the others arrived, Ben led Dan, Ginny, and Ellen into Vinnie's room.

The horde confused Vinnie. Was why his mother here? And Dan and Ginny? Dan introduced Vinnie to Ben—Vinnie had heard the name but had never met the man. Joe interrupted, asking them to wait for the doctor. Dan backed away, letting Ellen touch Vinnie.

If the numbers overwhelmed Vinnie, they annoyed Dr. Alvarez. "Only Joe stays. For the next few days, visitors will be limited and brief, except for Mrs. Briggs."

With the room empty but for Vinnie, Joe, and the doctor, Vinnie expressed his thoughts sequentially, as requested by Dr. Alvarez, to test Vinnie's brain function. The last time he had seen his mother was three months ago, Vinnie said; he was unaware that it was now over four. Vinnie gazed at Joe, an attractive man that had kissed him, and the unfamiliar doctor. He had no idea why he was bandaged, or attached to all these machines in an unfamiliar room. Had he been in an accident? When? Where was he?

Dr. Alvarez took Joe outside to give him detailed instructions, a thoroughness Joe appreciated. Once procedures were in place, Joe brought Ellen back into Vinnie's room. He adjusted her seat and added a cushion to prop her higher.

Dan and Ginny decided it was best to wait until another day before visiting Vinnie. Ben agreed, so the three of them entered the gym together, using the training as a diversion.

And, for the first time, Ben trained the couple together. Ginny and Dan had thought this would be a good idea, only to find out that Ben's workout was twice as hard as usual. Afterward, soreness silenced their conversation, but on the way home, Dan said, "Maybe wait before you talk to Ben about… about your… our plan."

"I'd already decided that. Vinnie takes priority. Our issue… my problem can wait. We're talking; that's progress."

"Yes, progress. Nothing can go wrong." Dan words wobbled like his legs.

# Chapter 43

## Reunion

The bedroom had somehow shrunk, at least for Ellen. Two words had changed her entire perspective: "Hi, Mom." Through wet eyes, she saw Vinnie and nothing more. She wanted to regain their lost years. What would Vinnie like to eat? Would he like her to make one of his favorites: aglio-olio linguini or melanzana al forno?

Vinnie reminded her of Dr. Alvarez's "fuckin' dietary restrictions."

But soon Vinnie changed their conversation. He wanted to understand what had happened. What did his mother know about Ben, Joe, this place? Where was this?

Ellen summarized. Ben's wealth, the Upper West Side condo, Ben's kindness and generosity.

Vinnie still didn't understand the help from Ben and Joe. "I don't get it. Why?"

"Why are they gay?"

"No, Ma, why are the helping me?"

Ellen couldn't answer that. Vinnie had been mugged, a homophobic attack, so Gary Del Vecchio, in gay solidarity, had generously allowed for private care—at least that's what she'd been told. She left out Dan's speculation that the mugging was job related. In short, she said that Ben's help was a favor to Dan. "What a nice man. You'll like him. He's not what I imagined of a bodybuilder. He's smart, kind, and gentle."

Vinnie remembered a different perspective on Ben—the one related to him by Dan. "I knew Ben was Ginny's trainer, but not Dan's. A lot's happened, hasn't it? And Dan did say Ginny's trainer was a bodybuilder. Have you seen his fuckin' size? He's like bigger than this fuckin' room."

Seeing his mother's finger wiggle, Vinnie apologized for his adjectives and smiled.

Ellen told her son that she had shared their family history with Ben, Joe, and Dan. Ben had become angry to learn of John's and Jack's gay-bashings.

"Holy shit, you told them everything? That's private and personal."

"Dan already knew most of it. Blanca too, from what Dan told me."

"That's different." Vinnie's voice was shaky, weak.

"No it's not. Do you want me to continue?"

Vinnie nodded.

The next shock was learning that both his father and brother had visited him in the hospital. In fact, Jack had been granted early release from Attica due to family circumstances.

"Leave it to Jack to use me. Fuckin' asshole."

A frown crossed Ellen's face.

They surfed family matters, their conversation weaving. Ellen avoided the topic of Vinnie's care, though; she thought it best for Dan to explain. She accidentally let slip that Dan had resigned from DV&N, which upset Vinnie. She claimed ignorance about the cause, which was true. And she had no information on Vinnie's work friends, not even Blanca.

Ellen took a deep breath. "You'll find this hard to believe. When you first arrived here, Ben offered me a bedroom—there are five on this floor by the way, each bigger than half our house in Queens. You can't believe the view."

Vinnie grinned. "Better than Queens, huh."

With a shake of her head, Ellen continued. "Anyway, I stay Friday through Sunday afternoon."

"Makes sense, given your job and Dad's demands on you too."

"Your father was against it, but he came to see for himself."

Vinnie was shocked. "Dad? Came here? Does he know about Ben and Joe?"

"Oh yes. Before he was through the door Ben told him he and Joe were gay. And believe it or not, he likes them. The feeling isn't exactly mutual in Ben's case. But Joe's accepted your father's change of heart. I have, too. Vinnie, it's real. He's different. Can you forgive him? I know that's a lot to ask."

A mute Vinnie looked down at his broken arm.

"Take your time. Anyway, when your Dad arrived, Joe took charge. Ben was angry, so he left the room. And Joe told your father about these machines." Ellen's arm swung around the room. "He described your medication and nursing needs. Your father was interested. Eventually Joe explained his role as your nurse and physical therapist. He said that your chances of waking up were slim. He was wrong on that, thank god. It's a miracle." Ellen's voice cracked. Vinnie closed his eyes on the word "miracle."

"Your father liked that Joe didn't mince words. You know how much your father hates people who BS him."

"Okay, I get it. Dad and Joe like each other. What about Ben?"

"Now that's a different story." Ellen looked over her shoulder and lowered her voice. She relayed Ben and John's first interaction, ending with Ben's handshake. "He nearly broke your father's fingers. John had tears in his eyes.

"After a few visits, your father began to ask Ben about him being gay. It was too personal. I thought a fight would break out. They were in the kitchen; Ben hasn't come down here since your first day, I don't think. Ben asked me to leave. He promised nothing would happen, just men talking over beers. I learned later from your father that Ben shared his entire life story, being gay and other stuff. I'll let Ben give you the details, but I'll just say that Ben's had a tough life."

"Fuckin' unreal."

"There's more. Your dad talked about the misconceptions of gay men, bodybuilders, and homosexuality. Even bigotry."

"Fuck and fuck. Oh—sorry, Mom, it's too much."

"That's okay. You've been in a coma, and it *is* a lot to believe."

"Dad actually said 'bigot'?"

"Yes. And then he admitted he's been one. He didn't realize how nice gay people could be. I almost went into a coma myself."

"I'm shocked. It's unbelievable."

"Your father really likes Joe and Ben. He hopes they'll be your friends."

"You're shittin' me. Oh, sorry, Mom."

Ellen smiled. "I am not shitting you."

* * *

Big John came by the next day. He and Vinnie talked a long time, and then Big John asked for Vinnie's forgiveness. Vinnie said yes—but in a way that meant, "I'll think about it." Vinnie's cynical mind wondered if his father's overnight epiphany was an angle to get at Ben's money. Vinnie would need a lot more time to empty his buckets of bitterness.

Her son's doubts triggered Ellen's own. While father and son talked, she and Joe drank chamomile tea in the kitchen and discussed her doubts.

"You know, Ellen, it's unusual, but not unprecedented. When parents disown their gay children, the break is generally permanent. Once they take a moral stand, their heels dig in. I've known gay men wither away, dying from AIDS, begging for their parents. I've called on their behalf, only to hear the mantra, 'We don't have a son, we don't have a daughter.' In your husband's case, I don't know, but something is different.

"Personally, I don't believe John wanted to disown Vinnie. He's a victim of society—he behaved the way he was expected, to prove he's a real man. My pop psychological explanation is that Vinnie's severe physical bruising and coma forced John to confront his own violence against Vinnie. I'm pretty sure this change has been coming for a long time. Vinnie's coma just pushed the change forward, but it would have come.

"But if a true reconciliation is to happen, we'll have to help. Right now, it's Vinnie's move. He'll have to allow his father a way to save face."

That acceptance from Vinnie came slowly, but it came. At first it was just words more than it was sincere feeling. But then it was more.

Ben was pushed too. If Vinnie could forgive, Ben begrudgingly admitted that he could at least act civil toward Big John.

That last gulf was crossed the day John squeezed Ben's bicep and thanked him for helping Vinnie. Ben knew the signal: John was being intimate, in a man's way.

Ben's manly response was to flex. Fibers moved, and a mushroom head stretched Ben's shirt.

"Holy shit. What a muscle. That's huge."

The choice was Ben's. He removed his shirt, giving Big John the visual to go with the tactile. Ben's biceps could sink ships.

"They've got to be twenty, twenty-one inches."

"Twenty-two, to be precise." To make his point, Ben wrapped his arm around Big John, tugging him into his chest, their faces only kissing distance apart. "We gays are not all puny. We're like everyone else. Small, medium, large, and super-size."

It was decision time. Crush John into powder and vacuum him off the floor later while drinking his protein shake? Or let him walk away?

With a rasp, John said, "I see that. I wish Vinnie would put on weight. Maybe he wouldn't have been hurt so badly. Would you help him, Ben? I'd appreciate it."

Ben's decision was made.

And without knowing it, Ben had made Vinnie and his father's reconciliation possible. Just in time, too. Vinnie would soon need his father's help.

# Chapter 44

## Paris Speaks

Monday's call came a month after Vinnie's miracle awakening. Dan was eating breakfast. He placed his coffee next to the *Wall Street Journal* and answered the phone.

"Hello."

"Bonjour, mon ami, ça va?"

"Oh, JJ, ça va, ça va? How nice to hear your voice. How's Marion?"

"Bien. From me she only wants sex. I have no rest. And how is your beautiful wife? I miss feasting my eyes on Ginny. Is the sex good too?"

Dan thought JJ was proving he was French. "She's fine." Dan frowned in his lie. "Are you and Marion coming to New York?"

"No, my friend, we are not. Soon we will be able to afford only to visit the next arrondissement."

"Is this a call to sell me the Eiffel Tower? Tightwad, spend your big salary."

"You know my big salary now, not in six months. I tell you I will not have a job. This is my reason for calling." Jean-Jacques's voice lacked its usual trill.

Dan sat up, his voice business formal. "What's up? You're too good for DV&N to lose you."

"True, I am good. That is not a brag, just the truth. The problem is our division shows underperformance. Not only us in France, but all our European markets. I have spoken to London, Milan, Cologne, Madrid. We have had dips in the last two months that no one can explain."

"Markets are down."

"No, not the markets. Our products sell well. Our stocks, they move up. I will tell you the error. It's that *folle*—what's the word?—yes, screwball. Linda Lords. Her numbers, they do not arrive to her prediction." JJ had slipped into faltering Franglais.

"JJ, I told you this months ago. I knew Linda's model was wrong. And for my honesty, I was fired on a trumped-up sexual harassment charge." Dan sounded like a squawking black-crowned heron.

"*Oui, mon ami*, but I can't figure out the model. I want to send you data for your opinion. Okay?"

It was not okay. Dan sighed. "I can't. It could be construed as corporate espionage, which carries a big fine and prison. It violates my confidentiality agreement. I'd lose my compensation, and that's money I need for my start-up consulting business."

The friends commiserated over their predicaments.  JJ apologized for putting Dan in a terrible position. Dan was sorry, too; he wanted to help JJ. And help himself, too: this was an opportunity for payback. Dan promised JJ he'd think about it and call next week.

* * *

The following morning an overnight air package arrived from Paris, with Jean-Jacques Gagnon's signature. The customs declaration listed a data CD and handwritten notes.

Dan twirled the package over lunch, his nearly empty glass of white wine pushed aside. Ginny listened to his excuse for not telling her earlier about his conversation with JJ. She sat back, crossing her legs. Dan poured wine.

"I didn't know he'd send me this."

The issues Dan had raised to JJ came up. The risk, the criminal implications, the legal fees, the loss of income. Ginny also pointed out that JJ faced the same risks. They'd both be unemployable in the financial services sector.

"This is a lose-lose situation," she said.

"But I feel like I should help. I know it's crazy."

"Help?  Or get revenge?  You should just destroy that now, Dan.  It's a felony just to have it here." Ginny stood to leave.

"Can I think about it? You too, please. I'll call JJ tomorrow, but can you give me that?"

Ginny turned. When she spoke, her voice was clipped. "Fine. But without a way around the corporate confidentiality clause, you tell JJ no."

* * *

Ginny started that night to examine Dan's confidentiality agreement.

"Nothing. Airtight. Myron sewed it up so even water wouldn't leak."

"Myron's good, I'll give him that," Dan said.

"You're without a pot to piss in. Ruination with a capital R."

"That doesn't invalidate my analysis."

Ginny nodded. Despite their earlier agreement, Dan had looked at the data CD. Ginny had too—she was just as curious as Dan.

Dan continued. "Linda skims the gross income with a stochastic variability algorithm. And DV&N headquarters is isolated, since all data must pass through Bill—which was his motive to back her over me. That's their fail-safe. All operational data passes through Bill. Linda's called it an espionage firewall, but in reality it's there to block whistle-blowers like JJ. If anyone circumvents the protocol, her hierarchical plan will result in immediate dismissal. What a sham."

Dan walked around, scratching his cheek and rubbing his forearm. He settled down across from Ginny. "What if I covertly inform Maria—maybe through Blanca? It's not like revealing something to an outside competitor, and I'd be helping DV&N."

Ginny shook her head. "And that would show you had inside data, which they'd learn came from JJ. Even if Gary overlooked *your* indiscretion, Bill would certainly move against JJ."

"But how would they know?"

"From you. Bill and Myron would threaten you with a suit unless you revealed your source."

"Damn. The game's rigged."

A crease formed on Ginny's brow. "That's it. Game theory. Remember the Prisoner's Dilemma lecture by Professor Hillborne?"

"Of course. Hillborne was our challenge contest."

"Wipe the smirk off your face. Think hard. Remember *mamihlapinatapai*?"

"Not really. Why?"

"Ah, so smartass doesn't remember everything. Mamihlapinatapai is the term used to describe the Tierra del Fuego indigenous people's situation when two people wish the other would offer them a prize—something valuable they both desire. Neither party will ask the other, yet each is unwilling to offer unless asked. The ingenuity comes from obtaining the desired gift without asking."

"Weird... but so what?"

"Okay. Professor Hillborne linked the classic game-theory Prisoner's Dilemma with mamihlapinatapai. He explained the first like this. Two criminals, say Harry and George, are isolated from each other upon arrest. The cops have insufficient evidence to convict them of a major crime, only a minor one. If both remain silent, they'll receive minimal sentences for the minor crime—let's say, one year. However, if George testifies against Harry, who remains silent, than Harry receives the maximum three years for the major crime and George's plea bargain sets him free. The reverse is true if Harry testifies and George keeps quiet. But if both testify against the other, then both are convicted, and each gets two years."

Ginny paused and waited for Dan.

"I know the problem," he said. "George and Harry both serve one year if neither testifies. Or George gets zero and Harry gets three if only George testifies. And if both testify they each receive two years. Their combined sentence will be either two, three, or four years. What's your point: they should have attended Harvard?"

"Very funny. These are criminals, not academics. They're interested in what's good for them individually, not the team total. Each knows the other is just as selfish. They expect the other will testify, so each feels they must testify or face the maximum term. DAs bank on this lack of trust. Do you know the only time this doesn't work?"

Dan shrugged.

"With the Mafia. Can you guess why?"

A schoolboy grin crossed Dan's face. "Because any prisoner that testifies has a short-lived freedom—literally. Your hypothetical George would have to enter witness protection."

Ginny pointed her finger like a gun at Dan. "Bingo. Now move on. We can assume Bill and Linda are not Mafioso. No *omertà*." Ginny used her best Italian accent.

Dan fidgeted. "I'm not with you."

"Go back to mamihlapinatapai. That's what the syndicated crime bosses impose. No one asks, but everyone offers to keep quiet. Their gift is silence."

Dan groaned. He didn't follow.

"Suppose Linda and Bill want the other to offer something without asking."

"And what would that something be?"

"A variation of the Mafia *omertà*. Suppose one testifies against the other, and the other does not. It forces a Prisoner's Dilemma solution."

"I'm lost."

"Pay attention. Let's try this. Linda wants Bill to give her permission to testify against him while he keeps quiet. Bill's gift is permission for Linda to testify."

"Still lost. What's the testimony? Rigging the proposal? Embezzlement? They haven't been charged with either."

"No, it has to be something new. Something illegal like heroin possession."

"Oh great. And how do we get them on drug possession?"

"That's only an example." Ginny paused. "You know, it might actually be a good one though. I'll need time to think." Ginny's eyes turned to the ceiling. "Okay, let's suppose they have heroin... and Linda wants Bill's permission to testify that the drugs are his. That's the mamihlapinatapai part and rigs the Prisoner's Dilemma. Bill agrees to not testify... this is going to require more thought."

Dan stood up and rolled his eyes.

"Sit down. I'm trying to help."

Ginny walked Dan through the scenario. Bill agrees because he'd get his payoff on release from prison. With Bill away, JJ could follow protocol to inform Bill's replacement, who would learn of Linda's embezzlement, hence blowing apart the scheme.

But the setup didn't exactly fit the Prisoner's Dilemma rules. Would Bill accept fifteen years, out in seven, no matter how much Linda offered? The mamihlapinatapai might not work.

Dan's jaw fell to his chest. "Pretty big caveats, don't you think? And I don't see the drug angle working."

Ginny stood behind Dan, rubbing his neck. "We'll improvise. I'm liking this more and more. With a little luck, it'll work."

"Luck?" Dan shook Ginny's hands off his neck. "Risk everything on luck? Look at my track record."

Ginny walked to the kitchen, made herself an herbal tea, and started jotting down notes. Moments later she ran to the dining room, startling Dan.

"What now?"

"We've missed it. This is big."

"What's big?"

"You've been right all along. It's Vinnie, not just you. He didn't get mugged at random. He was attacked on purpose and left for dead. He's in danger."

Dan stood, one arm reaching for the table.

In a few steps, Ginny was holding him. "You can be sure Bill was behind it. We need to find out. Who might know?"

Without missing a beat, Dan blurted out, "Blanca."

"Then we'll need Blanca's help. Damn, but you can't talk to her." Ginny pointed to the legal papers. "We'll need an intermediary." Her hand stretched over her head. "Ben?"

"Hmm. Yes, I'll talk to Ben."

# Chapter 45

## Sisterly Guidance

"Hey Ginny, how's my big sis?  What's up?"  Rachel's singsong voice gave Ginny a smile despite the serious nature of Ginny's call. The two sisters had a rhythm of their own, developed over years of care and fights.

"Hi, Rach.  Listen, I could use your help, and Ted's.  I have an idea that might fix Dan's problem at DV&N."

"Anything. I'll help. Ted too, I'm sure. What can we do?"

Rachel dropped everything, and two hours later she was with Ginny in a nearby coffee shop, hearing her big sister's plan.  The first sticking point was acquiring a sizable amount of drugs.

"What?  Ginny, you know how hard Ted's worked in rehab to break his habit. He's relapsed twice, and this is his longest recovery period. I'm sorry, but the temptation would be too much." Rachel was tense, her face hard.

"I know. And I wouldn't ask if there was another way. Ted wouldn't have to touch the stuff.  I'd go with him, and I'd hold the bag—or however it's delivered."

"You're crazy.  First, what happens if you're caught with eight ounces of heroin in New York? That's at least eight years' prison, up to twenty, and only if the charge is possession with no intent to sell. The feds are worse. For that amount they assume intent to sell and they'll throw your ass in prison for five to twenty.  And the fine is… oh, something crazy like two million. Ted had this drilled into him during rehab. Your career? Over. Your life? Finished."

"I understand.  But we won't get caught.  And we won't have it for long. Bill Barrington will.  That's the point.  Tough sentences for him and Linda Lords."

"And what about Ted?  If he even *sees* his former drug dealer and the bag passes in front of him, that's a trigger.  Maybe not immediately; maybe it's a day or two later, or a week.  But then all hell breaks loose.  He'll have cravings. The risk is just too great. I'm sorry, Ginny, but I can't ask Ted to do this. Not to mention I'm worried about you. It's a crazy idea."

Her sister was right. This *was* too much to ask, and she had no right to destroy Rachel's and Ted's lives. Ted already struggled to conquer his demons. He'd always be fighting them, but the longer he managed to control them, the better his chances.

"You're right. I shouldn't have asked; I'm sorry. It was an unreasonable request." Ginny's shoulders sloped downward as she picked up the luncheonette tab.

Halfway down the subway stairs Rachel grabbed Ginny's arm, stopping her on the landing.

"I have an idea—and I can't believe I'm even thinking this. Suppose I ask Ted for his dealer's contact? That *might* be a trigger, but it's far less likely. He already has access to that anyway. I'd make the call, and I'd identify myself with all sorts of assurances so the dealer knows it's not a sting. Ted can guide me. We make the purchase—*without* Ted. We'll go in disguise: two sisters with their shopping regalia. Bring Bloomingdale's bags." Rachel laughed. "You might as well fill my bag with a couple of blouses, jeans, and a pair of shoes—for authenticity. We'll blend in with our *Sex and the City* look."

Ginny laughed. "So, besides heroin, I'm buying your spring outfit too? By the way, how much is eight ounces of heroin?"

"How the fuck should I know? I don't do heroin. Probably less than my new Bloomingdale's outfit and shoes will cost, I'd say. This won't be cheap, but you and Dan can afford it. It'll be worth it, too, if Dan clears his name."

"Okay. Then call me with the arrangements. I haven't told Dan yet, so mention nothing. I've never kept anything from him, but this is different. The less he knows, the better, so he can have complete deniability."

"I agree. I'll let Ted know… and certainly not a word to Mom or Dad. Jesus, could you imagine Dad's apology to the police!" Their lion roar laughs caused nearby heads to turn in their direction, before the natives resumed their quick descents underground.

The details came a few hours later. Ginny answered her cell in the bedroom with the door closed. "Thirty grand. That's a lot. How can I withdraw that much from our account without Dan knowing? The bank would send an email alert. I don't suppose you could front this for me, Rachel?"

"You're joking. Sis, dearie, we're still digging our way out from Ted's habit of two years ago. Now you know why his addiction changed our lifestyle. I would if I could. Maybe you'll have to tell Dan."

"He'd explode. Dan doesn't do this kind of thing. He'd turn himself in to the police. Not an option."

"Okay, well… who do you know with lots of money? Mom and Dad, but they're out. You must have lots of rich friends. Who do you see regularly that has money?"

"Of course! Ben, my trainer. He's been around the illegal drug world—steroids. He won't take a moral stance, especially if I explain this is not for me or resale."

"Mr. America has money? I'll bet there's a good story there. I can't wait to hear it."

*No you don't,* Ginny thought. *No way.*

"I'm a little excited," Rachel said. "How about you?"

"Not really. I never went for the 'bad girl' image that you did."

"Bitch."

"Back at you. And thanks, Rach, I love you."

"Me too."

* * *

From the look on Ben's face, Ginny knew she had stunned him. He was speechless for several seconds, his eyebrows inches high.

"Ginny, do you realize what you're doing? Drug dealers are bad people. They kill and murder without a second thought. It's too dangerous. You have to tell Dan."

"Ben, I asked you in confidence. Dan can't learn about this until it's over. I understand if you won't float me the loan—it's a lot of money. But whether you do or not, please, say nothing to Dan."

"The money's not the issue. Thirty grand doesn't even put a dent in Davis's trust. It's your safety I'm worried about."

"Me too. But I need to help Dan, and I'm willing to take the risk. And my sister and I *will* be safe. This contact is Ted's friend."

"'Friend' is not a word with meaning in the drug world. Your sister's boyfriend would be the first to admit this, I'm sure. Here's the way it is, Ginny. Ted was this man's client until he stopped—at which point he became insignificant to his scumbag dealer. You and your sister will be in danger as soon as you meet this guy."

"I'll have mace on me. Ben, I'm desperate; I have to do this. We've had a tough time this year, as you know."

Ben leaned back and clasped his hands behind his head, his favorite thinking position. A few unconscious flexes drummed his biceps against his brain. His forearms returned to the desk surface.

"Here's my offer. I'll give you the thirty grand on the condition that I come with you."

"First off, it's not a gift. I'll pay you back once I tell Dan and can withdraw from our savings. Second, I don't want you involved. Rachel and I can take care of ourselves, and I'm not placing you at risk—which shouldn't be that big anyway."

With a kettledrum baritone growl, Ben replied: "What makes you think this is a negotiation? You don't set the terms—*I* do. The money's a gift, and I come along. Take it or leave it." Ben flung out his arm and flared his chest, his finger pointing at Ginny.

Ginny knew she had no choice. "Okay."

# Chapter 46

## The Gang

They met in the lobby of UltraFit and waited there for the taxi. Introductions were made. "Ben, this is my sister, Rachel. Rach, this is my friend, Ben."

Rachel looked at Ginny and flexed her arm in a mock pose. "Ginny, he's incredible. Where did you find him? I've never seen anyone this big."

"Yeah, he's huge. You should see him with his shirt off. Muscles all over."

"Hey, I'm standing right here," Ben said. "I'm not hanging on a MOMA wall. I can hear you." Ben was used to people staring at him, touching him, but not talking about him like this in his presence.

"Pipe down. This is between sisters, so shut it, big boy. Now let me have a feel. Flex those guns."

Ben didn't move. Rachel moved closer to pull his arm. She was altogether different from her sister. Ben gave her a side pose and Rachel mumbled something about melons that he didn't ask her to repeat.

"Fun's over," Ginny said. "The taxi's here, and we don't want to be late."

The taxi dropped them on the edge of Bensonhurst on the way to Gravesend toward the corner of Sheepshead Bay, a section of Brooklyn unfamiliar to all three. Rachel lived in the Heights near Henry Street's chic neighborhood, and both sisters had spent time wandering the remains of the Coney Island fairground, at the fringe of Sheepshead Bay, which was as close as they'd been to this location. Some parts of Brooklyn were an unknown landscape to the two sisters. Ben knew another Brooklyn neighborhood, buried long ago.

"So where are they?" asked Rachel. The two sisters held their Bloomingdale's bags; Ben stood a few feet back.

A whistle sounded, and two men appeared from nowhere. One was small and skinny; the other had a Michelin-man belly. Big—not the way Ben was big, but big.

"Youse lookin' for us?" came a voice with the harshest Brooklynese any of them had ever heard. *We'll need an interpreter*, thought Ben.

"I'm Rachel and—"

The small guy raised his hand. "No names, sweetheart. Nice to meet youse and all, but no need for formal introductions, if you get my drift."

"Yeah. Fine. We're here to buy—"

Again a hand went up. "We know what you're here for. Got the cash? And who's the body with you." His final words sounded like "witch youse," and Rachel nearly said, "God bless you."

"He's B—I mean, he's a friend. He carries our shopping bags."

"Ha ha ha ha. Hear that, Cheese. Carries the shoppin' bags." The little guy laughed a little too long and a little too strained.

Ginny had had enough. "Shall we finish and be gone?"

"Sure thing, *Cicciolina.* You've got the dough. Pass it over."

Ginny didn't understand the name the little guy had called her, but she didn't like the way it sounded. She looked over her shoulder. Ben started to open his jacket, and "Cheese" mirrored Ben's move, his hand moving inside his own jacket.

"Easy," Ben said. "I have the envelope in my jacket. I'll use two fingers— watch."

The little guy nodded and Cheese closed his jacket. Ben carefully removed an envelope from one side, then a second from the other side. He stepped forward and held them up. "I think you have something for the ladies."

"Oh, sure thing. Give 'em their purchase, Cheese. Want it gift wrapped, girls?"

Cheese dug into his coat pocket with his pudgy hand and produced a small donut bag. Ben stepped forward and opened it; inside was a plastic deli-bag. He removed the wire twist, stuck his pinkie into the white substance, then touched his tongue. He nodded to Ginny before handing over his two envelopes to Cheese.

Cheese opened the envelopes, then passed one to the smaller man.

Ben said to the women, "Not sure it's the best, but it'll do."

"Hey, my stuff's top quality!" said the little guy. "You don't go bad-mouthin' my stuff. *Capisce?*"

"No problem. I meant no offense. We're fine. Nice doing business with you." Ben knew he'd made a mistake. *Shit, why'd I say that? These two-bit bozo mafioso could lose it at any time.*

"Apology accepted. Have a good time. Call me if you need more."

They decided to use the subway to return to Manhattan. Once they were on the train, Rachel looked at Ginny.

"I was scared shitless. Thank god you brought Ben."

Ben sat between the two women on a long bench seat. He'd removed his jacket, and each woman held one of his massive arms, which they squeezed during the ride.

"We needed these. Feel them, Ginny. They're so hard. Makes me wet. Glad you thought to bring guns."

Ben rolled his eyes. "Hey, remember I can hear you? And for the record, *I* suggested I accompany you. *My* idea. And you're welcome."

He raised his arms and pulled Ginny's and Rachel's heads against his chest. Then he flexed, bouncing their heads; the sisters giggled like schoolgirls.

Ben was sweating, and not only from the vents blasting heat. His heart pounded. He chest tensed, his arms tightened, but this outer display of strength bore no resemblance to his thoughts. *I was scared shitless. Those thugs had come to rob us. They'd cut the heroin only as a contingency. That was going to end badly. And what could I have done?* Ben wasn't confident that, had the men pulled guns, he would have been able to reach them before they fired. *Maybe the little one knew I'd have gone for him. The dimwit lard would have shot without thinking—probably because he needs a calculator to add two plus two.*

Ben relaxed a little, which allowed Rachel and Ginny to struggle free. They complained he'd been too rough, although that was mostly from Rachel.

The train crossed into Manhattan, halfway to Uptown. Ginny and Rachel huddled down close to Ben's sides. Men gave fleeting glances at the two women, but they were awed by the hulk holding them. Women felt envious watching Ben's strong arms hold Ginny and Rachel, then resentful when they spied the big Bloomie's bags.

Ben remained vigilant. He stared back at his fellow passengers, noticing their glances at the bags. *You wouldn't want to know the real cost of these. You wouldn't want to know or you'd be scared shitless—like us. And it's not over.*

# Chapter 47

## Shopping Surprise

Throughout that week, Dan slept restlessly. And his dreams were bizarre, to say the least. In one, Ginny was the starting Red Sox pitcher, and he was the catcher. They were minor A-league players who had been called up due to the 1994 baseball strike. Ginny hit three batters in a row. Then Dan misjudged her ball velocity and trajectory, and two players scored. Umpires flooded the field, ejecting them for arguing on the pitcher's mound. So vivid was his dream, he told Ginny about it the next morning. She laughed—but not Dan.

* * *

As he opened his front door, Dan was surprised to find Ginny and her sister on the living room couch.

"Hi, Rachel, what a nice surprise." Dan kissed Ginny and Rachel on their cheeks and noted the Bloomingdale's bags between them. "Been shopping? Let's see what you bought."

Dan reached across, but each sister lurched, grabbing a bag.

Dan jumped back. "Hey, I'm not going to steal it! Just a peek."

"Honey, it's a surprise." Ginny used a sexy voice and batted her eyelids. "I'll show you later."

Dan shrugged. "Goody. A surprise. Well, I see Ginny has not been a good hostess, Rachel. We have a very nice rosé, which goes well after shopping…?"

"No thanks, Dan. I was just about to leave." Rachel stood up.

"Nothing for me either," Ginny said.

Dan walked past Rachel as if he was headed for the kitchen. Then he spun on the balls of his feet, reversed direction, and grabbed the nearest Bloomingdale's bag. He expected to pull out sexy lingerie in black or maybe bright red, but instead he found a plastic bag.

Ginny yelled, "No! Don't touch it!"

Dan knew. This was not face powder.

"Let me explain." Ginny snatched away the plastic bag and put it back inside the bigger bag.

"Please do. Is this what I think it is?" Dan's face masked his inner fury, but his shaking gave him away.

"If you think it's heroin, then you would be correct."

Dan's chin dropped and his jaw unhinged. His body lowered into the chair opposite Ginny.

"I guess I'm staying a little longer," Rachel said quietly. "I'll have that rosé, if it's still on offer. Anyone else?"

While Rachel was getting drinks for everyone, Ginny told their story. She explained how this all fit her game theory plan, the one they had discussed the week before.

Dan just stared the at the Bloomingdale's bag. "Eight ounces of heroin. How do you plant this in Bill's office? Some pretext to retrieve my personal items I'd left behind? After four months? What, you just saunter past and put the bag on his desk? Or maybe you plan a casual visit to see Bill?" Dan switched to a higher pitch, an attempt to mimic Ginny. "And Bill, do you mind if I keep this bag of heroin in your desk while I run out for an hour?"

Dan banged his fist on his knee and lowered his head. He mumbled, "Stupid." Shaking his head, he looked up. "You didn't put on your Paris show by buying a bunch of dresses. You planned every step—you always do. This is so unlike you." His cheeks sucked in. "The whole idea is crazy. Two smart people acting like dumb kids. What were you thinking? I'm really surprised at Ben, too."

Ginny had sat quietly for Dan's rant, but this last comment sparked her fury. "That's not fair to Ben. I blackmailed him into it, I'll have you know, and you should *thank* him—for the money, and for escorting us. We wouldn't have that bag if not for Ben. Don't even try to blame him."

"Oh, Ben, always the good guy." Dan paused—now wasn't the time to go there. "Okay, let's leave Ben aside for now. Now what? Frame Bill? Does this really fit the Prisoner's Dilemma and mamihlapinatapai? How exactly does that work? Because you need Linda too, and she's not here."

Rachel raised her hand. "What mammihappy?"

"Don't worry about it, Rach, I'll explain later," Ginny said, then returned to face Dan. "Yes, I will frame Bill and Linda. We have to get into the gutter like them. The high road hasn't worked. You could still face sexual harassment charges. Or you could become a data espionage criminal if you show JJ's data to anyone."

"We don't play dirty," Dan said. "*I* don't play dirty. I don't want to become like them. And we can't keep that here, either. Someone has to take it away."

"Don't look at me," Rachel said, folding her arms across her chest. "I can't bring it to my place. That'd be rubbing it under Ted's nose, metaphorically speaking and probably physically, too."

Neither Ginny nor Dan responded.

Rachel added, "Helloooo! Yoo hoo? Anyone home?"

"Sorry, I'm thinking," Ginny said.

"I figured that much out," Rachel said. "So, sis, what's the plan now? Sell it on the street? What was the point of all this if in the end you don't frame Bill? *He's* supposed to get caught with this shit, not us."

The sharp words struck Dan. "I'm thinking that it's not necessary for the package to be found in Bill's office. It could be anywhere that identifies it with him."

Rachel looked at Dan. "You mean like his home?"

"Yeah, but that's even harder than his office. Besides, the sleazebag might implicate his wife. I'm thinking his briefcase."

Ginny's eyes rolled.

"Not at his office," Dan explained. "Bill takes his briefcase to meetings, on trips, to hotels. Wherever Bill goes, his briefcase goes with him."

Ginny caught on. "And to go from one place to another, he takes a cab or he drives."

"His car." Rachel was gleeful.

With a renewed strength in his voice, Dan added: "His car's at his home or in the Hawthorne Building underground parking garage. DV&N pays for his personal reserved spot."

"And how do we get into the garage?" Rachel asked.

"I've still got the key entry code," Dan said. "My parking spot is paid until the end of June—it's all included in my severance benefit package."

Dan remembered his dream, the one where they were A-league baseball players. They were jokes because they weren't like the superstars. They were minor-leaguers. They needed professional help. Just like they did now.

Dan knew whom to ask. He tasted bile, and his chest tightened.

Ginny asked if Dan felt all right. Dan swallowed the bitter taste. Could he do this to achieve the goal?

"I have an idea," he said, "but I need to talk to someone first."

The way Dan took charge, gave orders, made decisions... it stirred something in Ginny. This was the return of the man she had married. She knew things were changing. Dan was changing.

What would he do next?

# Chapter 48

## Consultations

The street noise outside Ben's penthouse condo didn't make it up the multiple stories to penetrate his triple-thick sealed glazed windows. Add a few sheep and Ben's condo could have sounded like a remote farmhouse.

Ben entered the living room with two glasses of protein shake and held one out to Dan. He stood ready for his reprimand.

Dan took the shake. "I know what you did for Ginny... and her sister."

"You needn't say any more. It was stupid, we did it, over."

"Don't stop me—at least give me that. Suck it up. The whole idea was stupid. The risk was too great, and the plan's incomplete. What the hell were you thinking?"

"I agree. Never again, I promise. Satisfied?"

"No. Now I want to thank you—and not just for your generosity. From what Ginny told me, the situation was not good. She and Rachel would have been robbed, probably hurt... your money stolen. I'm surprised that two supposedly smart women didn't see that with the amount they were buying, they were targets. I can't thank you enough."

"Forget it. You know I love you guys. I have more than enough money. I'd protect Ginny under any circumstance. You have my word."

"I know. Which is why I can't remain angry with you. Here's the awkward part. I have to ask another favor."

Ben sat.

"I need help from the last person I want to talk to: Vinnie's father. I despise that man, I truly do."

Ben moved from his chair to sit beside Dan on the two-seat couch. He put his hand over Dan's. "No more than I do. But I'll tell you something—and don't think that I'm not still angry at the man, because I am. But John has changed. He shows remorse. I harbor bad feelings about him and his gay-bashing. I've had to put up with that shit ever since I came out. Acceptance hasn't been easy... and to tell the truth, I'm not sure I've forgiven him. But

Joe's a keen observer, and he says John falls into the fifteen percent of parents that recognize their bigotry—and change."

"It'll take more than that to convince me," Dan said. "I'm not on board with you or Joe, but I won't say anything to Vinnie, and neither should you. Still, I need John's and his son's criminal expertise." Dan's leg jackhammered; Ben stopped it with a hand on his thigh.

"It's okay, Dan."

"I'll have to go through Ellen. She'll know her husband best. Whether I can trust him and Jack. That's why I'm here. I'd like to talk to her, away from Vinnie. Would you ask her up here to see me?"

"I'll go get her." Ben squeezed Dan's hand.

Ben left, and after a few minutes, Ellen walked in with a slow gait, looking around the unfamiliar room. "Hi, Dan. What a lovely surprise." She kissed both his cheeks, then sat next to Dan. "Are you going to see Vinnie?"

"I'll stop by after we've finished talking."

"Good, he's asking about you. Are we waiting for Ben?"

"No, this is private. I have something to ask you… and it relates to John and Jack."

Ellen stiffened. Dan had noticed this before, whenever John or Jack were mentioned. He thought it was probably a reflex from the years when what followed would be bad news.

"Ask."

"I'll get to the point. I want to talk to John and Jack about helping me with a personal problem. Will you ask them if they'll talk to me? I'm not going to beat around the bush. This will be illegal… I want you to know that up front. I don't like it—and there's no violence, I guarantee that—but there are risks, especially for Jack on parole. I'd understand if you prefer not to have them involved. All I want to know is if they'll talk to me, give me advice. Will you do that?"

"No. I won't ask. I'll *tell* them they have no choice. When do you want to meet?"

Ellen's outstretched hand took Dan's, like Ben's had moments before. Dan looked down, wondering if there was something on his hand.

"Tonight, if possible, at my condo. I know it's short notice, but this is urgent." Dan couldn't wait to be rid of the heroin.

"They'll be there."

* * *

Big John and Jack held their Peroni bottles, refusing glasses. Dan didn't waste time with small talk.

"I asked to talk with you because I could use your advice and help," he explained. "Excuse me if this is insensitive, and I don't mean any disrespect with what I'm about to say. I know a little about your... er... your activities. That sounds terrible, doesn't it? I'm sorry."

Big John interrupted. "Just spit it out. We're criminals. Ellen told us a little, so don't mince your words. We admit it. Jack's just finished eighteen months upstate, and he'd still be locked up if not for compassionate leave for Vinnie. So say what you want."

Dan's mouth puckered. "O...kay. I need to plant heroin in someone's car."

A burst of laughter came from Jack. "Look at that, Pops, we're not the only criminals in the room. Fucking A."

Big John glared. "Shut up."

"Maybe I better start from the beginning," Dan said.

Forty minutes later, Big John and Jack were caught up to the present. Dan was fascinated to watch their criminal minds working out details. Big John was clearly the brain, Jack the brawn, but this was their home territory, and their banter sparkled. For each point one made the other had a counterpoint. It reminded Dan of DV&N planning meetings, except with criminal content. On second thought, maybe DV&N planning was criminal too—certainly in the case of Bill Barrington and Linda Lords.

Finally, Big John stood. "We'll need to work out a few more details and I need to talk to a few people. I'll call you tomorrow and we'll meet here. No discussions over the phone. Everything in person, understood?"

* * *

The coffee was good at Cafe dello Sport on Seventeenth Avenue in Benson-hurst, and the cannòli were filled with fresh ricotta. Big John Briggs was on one side of the table, with Officer Dominic Paganno facing him, two coffees between them, a cannòlo in front of the cop. Paganno was dirty, which anyone could have guessed if they didn't know already. No advancement in fifteen years, yet Paganno owned his Staten Island home and had a beach house down the Jersey shore. His wife drove a new Lexus and he had a two-year-old BMW. Of course, Officer Paganno used his four-year-old Ford Crown Vic to report for duty at Bensonhurst's sixty-second precinct, so as not to be seen in his Beemer. But today the BMW was illegally parked in front of the cafe.

"Sorry to hear about your boy, Vinnie. Terrible shame." Paganno's voice was a snake's hiss.

"Thanks, Dom. If I could only get the bastards that did this to him."

*If you did, you'd find yourself under the new extension to the Jersey Pike.* Paganno's thoughts reflected what he'd heard through the underworld grapevine about Vinnie's hit.

"Well, Dom, I have a favor to ask, for a friend of Vinnie's."

In traffic cop fashion, Paganno raised his hand. "Look, I'm not getting involved with whoever attacked Vinnie. That's not my thing, just so you know."

"Yeah, fine. This has nothing to do with Vinnie. It's about his boss. He was framed for sexual harassment and lost his job. This is payback. The idea is to plant heroin in the guy's car, then have him arrested. We want him to pay off the arresting officer to let him go free."

"And that would be me." Paganno grinned, his fingers moving around his cup.

"Yup, you'd be the arresting officer. Make up an excuse to let the guy go. Sweet talk him, you know the drill… not destroy his life. You'll take the shit and have it destroyed, glad to get it off the street. The guy agrees to a misdemeanor. Make some bullshit charge. There'll be a woman, too. Tell her she's an accomplice, so you'll need her contact information. We don't need it, but just take it. It's important."

"And what's in it for me?" His hand pointed to his chest as he looked out the window to his "old" BMW.

"Twenty large and the heroin's yours, making an additional thirty grand, maybe more. Let me recap. You stop a guy—I'll give you place, time, location of the shit in the car. You issue him and his woman companion warnings, taking both IDs. Your take is twenty plus the bag. Your part's done." Big John swiped his palms across each other.

Paganno's fingers tapped the table and his head swiveled from side to side as he spoke with a slow cadence. "If I come short on the thirty for the shit, you make up the difference. And half the twenty up front."

"No problem."

Paganno left, leaving Big John to pick up the tab, mumbling, "Fucking asshole."

# Chapter 49

## Chat

Freshly cut flowers matched the room in this condo that was bigger than any Blanca had ever known. She'd been surprised by Joe's phone call, and puzzled enough not to tell anyone. Her high heels clipped the hardwood floor as she took small steps to where Vinnie was sitting in a leather armchair beside a window view overlooking Central Park.

"Aw, Blanca, you're fuckin' gorgeous." Vinnie stood, hobbling on crutches.

"Please, don't exert yourself." Tears streamed down Blanca's smiling face. Of course everyone at DV&N had been told that Vinnie had awoken, but seeing him was a shock.

Joe steadied Vinnie. "Actually, sweetie, it's good for him. When his casts come off I'll make him *really* exert those atrophied muscles. I'm here just to check for emotional shock. I'll leave in a few minutes."

"Yeah, get a whip while you're at it." Vinnie stumbled as he moved to kiss Blanca's cheeks. Blanca's crying continued unabated.

"Hey, I'm the emotionally unstable one." Vinnie's hand wiped away his own tears, hiding his smile.

"I'm sorry, I'm just so happy to see you. Shareen and Maria and the whole gang send their love. They'll want to visit, but I was told not to say anything."

Blanca turned to Joe. "Mr. Malich, when can they visit?"

"Honey, it's Joe. Soon, but for now let's not broadcast Vinnie's location. I'm leaving. Vinnie, keep your sweet ass calm."

"Fuck you, Joe." Vinnie grinned.

"I'll take a rain check on that," Joe replied as he left. He laughed, closing the door behind him.

"Wow, Vinnie. He's gorgeous. Is something going on between you?"

"Ah… not really."

Blanca took a seat on a couch, removing her shoes and sitting on her tucked legs. Their conversation began with a mundane review of Vinnie's health and

Blanca's update on her family life. But finally Blanca steered the conversation back to Joe.

"Are you sure you two aren't an item?"

"Nah, that's just Joe."

"But there's *someone*, isn't there? I can tell. I'm not wrong."

"Well... Joe's desirable, but..." Vinnie stammered and shook his head. "Okay, the thing is... I think I've fallen for Ben. You've heard me talk about him? Dan's wife's trainer? But I'm not sure if he feels the same."

Blanca's hand touched Vinnie's lips.

"Fuck, Blanca, I'm always getting mixed messages. The funny thing is, Ben's everything I dislike in a man, physically I mean. He's a muscle-bound monster. I can't explain."

"You're doing fine."

"You'll meet him soon. He asked to speak with you, which is the real reason you're here, if you want the truth. I asked for you before—I can't tell you how good it is to see you—but they always told me it was too soon."

"Why would Ben want to talk to me?"

Vinnie picked up his coffee, took one sip, then another, then a third. A typical Vinnie stalling technique—one Blanca had seen him use at their inner-circle coffee klatch.

"He has questions about DV&N. Things Dan wants to know but for legal reasons can't ask."

Blanca nodded sideways, then took a breath. "Tell me more about Ben," she said.

Vinnie's hand was on his chest. "Ben has a heart of gold. He's sensitive, kind, generous... geez, I'm making him sound like a fuckin' saint. Our conversations are interesting, too. Ben's so comfortable talking to me, like he's been doing it a long time. He's doesn't hold back on personal stuff, either."

"I can't wait to meet him. Is he gorgeous, like Joe?"

"To be honest, no. He doesn't have Joe's pretty face—not that he's ugly. I'm guessing the steroids changed his head. He wears baggy clothing: polar bear chic. His arms stretch his T-shirt. I prefer him in long sleeves to cover the disgusting veins up and down his arms." Vinnie shuddered. "It's horrible. Ben's shorter than Joe, maybe five-ten. Did I mention he's a professional bodybuilder?"

"No. And wow, Vinnie, you're right: he's not your type. Is it your concussion?" Blanca laughed. "I remember how much you bad-mouthed muscle guys like your brother, calling them freaks. Hell, you give us girls shit if we admire a well-built man."

"Fuck you."

"Back at you."

Vinnie smiled. "But the thing is, there's so much more to Ben. He talks about movies, music, and fuckin' opera. He goes to the Met. Reads real books without pictures."

There was a three-knock cadence on the door. Even though it was his condo, Ben always knocked.

"Speak of the devil," Vinnie said. "Come in!"

Ben stepped inside and walked straight to Vinnie, kissing him on both cheeks the way Ellen had instructed. With his hand outstretched, he turned to Blanca. "Hi, I'm Ben Hausen. You must be Blanca. I've heard so much about you; I'm very pleased to finally meet you."

Blanca stuck out her hand to Ben tentatively, the way she might test bathtub water temperature.

"See, he's different," Vinnie said. "Ben, bring a chair over so Blanca can get used to having a gorilla in the room."

Vinnie grinned as Ben pinkie-carried a chair over.

"If I'm interrupting, I can come back," Ben said.

"Nope, we were expecting you. Blanca knows you want to speak with her."

Blanca looked to Ben and said with a soft voice, "I'm sorry for staring. I've seen pictures of bodybuilders, but never close up... well, from any distance, I guess. I'm sorry if I'm being rude."

"Happens all the time. I'm used to it, like most bodybuilders, which is why we don't parade around half dressed, unless you're on Venice Beach or Santa Monica. Us New Yorkers are less exhibitionist. Plus—wrong weather."

Without hesitation, Blanca quizzed Ben. He gave a rundown of his stats: two hundred eight pounds normal, two hundred forty-five in competition. Ben pointed to his flexed arm. "Twenty-two inches." He moved closer for Blanca to touch.

"Holy crap, it's so hard."

"Me too," Vinnie whispered to Blanca, then watched her grin spread.

"Should I leave?" Ben said. Vinnie and Blanca both shook their heads. "Okay, it's between you. Changing the subject, Blanca, I asked to see you about DV&N and what happened to Vinnie and Dan. Is that okay with you?"

"Of course."

Ben asked Blanca to relate the circumstances under which she discovered Dan with Linda on the floor in her boss's office. When Blanca finished, Ben looked to Vinnie.

"Vinnie, would you mind if I take Blanca with me to the kitchen? I need my afternoon protein shake."

The surprise was spray-painted across Vinnie's face.

Moving his head closer to Vinnie, Ben said, "I know this seems strange, but trust me. Can you do that?"

Vinnie stood and patted Ben's shoulder, muttering, "Of course I trust you, and always will, my love."

Using his crutch, Vinnie shuffled back to his bed. Blanca stood and took Ben's hand. On their way out, Blanca smiled at Vinnie and mouthed, "Bad boy." Vinnie stuck up his middle finger.

In the kitchen, Ben poured himself a protein drink and gave Blanca a glass of sparkling water. With a single swallow, Ben finished his drink, then sat.

"Blanca, we don't know each other, but I know Vinnie thinks the world of you. After we'd gotten to know each other better, I was going to talk to you about my feelings for Vinnie... how much I like him. I mean, really like him. Then he goes and says that. I'm not sure Vinnie likes me the way I like him." Ben stopped. "Excuse me. I need a minute."

He rose to get water. "Okay, that's an issue for later. The reason I wanted to see you, and Vinnie shouldn't hear this yet for reasons I won't go into, is to ask about your boss. My question is: can you tell me the next time Bill Barrington and Linda Lords will be together?"

Blanca made a cross with her index fingers. "Are you a sorcerer? How'd you know?"

"Know what?"

"Linda arrived from Paris last night. Too soon, since she'd only left New York days after Christmas."

"Why's that too soon? Business people travel all the time."

"True, but Linda needs to settle into her Paris job. The even odder part is that Bill made the request—almost a demand. I remember, because he had me make the arrangements just after Vinnie came out of his coma and we were all cheering in the office."

Ben shook his head slightly. "Well, doesn't matter why she's here. All I need to know is when and where Bill and Linda will be together outside the office. Can you find out?"

"Is the Pope Catholic? I know they'll be in Linda's hotel room, screwing themselves silly. Sorry. Is that too crude?"

Ben smiled. "Anywhere else besides the hotel?"

"I've made Bill a reservation this Friday at Bel Jour France. It's his favorite. I hear the food is fantastic, Michelin star-rated. Expensive, like a month's rent." Blanca smiled. "He'll take Linda."

"Is that it?"

"Well, Linda departs the following Wednesday, so there probably isn't much time for other get-togethers, other than at her hotel."

"Can you get me the details on the restaurant, and let me know if there are any changes? And say nothing to anyone, Blanca. It's important no one knows I've asked."

# Chapter 50

## Valet Parking

After serving beers to Big John and Jack, Dan began. "Barrington arrives after ten, so wait until eleven. He drives a black Mercedes XL and parks it on level two, space number four."

Dan handed Jack the Bloomingdale's bag. Jack removed the smaller plastic bag and placed it in the pocket of his leather jacket, then laughed.

"Pops, can you see us on Cropsey Avenue with a fuckin' Bloomingdale's bag. Might as well be a fuckin' queer like Vinnie." He laughed again.

Big John raised his arm as if to slap his son. Dan stood to intervene, but Big John just growled, "Shut the fuck up."

Instructions were relayed to Officer Paganno: Friday, Bel Jour France, Mercedes XL.

* * *

The Hawthorne Building's brightly lit garage made Big John wary. He really preferred garages with forty-watt bulbs spaced fifty feet apart.

On the second level of the stairwell, he cracked open the door, stopped, and listened. Footsteps were headed in his direction. Big John signaled Jack to descend another flight. A few minutes passed with no sound of entry into the stairwell, which confused Big John. Jack waited while his father went to investigate—it would be better to be alone if spotted, making less of an impression if someone was later questioned by the cops.

The reason why no one had entered the stairwell became obvious as Big John walked farther into the garage: there was a bank of elevators just around the corner from the stairs. A short all-clear whistle signaled Jack, who climbed the stairs two at a time.

Bill's Mercedes was parked in bay number four. Amateurs found high-end cars difficult to break into—but not Jack. He'd attended Attica's Auto Theft 101, which was given by professionals with PhDs in crime.

The Mercedes trunk was quickly breached using a specialty tool Jack had acquired from a cellmate's friend on the outside. Big John wrapped the plastic bag in a chamois rag he found inside the tire well. Once the heroin was secured behind the spare wheel, Big John wiped down the trunk; they'd worn gloves, but it never hurt to take extra precautions.

Then they slipped away to inform Officer Paganno of the chamois rag detail.

* * *

Bel Jour France: gourmet dinners at gourmet prices. The bill was for three hundred dollars, including fifty for wine, thirty for pre-dinner cocktail, and thirty for after-dinner cognac. But that was pocket change to Bill; after all, he had a big payday in his future.

As he pointed the valet to his car, Bill was imagining his fantasy night with Linda. Linda spotted the cop first.

"Bill, something's wrong. There's a policeman by your car. Maybe you shouldn't drive until he goes away."

"I can handle my liquor, don't worry." Bill slurred his words. "What's he doing?"

Brushing past the confused valet, Bill strode straight toward the officer. "Hey, officer, what do you want?"

Bill's arrogant tone pleased Officer Dominic Paganno. He recognized this privileged voice, a big shot's voice. Paganno smiled at Bill the way cheetahs smile at prey.

"Sir, is this your car?" Officer Paganno's voice reflected fifteen years of dealing with the goddamn public.

"Yes, it is. What's this about?"

"Your license plate is hanging off. The lot attendant spotted it. For a car of this quality, it might mean an attempted theft." Paganno waited. No response. "Or maybe someone stole yours and these are substitutes. I'll need to confirm."

Jack had loosened the license plate screws while John was stashing the chamois. Paganno had then completed Jack's handiwork, bending the plate while Bill and Linda were inside swirling their Courvoisier.

"It's mine. You can move along."

Dismiss me, you prick? This is going to be easy and fun.

"All the same, I'll need to verify," Paganno said. "Your license and registration, please."

"This is bullshit. It's fine."

"Bill, just do it and get this over with." Linda's voice quivered.

"Yes, *Bill*, do what the lady says." First names were hot buttons for privileged assholes.

"Screw you. I'll have your badge."

"Sir, if you don't cooperate I'll have this car impounded. We can check credentials at the station."

Linda looked to the policeman then to Bill, waving her hand. "Bill, for god's sake, just do it and we can be on our way."

Bill stepped to the passenger side and pressed his remote fob key. He retrieved his registration from the glove compartment and removed his driver's license from his wallet, then handed both over.

Paganno was annoyed with Bill's compliance. Smart girlfriend. If she'd been Bill's wife he'd have told her to shut the fuck up.

"Wait here while I check this out. I'll need your keys." Button number two.

"Fuck you. You have my registration and license—I'm not giving you my keys. Get the fuck away."

*Bingo.* "That's it." Officer Paganno grabbed Bill and pushed his face against the car as he handcuffed him. He picked up the keys Bill had dropped while being swung around.

"Oh my god. Officer, Bill shouldn't have said that. He can be an asshole." Linda stepped close to the policeman.

"You got that right, lady. Look, if you can calm your boyfriend down, let me check out the car, I might overlook his verbal abuse of a New York policeman. This is routine but necessary."

The German-engineered trunk opened smoothly and the bright interior light made inspection easy. Everything was sparkling clean, so Paganno easily spotted the chamois rag in the wheel well. But still, he took his time before making the surprise discovery. "Sir, what's this?"

"Fuck if I know. Looks like a shammy rag I keep to clean the car and wipe off fingerprints from scum like you."

Better and better. This guy makes my top ten biggest assholes.

"Bill, stop. You're not helping. Officer, please forgive my colleague's rudeness."

Paganno liked that: "colleague," not boyfriend, not companion. *She's dressed like a hooker and calls him a colleague. Here on business?* Paganno smiled. Maybe it was business—just a different kind.

Paganno opened the chamois and frowned at the plastic bag with white powder. He placed his pinkie inside, then touched a small amount to his tongue. Heroin, for sure. Not great though. Not enough to fetch thirty grand.

"Sir, do you know what this is?  About eight ounces of heroin.  That's a criminal offense."

"What? *Heroin*? You have to be shitting me. I don't do drugs. I have no idea where that came from. I'm sorry for what I said before. Linda's right, I'm an asshole."

Linda staggered.  "Officer, there's been a mistake.  That heroin, if it is heroin, must've been planted. I can vouch for this man. He doesn't do drugs. You have to believe me. This is a mistake."

Paganno hid his smile; this was going his way. Now to play good cop: a role he wasn't used to.

"Ma'am, I can see you're not bad people. Although your friend... I mean colleague... can't handle his alcohol. But I'm afraid this implicates both of you." Paganno held up the plastic bag. "This quantity qualifies as possession with intent to distribute.  I hate to ruin good people's reputation.  You're decent people... certainly *you* are, Miss." *Wow, that was a great performance.*

"We are," Linda said.  "We don't do drugs and we don't sell.  Can you help us?  What can we do to convince you?" Linda's eyes filled with water, something that hadn't happened in recent memory.

"Let me think." Paganno looked down at his feet for a few seconds. "I can't let you have this back."

"Of course, take it. It's not mine anyway." Bill awkwardly shuffled to the rear of the car. This sounded to him like a negotiation: his line of work.

More delay as Paganno rubbed his hand to his chin then realized he was overacting. "Okay, here's what I'm willing to do. I'll issue you a violation for an improperly displayed license plate. You'll get a warning in the mail, no fine for a first offense, and certainly not criminal. I'll need names and contact information from both of you. Miss, can you show me identification."

"Thank you.  Thank you.  Thank you," said Linda.  She fished inside her handbag and handed Officer Paganno her California driver's license.

"Any other identification?"

"I have my work ID," Linda said. "I used to live in California, now I'm in Paris, but my company headquarters is here, with Bill. We're executives with Del Vecchio & Neale." Linda's hand shook as she handed over her business card. "Do you want my Paris address too?"

Paganno copied down all her information on his notepad. "No need. We can contact you through your office here if we need to."

Bill provided his license and business card as well, writing both his direct line office number and his New Jersey home number on the back.

As the Mercedes drove off with a shaken Bill and Linda, Dominic Paganno called Big John. "All done.  I would've enjoyed busting him.  Could've had him on drunk driving too.  What an asshole.  The stuff's not great.  I expect you to pick up the shortfall.  Need their contact numbers?"

"Nope.  We're good for the difference, as promised." *Barrington's not the only asshole.*

The end of the call signaled the start of step two.

# Chapter 51

## Telephone Calls

The phone rang three times before a husky voice answered. "Del Vecchio & Neale, Linda Lords's office. This is Ms. Cooper speaking. How may I help you?"

"I would like to speak to Linda Lords." A gruff Brooklyn accent.

"I'm sorry, Ms. Lords is in a meeting. May I take your name and contact information? Ms. Lords will return your call as soon as she's available. If you tell me what this is regarding, perhaps I can be of assistance." Shareen used her formal DV&N phone voice.

"Nah. It's personal. When will Linda be available?"

"She's in meetings all day, but if you tell me your name I'll pass it along."

Big John hadn't anticipated that he wouldn't reach Linda Lords with a single dial. Calling Fortune 500 company headquarters was not among his life experiences. Steel-mesh barbed wire fences had never impeded Big John, but corporate gatekeepers were entirely different obstacles. Dan, however, *had* anticipated this hurdle. He sat next to Big John, listening in on an extension. When he heard Shareen's reply, he wrote instructions on a pad for Big John.

Big John read the script Dan jotted down, his mechanical voice sounding like a Coney Island machine recording. "What time is Linda's next meeting?"

"Eleven-thirty. Ms. Lords will probably not return to her office but go directly to her next meeting. I don't know when she'll return to her office."

More pad scribbling.

"I'll take a chance and call a few minutes before her eleven-thirty meeting. Tell her it's important and she'd better take my call, because it's about her meal with Bill Barrington last Friday at Bel Jour France." Big John pronounced the restaurant as Beel Jarrr Fraaance. "She'll know what I mean and she'll want to talk to me."

"Sir, if you would please tell—" *Click.* Shareen was astounded. The caller had hung up on her in mid-sentence. This was not a typical DV&N client—far too uncouth. She would tell Linda before her next meeting. Despite what she'd told the caller, she knew that Linda would return to the office before her next meeting to collect her notes.

Dan nodded to Big John. Time for the next call.

"Hello, this is Del Vecchio & Neale, Bill Barrington's office, Ms. Santos speaking. May I help you?" Blanca had a cheery voice, not as formal as Shareen's, but the same script.

"Yeah, I want to speak to Bill Barrington." More of Big John's Brooklynese, this time a counterpoint to Blanca's Bronx.

"Mr. Barrington is unavailable. May I take a message or may I help you?" Again Blanca used the same script Shareen had used. DV&N assistants were well trained, practically word-perfect. But Blanca wasn't as effective a gate-keeper as Shareen, for the simple reason that she didn't care who bothered her boss.

"Nah. This is personal. Bill's gonna want to talk to me, I guarantee ya. He had dinner last Friday with Linda, so he'll talk to me."

One of Dan's instructions to Big John was to use first names, giving cre-dence to the claim that the call was personal.

And indeed, Linda's name had proved to be the master key. Blanca patched the call through to Shithead Barrington, hoping this might ruin his day.

"Bill Barrington speaking. Har har, har har. So whom am I talking to?"

"Not important. All you need to know is that your shit wasn't any good. You owe me extra." Big John didn't require Dan's help for this part. He knew how to shake down a stooge.

"Who is this? What's this about?" A false bellowing sound.

"Cut the crap. You know exactly what I'm talking about. Here's the deal: you come up with ten grand and tell your bosses at DV&N, what's their names, oh yeah, Gary Del Vecchio and Myron Rosenberg, that Linda was caught with drugs and needs to be fired." Big John read off the corporate names Dan had written down for him.

"You're out of your fucking mind. It wasn't my shit, as you put it, and I'm not going to be blackmailed. Screw you."

"Doesn't matter to me. I've made the same offer to Linda. You or Linda lose your job, it's all the same to me. This is payback for me losing my street creds trying to unload your bad shit. You could both save your asses if you each come up with ten grand and one of you quits. You know, personal health reasons. You'll both keep your reputations, at least."

"Listen to me, asshole. Fuck you." The scream was audible in Blanca's office even with the door closed. Bill beat Big John to slamming down the phone.

"We need to reach Linda before Bill," Dan said. "This can't wait. Try

Linda's cell phone." His voice quivered. He had expected Bill to negotiate or stall for time.

Big John looked through the papers Dom Paganno had handed him. Paganno had decided not to throw them away, even though Big John had said they weren't needed. And there it was: Linda's cell number.

DV&N had a strict protocol: during meetings, all cell phones were to be on silent mode with minimal vibration. But Linda didn't believe in protocols. Her loud ring echoed through the room and she feigned an apology as she hurried from the boring meeting. An unknown phone number flashed on her screen.

"Linda Lords speaking."

"Hiya, Linda. Listen carefully because you don't have much time to make a decision."

Big John repeated to Linda the speech he had given Bill. She wasn't as crude as Bill, but she dismissed him all the same. Not her drugs, she said. Nothing to do with her, and she had no intention of losing her job over this. It was Bill's car, his problem.

"You have until three o'clock before I call Gary. Make a decision before two fifty-five. And toots, keep your cell on and take my call."

As Big John hung up, he saw in Dan's expression that the man felt the same way he did. This was not going down as Dan had planned, for the reason John had given Dan from the start. If it were him, he'd call the bluff. And he was certain Bill and Linda would make the same decision once they talked to each other.

* * *

Instead of returning to the meeting, Linda rode the elevator up a flight to the executive office wing, where she walked past her office and into Bill's corner office.

"Good morning, Linda," said Blanca, her voice as sincere as she could muster. "How can I—"

Waste of effort. Neither acknowledging Blanca nor knocking at Bill's office, Linda burst through the door. Before it slammed shut behind her, Blanca heard Linda say, "What the fuck, Bill."

Blanca smiled. This was a good morning.

"Did you get the same fucking call as me?" Linda asked.

"You mean that bullshit blackmail threat. Don't worry about it."

"Don't worry? What do you mean, don't worry? One of us will lose our job! We have to fork over ten grand each of our hard-earned money to a corrupt cop."

"Calm down and think about it. First, the drugs weren't mine. I can't explain how they were there. Maybe my goddamn wife is doing drugs, hiding them in my car. I don't know." The words came out in a measured cadence, managerial.

Linda couldn't be sure that Bill didn't sell drugs on the side; nothing would surprise her about Bill's morals after his setup of Vinnie and Dan. She shook her head.

"Second point: there's no written drug charge. How's the cop going to explain he suddenly remembered he confiscated a bag of heroin from the weekend? 'Chief, by the way, I have these drugs in my car that I forgot to report.' I don't think so. He's bluffing, and his blackmail works only if one of us confesses. Hell, confesses to what? It's all bullshit."

As much as Linda understood Bill's logic, wanted to believe him, she had doubts. Could Bill be trusted? He'd act in his best interest. That's what Bill always did. She needed more than his opinion that this was bullshit.

"Bill, is there any way we can track down this cop? I don't think the person on the phone was the cop. His voice didn't seem right."

"I had the same feeling. Might've been a bad line or he held a cloth over the phone. Let me think about it."

Linda looked at her watch. "We have until three. That's not much time."

"You go, and I'll get on this right away."

# Chapter 52

## The Check

"Hi Dan, it's Blanca. How are you? Vinnie? The girls can't wait to see him."

"Hi, Blanca. Vinnie improves every day. I'm fine too. Remember not to tell the others where Vinnie's staying, especially so neither Bill nor Linda learns Vinnie's location."

"I don't understand why, but I haven't, and I won't."

"How about you? Everything okay?"

"That's the thing, Dan. I know it's against the rules to talk to you about DV&N, but something odd's happened. Linda barged into Bill's office a half hour ago, then she and Bill stormed out." Blanca paused. "And here's the odd part. Just before Linda burst in, a call came from a Brooklyn guy. He told me it was personal, about Bill's dinner with Linda at Bel Jour France. I mean, Ben knew about the same dinner. Does this involve Vinnie or you?"

A few seconds passed. "It has nothing to do with me or Vinnie." The lie stuck in Dan's throat.

"I'm so relieved. When can I visit?"

His lying returned sooner than expected. "Maybe the day after tomorrow, after Vinnie's medical review." Dan's throat choked his voice.

As soon as the call ended he placed a new one. "Ginny, we may have a problem."

* * *

The valet for Ristorante Roma caught the keys thrown to him as Bill rushed into the restaurant. Sal lumbered over, pointing to Carmine at his back room table.

Carmine extended a limp hand for a pretend handshake.

"Thanks for seeing me on such short notice," Bill said. "I appreciate it."

Carmine didn't waste time with small talk, especially near lunchtime. He might postpone a meal for urgent business, but nothing else. Bill's business wasn't urgent.

Carmine looked at his watch. "Talk."

"It's something inexplicable. I had dinner at Bel Jour France with a friend last Friday."

Carmine chewed his lips while Bill summarized what had happened. He concluded with, "It's bullshit. The cop took the bag, then issued me a warning on a trumped-up vehicle charge."

"Dirty cop takes your drugs. Big deal." Carmine formed an onion tip with two fingers and his thumb pinched, shaking his wrist.

"Not *my* drugs. A guy calls me, says the 'shit's' no good. It's not the cop's voice." Bill told Carmine about the demand. "I can understand about the money—even though it's bullshit—but why does he want one of us to lose our job?"

Carmine shrugged.

"Okay, doesn't matter. Can you find out about the cop or the caller?"

"How am I going to find a dirty cop? Even if we narrow it to Brooklyn, the number is probably several hundred, maybe a thousand. In my line of work, I depend on the cooperation of New York's Finest." Carmine rubbed his Armani sweater.

Bill whistled when he heard the number of cops on the take. "I have a badge number with a scribbled name on the warning, unless it's fake."

Carmine took the paper, then waved it at Sal. "Know this guy? One of ours?"

Sal stared. "We used him once. Unreliable. Jammed up one of Mike's guys, so Mike won't use him again. I wouldn't either."

Carmine turned to Bill. "He wanted ten from you and your associate?"

"And one of us quits our job."

"Thirty, same as before."

Bill blinked.

"And you keep your jobs."

"Are you saying that for thirty grand this goes away?" Bill's mouth hung open.

Bill made an executive decision; there was no time to consult Linda, not with the approaching deadline and Carmine about to start lunch. "One more thing. Er... this needs to be done before three. Is that possible?"

"I'll let you know. My antipasto will be here in twenty and I need to wash up. You'll get a call after lunch."

* * *

At two forty-five the news broke across the New York metro stations. But

Bill heard it by phone. "Come for cannòli and an espresso around four," Sal Friscollo added, munching his words the way he chewed breadsticks.

On returning to DV&N, Bill went straight to Linda's office. His demand for fifteen grand rocked her executive swivel chair.

"You want me… to… to… to hand over… fifteen fucking grand after I've already… for what?"

"Shut your fucking mouth. You want to keep your fucking director's job? You'll cover this in a week with your new salary. Just get me the goddamn money, bitch."

"How do we know this is over? There won't be more demands?" A mouse squeal voice.

Bill puffed out his cheeks. "Trust me, it's over. Read the *Daily News* online."

Linda quickly pulled up the headlines. Her hand went to her mouth, stifling a scream.

"I'll get the money. Never again." She struggled out of her office to the ladies' toilets. She left the next day for Paris.

* * *

At three p.m. the New York Stock Exchange closing bell rang. Dan was checking the Bloomberg online closing summary, but he switched to the *New York Times* when a bulletin flashed across the bottom of his screen.

A New York City cop was shot and killed in Brooklyn this afternoon. Details are unknown. Updates will follow as more information reaches the news desk.

Crime stories didn't interest Dan, but this one did. Unfortunately, the *Times* had no more information than that, so Dan surfed to the *Daily News* web page—cop killings were right up their alley. And in fact, the *News* did have a bit more information. They were withholding the cop's name pending notification of next of kin, but they gave the precinct and added that the victim had died of a single shot to the head.

He called Ginny for a second time. "This is bad. Real bad."

"What could have gone wrong?" Her voice was unsteady.

"It was a stupid idea to begin with. Suppose they link this to us?" Dan asked.

Ginny's voice cracked. "How?" She paused, sucked air. "What's the connection between the cop and John?"

"I have a bad feeling. Come home as soon as you can. I'm worried." A sigh. "Ginny, I love you." He hung up before Ginny said, "I love you too."

Dan's next call was to Big John.

"Jesus Christ. A fucking disaster. It's got to be my guy." Big John's voice was strong, no fear.

"Brooklyn has a lot of cops. Are you sure?"

"Same precinct, so yeah. We've got to hope my guy didn't tell anyone about me or Vinnie. A fucking disaster."

That night Ginny and Dan huddled together, glued to the TV evening news, but came away no better informed. But they got the news they expected when the phone rang at eight-fifteen.

"I can confirm." No greeting from the gruff voice. "Tomorrow, Vinnie's place."

* * *

Big John and Dan sat in the kitchen, going over details. "We find out how far this goes, who knows, how it was discovered. What's the blowback to us? We trace Barrington's steps after my phone call." Big John stopped, then crowed. "No, we start with the restaurant bust."

The criminal's logical decision-tree process fascinated Dan. "Do we ask at the restaurant?"

"Not us—we can't be seen. The person has to fit in, which rules out anyone I know."

Dan had the opposite problem: he knew people that would fit the restaurant, but not the situation.

Ben walked in while they talked, piling food on the table. He'd overheard, and he offered a solution to their dilemma.

* * *

Without knowing why, Blanca arrived later that day to see Vinnie, two days ahead of her planned visit. She had hastily arranged for her husband to pick up their kids from school. It was a normal visit until Ben interrupted them, asking Blanca for another private conversation.

Vinnie agreed, but he did grumble, "This is becoming a fuckin' habit and *I'm* the fuckin' patient, remember?"

When Ben and Blanca were alone, he asked her, "Do you know the maître d' at Bel Jour France?"

"Yes, Lucien—not personally, but we speak often. His real name is Harry, Harry Finkelstein. Do you want his number?"

Ben shook his head and held up his hand. "I need a quick reservation for two, and I heard they're difficult to get on short notice. Could you…?"

"No problem. I'm sure Harry will do it for me."

"It would be for the two of us."

Ben's chin rested in his hand. Blanca's hands moved to her face.

"It's not a date—remember I'm gay. This is important for Vinnie and Dan. I can't explain, though; you'll just have to take my word. If it's too much to ask, I'll find someone—"

Blanca slapped Ben's arm, shaking her hand after. "Are you kidding? Anything to help, plus dinner at a posh French restaurant to boot! I'm in. Be forewarned though: I have one hell of an appetite." Blanca patted her stomach. "Not wafer-thin, and I drink too."

"That's great. Thanks, Blanca. When can you make it?"

"In two days Linda arrives from Paris, an unscheduled return visit. Bill always leaves early to 'help' her. Yeah, right." Blanca pumped her right arm. Ben turned crimson. "Anyway, it gives me leeway in the afternoon."

They made arrangements for the same day as Linda's arrival. Ben would pick up Blanca at six-thirty in front of the Hawthorne Building in his maroon Audi A8, vanity plate UFIT-1.

"And not a word to Vinnie about our dinner. Who knows what'd he say."

They laughed with their throats, but not their eyes.

# Chapter 53

## Dinner Date

The Audi double-parked outside the Hawthorne Building. Blanca flew out the revolving door, ignoring the cold and removing her overcoat with a twirl. She wanted to show off her perfect outfit: Ginny had selected it and Ben had paid. A Bloomingdale's courier delivery had arrived shortly before five.

Blanca's beige skirt, knee-length and straight, had small flecks of gold running in vertical spirals. Her off-white blouse, embroidered with pastel flowers, revealed sufficient cleavage, and the back was cut low, displaying a significant amount of Blanca's silky brown skin. Silver, tube-shaped earrings, long and thin, offset her round face; each tube contained five semiprecious rubies, and the theme was repeated in the necklace's two-inch silver cylinder with a large revolving ruby. The necklace dangled above Blanca's cleavage, accentuating her ample breasts.

With red, three-inch heels—open-toed, with straps wrapping her delicate ankles—Blanca danced in her shoes to the car. Her lipstick matched the ruby stones.

Stretching across the passenger seat, Ben opened the door with a whistle. "You're beautiful! I've just become straight, and to hell with your husband. Honestly, you look magnificent."

Blanca blushed, every bit a teenager. "This outfit is unbelievable. I could never afford anything like this. No sauce for me tonight. You'll be able to return it unmarked. The shoes stay, though. I'll take out a second mortgage tomorrow."

Ben's smile matched the glowing dashboard, and he shifted from first to third, both engine and man humming.

* * *

The Audi glided into Bel Jour France's parking lot and the valet opened Blanca's door. He had seen a lot of expensive jewelry and high-priced clothing, all crass on rich people with no taste. But this was something else, a rare elegance. He held the door while high heels hit the ground like syrup flowing on a sundae. Ben exited before the valet got around to his side. The refrigerator stepped out, causing the valet to step back.

Lucien escorted the couple to a choice location, their seats angled so both could see the entire room. As he returned to his dais, Lucien was perplexed. Why did Mr. Barrington bring trash to dinner when he had such a beautiful administrative assistant? He smiled at Blanca's pretentious title, without considering his own name change from Harry to Lucien by Bel Jour France's proprietors: Silvia and Arnold Grossman of Englewood, New Jersey.

Dinner conversation began with history. Blanca's troubled youth and her marriage to her childhood friend, Alejandro—Jandro. The two Puerto Rican kids escaped the gangs and the Bronx, and they now owed a mortgage on a small colonial in Garden City for their two boys. No dog or station wagon yet, but coming soon. When it was Ben's turn to tell his own history, he chose to skip over the tragedies in his life, skimming past most of Davis McGregor III only to reveal his ultimate acquisition of UltraFit. He had accepted his homosexuality in his mid-twenties, when he started bodybuilding.

"That was your entry into the gay world?" Blanca saw Ben's slight smile. "I'm sorry, did I say the wrong thing?"

"No. I was waiting for you to say that. Everyone does, like clockwork."

Now Blanca smiled. "You set me up, didn't you? I'd beat the crap out of you if I could."

Laughing, Ben tapped Blanca's hand. "In my case, I fit the stereotype, but I'm not the norm."

"Then why did you start bodybuilding?"

"Drawn to it, I guess. It happened in college. Something clicked. I started to lift weights, and good genetics or whatever, but my body responded. I became strong, and my size increased. I liked it. Why does someone become a professional tennis player? Money? Maybe, but before that they have an obsession with tennis. Same for any sport, really. But god forbid it's a sport society deems unusual, like ballet for men or boxing for women. The person must be a deviant."

This time Blanca tapped Ben's hand. "I sort of get it. But if I'm totally honest, playing tennis doesn't seem the same as bodybuilding. Don't you agree? I mean, tennis requires skill and dedication besides physical exertion." Blanca stopped. "Did I offend you again?"

"No offense taken. Sure, tennis requires skill. Now imagine lifting three hundred and fifty pounds over your head or five hundred pounds off your chest. Maybe it's not a skill in the same way hitting a ball is, but it takes dedication. And lifting isn't enough. Bodybuilders need to diet, understand nutrition, metabolism, and—unfortunately—take drugs. But you know body-building isn't the only sport with drugs."

"Did you do drugs? Can I ask you that?"

"You know, I'm enjoying this conversation. From someone else, it would be judgmental, but not you. I think you honestly want to know—there's no cruelty or mocking."

Blanca's hand covered her face. "I would never mock you. I want to know because I have two boys and I want to be prepared. One or both might be gay. Or be interested in bodybuilding, or ballet, or who knows what. I want to be ready to accept and support them. That's why I'm asking."

"To answer your question, yes, I did steroids. I'd never have made it into the pros without them. I didn't do as much as others—probably good genetics gave me quicker gains. I've quit using for reasons I won't go into. I've learned about nutrition. For example, tonight's entire meal is an antipasto to me. And when we leave, I'll go home, cook two steaks, a half pot of rice, and drink a quart protein shake."

"I wish I could do that. Look at me. I've gone to pot... no, I've *become* the pot. I wish I could lose some pounds."

"Now *that* talk I won't tolerate. You're beautiful. However, if—and I say this without trying to influence you—if you do decide you want to reduce, then let me know. I have a great nutritionist on my staff. And my personal trainers are the best. Of course, should you decide to take up bodybuilding, there's me."

The laugh from Blanca shook her water glass.

A serious look crossed Ben's face. "You've never been to a bodybuilding show, I presume?"

With a tilt of her head, Blanca said, "No, and I can't imagine going."

Ben wagged his finger. "I'm inviting you to the next regional. I'm the guest poser. You'll have the grand tour backstage and see men and women at different stages of development. And, again I say with no pressure, if you want to exercise, or lose weight, then you have an unlimited guest pass at my gym. Agreed?"

Blanca pretended to flex her arm and feel her muscle. "Let me think about it. I'm not sure I'm ready to look like you."

This time it was Ben's laugh that shook the glass. He flexed his pectorals so his shirt moved. "What, you don't want to do this?"

Blanca giggled.

"Want to touch?" Ben said. "I'll let you if you'll let me."

Blanca picked up her knife and said, "Just try."

Heads turned at the uncontrolled laughter.

Ben said, "Your threat might be more menacing if you hadn't picked up the butter knife."

The two companions finished their meal, along with a one hundred and forty dollar bottle of wine. Blanca consumed most of the latter, given that Ben was the designated driver. Blanca now slouched, smiled, and grinned at random.

"Jandro and I could never have afforded to come here. I can't thank you enough. And I meant what I said about returning my clothes. See, not a crumb anywhere."

"They're yours. My gift."

"No way. These must've cost a fortune. And the shoes... wow. I'll sleep with them. Jandro can move to the couch. But I'll box them up tomorrow."

"No argument: they're my gift, for being such a good friend to Vinnie, and for your help tonight. Please, it would make me very happy. Can't you do this for me? For Vinnie? I'm begging, really."

A small tear formed in Ben's eyes. Blanca didn't understand. What happened?

"Ben, you're the most wonderful man, generous and kind. I'll divorce my husband and marry you, even if you're gay. Vinnie will have to fight me for you."

Blanca stopped talking suddenly and covered her mouth.

Ben leaned forward. "What did you say?"

"Just that you're kind and I accept your gift."

"Blanca Santos, you tell me now. What about Vinnie?" Ben's face darkened and his chest expanded.

"It's not my place. I've had too much wine." Blanca leaned back, but Ben didn't. "Okay, fine, here's the lowdown. Vinnie really likes you. Uh, this is in confidence, I might add, so this screws me royally. Vinnie's confused. Please don't be mad at him... that's just Vinnie. Don't be mad with him, please."

"Mad? Are you crazy? This makes the night perfect. I've had strong feelings for Vinnie for a long time. I can't say I love him, but I want to give it a go. There's something that's grown over the last weeks... my heart pounds every time I'm with him. Should I say something? Ask him out when he's better?" Ben stared into Blanca's eyes.

"You'd be crazy not to, and Vinnie would be just as crazy if he didn't accept. He will, though. You two are right for each other; I can tell."

Ben smiled and stood. "Well, time to get to work. Follow my directions and ignore whatever I say that doesn't make sense. Just follow my lead. Lucien and I need to chat."

# Chapter 54

## Return to the Bedroom

Perhaps it was just relief, or fear, but Ginny found herself desiring Dan. Maybe it was his quick action, his mobilizing Ben and Big John. Dan's decision-making had been effective. This was unlike Paris—and here the stakes were much higher. This wasn't a ranting little Parisian, but mobsters that murdered with impunity.

But whatever the reason, Ginny felt a stir, a sense that she'd passed her stethy obsession. The only way to prove it was to have Dan in their bedroom. She'd test her theory, hoping to create a new beginning.

Dan felt her mood. Ginny started with shooting-star kisses. His arms curled around her, forcing their bodies to meld. He observed everything with predatory eyes. He lowered her zipper, each notch unfolding dress and re-vealing skin. His first date trembles returned, the shyness of unfamiliarity, the areas unknown, unexplored.

Her dress dropped, and Dan's shirt was flung aside. Dan's hand stretched out and held Ginny's buttocks, kneading rocks.

Stepping back, Ginny made a slow turn. Quotation marks formed Ginny's ass as her spindled calves toe-stepped over discarded undergarments. Dan struggled to keep himself from charging her; immolation was guaranteed. He wanted to crease her, fold her over, consume her.

Her disrobe was just a prelude. She bent at her waist, legs spread, ass spread, and her arch gave Dan all he desired.

She fanned his flame: "Come rub me."

His limbs flashed his response, pants and briefs dropping, arms out-stretched.

Ginny placed her forehead to the floor, her between-the-legs view showing Dan moving forward. When he made contact, the impact moved her legs. Ginny steadied herself with one hand on the side of the bed. With her free hand, she searched behind her to grab hold of Dan. Her desire intensified.

His actions came unplanned. He toe-lifted his body, his penis sliding up

Ginny's backside, his hands on her firm bulbous ass. Then, with his hands anchored, Dan gave way to his aching organs. His cock rubbed along Ginny's anus; the friction increased his craving. He dipped, allowing his spring-loaded penis to brush Ginny's vagina. Dan did not seek palliation but encouragement.

Ginny obliged—for him and her. She wrapped her hand around Dan's cock, wanting to pop the top and sate her appetite. She felt Dan's firm six-pack rub against her ass as his penis went farther between her legs. Harder, she thought. She wanted Dan's washboard abdominals to scrub her. She swallowed her breaths, appearing to inhale Dan. Her voice hushed instructions: "Closer, move your abs tight against me."

Dan accepted Ginny's direction. He acceded when he should have over-ruled. He moved in, waiting for her next directive, the initiative all hers.

He missed the subtle change. Ginny had barked instructions, and he had responded. He'd only wanted to quell his ache, his desire to enter her; his sexual drive took no notice of mental shifts. The point for him was climax, nothing more.

But not for Ginny. She had abandoned her thought to invite Ben for a re-turn session when she became convinced that Dan's recent actions had subli-mated her desire. For her, this night needed to prove her right. Dan would take charge, know what to do, show his strength in both body and mind.

"Hold my breasts. Press into my back."

With his arms outstretched, Dan clasped the firm mounds. Each hand grasp caused shivers. He twisted Ginny's Q-tip nipples, and for each swirl of his thumb and index finger his balls moved higher and his penis pulsed. Every ache in him was derived from Ginny's body. He'd take directions all night to feel like this.

She knew what Dan wanted—what she wanted too. She'd let him release, allow him his joy, take whatever she could. Her toes and legs pushed up, which raised her rear and pulled Dan along her back, his hand unwilling to release her breasts. Then she gave him a choice as a means of forcing him to take over: "Lipstick or Vaseline?"

"Shaving cream." Dan whispered.

"Kinky." He'd made a decision—and not one she had expected. Her smile was restored.

When Dan returned from the en suite, Ginny was on her back, her V-spread legs across the bed. He handed her the tube and kneeled between her legs, his flagpole at full parade.

"What's this?" Ginny said. "This isn't cream, it's shaving gel."

"I switched from cream to gel. I read it gives a better shave. Let's see how it works here."

*Assertive*, Ginny thought. She heated up. She squeezed, and her palm filled Texas oilrig style.

"Too much." Dan didn't want a soaking.

"Not from this angle." Ginny motioned Dan to kneel closer. But instead he shifted and moved to squat, his arrowhead aimed high, cool air entering his anus.

This was her decision. Ginny slathered, feeling Dan's hardness, wanting it to enter, the vein pulsing blood with her every stroke. She desired this, squeezing his root before returning to his mushroom tip.

A breeze tickled him; he balanced on his toes while using Ginny's breasts for support. His index finger extracted gel, which he spread across Ginny's nipples, twirling. They were perfect. Dan felt joy with every touch; he was at the pinnacle of his desire. And he saw Ginny's smile, another cause for joy.

"More gel. Lube me again." Dan's bass voice was stern.

Ginny massaged Dan's penis, pleased with his manly lecture. Her desire now matched his; she wanted him to insert, and pure animal instinct took hold. Her vagina was ready, yet she did not rush. She had Dan spit-polish shined, yet she held him back, making the eventual entry count for more.

Dan's mitten hands continued to palm Ginny's breasts. He gave her the next instruction. "Lift up."

If she did, Ginny knew this would complete his entry—and it was too soon for her. So she side-rolled underneath Dan's straddle. Every region inside her was excited. She wanted this, needed it. She raised her top leg, impeding Dan's passage further.

"Let me turn you over," Dan said. "I can't get into you this way."

Ginny moved her leg higher, enjoying Dan's barking order.

With years of yoga and gym training, Ginny had flexibility. Her leg extended to the ceiling, which allowed Dan to slide under. Her gymnastic movements had given Dan great satisfaction over the years. Now Ginny put human desire center stage, the physical expressing emotion.

Dan reciprocated, applying the skills of a truck driver to line up his cock with Ginny's vagina. Ginny helped with the final alignment. They had reached mutual satisfaction from their perfect coupling: male and female; love and desire; trust and faith.

He pushed. Ginny welcomed his thrusts. He breached her relaxed clitoris muscles, and her legs went Lincoln tunnel wide. Dan held her breasts throughout the coupling. This was everything he wanted.

The moment arrived.

Ginny grabbed Dan's arm, and he took his cue. His bicep rose in synchrony with his cock. He forced arm fibers to create muscle knolls, filling Ginny's hand.  She gripped the bulge, her merry-go-round brass ring.  His muscles belonged to her.  His strong body and his confidence had returned.  She'd found relief, had conquered her obsession; had forgotten Paris, forgiven.

Dan felt as if he'd need a transfusion; his blood surged from penis tip to bicep splits.  He lost control of his body, the pulsing, undulating, flexing.  He quaked in both body and soul.

Ginny's labia squeezed Dan's penis as her hands pressured Dan's arms.  The push and squeeze caused sweat to stream over her body.  The noise of their lovemaking crowded out her thoughts.

She felt his spurt on her cervical wall.  His tense biceps hardened in her hand.  Ginny screamed, her own ejaculate flooding the bedsheet.

Dan's arms cramped; he struggled to lower them.  His ejaculation had exhausted him, and he was fatigued, too, from flexing his muscles. He rolled his sinewy body to his side; each sigh an echo of his recent passion.  Dan's sleep arrived, quick and deep.

Ginny studied her sleeping husband.  She wanted him to mount her again. She wanted him to rise up, a power resurrection, body and control.  His muscular body was not laced with a bodybuilder's striated and hardened fibers. This had been a delusion.  She had not satisfied her stethy.  How could she think it would be so easy?  There had to be a reckoning for this self-deceit.  It wasn't over.  She'd talk to Ben.

# Chapter 55

## Twenty Questions

The small maître d's office contained a desk and swivel chair, a guest chair on the side, a desktop computer, and a Paris wall calendar. Lucien, a.k.a. Harry Finkelstein, sat behind his desk. Blanca sat in the side chair with Ben standing behind, his hands gripping the chair's back. Opposite Blanca, the parking valet perched on the desk's corner.

"How can we help?" Lucien used his formal maître d' tone.

"I'd like to know about the cop that gave Bill Barrington a ticket last week. Can you describe him or tell us anything about him?"

"Nah," said the valet. "Nothing special. He was an NYPD standard-issue cop. Showed his badge from the sixty-second in Brooklyn, which was unusual, but nah, nothing more."

Ben looked at the valet, then to Lucien, then back to the valet, then spoke with a soft growl. "You're telling me that for no reason a Brooklyn cop happens to be in your lot and sees something wrong with Mr. Barrington's car. Is that what you're telling me?"

The valet's posture shifted. His lips puckered his face as he turned to Lucien.

Harry Finkelstein replied, "I dunno whatch youse wants from us." Harry's Brooklynese replaced Lucien's faux French. "NYPD can issue tickets anywhere in the five boroughs. Nothing to do with us."

"Yeah, that BS might work on someone else, but you and I know cops don't roam out of their own precinct, much less out of their district, to give minor vehicle violations. You want to try again?" Ben was gruff.

Blanca decided to diffuse the tension, not knowing why Ben was concerned with Bill Barrington's automobile ticket. "Look, Harry, Mr. Barrington wants to know if he's a target for a shakedown. I think you can appreciate his concern. He needs to know if he can continue to come to Bel Jour France or whether he should tell Mr. Grossman he'll be switching to another restaurant."

Ben tapped Blanca's shoulders, careful to use fingertips only. He'd noticed that Blanca had switched from "Lucien" to "Harry," making this a discussion among friends.

"I don't think Mr. Barrington has anything to worry about. I'm pretty sure it was a one-time thing, probably related to business Mr. Barrington had in Brooklyn. I understand it's all taken care of… a one-off, nothing more."

"And how will Mr. Barrington know this, Harry?" Ben's voice was low and calm.

"I can't say exactly, but I know it's finished."

Ben turned to the valet. "What did the cop look like? What exactly did he do?"

The valet hesitated until he saw Harry nod. "I don't know. He was shorter than you, and stocky… well not your size, but bigger than me. Typical Brooklyn cop, all attitude. Said he saw the Mercedes come down the street and it had a problem with the license plate. He waited until Mr. Barrington and his date came out."

Blanca smiled. Date? Yeah right! Screw bunny is more like it.

The valet continued. "He asked Mr. Barrington about the car. Mr. Barrington argued. The cop claimed it was suspicious, then asked to look inside the trunk. Mr. Barrington was furious. I think he may have pushed the cop, so the cop handcuffed him. The woman pleaded for Mr. Barrington to stop acting like a fool. The cop pulled a rag from the trunk."

Ben knew what was pulled out, but Blanca didn't. "So, you have no idea why the cop came to this restaurant?" Ben looked to the two men; both shook their heads and shrugged.

Blanca gazed behind the desk to a stack of newspapers—the *Daily News*. It wasn't the reading matter she would have expected to see in an upscale restaurant. She pointed at the papers and asked Harry to pass over the top part of the pile. Harry said she could have them as they were for recycle.

Blanca shuffled through the pile until she found Tuesday's paper. She turned to page two, which had a picture of the cop murdered on Monday, who had now been identified as Officer Dominic Paganno. She extended the paper to the valet. "Is this the guy?"

"Yeah, that's him. Jesus, he was killed last Monday? Son of a bitch. Well I guess Mr. Barrington won't have to worry about his ticket." The valet chuckled, but no one else did.

Ben touched Blanca's arm, and they turned to leave.

"I wonder if they'll find the other guy dead too." The valet chuckled again.

Ben and Blanca spun back; everyone's eyes were focused on the valet.

"Shut up, Richie," Harry muttered.

Ben eyed the valet. "Richie, that's your name?"

Richie nodded.

"Okay, Richie: what do you mean 'the other guy'?"

"I'm sure Richie didn't mean anything," Harry said. "He just talks. That's the kinda guy he is."

The valet looked uneasy. "Uh, yeah, like Harry says, I talk. It don't mean nothing."

Ben stepped up to within inches of the valet. His voice was gruff as he said, "Well maybe Harry, or Lucien, or whatever the *fuck* his name is, should let you talk a little more."

"Nothing much to say, really." Richie backed toward the wall, but Ben followed, his chest pushing on Richie.

"I don't believe you, Richie. I think there was someone here to speak to Mr. Barrington, and I want to hear about it now." Ben growled, pressing forward, leaving no personal space between Richie and him.

"Look, I don't know anything. A month or two back this guy drives in, I park his car. He's a big guy like you, not muscle, but not the kind of guy you'd want to meet at night. He doesn't go into the restaurant, but he takes out his cell phone and two minutes later Mr. Barrington comes out. He's friendly to Mr. Barrington. Well, not friendly, but not hostile like the cop."

"What did he want?"

"I don't know. I just park cars."

"Richie, you must've heard something. People talk as they get into cars, and they never notice the valet. Isn't that right?"

Richie agreed with a nod. The valet was nobody unless your car was scratched.

"So talk," Ben growled.

The valet held up his hands in a sign of surrender. "Okay. I heard the big guy say, 'The fag's been taken care of.' Mr. Barrington handed him an envelope. That's it. I remember because it'd been a long time since I'd heard someone be so open in public about gays. Maybe I'm sensitive because I'm gay. Are you going to beat me up for being gay?"

Ben backed away; that was all he could do for the valet. This was not a moment for empathy; Richie had seen Bill pay off the man he'd hired to kill Vinnie.

Ben needed to tell Dan and Big John.

# Chapter 56

## Committee Decision

The following afternoon, Ben was in his office, about ready to start his afternoon workout. After his dinner with Blanca, he'd filled in Big John, Jack, Dan, and Ginny on what he'd learned the night before. Now it was waiting time. Wait for Big John to figure out what to do.

So when the name "John Briggs" popped up on Ben's cell, Ben closed his office door before answering.

"What's up?"

"Not much detail. The guy was Sal Friscollo, one of Carmine Aquafreddo's captains. Carmine's known as Cooler. He's a 'made man,' heads a small section of the Brooklyn mob. You don't want to have anything to do with him or Sal Friscollo—who goes by the name Chopin because of the size of his hands. Sal is worse than Carmine. He boxed in his youth, but he was too slow and found employment as an enforcer. He did ten years upstate for involuntary manslaughter—and he would have been convicted of second-degree murder if two witnesses hadn't 'gone missing' and a third suddenly changed his testimony and said the deceased had attacked Sal. 'It was self-defense. Poor Sal would have been killed.' That story was hard to swallow given the victim was five foot eight and weighed a hundred and forty pounds. But whatever. The jury convicted Sal on the lesser manslaughter charge. I'm telling you, with these two, it's a goddamn miracle Vinnie's alive. My boy's a strong one. But we have to drop this investigation, now. Trust me."

Ben wasn't interested in dropping anything. But Big John had a point. Was it Cooler or Chopin they wanted, or was it Bill Barrington?

* * *

Dan was with Vinnie when Ben knocked. Ben was holding an envelope marked "confidential." The package had been hand-delivered by Jack Briggs to DV&N's reception desk for Blanca Santos, and Blanca had brought it to the cute muscular Steve at UltraFit, saying that it was urgent that Ben Hausen receive the package as soon as possible.

Big John had instituted this elaborate procedure. John knew that Carmine Aquafreddo would learn that inquiries had been made regarding the dead cop and Sal Friscollo. So Big John ordered no more family visits to Ben's condo. Ellen Briggs had objected, but he'd convinced her that by going to visit Vinnie, she placed Vinnie in danger—and Ben and Dan, too. The same restriction applied to Blanca. Vinnie's location had to be kept hush-hush.

Vinnie, unaware of the unfolding events, was pleased to see Ben. But Ben just said, "Mind if I have a quick word with Dan in private?"

"What the fuck, Ben? First Blanca, now Dan. Fuck!"

Dan's questions began as soon as they stepped outside Vinnie's room, but Ben shook his head. They went upstairs to Ben's study, where Joe and Dr. Alvarez were waiting.

"It's nothing to worry about, Dan," Ben said. "I thought you all should hear and see what we have. We want your input. Everyone should have a say, as it concerns Vinnie."

Dan's surveyed the group. "If it's about Vinnie, shouldn't we include his parents?"

Ben nodded. "For reasons you're about to hear, Vinnie's parents will be staying away. They have full confidence in you."

"Okay, now I'm getting worried."

With his gentle tone, Joe explained. "Dan, sweetie, please sit. You're jumping to conclusions, or making assumptions, or… I don't know what. But just listen. This is good news."

It was Ben who did the explaining. The lowdown was that mobster Carmine "Cooler" Aquafreddo and his enforcer, Sal "Chopin" Friscollo, had been given a contract by Bill Barrington to kill Vinnie. Big John said that this meant a wall had to be put up between outsiders and Vinnie; only the four men in the room would have contact with Vinnie from now on. And these precautions would have to remain in effect until the street gossip went away.

Ben waved the opened envelope. "Vinnie's father sent photos of Sal Friscollo. Jack got them through his warden friend at Attica. They're from Sal's incarceration, so they're out of date, but Dr. Alvarez thinks the photos might help Vinnie's memory. Still, he has concerns."

Dan stood. "Wait. The mob nearly killed Vinnie, and this is *good* news? Are you proposing we help Vinnie remember so he can make an assault charge against the *mob*? This isn't good news!"

"Sit, Dan. You're missing the point. Dr. Alvarez says often one memory can trigger others. If Vinnie remembers the face of his assailant, he might make other connections. But there's a risk. You explain it, Dr. Alvarez."

"Ben's right," the doctor said. "The event we want Vinnie to recall was traumatic—he nearly lost his life. Showing him the photo of his assailant might cause psychological trauma."

"Then forget it," Dan said. "Why take the risk? What's the benefit? An off chance Vinnie might remember something else? What? Even if he does, what good would it do?" Dan stood and began to pace.

Ben stood too. "Dan, I couldn't agree more. However, there's the possibility Vinnie knows something that could exonerate you."

"I don't care about my reputation. I'm fine. I know I didn't do anything, and I can live with that. This whole thing started because Vinnie tried to help me over my stupid proposal. Well, I don't need DV&N. I can get along fine without them. Let it go."

Dan started to leave, but Joe stepped in front of him and lightly touched his arm.

"Honey, except for one thing," said Joe. "Vinnie may want to do this because it might get him closure—and justice."

Dan replied in an angry tone, "And how does that work, Joe? How does it get justice for Vinnie if Carmine and, what's his name, Sal, are untouchable? Explain that to me. I don't want that kind of *justice*." Dan's eyes bulged. He stood tense and shaking.

Joe knew Dan needed a few seconds to take in oxygen. Condescension would only make things worse, so Joe was frank. "Dan, it's not the mob we're concerned about. They were tools. The real culprit is Bill Barrington, and maybe Linda Lords. If this hurts Bill Barrington, then Vinnie will receive justice. Maybe you will, too, but you're not the central point. Your feelings are tangential. Vinnie comes first, not you—don't you agree?"

Dan stopped pacing. All eyes were on him.

"I'm out of my depth here. What happens next? What do we do?"

* * *

The four men gathered around Vinnie. Dr. Alvarez explained both the importance of the proposal and the associated risk: a setback, even the possibility of a shock-induced coma. The photo would surely upset him.

"If the risks are small, what's the problem? I mean—"

Dr. Alvarez interrupted. "Vinnie, listen carefully. I said small, not zero."

Ben chimed in. "Can you give us a number?"

"No."

Dan started to launch into a statistical explanation, but a cry came from Vinnie. "Thanks, Dan, but enough. If you continue anymore it might just put me into in to a math-induced coma." Vinnie looked to Ben. "Fuck this. Ben, what would you do if you were me?"

"Oh, no. *I'm* not making the decision for you. You're on your own."

The entire room agreed with Ben.

"Oh, what the fuck. I didn't even notice the last coma, and apparently I made some good friends while I was unconscious. Go ahead, let me see the photo." Vinnie stretched out his hand.

For all his bravado, Vinnie's hand shook a little as he opened the envelope and pulled out the photograph. Vinnie's reaction surprised everyone: he laughed, hard and loudly.

Dr. Alvarez approached Vinnie. "Is everything okay?"

Vinnie walked to the couch, chuckling. "Son of a bitch."

"Vinnie, I'm going to ask you a few questions. I want to keep your brain focused on the present. Do you know where you are?"

"Look, Doc, I'm fuckin' fine. Don't worry. I'm not in shock… well, I am, but not in the way you think. Really, I'm okay." Vinnie looked up at Dr. Alvarez and then to Ben, Dan, and Joe. Each of them appeared to be more in shock than Vinnie.

Dr. Alvarez continued his exam. "What do you see in the room? Who's here, and do you know where you are?"

Vinnie smiled. "I'm in the most wonderful place and with my fucking best friends ever. I am the happiest and luckiest man alive. I'm fine, Doc, really, don't worry. So this is the fucker that beat me up and tried to kill me? Jesus, look at the mug on this guy's face. And look at his hands."

"This is a good sign. I think we can all relax," said Dr. Alvarez. "The fact that Vinnie has no qualms about the person in the photograph and that he has expressed a strong emotional connection to all of you suggests a positive emotion rather than a fear reaction." Dr. Alvarez paused, then turned to Vinnie. "But can you explain what made you laugh when you saw the photo?"

"Because when I saw the face on this bastard, my first thought was that my coma was not from his beating the shit out of me but from me being forced to look at that face. Can you imagine that up close and personal? He probably sends people into comas everyday just by strolling down the street. He should call Disney for the role of the Beast in a remake of *Beauty and the Beast*." Vinnie laughed at his own joke.

After some refreshment, Vinnie started asking questions. First he asked them to identify his ugly assailant. Ben told him the man's name.

"Chopin? Fuck me. What tune was he trying to play on me? I'll bet it was a showtune since he knew I'm gay. Probably 'Hello Dolly' or 'New York, New York.'"

Ben filled Vinnie in on the connection between Sal Friscollo, his boss Carmine Aquafreddo, and Bill Barrington. Ben told him about John's fear that Carmine might worry the inquiries were about an investigation—and that he'd act mercilessly as a result—and that for safety reasons, Vinnie's family, Dan, and Blanca had been asked to have no direct contact with either Vinnie or Ben. Everything would go through Ginny on a pay-as-you-go disposable cell phone.

The group disbanded, and everyone went home, leaving Ben and Vinnie alone.

"Would you mind if I come back tomorrow?" Ben asked. "I think we should have a talk about your future here."

Vinnie agreed, but the idea made him more worried than observing Sal Friscollo's mug shot had. He understood: his days at Ben's condo were numbered. The longer he remained, the greater Ben's exposure as a mob target. Ben may have been the most powerful man Vinnie had ever seen, but muscles didn't stop bullets. Vinnie didn't want to leave, but he knew his time was up.

# Chapter 57

## Check-Out

Fresh flowers filled the vase on the dining table. A rhythmic rapping on the door interrupted Joe and Vinnie's conversation. Both men turned to the door.

"Come in," Joe said.

As soon as he stepped into the room Ben knew from Vinnie's red eyes. Joe had told Ben earlier, before Vinnie: no need for round-the-clock nursing. An UltraFit physiotherapist would replace Joe.

Joe turned to Vinnie. "Crying won't help, pumpkin. I'll be back to visit." Then he rushed out of the room, his own tears flowing.

Ben sat on the couch and tapped the cushion. Vinnie hobbled across on crutches.

"I know, I need to go," Vinnie said. "No need for you to say it. I'll fuckin' leave as soon as this leg cast is removed in two days." With the back of his hand, Vinnie wiped his nose.

Ben's eyes widened and his voice quaked. "God, no. You stay as long as you need to."

"Pity? Is that it, Ben? Don't worry, I'll cope fine in my apartment."

"Of course, except for one thing… er… it's just that… Dan and I think you might need to be hidden for a while."

"What?"

"You may be a target for another attack."

"A target? By who?"

"The mob."

"For fuck's sake, why would that be?"

"Can't say, exactly." Ben grabbed Vinnie's hand. "If you don't want to stay, I'd understand. I'll help you find somewhere safe." Ben sandwiched Vinnie's hand between his own.

Vinnie pulled his hand away and raised his voice. "*Want* to leave? You've got to be fuckin' kidding me. I love this place. A never-empty refrigerator, great wine cabinet." Vinnie grinned. "I should mention I sampled from it

236

once or twice."

"Four times."

"Fuck you. I thought you didn't count bottles."

"I don't. Empties in the recycle were a giveaway." Ben's lips curled up at the corners. "It's settled then."

Before Ben was halfway across the room, Vinnie called out. "I won't overstay my welcome. I don't want to mess up our friendship." He hesitated. "We *are* friends, aren't we?"

Ben skated back to the couch, put his hands on Vinnie's shoulders, pressing him against the back of the sofa. Then he lowered his head and his lips took hold of Vinnie's, his tongue exploring, his eyes tearing up.

Muffled sounds accompanied pounding fists. Vinnie panted, "Christ, Ben."

"I'm sorry. I shouldn't have done that."

Vinnie responded by untying Ben's sweatpants and guiding them to his ankles. Ben wore no underwear, and muscular colonnade legs flanked Ben's stiffened penis. With two fingers, Vinnie's long strokes bounced Ben's hard cock off his multi-layered abs. This was not dispassionate, a pickup, or a one-night-only with a friend of a friend. Vinnie kissed Ben's engorged tip and gyrated his walnut balls. Then his hand sank deeper, an extended finger probing Ben's anus. The jolt swelled rocket adductors, and hard muscled plates clamped down on Vinnie's arm. Blood circulated through capillaries, making Ben's lower body tingle. His white jet stream spurted, spewing for seconds or eternity, soaking Vinnie's cotton tee. A roar cascaded with each pulse: "Fuck. Yes. Fuck me. Don't stop. More. Fuck me."

Vinnie's eyelids shuddered open, and he pushed away. Grabbing his crutches, Vinnie swayed to stand, but he was blocked by a colossus.

"What's wrong? Are you all right? Vinnie, did I hurt you? Vinnie…?"

Ben lifted Vinnie off the couch so that his feet were dangling. Vinnie was embedded into Ben's pectoral cleft and encircled by a stay-forever crush. Vinnie's newly healed ribs ached, and he could barely breathe.

"Uh… uh…." Escape was impossible. But a knuckle tap to Ben's forehead brought Vinnie's release.

"Fuck, Ben. You nearly suffocated me." Vinnie touched his rib cage.

"I'm sorry. Shit, did I hurt you? I'm an idiot. What happened? Why did you stop? Are you hurt?"

"I'm fine." Vinnie poked his rib cage. "Something happened. Your words and the… well, your… goo, it made me remember something important. It solves the mystery. Fuckin' A, I've solved it."

"Solved the mystery? What mystery?"

Vinnie just stared, his mind racing.

"Vinnie, what happened? Are you sure I didn't hurt you?"

Vinnie put his arms around Ben's neck. "I'm fine. It was mind-blowing, if you'll excuse the pun. But I've remembered something and I need to write this down—is that okay? Can I have a rain check?"

* * *

The next morning, Vinnie made his call.

"Good morning, Vinnie. A bit early, isn't it?" Dan looked at the kitchen clock.

"Ben helped me remember!" Vinnie elected not to explain the circumstances of his epiphany. *Imagine how much I'd remember if he'd stuck his dick up my ass.*

"You okay, Vinnie?"

"Yeah. Now let me tell you about the recordings."

* * *

Vinnie's next call was to Maria Benfatto.

Maria, following Vinnie's detailed instructions, found the USB memory stick behind the cleaning fluids on the top shelf of the supply closet.

She listened to the recordings with Shareen. Here was proof of Bill and Linda's embezzlement plans, and circumstantial motivation to suggest Linda's "rape" had been a hoax.

With ears still burning, Maria called Gary Del Vecchio at his West Palm Beach getaway house. That call ended with a meeting scheduled for Monday morning—a meeting of senior partners, corporate counsel, and Dan and Ginny; Bill Barrington was not invited.

* * *

Jammed in a crowded elevator with bleary Monday morning workers stood Dan and Ginny holding hands, their visitor badges hanging from their necks and their anxiety mounting with each floor.

Bill saw them enter the conference room, and turned to Blanca. "What the fuck are *they* doing here?"

"Who?"

"Dan Livorno and his sweet-ass wife. I saw them come off the elevator and head to the conference room. What's that about?"

Blanca didn't know, but she guessed maybe it was a review of Dan's benefits. That answer satisfied Bill, and he returned to his office and closed the door. *Stupid Rican bitch would have heard about it if it involved anything more.*

Gary was seated at the head of the conference table and presided over the knotted toads lined to one side: Maria Benfatto, Shareen Cooper, Brian Neale, and Myron Rosenberg. Dan and Ginny Livorno sat on the opposite side of the table, separated by tabletop speakers.

Maria was in charge. "If it's all right with everyone here, I'll fast forward through certain sections that may cause… embarrassment. Is that acceptable?"

"No, it is not." Ginny's voice was hard. "My husband was hurt. Vinnie nearly lost his life. Play it all, in its entirety, and to hell with who's embarrassed."

Gary nodded.

Maria played Bill's recording first, then Vinnie's tape. Silence gave way to gasps, even from those that had heard it before.

At the end, Ginny spoke. "That's even more outrageous than I'd imagined—in addition to being disgusting and obscene. My husband was vilified, painted as a pervert, and you all believed it!" Ginny was furious.

"Ginny, it's all right," Dan said, trying to calm her.

Ginny scowled. "It is *not* all right."

Gary pressed his hands together in front of him. "Dan, Ginny's right. You *should* be angry. Both of you."

Myron interrupted. "Gary, don't say any more at this time. We can prepare a statement later."

Gary leaned across the table toward Myron, his hands balled into fists, his knuckles white. His anger matched Ginny's. "Myron, *shut the fuck up.* Another fucking word and you're fired. Keep your goddamn lawyer's asshole of a mouth shut. Not. Another. Fucking. Word."

Myron's eyes went wide, but he shut his mouth and leaned back in his seat.

The group became salt pillar stiff, except for Maria. She walked behind Gary, put one hand on his lower spine, the other stroking his neck, then touched his face. She turned him around, hugged him, and whispered, "Sit down. Have a drink of water."

Everyone sat silently as Gary drank his water. Fingers fidgeted underneath the table. The room chilled. No one doubted that Maria had prevented violence, least of all Myron. She'd shown her worth.

With an earnest tone, Gary spoke. "Dan, Ginny, I apologize with all my heart. I am responsible, and I take full responsibility for the wrong we—*I* did to you. I can't find the words, but you will be compensated." Gary shot a look at Myron. "I turned my back on the best person—the best people I've ever known. Dan, I don't expect you to forgive me."

Dan rose and walked over to Gary. He placed one hand on Gary's shoulder and the other on his arm. "I do forgive you. You acted based on the facts available. I would have done the same. You were... you *are* my friend. Our friend. Right, Ginny?"

The crinkling eyes above Ginny's penciled lips belied her nod. She remained upset—not for her hurt, but for Dan's.

Gary hugged Dan. "Thank you." He sprinted from the room, wiping his eyes, and lowering his head.

Brian Neale, the named senior partner at Del Vecchio & Neale, Inc., followed Gary into his office. Brian confessed his unwitting complicity with Bill and Linda, including providing his support for Linda's proposal even before the presentation.

"Gary, I was played. Bill knew I'd do whatever was easiest. He knew I just wanted to bury myself in my office, away from board member small talk. I'm as culpable as you. More, even."

"Yes, you are." Gary showed teeth.

Brian's shoulders slumped. "What now?"

"Now we act. We take legal action, both criminal and civil. We recuperate embezzled money. We dismiss Linda Lords, effective immediately. As for Bill Barrington, given his status as partner and board member, two thirds of the board must vote for his dismissal. But I don't think that will be a problem, do you?"

Brian stood up straight. "As the senior partners, we can take temporary emergency action against any junior partners. I vote yes to remove Bill Barrington. You?"

"Yes."

"Good. We have forty-eight hours, at which time the entire board must vote."

"Brian, one more thing. We *will* make this up to Dan. Understand? That is not negotiable. You tell Myron that, because Maria won't stop me the next time. I'll bring this whole goddamn place down if need be."

* * *

Disregarding the firewall protocol, Blanca went to Vinnie on her lunch hour. "Vinnie," she said, "I could take two hours if I want. I don't have a boss!" She was giddy with joy. Bill had been escorted by security out of DV&N—and Linda had, too, only a day before her return to Paris.

Vinnie's Pacific Rim smile could have cracked his face, requiring a cast to replace those removed two days before. He laughed at Blanca's jokes about Bill's departure.

# Chapter 58

## Shebang Office Politics

Ginny gloated that the results fit her theory of the Prisoner's Dilemma game theory plan—although not exactly in the way she'd anticipated.

Linda had spilled the beans in Gary's office, even though she received nothing in return. She admitted that Bill had withheld Paris data, that they'd trumped up the Northrop crisis, and that she'd devised the embezzlement scheme. The fake rape, she said, was Bill's idea. She blamed Bill's arrogance and stupidity. Her plan would not have been discovered had Bill not provided Gary with the smoking gun.

"Son of a bitch," Brian said. "I hope you rot in hell. I will do everything to see you incarcerated for years and years. You disgust me. Gary, I had no idea how far this went. I am sorry. I'll resign. I'm a fool."

Before Brian reached the door, Gary spoke. "Sit down, Brian. We were *all* fools, and I was the biggest. Myron, too."

Myron nodded in agreement.

Gary continued. "Linda, we will press charges, you can bet your crooked ass on it." He looked outside where the winter sky pushed on the window. "You have fifteen minutes to leave the premises. A security guard will escort you to retrieve your personal items; we'll have someone ship whatever personal effects you left in Paris. You won't need much in Attica."

Instead of leaving, Linda remained seated, an index finger pointing to the ceiling. "If I give you something even bigger... can I avoid prosecution?"

No one breathed.

Gary scowled. "There is nothing you could provide that would make a difference."

"Now, now, Gary," Linda said. "Don't you want to hear what it is first? You'll find it very interesting,"

Gary sighed and looked to Myron for an opinion. Myron nodded his assent; so did Brian.

Gary's lips barely parted as he spoke. "Fine. Go ahead, Linda, tell us something interesting that you think will save your ass."

"Vinnie's mugging was a hit job. He was supposed to die. Bill paid for a contract hit on Vinnie. And when Vinnie comes out of hiding, the contract will be fulfilled." Linda's state fair pie-eating face was blue-ribbon certified.

Myron's jaw dropped—and his wasn't the only one. This just went from state to federal.

As if waiting to gain control of her tongue, Linda took her time. "I want witness protection. I won't testify if I'm sent to Attica. You want justice for Vinnie? Then you're going to need my testimony." Linda had moved closer to satisfying Ginny's Prisoner's Dilemma criteria. Linda felt in charge, top dog among these two-bit turds.

Gary shot out of his chair, pointing to the door. "Leave *immediately*. Not the fifteen minutes I said before. Maria will have your coat and handbag delivered to the lobby. She'll even send toilet paper to wipe that shit-eating grin off your face. You haven't won. Get out of my sight."

This time, Linda did as ordered—and quickly.

Maria marched Linda by her elbow to the elevator, taking away her pass and employee ID.

* * *

That fucking little faggot broke into my office. He had no right to copy data from my computer. He should be fired. Fucking faggots stick together. I'll shit on you and everyone else here.

Bill's thoughts raced while he emptied his desk, supervised by two guards. He'd been given the same fifteen minutes as Linda. Shareen stood with the guards, inspecting everything Bill put into the cardboard box provided by Hawthorne's security team.

Blanca had been told to wait in Maria's office with the door closed and the corridor window darkened. Maria filled Blanca in on events. Neither Shareen nor Blanca was surprised about Linda's dismissal, but they had assumed that Bill, as a partner and board member, was protected. And Blanca's fears for Vinnie intensified when she learned that Bill had orchestrated the hit on Vinnie.

Finally, Maria gave Blanca permission to take a long lunch break. Maria walked out, thinking about Officer Paganno's death. This needed to be shared, with Vinnie, Dan, and Ben.

* * *

"I'll call Lenny Cohen. He works closely with the attorney general and has connections with the feds." The lawyer tone fitted Myron better than his own skin.

"Isn't that the guy who advised we dismiss Dan?" Gary shook his head; this was a rhetorical question.

"Yes, and he was right. I'm sorry—I know you don't want to hear it, but based on the facts we had, Lenny made the right call. Even Dan said as much. But we were played. With the true facts, we'd have made a different decision. Don't go back on old history. We're in way over our head, and to tell the truth, I'm not prepared to deal with the mob."

Myron left to make his call, but first he added, "I don't suppose I need to say this, but not a word to anyone, especially Bill, about what Linda said."

A half hour later, Myron returned to Gary's office.

"Lenny said we say nothing to *anyone*. And we need to impress that, strongly, upon everyone that was in the room with Linda. Lives are at risk. Lenny's going to talk to Linda and advise her not to have any contact with Bill from this point—or else she becomes an accessory after the fact to murder in the commission of a crime. The feds will secure a wiretap for Linda's cell under RICO, the Racketeer Influenced and Corrupt Organizations Act. Bill must be kept in the dark, so focus your accusation on the sex entrapment and fraud. And Lenny agreed that we had every right to remove Bill from the office immediately. Like, no shit. I told Lenny even *I* knew that."

* * *

Neither Dan nor Vinnie seemed particularly surprised to learn from Blanca that Vinnie's mugging had been not a hate crime but a mob hit. Dan had suspected it all along, though he took no joy in being proven right. Vinnie looked on the bright side: it gave him all the more reason to remain with Ben; plus, Blanca hinted that DV&N might make him a hefty compensation offer—or at least she felt they should. Vinnie felt freedom turning the corner, if he survived. All he needed to do was sit tight in Ben's condo. Preferably on Ben's lap.

# Chapter 59

## Leave a Message

Linda cringed as she surveyed the New Jersey motel in Hackensack, a fleabag off Route 46, an unbearable contrast to the luxury she was used to. Drab brown walls, off-white ceiling, faded mocha drapes, double bed, faux dark walnut chest of drawers, tiny bathroom. Her indefinite stay here was paid for by DV&N—surely they could have afforded better than this budget rat trap.

Her cell phone sat on a tiny table, its battery removed. She had been told that Maria would contact her on the room phone.

* * *

Bill heard Linda's low-pitch voice mail message for the umpteenth time. He waited for the beep, then left a message that varied only a little from his previous: "Bitch, you think you can freeze me out? You're a son-of-a-bitch cunt." His words echoed around his locked home office.

Bill's wife, Joan, heard the cursing, and she was baffled by him being home in the afternoon in the first place. When he'd entered the house earlier, he'd screamed, "Move out of my fucking way and don't say a word! And by the way, don't spend another goddamn cent—it's all going to my lawyer. Same for your goddamn kids. Now fuck off."

He had walked right past her to the liquor cabinet, removed a full bottle of scotch—bypassing the already-open, half-full bottle—grabbed a tall whiskey tumbler, and locked himself inside his office. The incoherent cursing had continued on and off ever since.

Joan had never seen her husband like this. Oh, sure, he'd cursed her after they'd argued, and he had struck her that one time, but he had never come home in a rage, and he had certainly never cursed the children.

Frightened and confused, she made her way to the master bedroom to call Bill's secretary, Blanca Santos. She used her cell phone in case Bill picked up the house phone; she knew that would only make things worse. Joan remembered Blanca from the office picnic; she was courteous, even showed a touch of kindness. She hoped Blanca could explain, because Joan needed to know what had caused Bill's fury. And why was he home from DV&N in the middle of the day?

Exhausted and worried after her visit with Vinnie, Blanca had just returned to the office when she took Mrs. Barrington's call. Blanca knew she would have to tread a thin line between helping an innocent and upset woman and overstepping the bounds of confidentiality. Deep down, Blanca felt that Mrs. Barrington had a right to know; and Blanca certainly felt no loyalty toward Shithead, even less now that he was no longer her boss.

"Mrs. Barrington, I'm sorry, but it's not my place to tell you. Mr. Barrington should explain. All I know is that Mr. Barrington was asked to leave DV&N, and he cleared out his desk."

"What do you mean, leave? Fired? What happened? He won't talk to me. I've never seen him this angry. He's in his home office now with a full bottle of scotch. I can hear him screaming and cursing in there."

Blanca recognized Bill in Joan's description. Blanca knew that Bill was the kind of man to blame everyone and anyone, especially women. She'd never seen Bill become violent, but she knew that alcohol brought out the worst in an angry man. Blanca had seen this volunteering at the woman's shelter. She'd also seen Bill's crude venom directed at female staff or at Vinnie, especially after a liquid lunch or excessive drinking at an office party. It was important that she warn Mrs. Barrington—and the children.

"Look, Mrs. Barrington, I can't tell you what to do, but my advice is to take your kids and go stay with friends or relatives. Do you have family you could stay with? I don't want to alarm you, and I'm saying this not as an employee of DV&N, but as someone who wants to help. You called me, and I'm telling you this as one woman to another. This is a very difficult time for your husband, and you need to be out of his way for at least twenty-four hours. Leave a note. Don't write anything about his behavior. Just make an excuse, like there was a pre-arranged event and you'd assumed he would be too busy to attend so it wasn't on his calendar. I wouldn't wait another minute."

"What? Why should I leave? Shouldn't it be Bill? Isn't this a bit drastic? Maybe he'll calm down in a few hours." Joan's flat voice softened at the end.

"It's up to you. But if it were me, I'd take the kids and be gone immediately. Please, think about it… and I wish you the best. Bye."

As Joan descended the staircase, Bill came out of the downstairs bathroom carrying his empty whiskey glass.

"What the fuck are you looking at, you fucking cunt? I'll beat the crap out of you if you look at me like that again. And make sure your shitty kids don't bother me. I'll beat them to a pulp too. You women are all the same. Fucking bitches." He slammed his study door and clicked the lock.

That dispelled any doubts Joan had about following Blanca's advice.

Joan didn't bother with clothes, a suitcase, or toiletries, and she wrote her note according to Blanca's prescription. Her goal was to drive fast, pluck her children from school, and seek safe refuge.

Two hours later, Joan pulled into her sister's driveway in Connecticut. The kids' complaining ended with the fuss Aunt Roz made over them. Uncle Dave would be home in an hour. For the children it meant more spoiling, but for Joan it meant the safety of her state trooper brother-in-law. Bill wouldn't mess with Trooper Dave, all six foot five inches, two hundred thirty pounds, and hip revolver.

The evening darkness, combined with the alcohol, left Bill struggling to use the toilet. Staggering, he peed on the floor and then slipped in it. "What the fuck! Bitch maid will clean it up. Fuck it. That son of a bitch Linda thinks she can screw me? I'll show her." His words slurred.

The rest of Bill's evening was filled with more unanswered calls to Linda's cell—and more scotch. He didn't even notice the empty house, and he never saw his wife's note. Not that he would have cared.

* * *

"Hi, Sallls… Ishh… It's Bill Barringggton."

Sal "Chopin" Friscollo needed a moment to decipher the caller's identity. "Oh, hello Mr. Barrington. How can I help you?"

With effort, Bill slurred his request: he wanted to talk to Carmine.

*No way am I passing this cazzo fucking drunk to Carmine*, Sal thought. "Sorry, Mr. Barrington, but Mr. Aquafreddo has stepped out. How can I help?"

"Fuck. I need Carmine. I've got another job. Fuck it, you do it anyway, so maybe I should talk to you. I need you to bump off that cunt partner… former partner, motherfucking cunt, Linda Lords. Same as last time."

No one said this on the phone, not to Sal. "I'm sorry, Mr. Barrington, I have no idea what you're talking about. Do you want a reservation? We have a great special tonight. How many in your party?"

"What the fuck are you talking about? I don't want to eat. I want—"

Sal hung up. Then he blocked all calls from Bill's cell before informing Carmine that they might have a problem with a former client.

# Chapter 60

## DIY

Winter's low morning sunbeam crossed Bill's face, igniting his hangover. He raised himself off the floor, zigzagged to the bathroom, and slipped again on his nighttime pee.

"What the fuck? Piss all over. Clean this up!" Bill yelled to an absent Brazilian maid, who had been told by Mrs. Barrington that she should take an indefinite vacation, her leave paid, her job secure.

Bill grumbled, "I'll bet that pussy Gary gave pussy Linda a sweet deal. Two pussies. Har har, har har." His dark eyelids lowered. "Fucking traitor…"

He removed a thirty-eight caliber handgun from his wall safe and a thousand dollars cash.

* * *

Standing across from the Hawthorne Building, Bill craned his neck back, unable to see his office thirty-five stories above. *Every one of the stupid bastard guards knows me. I'm a god to them, the jealous fuckers.*

And they did know him—as "the offensive prick."

Security post 9/11 among New York's skyscrapers was high. But Bill believed security did not apply to him. Vengeance fueled his brain, malice was his motivation, and the garage was his entry point. Building security had forgotten his garage elevator passkey when they confiscated his ID badge. An understandable oversight, since few employees could afford the monthly two-thousand-dollar parking fee anyway; it was a corporate bonus for senior executives. Each parking location included an elevator passkey to bypass the lobby. Bill smiled as he fingered his own passkey.

The sticking point was entry into the garage. Registered cars had access with automated telepass. Unfortunately, garage security *had* remembered to take his telepass.

Bill's reconnaissance moved from Second Avenue to the garage entrance on East Forty-Fourth. Two cars with passengers entered and the driver's ID was checked. *Hm, they didn't check the passengers' IDs. That's a security hole. I'll bring it up at the next exec meeting.*

Minutes later a car descended the ramp with a telepass—and this time there was no stopping and no guard check. Behind the car was a large FedEx courier van. Most couriers double-parked at the main Second Avenue entrance for quick drop-offs. The exceptions were deliveries containing multiple boxes, large equipment, or construction materials. These entered via the garage's loading dock for the freight elevators.

Bill had discovered his entry. He waited a half hour until a Staples truck turned from Second Avenue onto Forty-Fourth. Unlike other vehicles speeding past, this truck crept along slowly. Bill reacted.

A hundred feet before the truck reached the garage, Bill stepped out. Taking a New Yorker's mid-street stand, his arm overhead, Bill signaled the truck to stop. Hurrying to the passenger side, he jumped in. "You delivering here? I've been waiting for an hour. What's your schedule?"

The driver opened his mouth, but his words were caught on his tongue.

Bill had hoped the manifest would be on the dashboard. But even better: red LEDs on a GPS tracking system flashed the details he needed: Hawthorne Building, Fuller Associates, twenty-sixth floor, Room B.

"I'm with Fuller," Ben said angrily. "We were promised delivery before ten. What the fuck is going on?" Bill's opening salvo suited his personality. But then he adopted a tone of false empathy. "No, not your fault. Some dumb nuts in headquarters, no doubt. I'll cover for you, say you saved them from losing the account. I'm sorry if I landed into you. This cost Dee Vee and—er, Fuller my time standing on the street. Let's get this unloaded."

The driver mumbled something—thanks, perhaps—then drove down the ramp.

Talk about your retards.

With the Fuller delivery on the garage manifesto and the passenger unverified, the truck moved to the loading dock. Bill leapt out, telling the driver he'd alert Receiving about the delivery.

* * *

Pinging elevator doors opened on the thirty-fifth floor, opening to a wooden panel embossed with the logo of Del Vecchio & Neale, Inc. Bill's name had already been scrubbed from the partners list.

*Fuckers didn't waste any time.* Bile rose in Bill's throat. *Steady. Do what you came for.* Bill's head lowered, eyes on feet, face hidden, revenge propelling him forward.

He neared Linda's corner office, yet felt no closer. Sunlight brightened the glass corridor wall, and Bill squinted; a woman held file folders. *Goddamn traitor.* His pace picked up, and the .38 emerged from his winter coat. His eyes red, his mind and vision clouded, Bill passed through the secretary's office. There was no communication between his brain and optic nerve. He took no note of the fact that this woman's short dark hair and brown skin looked nothing like Linda's long blond hair and fair complexion. In fact, nothing about the African-American resembled Linda's Nordic WASPiness. But Bill's brain's malfunctioned; to him, this woman was Linda. He saw nothing else.

Bill raised his gun and shouted, "You motherfucking cunt, you think you can double-cross me?!"

He fired.

Brian Neale's office was diagonally opposite Shareen's. But he was in a personal crisis, unable to concentrate on finances, so at that moment he was strolling the corridor, approaching Shareen Cooper's office. When he heard the shot, he jumped; he smelled the gunpowder before he saw Shareen holding her shoulder, leaning against the glass wall, eyes wide with terror. Then he spotted Bill.

Brian sprinted toward Bill Barrington and slammed into him. The gun was knocked from Bill's hand. His adrenaline high, Brain lunged for the gun, grabbed it, pointed it at Bill.

"Hey, little man," Bill growled, "don't play with big boy toys. Give it to me and get the fuck out of my way."

Bill grabbed for the gun, turned it aside.

For the second time that day, a gunshot echoed through the offices of DV&N.

Brian's shot was wild. A thud sounded from beside the two men. They both turned.

Shareen had collapsed onto the floor, and serpentine blood flowed under the desk. Only now did Bill's brain catch up with his eyes: this wasn't Linda.

"Wrong bitch," Bill said. "We shot the wrong bitch."

Brian panicked and ran to Shareen, dropping the gun. He bent over Shareen's body. There was a gaping hole in the back of her head; brain matter painted the wall where she had stood.

Brian cried out, then turned and vomited. In his shock, he had forgotten all about Bill Barrington. He didn't notice when Bill calmly picked up the gun and stood.

Bill fired two rounds into the ceiling, then two into Brian's chest. More screams echoed from the corridor. Any staff who lingered after the earlier gunshots were now packing into stairwells.

"Where's fucking Linda," Bill growled at the corpse.

Then he realized. Linda had been promoted.

As he approached his former office, Bill saw the confluence of the East River and the Hudson, Lady Liberty's torch reflecting the low winter sun. "Yoohoo… Linda… I'm here. Yoohoo… Linda Lords… I'm here for you."

The childlike singsong changed to a growl. "You fucking slut, traitor, bitch."

Blanca was crouched behind a filing cabinet, trying to decide whether to run from the office or stay put. She'd heard the gunshots, but had no idea who was responsible or what was going on. She went from puzzlement to shock when Bill entered the room, calling for Linda Lords. His stiff posture, wide stance, and raised gun formed the portrait of a deranged man. Blanca knew in that instant that her advice to Mrs. Barrington had been good.

Blanca rose from behind the filing cabinet. "Hello, Mr. Barrington," she said as calmly as she could muster. "Linda's not here, and you shouldn't be either."

"Don't hand me that bullshit, you Puerto Rican slut. Oh, another brown baby on the way?" Bill pointed the gun barrel at Blanca's swollen belly. He had ignored the pregnancy announcement a week before, but today Blanca had donned maternity clothes for the first time.

Blanca stood firm. "Excuse me. You need to leave before I call security."

"What do I care, bitch? Out of my way. That cunt's in my office."

"Linda is… is… is not in your office." Blanca folded her arms. "You don't have an office. And you will not use sexist and racist language around me. You don't work here, and you have no authority."

With his gun pointed at her, Bill bellowed, "Move it, you Puerto Rican bitch."

Just then, Maria appeared in the doorway to Blanca's office. She had seen Shareen, and now she carried sorrow, indignation, and resolve on her shoulders.

"Bill, put that gun down," she said. "You've done enough already."

"Oh, look who's here, the queer's queen bee. The queen has a queen. Har har, har har. I'm senior to you, so *I* give the orders."

"Not anymore. Give me that gun while we wait for the police in the conference room." Maria held out her hand.

"Bitch, didn't you hear me? *I give the orders!* Where's Linda?" Bill looked over Maria's shoulder.

"She's not here." Maria flicked her hand by her side, a signal for Blanca to move into Bill's old office.

"Don't you move, you goddamn Rican bitch. Tell me now where that cunt is hiding."

Blanca said nothing.

Maria belted out her words. "How dare you speak to Blanca like that? Give me that gun right now." Maria stepped forward. Bill used his height and strength advantage to knock Maria down.

"You're a little cunt, just like this one!" Bill turned back to Blanca and pointed the gun at her belly. "Now, for the last time: where's Linda."

Blanca's calm demeanor broke; she began to sob. "I don't know. Probably in California."

"More lies! You have two seconds to tell me, or I'll do the same thing to you that I did to Shareen."

While Bill yelled, Maria shifted to her knees. Fueled by rage, she leapt, throwing her body into Bill's legs. As he fell, Maria grabbed his arm, jerking it down, twisting their bodies. But her hold gave Bill buoyancy, enough to toss her across Blanca's desk.

He pulled the trigger three times.

* * *

Bill was charged with three attempted murders. Shareen's death was caused by Brian's misfire. Blanca and Maria had lived only because Bill had failed to check the gun chamber.

During his interrogation by the police, Bill spit out his responses. "I'll have your badges! I know people! You little people can't touch me. Har har, har har."

# Chapter 61

## Yes

Bloomingdale's bustled at Easter, but Ginny wasn't feeling it. She'd refused the Paris position over Dan's objection, smiling at the irony since Dan had declined the recently opened European executive director position.

"Not interested," Dan had said. "Besides, I can't leave Vinnie now, can I?"

Ginny had countered that Vinnie would be fine. He was wealthy now—Dan too. Gary had kept his word, and the men's compensations had been kings' ransoms. Myron hadn't even complained.

"It's not just Vinnie, and it's not about the money," Dan explained. "It's just… I've changed." Dan didn't mention that the thought of Paris conjured up his irrational jealousy and memories of his moment of weakness.

"Me too," lied Ginny. She hadn't changed; she still had bouts of stethy.

But they agreed about their love for each other, and so they resolved to reformulate their lives.

Dan abandoned his economic forecasting career. And his temperament changed, which was obvious to anyone who knew him. The funerals and the reproaches weighed on Dan. Depression had come with Vinnie's coma, then anxiety had come over Ginny, drugs, and the mob. And his self-recrimination trailed him always: an appendage he could not amputate. His latest worry was the prosecution of Bill and Linda, and its implications for Vinnie's safety. His transformation could not be denied, not by Ginny, not by friends.

The one thing that hadn't changed was his concern for Ginny's obsession. She'd become moody without reason and would snap over nothing. "Dan, can't you get the milk from the refrigerator yourself?" "The newspaper's behind the table where you left it!" "Do you need to know everything I'm doing?"

He didn't, but it wasn't much to ask. He noticed Ginny attended more bodybuilding competitions, even minor events. She supported young Billy, UltraFit's champion on the rise; she would excitedly recount Billy's routines and his first-place trophy. She'd been giddy over her backstage tour with

Blanca—they were both Ben's special guests—and wowed by the room filled with muscle glued to bone.

Dan spent less time with Vinnie, giving more attention to Ginny. She appreciated it, but did not reciprocate the effort. The imbalance bothered Ginny more than Dan—more proof of how much he'd changed.

So Ginny daydreamed at Bloomingdale's, unfocused on either Easter or the summer collection. With self-analysis came realization: weeks before the DV&N perdition she had relapsed. The tragedies aside, her apathy had grown from her obsession. The fault was hers. The solution, too.

Her solution needed cooperation. She counted on Dan's new persona. He had shed his self-consciousness and his jealousy. This was her opportunity, the time for bold action.

And if she planned to be bold with Dan, the same held true for Ben. Forget the pretext of a friendly dinner or the critique of his posing routine. She'd be up front this time, and tell both men that this was nothing more than her attempt to satisfy her obsession. The direct benefit went to her and her alone.

They would accept or they'd tell her to drop dead.

* * *

Ginny approached Ben first. As she took the protein shake from him at the end of her workout, her hand was shaking.

Ben's fingertips steadied her. "What's wrong? Did we overdo the work-out?"

"The workout's fine. This is about you, me, and Dan." Ginny swallowed her shake. "Dan and I… our sex is mechanical, no passion."

Ben's jaw dropped. Ginny raised her finger. "I know this is uncomfortable for you—it is for me, too. But I have to talk about it."

Seeing Ben's head tilt backward, she continued. "You know what I'm going to say, don't you?"

"I guess."

"It goes back to us. I've given it thought, with Sarah and Betsy's help."

A smile appeared on Ben's face. "Cauldron on full heat, chicken hearts and toad legs included?" He mimicked stirring a large spoon in a big pot.

"Very funny. You can't blame them for our fiasco. It wasn't their fault."

"And pigs fly."

"Fine. I'll leave now." Ginny stood up, playing her trump.

"Sit. That was rude of me to say about your nice witch friends."

Humor felt good to Ginny. She pretended to put a hex on Ben. "Apology accepted." She put down her protein drink and used her lecturing voice. "I'm going to be blunt. You know about my sthenolagnia obsession." *God, my mother's words.*

Ben raised his arms for a double-bicep pose. Tensing, balloons inflated, veins crisscrossed high. "Ginny, you know I'll flex for you any time you want."

"I'm serious, Ben. Thanks for the show, but it's not that. Stop pretending. You know, don't you?"

Lowering his arms, Ben's voice was one tone short of a trill: "I'm a homosexual man. This can't be right for Dan, or for you."

"Not if you've observed the change in Dan. It's in his face, his attitude. He sounds different. He's not the same. He won't behave like last time. The question is: will you?"

Ben's consent came with no conditions.

* * *

The clues butted Dan: the dining room table set with china and crystal glasses, the lit candles, an open bottle of red Montepulciano, the fresh flower centerpiece.

"What's this going to cost me?" he asked.

"You're such a cynic."

"The cynic wants to know the bottom line."

Ginny stuck her tongue out. "Eat first."

When the bottle was emptied, Dan retrieved a second. He knew he would need more when Ginny motioned him to the living room, her shoes off, toe-stepping so her rear end oscillated.

On the couch, Dan handed Ginny a full glass. "Okay, I'm ready," he said, knowing he wasn't. He looked at Ginny's soft, tight jeans sewn to her skin; her T-shirt tinged with pale purple that accented skin, the fabric hugging braless breasts and protruding nipples; the rippled abdomen of her exposed midriff. *She's gorgeous*, he thought.

"I need to spice up our sex."

The directness startled Dan, and his tin voice replied, "Of course. We can have great sex."

Ginny's harsh staccato ground out her words. "We can't. Let's stop pretending. I'm going to say something I never thought I'd admit out loud. My mother was right—*is* right. I have sthenolagnia."

Dan leaned back, and his empty glass dipped forward. His mother-in-law's words from years before replayed in his mind: "Dan, obsession can increase or decrease over time. You'll need to keep watch. Ginny won't be unfaithful, but if she's driven by her obsession she might ask for a divorce so as not to hurt you… or do something to hurt herself, or…" Anna Swinburne had stopped there, her shoulders stooped as she walked away. Dan had understood, afraid to ask more. He had tried to forget.

His pursing lips and short breaths alarmed Ginny. Rejection? She thought Dan was about to cry. Why? She hadn't demanded, had made no threat, had said nothing definitive.

Dan's glass dropped to the floor.

"Are you all right?" Ginny moved closer, touched Dan's knees, felt his face. She had miscalculated, had not considered his months of depression.

His hands covered his face. His muted voice spoke through fanned fingers. "I know. We both know… *have* known for a long time. I don't know what to do, what's best." Dan sobbed. "I swear that whatever it is I'll do it. Please don't do anything to harm yourself, I beg you. I can't take any more loss in my life."

Shaking her head, Ginny said nothing for several seconds. "I don't understand, Dan. I'm asking you for another chance with Ben. That's what I'm asking. What did you think? Why would I harm myself?"

"I don't know. I'm confused, so confused." Dan stopped to rub his eyes. "If that's what you want, need, I'll do it. Anything to protect you."

Sobs came from Dan, and Ginny's head lowered, her long hair falling to her lap. She pulled Dan's hand away from his face and saw his red eyes, felt him shaking. Her own words fluttered. "I've spoken to Ben, and he agrees. Are you saying you do, too? No reservation, anything goes?"

"Yes."

"It'll be different this time, I promise. We'll have sex in front of another man. Do you care? Can you manage?"

Dan nodded and answered in a barely audible voice. "I don't know. I'll try."

"Dan, are you all right? You can't feel coerced. You have to be fully supportive. Can you do that?"

Dan honestly didn't know.

* * *

Later that evening, after ruminating in his study, Dan found Ginny reading in bed. She started to speak, but was stopped by his lips on her cheek.

"I don't care about anything except you," Dan whispered. "I'll do whatever you ask. I've suffered from my hang-ups—and you from yours. We had a comatose friend and two of my colleagues died. Why should I care if we have sex in front of a man? It wouldn't be my choice for a thrill, but that's not important—*you* are. I commit to this with my body and soul if it keeps you safe."

# Chapter 62

## Bedroom Lifts

The two men stood in the living room, surprising Ginny. Waiting was not an option for either—better sooner rather than later, get it over with. Ginny's wish had been granted in a day.

With a commanding voice, she stated the rules. "Stop if anyone wants to talk. No one walks away." Ginny looked to Ben's lowered head. "This is for me, but I believe you'll have a good time too." Ginny grinned at the stone-faced men.

In the en suite bathroom, Ginny helped Ben apply oil to his muscular canvas. Then she left him there and returned to the bedroom, where Dan waited. She undressed Dan, caressing him as each item of clothing was removed. She cooed over his sculpted body, the results of five months at UltraFit. For each zippered tooth she lowered came a crotch rub and a pole rise.

Dan became impatient with Ginny's leisurely pace. His hand rushed to her breasts the instant she exposed them. He loved her firmness, her perfect knolls crowned with pigmented areolas and hard nipples. He surged as silk panties rubbed his penis. She held back, prolonging his wait. Dan sweated with desire.

Cool bedcovers bunched up as Dan's ass shimmied up the bed. Ginny straddled Dan. Practical instructions were whispered. Dan held on to her breasts as if they were life buoys. Candle fragrances filled the room, flames flickering.

"Honey, close your eyes and slide down to the foot of the bed. Think of how much I love you, nothing else." Dan exhaled with her brush touch of his penis, the powdering of his testicles, the kissing of his chest.

"Come in," Ginny said to a closed bathroom door.

Ben entered, his muscles like carried luggage. Dan's eyes opened, and his gaze lowered to the small poser suit, the pouch a mere string on Hellenic legs, this poser for partners, not contests.

All waited for the sounds of "Nessun Dorma"—Ben's idea for the evening's theme. When it began, he performed a routine tailored for Ginny. Crushed stone realigned with each beat. Three minutes and one second into the music—when Pavarotti belted *"Vincerò!"*—Ben's butterfly stroke sequenced into Da Vinci's "Perfect Man X" pose.

Ginny shouted her approval. "Ben, you're perfect! You won."

Two heads turned to Dan, who replied, "I'm with Ginny. I never expected this. I can't believe all that muscle—every part of you is rippled. You look like marble, yet move like ballet. I'm blown away, really."

The professional emerged in Ben, and he started to explain his routine and diet. Ginny barked, "Not now! Tomorrow you guys can talk. This isn't a bodybuilding seminar. Ben, come over here."

Stepping forward, Ben saw Dan's full-on erection. "Enjoy yourself, Ben. No need to be self-conscious." Ben laughed and looked down. "Me too." Ben shed his poser, then raised his arms for a double-bicep pose, his log legs making a twig of his stiff penis.

"Enough." Ginny's loud voice caused both men to shrink. She turned to Dan, her breasts rubbing his jacked-up penis, aware that her ass was in Ben's face. She signaled for Ben to move to Dan's left side.

Whispered words of affection and love soothed Dan. He entered a trance, unsure if Ginny had given Ben permission to touch until Ben's pipe-wrench hand stroked Dan, nuzzling his scrotum. Dan held back his protest. He allowed this man to touch him. This had been his vow to Ginny, and it was also a result of the gratitude he owed Ben. Dan's head lowered; his lips sealed to the crevice of Ginny's breasts, seeking her hardened nipples. He knew these hands kindling his cock and balls were familiar with the apparatus, and not the hands of a woman.

The time had come for Ginny to reap her pleasure. She massaged Ben's billowing sinuous arm. Ben's flexed steel fibers didn't even feel Ginny's puny grip. He relaxed before tensing again, then repeated this maneuver twice more. Each time the bulge grew higher, until the mound split into a cleft wide enough for Ginny's pinkie. She panted steam.

Dan was near apoplexy with stimulation. He didn't care if the source was woman or man, he had descended into a pleasure warren.

Ginny looked at Dan for signs that he would panic—that his anxiety and jealousy might explode. She examined Ben just as carefully. But so far both men kept their word.

The time had arrived.

Leaning across the bed, Ginny lined up her legs. She lifted herself to her knee, her ass spread. She waited for Dan to object, but heard nothing. Dan had changed. His jealousy was gone; his fear, too.

Dan knew why. He'd been battered by life's capricious uncertainty. He would accept love and friendship when it came. If this act gave pleasure to Ginny and Ben, then wasn't he rewarded as well? And he was, both emotionally and physically. The sensuous tingling in his spine was proof.

Ben's feelings were similar. He didn't like this kind of trio. It would never have been his choice, even allowing for his fantasy about Dan. But his life had been full of choices he didn't want: loss, years of emptiness. Ginny and Dan were his best friends. He'd willingly give them what they needed. He wanted this to be Ginny's special night, and he'd find some way to make that happen. His exhibition alone wasn't enough, but what was… he didn't know. He would wait and provide what she needed.

A prod from Ginny awoke Ben to her instructions. He sat behind Dan, his legs spread into a V, and his bookshelf pectorals held Dan upright as Ginny mounted her husband. Dan's embrace pulled Ginny deeper into coitus. He loved her smile, and he loved the way she fucked him. He focused on her, blotting out thoughts of the half-ton man behind him.

Impatience and desire quickened Dan's pace. But it was too quick for Ginny. "Slow down. Take your time."

Slowed to four-quarter rhythm, Ginny's labia relaxed and widened. Dan's penis sank deeper into her, and Ben helped Dan rise up by lifting him under his armpits. Inadvertently, Ben's shaft slid along Dan's spine. Dan's rising anus lifted above the bed.

Dan lost his libido momentarily, fearing he'd exposed too much to Ben. "Ben, don't, please."

"Don't worry Dan, I understand." He did understand, but he didn't reveal that he had wanted full access. He wished he could have raised Dan higher. He tapped Ginny's back.

She dismounted and complained, "What happened?"

Ben arranged Ginny and Dan like Barbie and Ken dolls, the couple facing each other. Then pushing Dan's shoulder, Ben forced Dan into a squat. Ben directed Ginny to straddle Dan's legs, her vagina on Dan's straight-up glowing lust. She obeyed, and Dan entered her, her rhythm matching his thrusts. Summoning his willpower, Dan overcame his embarrassment as Ben stared.

Ben moved closer, his legs and penis now touching Dan. With ease, Ben moved Ginny and Dan to their haunches. Ginny's full squat now matched Dan's bent legs; his chest rubbed her breasts and his penis penetrated even deeper than before. They moaned their desire and pain, their balance precarious.

Ben squatted too, letting his forearms become resting posts for Ginny's and Dan's buttocks. He clasped his hands together, then flexed to seal the union.

His balled biceps pulsated against Dan's anus and lifted Ginny up, pressing her breasts into Dan. She grabbed hold of Ben's popover mounds. The odor of muscle wafted throughout the room. Ben held his squeeze. Ginny grabbed Dan's neck, and he clasped Ginny.

With an inhale, Ben squatted lower. His deep bends allowed his arms to span the flared cracks. Ben pushed with the power gained from lifting hundreds of pounds ten thousand times. Ten-inch snowballs formed his pectorals. As he squeezed, Dan's penis was pressed into Ginny.

Grunting, Ben's nose invaded the copulating space, and sex trailed up each nostril. His aching cock swelled with the vision of Dan's penis. Ben's scrotum pumped iron, lifting his ball sack.

Ben's oak legs straightened, lifting Ben, and Ben lifted Ginny and Dan into the air. He had squatted seven-hundred-pound barbells for warm-up.

Ginny said to no one, "Yes, yes, I love this feeling."

Reaching the bed, Ben lowered the pair, holding them until they found their footing. Spreading his stance, cupping his hands like gloves, he made custom seats. His middle finger lined up with each anus. Dan initially grunted protest, but with a look at Ginny, he soon acquiesced.

With one leg back, Ben genuflected before raising his arms. The copulating couple moved to the ceiling. Every muscle strained. Arms, legs. Penis, too. Ginny and Dan fucked while suspended in air.

Ginny called out an invented alphabet. Her hands rested on Ben's python-headed trapezoids, on shoulders torn from the Alps. She produced new words for each of Ben's hydraulic pumps. The mirror reflected a portion of Ben's deltoids, spreading from one wall to the other. Ginny's syllables made soup.

Dan fucked his brains out. Was it possible? Could anyone be this strong? Ginny screamed as her wetness covered Dan's stiff member. Dan's sweat rained down his chest; his penis felt like it was as long as a broom handle.

With a grunt his only warning, Ben crushed Ginny and Dan's coccyges, ramming Dan deeper into Ginny. Ginny slobbered words of strength and power until her sounds had no meaning. She finished her second climax with, "I can feel the strength... I feel it... I... I... the muscles and power."

The joyous outburst gave Dan insight into Ginny's obsession that he'd never had before. Her hummingbird lips fluttered between smile and scream. Her rising chin beseeched, her elongated neck twitched. Dan saw his wife consumed by ecstasy.

His desire was wrung from a dishcloth. Ginny's heat poured out from a ladle. Dan burst with a choir's cry.

The explosion forced Ginny's nails into Ben's sinew, moored by tendons that tethered ocean liners. Her hands moved along shoulders bigger than

Ben's head, fingers curling inside triceps as her pussy fucked her husband. Her fingertips skirted the ridges of Ben's biceps.

A crawling anticlimax released Ginny and Dan. She had what she wanted. She loved Dan, yet she needed her Ice Cream Man.

The couple's cries were a blend of joy and pain. Ben's deltoids and trapezoids were fatigued, yet Dan's concave ass gave Ben's cock the force to spew while he lowered his friends.

As all three toppled to the bed, no one spoke, nor did they need to. Their feelings spoke on bedspread stains.

# Chapter 63

## Incentive

Heavy breathing dominated the room, and rising heat circulated from floor to ceiling. The three of them were completely spent.

Ginny rose from the bed, glancing over her shoulder at the two bodies side by side: the man she loved, beautiful and intelligent, his eyes closed; and the man she craved, caring and log cabin big, eyes wide open. As she entered the bathroom, she felt sated and content. She had what she wanted, what she needed.

The sound of Ginny's shower reawakened Ben's desire. He turned on his side, examining Dan. "You okay, Dan?"

"Uh-huh."

Ben's left hand reached under Dan's legs to massage Dan's ass. His middle finger pressed against the perineum.

Dan sat up. "Fuck." His penis started to rise.

"Still okay?"

"What? Dunno."

With his forearm extended, Ben moved his hand farther under Dan. Two fingers lifted Dan's sack and balls with the skilled touches and sensuousness of a gay man. He released then pushed repeatedly, each act prickling Dan's testicles. It was good, Ben knew, and Dan's excitement was rising. Ben waited for Dan's words.

Embarrassment prevented Dan's objection. His rising penis was not excitement, not emotional. He wished Ben would stop, but he couldn't say it. His erection wasn't hard like it had been with Ginny. He wanted to shout "enough," but he did not. Did he feel an obligation to Ben? Was this part of his promise to Ginny? Why he said nothing, Dan didn't know. Six months ago he would have protested, would have expressed both disgust and repulsion. But now he didn't know what he felt, except that this didn't matter. Not in the long run, not in a big picture way.

The new Dan Livorno was freed from conformity. Which didn't mean he liked what Ben was doing, but he wasn't repulsed by it.

Unlike Dan, Ben was enjoying this exploration. He loved everything about this gorgeous man, and Ben's excitement was real and very hard. Ben's hand centered on Dan's ass, and his finger moved between the tightly clenched buttocks. With skill, determination, and strength, Ben separated Dan's tight cheeks, pushing his middle finger deep into Dan's hole, his sphincter stretched from recent coitus. Ben breached, and if Dan had leaped before, this touch produced flight. Ben waited for Dan to catch his breath before going further.

The cry to stop did not come, so Ben continued. This was the moment he'd imagined since the day he met Dan, the thought repeated at every training session. His request that Dan touch his muscles was an excuse. He had fantasized that Dan meant it. Dan had Davis's beauty, fluidity, and intelligence. Ben sought peace, maybe joy, certainly serenity in Dan, as he had in Davis. Ben longed for pleasure given by a friend, not a one-night pickup with a muscle worshipper.

The fingers found the spot. Dan reacted. "Oh, fuck."

Ben's lips stretched and he smacked his words. "Everything okay?"

"Don't know. I'll manage."

Not typical words for this kind of foreplay, but good enough. Nor was this foreplay, not in the real meaning. This would go no further; this would have to be enough. Ben was content to watch Dan's dick grow, was surprised that he ejaculated so soon, a rapid-fire sluice.

Pumping his own hard penis, Ben masturbated, coating Dan's legs and stomach.

Dan's eyes retreated and his eyelids vaulted closed. He did not want to see what he knew to be true. Liberation had its limits.

Ben spoke. "I appreciate this. I hope you're not offended. This has meant more to me than I can say."

"Sure. I'd never considered doing anything like this, and I don't expect I will again."

"Yes, well… er… er… never mind."

Dan's eyes did not open again. His breathing grew even, each inhale yielding a slight rise of his chest, and purrs of satisfaction dotted his sleep.

But although Dan slept, Ben did not. He rested on his side, his hand atop Dan's pectorals, moving around his nipples. Ben commiserated with Ginny's obsession like never before. He understood her desire. He needed someone—and that someone could not be Dan. But he would enjoy the now; tomorrow he could worry about a new life.

Dripping wet from her shower, Ginny peeked into the room. The scene had changed. Ben rested on his side, his hand on Dan, nude on her bed. It was a strange sight; Dan was always clothed, even when alone.

Ginny pedaled to the bed for a closer look, but Ben's laterals obscured Dan. Ben's arm craned over Dan's chest. A few candles had extinguished, and the room was darker than before. Ben's striated legs bent into Dan. Ginny's unexpected damp touch caused Ben to shudder.

Ben removed his arm. Ginny leaned across, water droplets falling on Ben back. Dan's face was a portrait, every facial fixture perfect in form, size, location, and color. "He's beautiful," she whispered, and Ben agreed.

Ben swiveled upright, putting his feet on the floor. He mouthed "thank you" to Ginny. Using two fingers, Ginny touched her lips, then Ben's. She shimmied back into the bathroom, her neck craned backward for one more look. Ben was kneeling at the bed as if in prayer, his words whispered yet heard by Ginny: "Thank you, Dan."

A guttural reply: "You're welcome."

His clothes bunched under his arm, Ben looked to Ginny, walking out with no goodbye.

* * *

Under the bedcovers, Ginny disturbed Dan with her snuggle. He asked that she roll on her side, allowing him to candy wrap around her. He kissed her neck, snuggled her buttocks. One hand was secured to his pillow, the other to Ginny's breast. Sleep took over again.

There was no sleep for Ginny. She smiled, her hand on Dan's, pushing his to flatten her breast. Her face teemed with the night's pleasure until a shadow draped her thoughts. Dan had had sex with another person—a man. Not penetration, but how else could you define masturbation? It had been sex, and she'd permitted it.

"Fuck." Ginny said it out loud, but Dan didn't hear. *I'll have only myself to blame if Dan's become a homosexual.*

*That's stupid.* People did not become homosexuals by choice. Maybe Dan had always been gay, though? No. She found that idea inconceivable. He'd had opportunity: Vinnie, Ben, or even his former boss, Gary Del Vecchio. She'd have known. Tonight he may have been bi-curious, is all. That shouldn't have bothered her, but it did. Why? Dan bi-curious? No, not that. Her thoughts followed the flickering wall shadows. Ben gave Dan his climax. So? She recalled Ben's tender touch. The two men had thanked each other. Ben was the reason for Dan's enjoyment, not her.

She nudged Dan to roll over so she could rest on her back. Was this betrayal? An extramarital affair of her doing? She'd miscalculated. She was jealous.

Jealous. That was Dan's affliction, not hers, so what was this feeling? Was this how Dan felt, the reason for his outrage? His constant complaints about her touching bodybuilders, his indifference to her comments about men's physiques, his nagging her over time spent with Ben. She had never understood his jealousy. She did now. Her stomach knotted knowing that Ben had substituted for her, had fulfilled Dan's needs. She thought of her own desire for Ben's muscles and strength. Did Ben need Dan for masculine intimacy? Had both been sexually satisfied? Now she desired Dan's body, she wanted to satisfy Dan's sexual and intimate needs, and she had allowed Ben to do it for her.

Holding the fingers of one hand in the other, she pulled each. She wasn't only jealous that Dan had sex with Ben—not entirely. She had lusted for Ben's masculinity herself, and had seen that Ben had had the same feelings for Dan. This was the lust for attention. Ben wanted Dan's attention, and she feared Dan would now seek his from Ben—the same attention she had denied Dan all year.

Fear fueled her jealousy. Ben was unstoppable in his lust; Dan would succumb. She imagined that Dan had conquered Ben's desire, and soon the reverse would happen. She understood like never before: jealousy was all-consuming.

The night's success vanished. Ben had solved her obsession, her stethy problem, only to create a new obsession. *I'll make sure Dan knows he's all I want. He'll see I lust for him alone. I'll make him mine again.*

* * *

Shuffling across his living room to glowing wall lights, Ben thought about his bedtime music. "Nessun Dorma" had set the evening mood earlier, but now the mood had changed. Surprise, pleasure, and fulfillment were mixed together. Ben was surprised by his own strength; and more surprised by Dan's submission. He was pleased he'd helped Ginny overcome her sthenolagnia, although he doubted this success would be more than momentary. He was pleased that Dan's first sexual experimentation had succeeded, and his months of desire for Dan been satisfied.

Ben fingered the CD collection with thoughts of Dan snuggling into Ginny. This was love, the fulfillment he wanted, needed. That had not come. Dan would not fulfill this need, but Ben believed there was a person that could. And that person was only a staircase descent away.

Reaching for Etta James, Ben sank into the couch, waiting for her rendition of "At Last." As Etta crooned "My lonely days are over," Ben made his decision.

# Chapter 64

## Watershed

After a poor night's sleep, Ginny rose at seven on Saturday morning. Dan was still curled up in a deep sleep. A few blocks away, Ben's sleep matched Dan's; both were oblivious to the dawn. Of the three, it was only Ginny who had the restless night, as anxiety surfaced in dreams mixed with reality.

She'd had her perfect night until the end. Now, sitting sideways on the bed, her bare feet waxing the wood floor, Ginny stared at the extinguished candles. She rose and entered the en suite bathroom, finding Ben's oil open on the vanity.

The bright lights did not illuminate her mind's dark disquiet. Something had changed. Ginny sensed it. Her life had changed. *She* had changed. Was it possible that a night of incredible sex, of her fantasy realized, could have this impact? She had said this to Dan and Ben, but it had only been her way to persuade them—she had not fully believed it.

On her return to the bedroom, her brow furrowed, she again marveled at her husband curled under the sheets. She loved him. As if for the first time, Ginny saw what had been said repeatedly to her by family and friends: Dan was perfect. He was handsome; his sinewy body was the work of a talented sculptor; his face was a personal sketch by God; and his intelligence was superior to most. Last night he had proved his commitment to her, his devotion, his willingness to act against his own wishes. Of course, he did not have Ben's bulging muscles. Nor was he without flaws, especially his jealousy, which she now understood. His fear, too, could be explained. Yet Ginny could not think of anyone without some flaw, some imperfection. She saw, too, that that applied to her even more. So what had happened? What was happening?

Ginny went to the kitchen for answers.

"It's me. That's what's happened," she said out loud. She'd vanquished her most desired sexual fantasy—and she had lost her need to feel immense power while engaged in sex with Dan. This was real. The image of bulging muscles had lost its appeal. She had beaten her sthenolagnia. But she needed confirmation.

* * *

Two hours later, Dan entered the kitchen. "Geez, Ginny. You should've woken me. Look at the time."

"It's Saturday, and you've nowhere to go. You were exhausted from last night. Do you remember last night?"

Dan shuffled to the refrigerator. "I don't want to talk about it."

"Yes you do. Did you not have a good time?"

"Yes. But I'm not like that. I don't know why I let that happen. I mean, Ben was great, and gentle—well, not the lifting us in the air part. Can you believe that? I mean, how strong *is* that?"

"Yes, he's strong. And guess what? It's gone. I don't feel it anymore."

"What's gone?"

"My stethy. I can tell. Even when you mentioned Ben's strength just now, it didn't feel the same. I've no desire inside. I think it's gone."

"Ginny, that's great! Can it be true? Will it last?"

"I don't know. All I know is that I haven't felt this way for a long time. Maybe never. Before, any mention of strength, power, muscles, body-builders… it would have given me tingles and I'd zone out. But not now. It feels different."

Dan walked over to Ginny and took her in his arms. He was about to flex, but decided that might tempt fate. Ginny leaned in to kiss him. "I love you, Dan Livorno."

"I love you, Ginny Livorno. Can we eat?"

"Sure, loverboy, you'll need energy for what I have planned."

"Ginny, I don't know if I could. I'm feeling a little sore in strange places."

"I'm sure you are."

* * *

The way Dan stared into his cereal bowl gave Ginny her excuse to leave him alone. And she had her weekend jog with Sarah and Betsy. Before giving Dan his space, she mentioned that he could take the weekend to recuperate, but he'd better be ready on Monday. After her jog, Ginny planned to spend the weekend in Connecticut with her mother. After last night's sex arcade, the last thing Dan would have wanted was a visit with his mother-in-law, and he'd appreciated not being invited.

During their cafe sit-down, Sarah and Betsy had more questions than answers for Ginny. They'd been shocked, excited, curious, and envious of all that Ginny had told them, and, as always, Ginny had told them everything.

"Ginny, that's the most erotic thing I've ever heard. Why didn't you call me?" said Sarah.

"Me too, after all I've done for you! Did Ben really press you and pump-fuck the two of you overhead? I'm so envious. I'm getting wet just sitting here thinking about it," said Betsy, the senior VP financial executive and a married woman with two kids.

Neither friend could be sure if Ginny had changed or, if she had, whether it would be permanent.

"Let's hope there's no relapse," said Sarah. "But if there is, put me down for the repeat treatment."

"Fuck you, Sarah."

"That's what I'm talking about. That's the spirit, Ginny."

"I'll say it again, in case you didn't catch my drift. Fuck you, Sarah."

*This is a lost cause*, thought Ginny. Her friends were fascinated only by the sex—though to be fair, what had happened *was* fascinating.

The banter stopped when Ginny told her friends that she'd arranged an impromptu weekend in Connecticut. Nothing stopped silly talk like mentioning Anna Swinburne.

Yet Ginny's mind lingered on Dan's question during the train to Connecticut: *Is your stethy gone forever?* She'd like an answer to that question herself. Was her psychological change permanent, and was she sure about her altered sate? She needed to understand how her years of obsession could dissipate in one night. Was this typical? How could she prevent relapse, notwithstanding Sarah's hope she would?

Was her sthenolagnia truly gone?

* * *

Dr. Anna Swinburne started with questions. Most daughters would have been evasive, but Ginny had learned this didn't work with her mother—and besides, she wanted to be honest. So Ginny told her mother every detail of the prior night: the overhead lift, the pushing of buttocks, Ben's anal incursion into Dan, and Ben's rubbing Dan's chest. Anna listened, asked questions, and never judged.

"Do you realize what this means? Your sthenolagnia syndrome has evolved—and for the better, from my perspective. This is good news." Anna did not go so far as to say that Ginny was fully cured. She explained that Ginny had learned to enjoy bodybuilding and had bodybuilder friends. She told Ginny not to abandon her friends, which would be a mistake. But perhaps she could consider the bodybuilders as a hobby, not a desire.

"You mean I'll still want to feel their muscles?"

"Yes. But as an art form, as sport, in admiration for their dedication—not as a sexual desire, or as a part of your deeper issue: your need for powerful musclemen to protect you. You don't need Ice Cream Man. From this point forward, you'll enjoy looking at muscular physiques in and of themselves."

* * *

Neither Ginny nor her mother could know the full extent of the change. That knowledge would come five weeks later, with a new obsession that they'd share: shopping for maternity clothes and layette paraphernalia.

Ginny's pregnancy changed everything. With his usual precision, Dan calculated the moment of conception, and there was only one possible date. Their baby was conceived in an impossible air-fuck squeezed out by a muscleman. The same day the new daddy had had his first and only homosexual relation. Ginny, Dan, and Ben would forever celebrate that day every year under the heading "AFF": Air-Fuck Friday.

The pregnancy was not the only big news to affect the Livorno household. Even before the pregnancy was known, an event at DV&N shook their lives, on the Monday after AFF.

# Chapter 65

## Roommate

Sunlight glinted off Ben's bare chest as he leaned back against the headboard. The previous evening's physical exertion, a fraction of his usual workout, could not account for his drowsy state. He had dreamed of being with a man, but the face had been unseen, so naturally he concluded it was Davis McGregor III. Yet the figure did not have Davis's short-cropped hair. For thirty languid minutes he reviewed the night spent with Dan and Ginny. He had given them joy—and himself, too.

He also remembered that his joy had stopped when he'd entered his empty bedroom. He'd made a decision last night, and here it was mid-morning with him still in bed.

After his trademark knock, Ben entered Vinnie's room and took a seat on the couch opposite Vinnie in his usual window chair, his feet up on the ottoman. Ben fidgeted with the throw pillow. Nothing was said about the evening with Ginny and Dan.

"Vinnie, we need to discuss your living arrangements. I'd like to move you from this room and—"

Vinnie shouted, "Fuck! I knew this day would come." He burst out crying.

Ben's head jerked up and his mouth dropped. "Wait, let me finish. I want you out of this room... if you would consider moving into mine."

Vinnie jumped off his chair and kissed Ben with open lips. Ben waited for Vinnie to back away.

"I'm so happy I could cry," Vinnie said. And he did.

Ben hugged Vinnie until he winced. "Too hard? I'm happy too. Now *I'm* going to cry," said Ben with a dry-eyed smile. "I've wanted to ask for days, but I wasn't sure you liked me. It wasn't until I had dinner with Blanca..." Ben looked away. *Fuck, I wasn't supposed to say that.*

"Blanca? She *told* you? That traitor. I promised her to secrecy."

"It's not like that. She was making a joke. I can't explain, it just happened. Blanca asked me not to tell you... you should thank her."

"You're afraid of *me*?  Think I might beat the crap out of you or some-thing?"

"Let's say 'or something.'"

Vinnie jumped full straddle onto Ben's lap.  Ben resumed his bear hug, and Vinnie gasped.

"Oh, sorry.  Did I hurt you?"

"No.  Well, a little.  We'll need to adjust to our size difference."  Vinnie looked down at Ben's pants.  "In more ways than one."

With a glance down at Vinnie's pants, Ben answered, "Looks like I've got competition in one area.  We'll explore that later."

"That's not a hospital cast, in case you're wondering," Vinnie said, stroking Ben's head.  "You need to be somewhere?"

* * *

Ben carried Vinnie up a wide staircase to the top floor and into his bedroom—now *their* bedroom.  Vinnie was in uncharted territory: a man twice his size and a new floor of the condo.  Ben's bedroom was smaller than the one he'd been staying in, yet twice his entire Village apartment.  It was plainly fur-nished though, with a bed, a couch, table, and an easy chair with ottoman.  That suited Vinnie fine for what he imagined would be the room's only two uses.

Laying Vinnie on the bed, Ben removed Vinnie's clothes and tossed them into the corner of the room.  His own clothes joined Vinnie's.  At first Ben explored Vinnie's upper body, testing each part.  Vinnie wasn't anywhere near as fit as Dan; in fact Vinnie was thin, partly due to his injury and partly his stature.  And his face didn't match Dan's crystal eyes, his symmetrical face, sculpted nose, high cheekbones, dimpled chin, and velvet lips.  Vinnie was standard off-the shelf; Dan was one-of-a-kind.

Yet Ben stirred.  Unlike his physical attraction to Dan, this went further.  Vinnie was not a gorgeous body but a beautiful *person*.  His months convers-ing with Vinnie had created a bond.  They had shared laughs, cries, stories, histories, and created their own narrative.  Ben desired Vinnie.

If Ben overlooked Vinnie's physical attributes, the same could not be said of Vinnie.  He had no idea what could have created the lumps that covered Ben's body.  There were too many to count, and nowhere to grab hold.  Vinnie rubbed Ben's pectorals with the sensation he was cleaning a granite coun-tertop; he smiled, thinking that an electric buffer would be more efficient.  Nothing about Ben's body excited Vinnie: the grotesque size and checker-board veins, the hardened sinews.  And yet, as repulsed as he was, Vinnie, too, desired Ben, needed him.

They explored—touching, looking, kissing. Ben saw Vinnie's eyes shift from side to side, up and down. So Ben did what he always did: he flexed. He puffed out his chest and pressed his hands together, creating globes. Vinnie's hand was too small to cover more than half. Ben flexed a double-bicep pose, and Vinnie looked away, surprising Ben.

Their desires didn't match their understanding of how to proceed. Ben moved off Vinnie, suggesting Vinnie be on top. Vinnie rested above Ben's crouch, his fingers on Ben's abdomen to steady himself. Leaning over, Vinnie looked into Ben's eyes, at his lips, watched the small breaths slip in and out. These held Vinnie's attention more than mounded meat. Ben's face reflected all that Vinnie desired: kindness, generosity, empathy, and maybe love. Vinnie leaned across, his mouth touching Ben's, and their tongues engaged, Vinnie pulling Ben's neck.

Encouraged, Ben spread his legs, his hard penis springing across Vinnie's backside. Vinnie responded with his own erection poking into Ben's chest.

Ben's coarse tongue explored Vinnie's mouth. The men devoured each other, restraint swept aside. Ben lubricated Vinnie with gel from his side table, marveling at Vinnie's symmetrical, puckered, perfectly round balls. They made Ben wish he'd had bigger implants.

The curiosity over equipment made Vinnie look around. He estimated their cocks were about equal in length, though Ben's had a greater circumference. The lower side of Ben's penis had a prominent vein, as if he'd lifted weights with it. Vinnie stroked the vein, and got a soft sound from Ben in response. Ben's balls were big too, which surprised Vinnie, who knew the side effects of testosterone injections. Even so, Vinnie knew that his surpassed Ben. Yet Ben's were harder—a curiosity he'd ask about later.

With ease, Ben lifted himself up and guided Vinnie into his hole. Ben's smile anticipated the penetration, the joy drifting from face to body. Vinnie followed Ben's instructions, not caring how he made entry.

"Fuckin' great."

"Glad you like it, Vinnie. There's more to go."

Neither man wanted a long conversation; they were mostly content to moan. Neither worried about protection either, each having logged six months or more in abstinence.

Vinnie cried out as Ben pulled him in. "Keep going, I love this."

And Ben did, lifting Vinnie's ass, pushing him deep. Vinnie tried an embrace, but barely reached the sides of Ben's jumbo jet lateral wings. Vinnie grabbed Ben's throbbing dick, grinning with approval at his other ballast choice.

Excitement coated them like sprinkles. Ben stuck his finger into Vinnie's crack, giving the same tambourine play to Vinnie's balls that he'd given to Dan. Then Ben moved his finger deeper inside, pressing Vinnie's prostate until he felt the surge. Vinnie burst inside and out with a shout; he filled Ben to capacity. Seconds later Ben shot as well, his sizzling jism smacking the headboard. Their rhythm continued until they were spent.

"Fuckin' fantastic. Thank you, Ben. That was my best fuck ever."

Ben's response seemed flat to Vinnie.

"Was it not okay for you? What's the matter?"

"Nothing. It was, as you say, fucking fantastic."

"So?"

Ben was quiet.

"Ben, say something."

"I will, but not now. That was probably your first exercise in months, so let me give you a massage to prevent soreness."

From his nightstand, Ben produced an oil lubricant, and wasn't shy in its application. He covered Vinnie's legs, being careful with the healed fractures. He rubbed Vinnie's chest then pancake-flipped him onto his back. Vinnie winced with each pressure point.

"My turn," Vinnie said. "Let me do you."

"It's all right."

"No, I want to. I mean, I'm going to have to get used to it, won't I?"

With a short laugh, Ben said, "No one's ever put it like that. Don't you like these?" Ben shot a double-bicep pose. Vinnie's face puckered.

Like Vinnie, Ben faced down, and Vinnie prepared for overtime facing a sprawling back wider than the bed, the ridges calling for a ski patrol. Vinnie feather-kneaded, then gave his best pizza-dough massage to Ben's bulbous ass.

"Ben, what the fuck do you have inside this ass? I can't move them."

"You're not supposed to; that's the point."

"Not for me."

Ben rolled over, his chest mile-high. Vinnie tried again, working the mounds that loomed up. He might as well have done jumping jacks for all the impact he had.

Ben flexed his arm again, and the dual cannonball lifted, the veins surfacing the almost non-existent skin. Vinnie felt the rebar-reinforced veins. Ben was skin, muscle, and nothing else.

"I don't get it," Vinnie said. "Maybe never will. Do you really need to have veins showing?"

"You do if you want to win a contest."

"I don't."

"Um… do we need to talk about this? Is it a problem?"

"Don't think so. Like I said, best fuck ever, so, not a problem. And what about you? Want to talk about it? I'm not good enough for you, am I?"

"Hell, Vinnie, you are. The sex was great, and it'll get better once I know I won't hurt you. You still need weeks to recuperate fully. It's not you."

"Then what?"

"Can we talk about it later?"

"Why wait?"

"Because I loved it too much to analyze my feelings. Is that good enough for now?"

"Yes, as long as I know I satisfied you."

"You did. In fact, I'm ready for another round. How about you?"

Without warning, Ben pulled Vinnie on top, bench-pressing him overhead, this human barbell much lighter than Ben's normal iron-plated version. With slower buildup, the two men had another session, with Ben on bottom, a precaution to safeguard Vinnie. They both knew this was good, and they both worried it might end too soon.

Ben had waited a long time for sex that had affection—ever since he'd lost Davis. He had forgotten the feeling. The unrequited yearning played in Ben's mind and his loins. His penis was excited, his hypothalamus energized, his scrotum winch-tight. Ben knew he'd cum before Vinnie this time.

Afterward, Vinnie rested on his back, exhausted. "Even better. This will work, won't it? Us, together?"

"I think it will. There's nothing to stop us."

That was Ben's one sentence too much.

# Chapter 66

## California Bound

Ristorante Roma was typical of hundreds of Italian restaurants sprouting across New York City's five boroughs. The decor followed a single design: small wooden tables and chairs in the room's center with leatherette booths lining the sides. Each table was covered with a checkered tablecloth and had silverware around a small antipasto plate; a tall water glass with a fan-shaped napkin stuffed inside it was set beside an upturned wine glass. A sugar bowl and toothpick glass surrounded matching silver-topped salt and pepper shakers The wall murals depicted the Coliseum, Trajan's Monument, the Capitoline Hill, and St. Peter's Basilica. Big John had been to many restaurants like this, but never to Ristorante Roma.

"Carmine, this is John Briggs, father to the poor kid that you read about—the one that was beaten for being a homo. Remember, it was in all the papers?" Sal "Chopin" Friscollo addressed Carmine like he was talking to an old man with dementia.

Carmine remembered well—he had assigned Sal the "hit" on Vinnie. And the meeting with the homo's father had been prearranged, making Carmine's pretended surprise a farce.

Big John knew that Carmine was expecting him and that Sal was the man who had nearly killed his son. Yet pretense took precedence over reality. "You don't know me, Mr. Aquafreddo, so I hope you don't mind my coming here to talk with you. It's about my son, Vinnie."

"Want a cappuccino? Espresso? Good cannòli, too." These words signaled Carmine's agreement to the meeting.

"Thanks. An espresso would be great," said Big John, as a return signal that he understood the meeting was a favor.

"What's on your mind?"

"Well, Mr. Aquafreddo, it's a long story; can I make it short?" You know what this is about, and you know the details of my son's beating, so let's cut the crap and get on with it.

"Take your time. I don't eat dinner for another twenty minutes." *Hurry up and spit it out.*

"This won't take long." *I got it, you sob. I'll talk fast.* "My son Vinnie recently had trouble with Bill Barrington, a big-shot exec at Del Vecchio & Neale, where my son worked. My son had an unfortunate accident, and he can't remember anything about it, but he thinks it involves this Barrington guy." *It was Barrington's contract with you that resulted in Vinnie's beating and near death.* "Vinnie would like to put this behind him." *My son understands this was a business transaction and he's willing to accept it was nothing more.*

Carmine sipped his cappuccino. "We all like to forget accidents. I've heard about this Barrington guy… maybe I read it in the *News*." Carmine didn't need the *Daily News* to know about crimes committed in Brooklyn, but he enjoyed reading the way the real facts were twisted. "Am I right, Sal? Was it the *News* that had this?"

"That's right. The *News* had two pages. What a shame. Guy went nuts, from what I remember."

Big John saw his opening. "That's right. He mumbled a lot of stuff. My son Vinnie thought he was crazy for a long time and doesn't believe a single word. Vinnie wants to forget everything that relates to his terrible time with Barrington and DV&N. Actually, Vinnie doesn't *need* to forget, since he's lost his memory."

The waiter delivered Big John's espresso. "*Grazie*, Alberto. *Nient'altro*," Carmine said, and waved the waiter away.

"There's one more thing. How should I put it… Barrington went 'postal' after he was fired. Vinnie tells me that Barrington and a woman accomplice named Linda Lords had planned to embezzle something like seventy-five million."

Carmine looked up at Sal. "Imagine that, seventy-five million. We'd have to sell a lot of pizza and cannòli. No more discounts for friends either, right, Sal?"

"Yeah, maybe we should start charging more for our pizza when we deliver to Manhattan," said Sal with a pukeface grin. Big John knew this was a communication he couldn't decipher and didn't care about.

"Mr. Aquafreddo, I'd like to let you know a little more about my son and Barrington. Nothing to do with you, but I thought you'd find it useful to know of events that might help your restaurant business." *I'm giving you advance information so you can prepare your options.*

Carmine nodded, and his hand wave signaled for John to speed it up.

"The word is that Barrington will get life. Vinnie said the guy is missing his top drawer, and the office shooting proves he's right. Anyway, Barrington's made up a story about Vinnie's accident to get a reduced sentence. Vinnie says Barrington's a liar."

Here, Big John related "Vinnie's version" of the attack. It placed the full blame on Vinnie's drinking, drugs, and a stupid adventure into the alleyway on an icy night. Big John gave Vinnie's fictional recall to the DA.

Carmine understood. Vinnie had contradicted Barrington's plea bargain, and Vinnie was more believable than the deranged Barrington.

Big John finished his espresso. Now for the tricky part. "Barrington's a nutcase, and his story would be dismissed easily except for this Linda Lords—the woman I mentioned before. Well, she wants to save her ass too. Rumor has it she's willing to corroborate Barrington's story."

Another pause. Was Carmine following this? Even Big John was having trouble with his storyline. But Carmine's brain was sharp, and uncluttered by emotion or morality.

"Yeah, very interesting. What's the end?" *Get to the finale. Your time's nearly up.*

"Lords told someone, I don't know who exactly, that if she could show that Barrington and she were set up, and it all relates to my son Vinnie, then she thinks she could get the embezzlement and fraud charges reduced, even dropped. She wants to go into protection."

Carmine nodded. He knew all about the Federal Witness Protection Program.

"Crazy, I know, but Vinnie's worried he'll be involved in a long trial. He says Lords is smart and might sell her story to the DA. Barrington will have to answer for the killing, but he'll use an insanity defense, which might work. Vinnie's says their story is bullshit. Vinnie's the one who uncovered their embezzlement scheme, so they're trying to get at him."

Carmine increased the stirring of his teaspoon in an empty espresso cup.

"Let me get to the end," said John. "Mr. Aquafreddo, Vinnie thinks he should stop talking to the prosecutor, who twists everything. He's made a video confirming that Barrington and Lords are liars. He's left it with his lawyer. Vinnie's had a rough time recuperating. I think he needs sunshine, maybe to move away from the New York winters, nothing to remind him of the past." *He'll be away from any state prosecutors. Vinnie's not going to remember anything.*

A chin nod from Carmine.

"I thought he should try California. But you know, kids today think their parents are stupid. That's why I thought he might respect your opinion, a businessman with lots of experience. That's why I'm here. What do you think? Should I tell Vinnie someone like yourself thinks this would be good for his recuperation?" *Do you consider Vinnie a threat? Do you accept that Vinnie's not going to testify?*

Carmine looked to Sal, who said nothing. Which said everything.

"Tell your boy I think California's a nice place. People who suffer accidents in New York can recuperate and have good health in the Californian sun. He should buy Californian olive oil until the price of the better Sicilian drops, which I'm guessing might happen in two years. I hear the airfares are cheap over the next three days."

Sal took Big John's espresso cup. *Meeting over.* Vinnie was a free man if he moved to California and remained out of New York for two years. He had three days' reprieve.

# Chapter 67

## Bags Packed

Three days flew by. They were unhappy days for Vinnie, Ben, Dan, and Ginny.

Vinnie's older brother Jack arrived Thursday morning, dropping Vinnie at the Forty-Second Street entrance to the Port Authority building. Big John and Jack knew better than anyone the criminal mind, so—Carmine's assurance aside—Vinnie needed to be hard to find.

Ben had wanted to drive Vinnie to JFK himself, but Big John won that argument. Vinnie had to depart New York with minimal contact with family and friends—who needed to be kept in the dark as much as possible.

But only Ben knew Vinnie's final location—because he'd arranged it. Jack knew the departure was from JFK and nothing more. DV&N colleagues, friends, and the Briggs family had no idea. Even Vinnie himself was in the dark. Ben alone knew, and Vinnie would learn when he landed at Los Angeles airport.

The hug was hard, the lift high, and the kissing and crying didn't stop until Vinnie exited the condo building using UltraFit's staff-only rear exit after hours. Ben had shut off the security cameras. Vinnie walked alone to Columbus Circle and caught the Eighth Avenue downtown—a journey he hadn't made in months. He held a single piece of hand luggage.

On board American Airlines non-stop from JFK to LAX, Vinnie relaxed in his business-class seat, the ticket purchased with cash by Ben—his parting bon voyage gift.

The single carry-on made Vinnie's transfer in LA to Amtrak easier. The train took him to Ben's San Francisco condo, his final destination, and another example of Davis McGregor III's legacy. The flight would be the last time Vinnie used his full name. He'd receive a duplicate platinum AMEX under the UltraFit account and Ben Hausen's name, with the card issued to Vincent DePaul. Jack had planned to ship Vinnie's additional personal items to a P.O. box in LA, but Ben suggested that Vinnie buy everything new. Vinnie liked that idea. He wouldn't be sponging off Ben, either. He fully intended to reimburse Ben once his million-dollar settlement check cleared and he could again become Vinnie Briggs. Myron Rosenberg's apoplectic fit over the offer had been cured when Gary Del Vecchio's mug had hit him on the forehead.

Ben and Vinnie stayed connected, the two having to contend with several phone calls every day on cell phones that were untraceable by anyone aside from the NSA. Ben was reminded of living through the same scenario when Davis had gone away; their only contact had been phone conversations, until even that stopped.

The days dragged by, and Ben stared out his bedroom window. It was a view he'd imagined sharing with Vinnie. Their time as lovers had lasted only three days before it was over.

* * *

Bright fluorescent recessed lights made the gray cell seem larger than it was. On this day a small spot flickered around the floor from reflected sunlight that bounced off the steel toilet bowl and washbasin on the back wall. Two men sat across from each other, one unshaven with prison muscle, the other clean-shaven and fit, not up to par with the other man.

"I'll be out of this stinking hellhole and away from your dirty mug in no time, no offense. Har har, har har."

The upgrade to a bigger cell and more freedom in a federal white-collar country club prison was all Bill Barrington thought about.

"When I go before that federal prosecutor next week and tell him what I know about that fucking Carmine Aquafreddo and his illiterate fucking Guinea goombah Sal Friscollo, I'll be out of here before you take your next shit. Har har, har har."

The guards heard the commotion three days later. Bill Barrington had committed suicide by stabbing himself in the back five times with two different homemade shanks. This was the only possible explanation for his death, since not one of the fifty eyewitness prisoners had seen anyone attack him. As corroboration, Bill's cellmate had reported that Bill had been depressed. The upside was that Bill Barrington had achieved his removal from Attica— to a cemetery in New Jersey. His family hadn't attended the burial, although flowers had been sent from a restaurant in Brooklyn.

Linda Lords's conviction of fraud with intent to embezzle should have resulted in a twenty to twenty-five-year sentence, but her cooperation with the DA in return for her testimony against her partner resulted in only twelve years at a minimum-security federal penitentiary. In the end, Ginny's vision of the Prisoner's Dilemma had come true. With good behavior, Linda might be released in five years and find employment in the promising service sector, living on minimum wage plus tips.

* * *

The birth came a week early: eight pounds, four ounces. The baby boy had big feet and big hands, and was beautiful like his daddy. Dan believed Anthony Benjamin Vincent Livorno was happiness incarnate. Ginny's son became a member of her running group, and his new baby-style running buggy was a gift from Uncle Ben. The crayons in two hundred colors were sent from California—a little too soon for a baby, said Dan, but Uncle Vinnie disagreed, saying it was never too soon to learn color coordination.

Dan was happy with his new life, away from high-pressure investment models. He and Ginny began a specialized import/export business from small fashion houses across Europe, and sold to boutique stores in five select US cities. Dan used part of his forty-five-million-dollar DV&N compensation as initial capital, and placed a good chunk of it in sound investments for his son's future.

* * *

Happiness was not part of Vinnie's vocabulary. His San Francisco living quarters in Lower Pacific Heights weren't as spacious as Ben's New York high-rise, yet the eight thousand square feet of living space weren't exactly shabby, either. Vinnie may not have been cramped, but he was lonely. He missed his friends. He missed Ben. He worried that Ben would have a change of heart, or would fall in love with someone else. Would Ben really move to the West Coast as he had promised?

Disappointment was nothing new to Vinnie. His few past lovers—all two of them—had ended nowhere. Doubts shadowed Vinnie in his lonely state. Was he wrong about Ben? Did Ben ever really want him? He'd have to wait until the day he'd be reprieved to know for sure.

Vinnie lay in the bed. He recalled the Wednesday in September, not yet a full year gone, his past life. *I loved my boss. Best fuckin' boss ever. I love Ben.* Vinnie stopped talking to himself and looked around the interior of the unfamiliar bedroom. Tears formed in his eyes. *Does anyone love me?*

If you enjoyed reading ICE CREAM MAN, please rate this book and leave a review for other readers. It means a lot to me—and to Vinnie, who is busy investigating crimes and complicating his relationships with Ben, Dan, and Ginny. Thank you!

Remember to sign-up on my email list at charlespuccia.com for pre-release information on Vinnie's next story.

Sincerely,
Charles J. Puccia
vbstories2@gmail.com
www.charlespuccia.com